The Lonely Hearts Club

The Lonely

Hearts Club

ELIZABETH EULBERG

Point

• No part of this publication may be reproduced, stored in a retrieval system, or transmitted in any form or by any means, electronic, mechanical, photocopying, recording, or otherwise, without written permission of the publisher. For information regarding permission, write to Scholastic Inc., Attention: Permissions Department, 557 Broadway, New York, NY 10012. • This book was originally published in hardcover by Scholastic Press in 2010. • ISBN 978-0-545-14032-4 Copyright © 2010 by Elizabeth Eulberg. All rights reserved. Published by Scholastic Inc. SCHOLASTIC, POINT, and associated logos are trademarks and/or registered trademarks of Scholastic Inc. 12 11 10 9 8 7 6 5 4 3 2 1   11 12 13 14 15/0 • Printed in the U.S.A. 40 • First paperback printing, January 2011 • The text was set in 13-pt. Centaur MT; the display type is Bickley Script
Book design by Becky Terhune

For my beloved EEC.
Especially Dav Pilkey,
who was the first person
to encourage me to write.
This is all his fault.

I, Penny Lane Bloom, do solemnly swear to never date another boy for as long as I shall live.

All right, maybe I'll reconsider it in ten years or so when I'm no longer living in Parkview, Illinois, or attending McKinley High School, but for now I'm done with guys. They're all lying, cheating scum of the earth.

Yes, every last one of them. Pure evil.

Sure, there are some that seem nice, but the second they get what they want, they'll dump you and move on to their next target.

So I'm done.

No more dating.

The end.

Yesterday

"Love was such an easy game to play . . ."

One

WHEN I WAS FIVE YEARS OLD, I walked down the aisle with the man of my dreams.

Okay, make that *boy*. He was five, too.

I'd known Nate Taylor pretty much since birth. Our fathers had been friends since childhood, and every year, Nate and his parents would spend the summer with my family. My baby book was filled with pictures of me and Nate — taking a bath together as infants, playing in our tree house in the backyard, and — my favorite — dressed up as a miniature bride and groom at my cousin's wedding. (Soon after, the picture of me in my white dress and Nate in his tux was hung proudly on my bedroom wall.)

Everybody always joked that one day we'd get married for real. Nate and I used to think so, too. We thought we were the perfect couple. I didn't mind playing war with him, and he would even play with my dolls (although he'd never admit it). He'd push me on the swings and I'd help him organize his action figures. He thought I looked pretty with my hair in pigtails, and I thought he was cute (even during his brief pudgy stage). I liked his parents, and he liked my parents. I wanted an English Bulldog, and he wanted a Pug. Macaroni and cheese was my favorite food, and it was his favorite food, too.

What else could a girl want in a guy?

To me, looking forward to summer was the same thing as looking forward to Nate. As a result, so many of my memories revolved around him:

❤ My first kiss (in my tree house when we were eight; I punched him, then cried afterward).

❤ The first time I held hands (when we got lost during a third-grade scavenger hunt).

❤ My first Valentine's Day card (a red construction-paper heart with my name on it).

❤ My first camping trip (Nate and I put up a tent in our backyard when we were ten and spent the entire night out there by ourselves).

❤ The first time I purposely deceived my parents (I took the train into Chicago by myself to see Nate last year; I told my parents I was spending the night at my best friend Tracy's).

❤ Our first *true* kiss (fourteen; this time I didn't put up a fight).

After that kiss, my anticipation for summer intensified. We weren't playing make-believe anymore. The feelings were real, they were different. The heart involved wasn't made from construction paper — it was living, beating . . . real.

When I thought about summer, I thought about Nate. When I thought about love, I thought about Nate. When I thought about anything, I thought about Nate.

I knew that this summer it would happen. Nate and I would be together.

The last month of school was unbearable. I started a countdown clock to his arrival. I took shopping trips with my friends to buy "Nate clothes." I even bought my first bikini with him in mind. I set my work schedule at my dad's dental office around Nate's work schedule at the country club. I didn't want anything to get in our way.

And then it happened.

He was here.

He was taller.

He was older.

He was no longer cute — he was *sexy*.

And he was mine.

He wanted me. And I wanted him. It seemed that simple.

Soon enough, we were together. Finally, really together.

Only I didn't get the fairy tale I was hoping for.

Because guys change.

They lie.

They stomp on your heart.

I found out the hard way that fairy tales and true love don't exist.

The perfect guy doesn't exist.

And that adorable picture of the innocent miniature bride with the guy who would one day break her heart?

That didn't exist anymore, either.

I watched it burn in flames.

Two

It all happened so fast.

It started like every other summer. The Taylors arrived, and the house was bustling with people. Nate and I flirted constantly . . . it was the routine we'd been going through for the past few years. Only this time, there were things underneath the flirtation. Like desire. Like the future. Like sex.

Everything I dreamed of started to happen. Nate was perfect to me. The guy I held everyone else up to. The one who always made my heart beat fast and my stomach flip.

This was the summer that my feelings were finally returned.

It started with a couple of dates, nothing big. Just movies, dinner, etc.

Our parents had no idea what was going on. Nate didn't want to tell them, and I went along. He said they'd probably overreact, and I didn't disagree. Even though I knew our parents always wanted us to eventually end up together, I wasn't sure they would've been prepared for us to be together yet. Especially when he was sleeping downstairs in our sound-proofed basement.

It was all going so well. Nate said all of the things I wanted to hear. How I was beautiful and perfect, how I made him lose his breath when we kissed.

I was in heaven.

We kissed. Then we kissed and kissed. Then we kissed some more. But soon that wasn't enough. Soon hands started wandering, clothes started coming off. This was everything that I'd been waiting for . . . but it seemed fast. Too fast. No matter what I gave him, he wanted more. And I was fighting it. Everything we did turned into a constant struggle over how far I'd go.

It took so long to get to this place, I didn't want to rush it. I didn't understand why we couldn't just enjoy the moment, enjoy being together, and not hurry to the next step.

And by next step, I meant physically.

There wasn't a lot of discussion about next steps in terms of our relationship.

After a couple of weeks, Nate started talking about how he felt that I was the one, his true love. It could all be so amazing, he said, if I just let him love me the way he wanted to.

This was what I'd been fantasizing about for so long. This was what I'd always wanted. So I thought, *Yes, I'll do it. Because it will be with him. And that's what matters.*

I decided to surprise him.

I decided to trust him.

I decided to go for it.

I had everything planned, everything in place. Our parents were going to be out late and we'd have the house to ourselves.

"Are you sure you want to do this, Pen?" Tracy asked me that morning.

"I know I don't want to lose him," I replied.

That was my reasoning. This was for Nate. This had nothing to do with me and what I wanted. It was all for him.

I wanted it all to be spontaneous. I wanted him to have no idea, and then be overwhelmed with how perfect it (I) was. He didn't even know I was home; I wanted him to think that I was gone for the evening, to make it even more of a surprise. I wanted to show him that I was ready. Willing. Able. I had it all figured out, except what I was going to wear. I snuck into my sister Rita's room and went through her drawers until I found a white silk camisole that didn't leave much to the imagination. I took her red lace robe as well.

When I was finally ready, I crept down the stairs to Nate's room in our basement. I began to untie the robe, feeling a mixture of excitement and pure nervousness. I couldn't wait to see the look on Nate's face when he saw me. I couldn't wait to prove to him how I felt, so he would finally feel the same way.

I started to smile as I turned the lights on.

"Surprise!" I called out.

Nate popped up from the couch with a look of panic on his face.

"Hi . . ." I said meekly as I dropped the robe on the floor.

Then a second head popped up from the couch.

A girl.

With Nate.

I stood frozen, not believing my own eyes. I looked between the two of them as they fumbled for clothing. Finally, I reached for the robe and put it on, trying to cover as much of myself as possible.

The girl started giggling. "I thought you said your sister was gone for the evening!"

His sister? Nate didn't *have* a sister. I tried to tell myself there was a good explanation for what I was seeing. There was no way Nate would do something like this to me. Especially in my own house. Maybe this girl had been in a car accident right outside and Nate had brought her inside to . . . um, comfort her. Or they were just rehearsing a scene from a summer production of . . . *Naked Romeo and Juliet.* Or maybe I had fallen asleep, and it was only a nightmare.

Only . . . no.

The girl finished putting on her clothes, and Nate, avoiding my eyes, walked her upstairs.

Such a gentleman.

After what seemed like an eternity, he returned.

"Penny," he said, putting his arms around my waist, "I'm sorry that you had to see that."

I tried to speak, but couldn't find my voice.

He ran his arms up to my shoulders and started to rub them through the robe. "I'm sorry, Penny. So sorry. You have to believe me that this was something so stupid. I'm an idiot. A complete idiot."

I shook my head. "How could you?" The words were barely a whisper, my throat was tight.

He leaned in. "Honestly, it will never happen again. I mean, nothing *did* happen. Nothing. It was nothing. *She* was nothing. You know how much you mean to me. You're the one I want to be with. You're the one I love." He moved his hands down my back. "Maybe this will make you feel better? Tell me what I can do, Penny. I would never want to hurt you."

The shock was slowly wearing off, revealing the anger underneath. I pulled away. "How could you?" I said. *"HOW COULD YOU?"* (I screamed the last part.)

"Look, I already apologized."

"You *APOLOGIZED*?"

"Penny, I'm so sorry."

"SORRY?"

"Please stop doing that and just listen to me. I can explain."

"Fine, then." I sat down on the couch. "Explain."

Nate glanced nervously at me — clearly he hadn't expected me to actually sit down and listen to what he had to say.

"Penny, that girl is nothing to me."

"Didn't look like it was nothing." I tightened the belt around my robe and grabbed a couch cushion to cover my legs.

Nate sighed. A full-blown sigh. "Oh, here we go with the dramatics," he said. Then he sat down next to me with his arms folded. "Fine — if you aren't going to accept my apology, I don't know what I can do."

"Apology?" I laughed. "Do you think saying 'sorry' is going to erase this? I thought you said I was special." I looked down at the floor, ashamed of myself for even bringing it up.

"Penny, you *are* special. But, c'mon, what did you think was going to happen?" Nate's face turned bright red. "I mean, here's the thing. You and I . . . we're . . . we're . . . well, it is what it is . . ."

I couldn't believe what I was hearing. The Nate from just a few short days ago was gone and some . . . *beast* had taken his place.

"What does *that* mean?"

"Jesus Christ." Nate got up from the couch and started to pace. "This is exactly what I'm talking about. Look at you, sitting there like you did when we were little and didn't get what you wanted. Well, I wanted you for a long time, Penny. A very long time. But even though you think you want me, you don't want *me*. You want your childhood sweetheart version of me. The holding-hands-kiss-on-the-cheek Nate. Well, that Nate grew up. Maybe you should, too."

"But I . . ."

"What? You what? Put your sister's nightie on? That's child's play, Penny. In your mind, it's a perpetual wedding day, no honeymoon, no taking off the wedding dress, nothing. But guess what. People have sex. It's not a big deal."

My body began to shake. It was hitting me.

Nate shook his head. "I should've known better than to get

involved with you. What can I say? I was bored, and it was much easier to give in to your fantasy than to fight it. And, I will admit, you do have that cute little suburban thing going for you. I just never thought you'd turn out to be nothing but a tease."

I felt sick. Tears started to streak down my face.

"Oh, come on." Nate sat down and put his arm around me. "Just yell at me some more and you'll feel better. Then we can move on."

I shook myself free and ran upstairs.

Away from Nate.

Away from the lies.

Away from it all.

But I couldn't run away. He was living in our house for two more weeks. Every morning I had to get up and face him. Watch him leave the house, knowing he was probably going out with *her*. Knowing that he had to look elsewhere because I wasn't good enough for him. He would never see me "that way."

Every day I was reminded of what a failure I was. How what I'd wanted for years had ended up hurting me more than I could imagine.

My older sister Rita was the only one in my family that I told, and I swore her to secrecy. I knew this would hurt our parents' longest, deepest friendship, and it didn't seem fair for Nate to destroy that, too. Plus, I was embarrassed. I couldn't bear to let my parents find out how stupid I was.

Rita tried to comfort me. She even threatened Nate's life if he came within ten feet of me. But even a hundred feet would've been too close.

"Penny, it's going to be okay," Rita promised as she wrapped her arms around me. "We all run into a few speed bumps along the way."

I didn't run into a speed bump. I ran into a brick wall.

And I never wanted to feel that pain again.

Three

I FELT LOST. I NEEDED TO hide away. Escape.

There was only one thing I could do to ease the pain. I turned to the only four guys who'd never let me down. The only four guys who'd never broken my heart, who'd never disappointed me.

John, Paul, George, and Ringo.

Anybody who has ever clung to a song like a musical life raft will understand. Or put on a song to bring out an emotion or a memory. Or had a soundtrack playing in their head to drown out a conversation or a scene.

As soon as I got back to my room, devastated by Nate's rejection, I turned up the volume so loud on my stereo that my bed began to shake. The Beatles had always been my security blanket. They were a part of my life before I even existed. In fact, if it wasn't for the Beatles, I would've never been born.

My parents met at a makeshift shrine in a Chicago park the night John Lennon was shot. Both were lifelong Beatles fanatics, and later on they felt they had no choice but to name their three daughters after Beatles songs: "Lucy in the Sky with Diamonds," "Lovely Rita," and "Penny Lane."

Of course, my older sisters were lucky enough to get normal middle names, but my parents gave me the full Lennon/

McCartney treatment: Penny Lane. I was even born on February 7 — the anniversary of the Beatles arriving in the United States for the first time. I didn't believe it was a coincidence. I wouldn't have put it past my mother to have refused to push just so I could be born on that day.

Most of our family vacations were spent in Liverpool, England. Every Christmas card we ever sent had us re-creating various Beatles album covers. Truth be told, I should have *hated* the Beatles. That should've been my rebellion. But instead, the Beatles became part of me. Whether I was happy or sad, I was comforted by their words, their music.

Now, I tried to drown out Nate's words with a blast of "Help!" While I did, I reached for my journal. The leather-bound book felt heavy in my hands, the years of emotion inside weighing it down. I opened it up and scanned the entries, most of them filled with Beatles lyrics. To anybody else, it would seem like nonsensical associations, but to me, the lyrics meant so much more than their words. Snapshots of my life: the good, the bad, and the boy-related.

So much heartache. I started to scan my past relationships.

Dan Walker, senior and, according to Tracy, a "major hottie." We dated for four months at the beginning of sophomore year. Things started out decent enough — if your definition of decent was going to the movies and then for pizza every Friday night with every other couple in town. Eventually, Dan started to mistake me for this character in the movie *Almost Famous*, also named Penny Lane. She was a glorified groupie, so Dan got it in his thick head that if he played "Stairway to Heaven" on the guitar, I would give it up. I quickly learned: Looks does not a decent guitar player make. Once Dan realized my pants were staying on, he changed his tune.

Then there was Derek Simpson, who I was pretty sure only dated me because he thought my pharmacist mother could get him drugs.

Darren McWilliams wasn't much better. We started dating right before this summer's Nate-craziness set in. He seemed like a sweet guy, until he started hanging out with Laura Jaworski, who happened to be a good friend of mine. He ended up double booking us for the same day. Little did he realize we would compare our calendars.

Dan, Derek, and Darren — and that was only sophomore year. I was cheated on, lied to, and used. The lesson I'd learned? To stay away from guys whose first name began with the letter *D*, since they were all the Devil.

Maybe Nate's real name was Dante the Destroyer of Dreams. Because he was ten times worse than the three *D*s combined.

I put the journal down. I was mad at Nate, yes. But mostly I was furious with myself. Why did I let myself do it? What did I get out of any of these relationships besides a broken heart? I was smarter than that. I should've known better.

Did I really want to keep getting used? Was there anybody out there who was worth it?

I'd thought Nate was, but I was wrong.

I got up to call Tracy — misery needed her company — when something caught my eye. I went over to my favorite Beatles poster and started to run my fingers across the lettering: *Sgt. Pepper's Lonely Hearts Club Band.*

I'd stared at that poster every day for the past seven years. I'd listened to that album, one of my favorites, hundreds of times. It was like it had always been a single long word to me, *SgtPepper'sLonelyHeartsClubBand.* But now three words separated themselves, and I saw something completely new inside.

Lonely

Hearts

Club

And that's when it happened.

Something about those words.

Lonely. Hearts. Club.

In theory, it may have sounded depressing. But there wasn't anything depressing about the music.

No, this Lonely Hearts Club was the opposite of depressing. It was alive.

The answer had been in front of me all along. There *was* a way to stop getting cheated on, lied to, and used.

I would stop torturing myself by dating loser guys. I would enjoy the benefits of being single. I would, for once, focus on *me.* Junior year would be my year. It would be all about me, Penny Lane Bloom, sole member and founder of The Lonely Hearts Club.

Come Together

"... you've got to be free ..."

Four

BOYS WERE DEAD TO ME. The only question was: Why hadn't I thought of this sooner?

I knew the idea was genius. But it would've been nice if my best friend was able to stop looking at me like I was an escapee from a mental institution.

"Pen, you know I love you, but . . ."

Here we go.

We were having an emergency meeting (complete with the cheese fries required to get over a breakup) at our local diner, less than an hour after my inspiration hit. Tracy took a sip of her milk shake, taking in my tirade about all the problems guys have caused me over the years. I hadn't even gotten to the part about the club yet and my decision to not date.

"I know you're upset, and you have every reason to be," Tracy said. "But not *all* guys are evil."

I rolled my eyes. "Oh, really? Should we go through your lists from the last two years?"

Tracy slumped down in her seat. Every year she made a list of guys she wanted to date. She would spend all summer weighing her options before putting the list together for the school year, with each guy ranked in order of preference based on a ratio of looks, popularity, and looks.

The list definitely caused more heartache than it was worth. Tracy still hadn't been on a date with any of the candidates. In fact, she'd never had a boyfriend. I couldn't figure out why. She was pretty, funny, smart, and one of the most loyal and dependable friends anyone could ask for. But, as if I needed another example of why boys sucked, none of the guys at McKinley seemed to feel she was girlfriend material.

Lucky her, I thought. But she wasn't seeing it that way.

"I don't know what you are talking about," she said.

"Right. So you're telling me you don't have a new list ready for inspection?"

Tracy moved her purse onto the seat next to her.

Of course she had a new list. We only had a few more days before the start of junior year.

"What to the evs," she huffed. "I guess I should just throw the list away since, according to you, all men are jerks."

I smiled. "Now we're getting somewhere. Let's burn it!"

Tracy groaned. "You've clearly lost your mind. Can you be serious for a second?"

"I *am* being serious."

Now it was Tracy's turn to roll her eyes. "Come on — not every single male on this planet is a horrible human being. What about your dad?"

"What about Thomas Grant?" I shot back.

Tracy's mouth dropped open.

Okay, maybe that was a little harsh. Thomas had been on

last year's list. She'd spent an entire semester flirting with him in Chemistry. Finally, he'd asked her if she was free one weekend. Tracy had been thrilled . . . until he texted her an hour before they were supposed to meet and told her that something had "come up." Then he'd ignored her the rest of the year. No explanation, no apology, nothing.

Typical male.

"And Kevin Parker?" I pressed.

Tracy glared at me. "Well, it's not my fault that he doesn't know I exist."

There was always one name on the top of Tracy's list — Kevin Parker, senior football player extraordinaire. Unfortunately, Kevin had never acknowledged that Tracy was even alive. When I'd been dating Derek, I'd invite Kevin and his friends over to my house for the sole purpose of letting Kevin get to know Tracy. But he never paid any attention to her. One of the only reasons I put up with Derek for as long as I did was because Tracy needed her daily Kevin Parker fix.

Thinking about that list and how much it dictated Tracy's happiness made me want to rip it out of her purse and tear it apart. Because I knew — one by one, she'd have to cross their names off, and she'd end up in tears.

Tracy sighed, then collected herself. "This year is going to be different," she swore. "I don't know — I've got a really good feeling about it." She took the list out and started wistfully looking at this year's contenders.

Had I seriously believed that Tracy would understand my need to stop dating? All she thought about was going on dates.

I gave up . . . for the moment.

Tracy wasn't the only one who had a good feeling about this year.

Five

THE FIRST DAY OF SCHOOL. I wasn't even at school yet, and I already had to face the enemy. Not Nate — he was gone. But Nate's kind.

"Aw, can you believe my baby brother is in high school?" Tracy gestured to the backseat of her car, where her brother Mike was blaring his iPod. "And you know, Pen, I don't see any horns on the top of his head."

"Yet." I smirked at her.

Little Mikey Larson was a freshman . . . a guy . . . one of *them.*

I wondered when he would start acting like every other guy at McKinley. Was there some sort of secret class where they taught boys to become himbos?

As Mike got out of Tracy's car, I couldn't help but notice how much more alike than ever they looked, with their dirty blond hair, hazel eyes, and heart-shaped faces.

Tracy looked me up and down. "Pen, those shoes are *adorbs.* You look smokin' *hawt* today." She applied a fresh coat of lip gloss in the rearview mirror. "Looking to impress anybody in particular?"

I groaned. "No — I just wanted to look nice for me."

Tracy gave me a look that said she didn't believe me.

I didn't care. This was going to be the start of an amazing year. I opened the door to school, excited about getting a fresh start, minus all the boy craziness.

The smile on my face quickly vanished when the first person I saw was Dan Walker, wearing the letter jacket I'd "borrowed" when we were dating. How fitting that I would be greeted by a reminder of hideous boyfriends past. I was just thankful that Nate was miles away back in Chicago. I turned the corner to get away from Dan and saw Kevin Parker, who was apparently still too cool to give Tracy the time of day.

My frustration grew as I continued to survey my classmates. I'd walked these hallways thousands of times, but it was as if my eyes were open for the first time. All I saw were girls falling over themselves to flirt with guys, couples walking hand in hand, guys being . . . well, guys: loud, obnoxious, egotistical. They didn't go to girls; girls came to them.

My bag vibrated and I pulled out my cell phone. I stopped dead in my tracks and Brian Reed bumped into me. "Watch it!" he yelled as his girlfriend, Pam, glared my way. Heaven forbid they weren't able to hold hands 24/7.

I snapped out of my daze. I was convinced there was some sort of mistake. But no — the phone cruelly confirmed the truth: It was a text from Nate. Of course he would find a way to torture me even though he wasn't around.

Have a good first day.

What? First, he knew I wasn't talking to him. Second, it had only been two weeks — did he think I'd forgotten? Third, could he have been any lamer? I deleted the text and shoved my phone back into my bag.

I refused to let Nate Taylor ruin one more day of my life.

"You're in so much trouble, Bloom!" Ryan Bauer was leaning against his locker, arms folded, with a mischievous grin on his face.

Fabulous. I was so not in the mood to deal with his crap.

"What is it?" I asked impatiently as I opened my locker, three doors down from his.

Ryan looked at me, confused. "Um, never mind." He grabbed my class schedule from my stack of books.

Ryan Bauer was one of those guys with a clingy girlfriend whose life revolved around him. He was the biggest cliché at our school: a star athlete with good grades, who just happened to also be gorgeous. He was over six feet tall with a lean build; he had amazing blue eyes; and he was always running his hands through his black, wavy hair. Naturally, he was also one of the biggest flirts in school. I used to go along with it, but this time I didn't have any desire to further feed his ego.

He was a guy. A *guy* guy. As far as I was concerned, he probably had the dead bodies of small children and puppies hidden in his locker.

I almost didn't recognize him without Diane Monroe hanging on his every move. Ryan and Diane had been dating since forever. Well, technically seventh grade, but in high school that *was* forever. Diane was the classic girlfriend for an over-achiever like Ryan: shiny long blond hair, pale crystal-blue eyes, model-thin frame, and always, *always* put together — your standard Cheerleader/Student Council President type.

"Man, it looks like we only have World History together," Ryan was saying to me now. "Todd is in that class, too. That totally sucks."

"Yeah, sucks." I didn't even try to hide the sarcasm in my voice.

"Hiya!" I looked down the hallway and saw none other than Miss Diane Monroe walking toward us with a huge smile on her face. She probably had some sort of sixth sense telling her that Ryan was talking to another girl. I tried not to roll my eyes as I started fishing my books out of my locker. "Happy first day of school!" she said.

I slammed my locker shut and tried to head to Spanish class — but my path was blocked by Diane, standing in front of me with her smile getting even wider, which freaked me out somewhat.

"Hey, Penny," she said. "How was your summer?" Her eyes were practically sparkling with enthusiasm. It was almost enough to make me gag.

I looked at her in confusion. Why was she talking to me? We hadn't spoken in forever.

"Uh, hi, Diane." I didn't understand why everybody felt the need to bring up summer on the first day of school. It was so annoying. Summer was over. There wasn't a need to think about it. Ever again.

"So, notice anything?" Diane started to twirl around. Everything about her screamed *perfect* — no big changes there — so I just shrugged. "Penny." Diane looked stunned. "My outfit — don't you remember?" I scanned her clothes: fitted denim blazer with a black sequined shirt underneath, pink layered miniskirt, and four-inch pink strappy sandals. I shrugged. Clearly, I didn't remember.

"Penny!" Diane opened up her blazer to reveal that the sequined shirt had a Beatles logo. "Now do you remember? We always wore a Beatles shirt on the first day of school."

My mouth dropped open. Yeah, when we were ten . . . and on speaking terms.

"Um, sorry," I said. "It's been a long time."

Diane's shoulders slouched. I wasn't giving her the response she'd been hoping for.

What did she expect? The last time I'd kept our first day of school ritual was in eighth grade. That was the day I'd been late for school because Diane hadn't come by my house to get me like she always did. That was the day my best friend forgot to wear her Beatles shirt. And it turned out to be the day I'd finally realized our friendship was over. We had been best friends for almost ten years. Our mothers had met at a book club when we were in diapers and had decided to make regular playdates for us. Her mother would pick us up from school and take us to the park, or we'd go back to my house and play in the backyard.

But none of that had mattered. Nothing else had mattered to Diane once Ryan came into the picture.

Diane had decided she only had room in her life for one person.

It had been between her best friend and her boyfriend.

Guess which one she'd picked.

Six

I GOT AWAY FROM DIANE AND Ryan as quickly as possible, before they could become DianeandRyan in the middle of the halls. But Diane's name popped back up at lunch.

"So guess who tried to make small talk with me in Biology *and* French like we're friends?" Tracy asked while we walked to the cafeteria after morning classes. "Diane Monroe — can you believe that? I think she is probably jockeying to get as many votes for Homecoming Queen as possible."

"Yeah, she's acting weird," I agreed.

"Ugh, I can't stand her."

Tracy had never really been a big fan of Diane's — not many girls in school were. Maybe it was her perfect appearance or the fact that she excelled in everything.

But that was just petty jealousy.

There was really only one person at McKinley who had a valid reason to hate Diane Monroe.

Me.

If it wasn't bad enough that she was a prime example of A Girl Who Gives Up Her Identity for a Guy, she'd also given *me* up. I'd always thought those girls who'd dump their friends whenever a guy showed interest in them were pathetic. But when I became one of those friends, I'd found out how much it hurt.

Just another example of what guys had done to ruin my life. As if treating me like crap wasn't enough, they stole my friends.

Even though I hated Tracy's list for how much it upset her, I was usually secretly glad when it ended up being a big failure. I never wanted to lose Tracy like I'd lost Diane.

Once we made our way through the long line of confused freshmen who were not yet aware of the cafeteria poison, Tracy and I established ourselves at our lunch table — the same one as last year. Our friends Morgan and Kara soon followed.

"Hey, guys," Morgan greeted us as she and Kara sat down. "My parents are so riding me about having more extracurricular activities on my college applications. Can you believe that? I have to start worrying about college already. Didn't we just start junior year?"

We all nodded in agreement. Kara shifted uncomfortably and fiddled with her apple as the rest of us dove into our lunches. It was hard not to notice the fact that she had lost even more weight over the summer — if that was even possible. She was practically drowning in her gray McKinley High hoodie.

Suddenly, Kara's body was pinned against the table by a short, curly-haired girl who must've slipped on the floor. Her tray hit Kara's head and her soda spilled on Kara's shoulder.

"Oh, no!" the girl screamed. "My soda!"

We all looked in shock as she picked up her plastic cup and surveyed her outfit, ignoring Kara completely. I'd never seen this girl before, so I figured she had to be a freshman. There was no way I would've missed her, even though she couldn't have been more than five feet tall. Everything on her was done to the extreme — acrylic nails meant to look like a French manicure, dark brown hair that had been over-highlighted with blond streaks, eyebrows narrowly plucked, and lips overly penciled in. She was wearing a very mini denim skirt and a lace tank top — in other words, looking like she was going to strut down a catwalk instead of eat lunch at the school cafeteria.

"Are you okay?" Morgan handed Kara some napkins to clean up.

"Ash-ley!" the girl screamed at her friend. "Did I get anything on my shirt?"

Tracy whipped her head around. "Excuse me — what about apologizing to my friend who you just soaked?"

The girl looked at Tracy like she was speaking a foreign language.

"What? I spilled my soda."

Tracy shot her the patented Tracy Glare — eyes squinted into tiny slits, lips pursed, a look of complete disgust. "Yes, you spilled your soda — on *my friend*. Do you understand what an apology means?"

The girl opened her mouth in annoyance. She mumbled

something that I guess was supposed to be an apology (it sounded more like a question: "saw-reh?") and walked away.

Tracy sat back down. "Unbelievable. It's the first day of school and already these freshmen think they own the place. Oh, and, what a shock, look what table they're going to."

There was a long group of tables against the windows that would always hold the jocks and cheerleaders, including the infamous Elite Eight: Ryan Bauer and Diane Monroe, Brian Reed and Pam Schneider, Don Levitz and Audrey Werner, Todd Chesney and one of his many revolving girlfriends.

Tracy and I were among the few girls left in our class who hadn't made it to the table as Todd's girl of the moment. I'd never had a desire to be part of their demented version of Noah's Ark, where you could only survive if you were paired up with a member of the opposite sex. If I had to choose between dating Todd and missing the boat, I was fully prepared to drown.

Both Kara and Morgan had dated Todd. Morgan had dated him in eighth grade, and he would go around and lie to the basketball team about how far he got with her. After he'd dumped her, Morgan had become increasingly popular with the other guys in class, until she'd realized it was because they all thought she was easy.

You would've thought that Kara would've learned from Morgan's mistakes. But no. Todd had managed to disarm all common sense in a girl. Kara had thought it would be different, so she'd taken the plunge . . . and found that this girl named Tina McIntyre was swimming in the same pool at the same time.

I couldn't help but wonder why it was that a guy could find two good girls to date at the same time, when we girls couldn't even find one decent guy.

My face became hot as I thought about how much trouble Todd had caused — not just with Kara and Morgan, but with practically half our class. I never understood the power he had over girls. He was your typical dumb jock: a big guy with a dirty blond buzz cut and an outfit that always showed off at least two sports team logos.

Thinking about Todd made me realize I wasn't the only girl at McKinley who would benefit from a boy boycott.

Those nasty freshmen girls were all over him now, and he was enjoying every minute of it.

"Guys are jerks," I practically shouted.

A laugh escaped Tracy's throat. "What to the evs — like you don't spend your time flirting with Ryan and Todd!"

Like I WHAT?

"What are you even talking about?"

"Are you even kidding me? Every time you're around Ryan, you flirt up a storm."

Yeah, well, that was the old Penny. New Penny was done flirting. I'd be happy if I never had to speak to any guys for the rest of the year.

"The guys in the Elite Eight aren't the problem," Morgan said. "Those girls are so shallow and have zero — and I mean *zero* — things to discuss outside of their boyfriends."

"Well," Kara interjected, "Diane is always nice to me. But Audrey and Pam are a little full of themselves."

Morgan glared at their table. "Please. Sure they're cheerleaders and date the star athletes — *how boring!* — but nobody really likes them. You know that's what's totally ridiculous about all of this — all those guys who are allegedly the popular ones are despised by most of the students. And anytime they're nice to somebody outside the group, it's always, *always* because they want something."

"Exactly!" Tracy chimed in. "Today in class, Diane pretended she wanted to be BFFs with me. *And* she tried the same thing with Pen this morning."

Morgan nodded. "Exactly. It's obvious she wants something."

"Yeah, well, whatever it is," Tracy said, looking over at the Elite Eight table, "she's *not* going to get it."

Seven

I GOT INTO WORLD HISTORY class and was completely surrounded.

Ms. Barnes, our teacher, did the seating assignments in alphabetical order (how original!) and I was placed between Ryan and Todd, with Derek Simpson sitting two rows behind me, and Kevin Parker (Tracy's main obsession) and Steve Powell (lower on the list) close by.

There were only three other girls in the class, and they ended up seated as far away from me as possible.

"Hey there, Señorita Penny," Todd welcomed me to my seat. We'd had Spanish together that morning and (much to my displeasure) had been assigned to be conversation partners. Todd had spent most of the time making up words by placing an *o* at the end of them — el chairo, el sandwicho, el footballo.

Ryan sat down next to me. "What a surprise," he said.

Todd leaned over to my desk. "Hey, Penny, what are you going to have your Spanish name be?"

I shrugged. I'd never really thought about it.

Todd continued, "Because I was thinking of using Nacho and figured you should pick Margarita, so when we have projects together Señora Coles will have to call on Margarita y Nacho." Todd laughed, then leaned forward and lifted up his hand.

I did my best to ignore him.

"What's this?" Ryan asked. "Bloom, are you two-timing me with Chesney? Seriously, I thought you had better taste."

Yeah, like I'm the one two-timing. I'm not the one with the girlfriend.

Todd made a rude gesture to Ryan and then the two of them started trash-talking about who was going to do more laps at practice that night.

I wondered if there were any all-girl schools in the area.

I'd never been so relieved to hear the last bell of the day. I jumped from the classroom like it was on fire and headed straight to my locker. There I found Diane waiting. Not for me. For Ryan. Of course.

Still, she waved.

Did she even have her own locker?

"Hey, Penny!" she said when I got closer. "Are you going to the game on Friday night?"

"Yep." I tried to seem busy finding my Biology textbook. I didn't know why she was all of a sudden so interested in my social calendar.

"Like anybody would want to miss that ass-kicking," Todd said, coming over with Ryan, then stopping to give him a high five. "Even Bauer's dad is going to be there! So that alone is something to show up for. That, like, happens about as often as, what, a lunar eclipse or something. . . ."

Ryan glared at Todd and slammed his locker shut. I'd known Ryan since grade school, and I'd never seen his dad. His mom and stepdad, sure. But not his dad. All I knew was that he was some hotshot lawyer in Chicago.

There was an awkward silence in their group — a group that I didn't want to get involved with. I reached for my phone and my stomach dropped when I saw I had another text waiting from Nate.

You can't ignore me forever.

I hit the DELETE button. I was sure going to try.

"Penny?" It was Diane's voice.

"What?" I looked up and noticed that she was alone. I hadn't heard Ryan and Todd leave. Why was she still here?

"Oh, um, I was just wondering . . ." She started nervously bending down the corner of her notebook. "I mean, I feel like we haven't really spoken in so long, and I'd love it if we could go out sometime — to a movie, or dinner, whatever you're up for."

She can't be serious, I thought.

"Oh, well, um . . ."

Why don't you tell me what you want so we can get this over with?

"Are you free tomorrow night?" she asked.

"Um," I stalled, trying to think of a reason why I couldn't go out with her.

"I was thinking we could go to the mall and then grab a bite to eat. Wouldn't that be fun?"

No, not really . . .

I looked at Diane. Her eyes were wide, and it seemed like she genuinely wanted to spend time with me. That, or she was so desperate to become the first junior to ever win Homecoming Queen that she was willing to take her campaign past enemy lines.

Wait a second, I thought. *This is Diane Monroe. The same Diane who cancelled on me a million times. Who would never put a friend before Ryan. If I agree, she'll no doubt cancel to do something with Ryan. Some things never change.*

"I think that could work," I said. I knew I could always make up an excuse (like that I needed to work at my dad's dental office) if she didn't cancel on me first.

Diane did a little jump. "Yay! I'll stop by tomorrow after class!"

I wasn't going to hold my breath.

Eight

"YOU AGREED TO DO WHAT?" Tracy practically ran off the side of the road when I told her the next morning. "Seriously, Pen, she's on some sort of medication. There's something off upstairs."

"I know — I see her talking to *everybody*." I tried to not laugh.

"You don't understand — you don't have any classes with her. I've got two — *before* lunch. And all she did yesterday was come over and talk to me in that cheerleadery way she has."

"Yeah, well, I'm not that worried about it. She'll cancel on me. End of story."

I guess in a way Diane prepared me for being dumped by guys. With her it was the same thing as any guy — the calls not being returned, avoiding me in the hallways, talking behind my back.

Tracy's cell phone rang. She threw her headset on, answered, listened for about three seconds, then screamed, "WHAT?"

I instinctively grabbed the wheel to steady her driving.

"Are you even serious? When?" Tracy grabbed my arm. "Oh my God!"

I wanted to hit her, but didn't want to die on my way to school. Tracy just kept on screaming and asking questions.

When she finally got off the phone, a look of smugness settled on her face.

"You're not going to believe it," she said. "Ryan broke up with Diane."

"WHAT?" I screamed so loud, Tracy winced. "You can't be serious. I've seen Diane at Ryan's locker —"

Tracy shook her head. "Jen went in early this morning with the volleyball team to practice, and the news broke. From what she knows, he broke up with her at the start of summer before she went away on vacation, but nobody really knew about it since Ryan didn't want to, I don't know, spread gossip or whatevs while she was away. They wanted to wait a few more days to tell people, but Todd ended up spilling it to Hilary Jacobs, and you can imagine where it went from there."

"That's impossible," I replied. Diane Monroe and Ryan Bauer had been together for four years. They were supposed to get married, have 2.4 kids, and have a 50 percent chance of living happily ever after.

"It all makes perfect sense! This is why she's being so nice to everybody, that fake little bee-yotch." Tracy glared at me. "And now we know exactly what she wants."

I looked at Tracy in confusion. What did Diane want?

"She thinks that now she's single, she can come running back to her good old friend Penny."

I tried to wrap my head around it. Diane dumped me for Ryan, Ryan dumped Diane, and now she expected us to be friends again.

I don't think so.

"Wait a second," Mike interrupted. "You're friends with Diane Monroe?"

"No, we *used* to be friends."

"Wow." Mike looked impressed. "She's hot. Do you think you can introduce her to me?"

"Get out of the car!" Tracy screamed. Mike rolled his eyes, and he jumped out as soon as Tracy pulled into the parking lot.

"How stupid does she think I am?" I asked. "After not talking to me for four years, she wants me to mop up after Ryan. I've got my own guy problems, thank you very much. I'm *so* canceling on her."

"What?" Tracy's eyes opened wide. "No way — you have to go!"

I couldn't believe she was even being serious. Tracy hated Diane and she wanted me to hang out with her?

"You have to get the scoop. Find out why he dumped her skinny ass and then get up and leave. You don't owe her anything. See how *she* feels being used for once."

"But I . . ."

"Come on, Pen. I wish I could go and hear her poor sad sob story. Oh, I'm so happy Ryan finally came to his senses. Hmmm, I wonder if I should put him on the list." Tracy looked thoughtful for a moment. "Nah, I've always thought he'd be better for you. Not that you're dating or anything."

I felt a migraine coming on.

❤ ❤ ❤

My headache wasn't going to go away once I got to my locker and saw Ryan. I was so preoccupied with Diane that I had forgotten that I'd have to deal with him, too. There was no way to avoid him.

Not only didn't I know what to say to him, but I didn't know how I was supposed to feel. Should I be mad at him? Should I be grateful to him for confirming once more that guys only use girls? Granted, I didn't know what had happened, but I felt it had to have been his fault.

"Hey there, Bloom," he said as I opened up my locker.

"Hey, what's new — I mean, not what's new, um . . ." I closed my eyes, hoping he'd just turn and walk away.

"Well, I see it only took twenty-four hours for the news to make its way around the school," he replied.

I looked over at him and didn't know what to say.

"Anyways," he went on, "I hear you and Diane are going out tonight."

I stared at him blankly. How did he know that?

"Hey, it's okay. I'm glad you guys are hanging out. To tell you the truth, I'm a little worried about Diane. You know how catty some people can be."

I tried to not think of Tracy . . . or myself.

"What up, Bauer?" Todd came from around the corner. I'd never been so happy to see him in my life . . . at least until he walked over and put his arm around me. "I don't give a crap that you're single now — you best stay away from my girl."

For the first time, Ryan seemed thrown off.

Todd, however, didn't pick up on this. He went on, "Now why don't you run along and start breaking some hearts while me partnero *en español* and I head to class?" As he grabbed my arm and guided me toward class, he started shaking his head. "I'm telling you," he said with an overdone sigh, "having Bauer be single is going to be trouble."

Ryan was right about news traveling fast through the school — it was all anybody could talk about. I tried to not get caught up in it, but as the lone member of The Lonely Hearts Club, I couldn't help but notice how unfair everybody was being. Nobody seemed to worry about Ryan. Of course, he would have a new girlfriend soon enough, but if he didn't, it wasn't a big deal. It was his choice. Guys rule.

But Diane was treated like damaged goods. The victim. A heartbroken, devastated shell of a person.

When people talked about Ryan, they were high-fiving, talking about his freedom.

With Diane, people were speaking in low voices, like she should've been ashamed to be single again.

So. Unfair.

I knew this. But it was still extremely awkward to be with Diane after school. I kept hearing a voice in my head that said, *The only reason she didn't cancel on you is because she doesn't have a boyfriend.*

On our way over to the diner, we talked about our families,

and how Rita was doing at college, and how her mother was remodeling their kitchen . . . again. When we got there, we talked about classes. Then what we were going to order. Then, when it seemed like the only thing left besides the breakups (ours, hers . . . pick one) was to discuss the weather, we simply stared at each other.

"So," Diane finally said as she picked at her salad. "How's Nate? Does he still spend the summer with you guys?"

My stomach tightened. "I don't want to talk about it."

"Oh." Diane looked down, realizing her question had backfired. She seemed so sad as she pushed her fork around her plate.

Finally, she looked up again. "Can I tell you something?"

I shrugged.

"I've always been a little bit jealous of you."

"Excuse me?" How could Miss Perfect, blond-hair, blue-eyes model Diane Monroe be jealous of me?

"Seriously, Penny — I mean, seriously! Look at you! Do you have any idea how hard I have to work to look like this? I mean, look at what I'm eating, for the love of carbs!" Diane motioned toward her garden salad with fat-free dressing and then looked over at my turkey sandwich with cheddar cheese and mayonnaise and potato chips.

"First off," she began, "you can eat anything and you have an awesome body."

Whatever.

"AND you have the coolest style. I choose what I'm going to wear based on what magazines tell me. I look the same as everybody else. But you have your own funky style that nobody else could pull off. You always have."

In other words, I was a freak because I preferred All Stars over stilettos.

"And, you know, I'm not stupid. I know people like you a whole lot more than they will ever like me."

As Tracy would've said, what to the evs.

Diane shifted uncomfortably in her seat. "Well, I just wanted to tell you that."

"Oh . . . thanks." I tried to give her a smile.

She picked at her salad again. "Do you remember how when we were little we used to put on those concerts for your parents?"

I nodded, surprised that Diane remembered the Beatles shows we'd performed in our basement.

"What did your parents call your basement?"

I sighed. "The Cavern." (The Cavern was the club in Liverpool where the Beatles had gotten their start.)

"Right! I remember that you had to be John and I was Paul and we had stuffed animals be Ringo and George." She started to laugh, leaning in. "And then we did that little routine in the cafeteria that summer up at the lake."

"When we went white-water tubing?"

Diane's eyes lit up. "Exactly! What were those guys' names?"

I looked down at the table, trying to remember the two brothers who'd hung out with us for that week.

"I just remember you completely schooling that one guy in air hockey." We both started to laugh. "Seriously, Penny, I thought your arm was going to come out of your socket, you were swinging it around so much." Diane started to flail her arms around fiercely and nearly knocked over her water.

And then something unexpected happened.

It was if the past four years had disappeared. As if it was just the other day that she was carrying around my books while I hobbled on crutches with a sprained ankle. The two of us began to reminisce about our friendship, and before we realized it, over an hour had passed. Diane looked thoughtfully at me. "Wow, Penny, it's been too long. We always had the best time together."

I smiled at her. We'd done everything together, made the promises that best friends make when they're in grade school — we'd go to the same college, get an apartment together, be each other's maid of honor . . .

Diane started to tap the table nervously. "I also wanted to tell you that I'm sorry." Tears were forming in her eyes. "I'm sorry that I threw our friendship away. I'm sorry that I treated you so poorly. And, most of all, I'm sorry that it's taken me so long to come to my senses. I can't begin to imagine what it must've been like for you. I couldn't help but think of you when Ryan and I broke up." Her voice cracked as she said his name. The tears were now flowing down her cheeks. "At first, I was fine. My family was going on summer vacation. I had tennis lessons to keep me occupied. But a couple of weeks ago I had nothing to do. Practice hadn't started yet. I was on my own."

She grabbed her purse and took out a tissue. She started sniffling. "I would call Audrey and Pam, but either they had plans with their boyfriends or, if they made plans with me, they'd cancel the second Don or Brian called. And I know — I *know* — that I used to do that same thing to you. That's something else I'm sorry about."

Flashes from years ago. The moments that I realized that I was losing my best friend and feeling alone, having no one.

Diane wiped the tears on her face. "It was hard for me to realize that I really didn't have any true friends. Not the kind of friend that you were. Now that school's started, it's making everything worse. I used to have a routine — Ryan would pick me up for school, I'd go to his locker, I'd . . . well, you know. You saw it. I made him my everything, and now, now I have nothing." Her sobs turned into sharp staccatos while she tried to steady her breathing.

"I . . ." I tried to find some words to comfort her, but felt so conflicted. "Diane, what do you expect me to do?"

She looked up at me with her bloodshot eyes.

"I'm really sorry about what happened with you and Ryan. Really. No one should feel that way, especially over a guy. But still . . . I don't know what to do. Because I can't forget that you completely abandoned me. I don't know what I would've done if Tracy hadn't moved to town the next year."

Diane struggled for air. "No, you're right, you're totally right. It's just . . . I don't know who I am anymore. Everybody knows me as Diane, Ryan's girlfriend, or the cheerleader, or class president. I feel so lost. Part of me thinks it's best to continue like nothing has changed, but there's another part of me that wants to just stop doing what everybody expects me to do. I don't know . . ." She shook her head. "I don't know if I want to cheer anymore. I really don't feel like cheering. I don't know what I feel like doing. I'm just . . ."

I felt sharp prickles of moisture behind my eyes. Who would've thought that I would still have something in common with Diane? I felt lost, like her.

Diane looked at me with a mixture of surprise and sympathy. She quickly handed a tissue over to me. Before I knew what was happening, I was telling Diane all about Nate. I felt stupid, knowing that I'd only dated him for a few weeks, not a few years. But for some reason, I knew she would understand. It took me a moment to comprehend that the tears that were now running down Diane's face were because of Nate.

"Oh, Penny, I'm so sorry. That's horrible! You trusted him, and he . . . Penny" — she made sure I was looking at her — "you did nothing wrong."

Although so much time had passed, I hadn't completely forgotten this Diane. The Diane who always knew the right words to say, the Diane who supported me no matter what. *This* Diane was the reason we had been best friends.

I tried to smile. "Yeah, well, I'm not making that mistake again, ever. I've decided that I'm basically done. You know, with guys." I tried to laugh, so she wouldn't think I was mental. "I just . . . I'm sick of it all. Look at us, both in tears — and for what? Because we decided to trust a guy. Big mistake. I actually formed a little club."

"A club?" Diane leaned in. "What club? Who's in it?"

"Me, myself, and I — The Lonely Hearts Club. I bet you think I'm pathetic, huh?"

Diane grabbed my hand from across the counter. "Not at all. I think you've been through a lot, and you've got to do what you need to do to get through it. If only you would've thought of this years ago, imagine the trouble you would have saved both of us. But . . . there's only one problem." Diane started to smile.

"What?"

"You can't really have a club with one person."

I laughed. "Well, I know that, but . . ."

"So how about adding another member?"

I looked at her in shock. "What?"

"Penny!" Diane wiped away her tears and looked genuinely happy. "Do you really think the next thing I want to do is date again? I'm so done, too. I just need to figure out what's next for me. Not me and Ryan. ME."

A surge of excitement rippled through me. "That's exactly what I've been thinking!"

"You have to let me in. I know I have to earn your trust back, and I will. But for now, can you at least *consider* for-giving me?"

She reached her hand out to me. I didn't even hesitate.

Now, there were two of us.

Nine

WHEN I LEFT MY DINNER WITH Diane, I felt truly happy and hopeful for the first time in weeks. Having a partner in crime, especially one who was also going through a breakup, was exactly what I needed.

I reached for my phone and saw that I had three texts.

The first two were from Tracy:

Has she started crying yet?

If she does start sobbing, take a picture for me!

And the third was from Nate:

I'm going to keep txting you until you reply.

I ignored Nate and called Tracy.

"Spill it," she answered.

I tried to fill her in, but she wouldn't let me get a word in edgewise. She kept making fun of Diane, which started to frustrate me.

"Tracy, stop it." My voice started to rise. "You know, this

has been hard on her. Imagine what she's going through. She feels lost —"

"Oh, please," Tracy interrupted. "Do you hear yourself? Next thing you know, you're going to be inviting her to eat lunch with us."

Dead silence.

Tracy sighed. "Are you kidding me? Please tell me this is a joke."

"Tracy." I spoke slowly, choosing my words carefully. "Everybody is being really mean to her. Consider it an act of charity."

"I already gave at the office," Tracy deadpanned.

"Please. For me?" I didn't even try to hide the desperation in my voice.

"Fine. But you owe me."

I got off the phone with her before she had a chance to change her mind.

"You do realize that I am going to kill you for this?" Tracy reminded me for the fourteenth time as we headed to lunch the next day.

"Just please give her a chance," I begged.

"Highly unlikely. I don't know — call me crazy, Pen, but I'm just not very excited about watching my best friend get used."

"I know what I'm doing." I headed toward a small table in the corner in case there was any hair-pulling or biting. I told

Morgan and Kara it was better for them to eat elsewhere today; I didn't want to make them an accessory to any violence that ensued.

"Yeah, I think you said the same thing at the start of the summer."

I froze in place.

Tracy grabbed my hand. "I'm so sorry, Pen — that was an awful thing to say."

I tried to shake the thought from my mind. This was going to be hard enough without having to think about . . . him.

"Just please, Tracy. For me. Be nice."

Tracy sat down and didn't say a word.

"Hey, guys." Diane sat down at our table. "Thanks so much for having me!"

Tracy forced out a smile.

"Oh!" Diane set a small cardboard box on the table. "And as a thank-you . . . cupcakes!" Diane placed two fancy cupcakes on the table.

"Thanks." I grabbed the bigger one and started licking the pink frosting. I glared at Tracy.

"Yeah, thanks."

Diane beamed, probably because that was the first positive thing Tracy had ever said to her. "You know, Penny, after last night, I feel so much better. Swearing off boys was the best decision ever. The Club is going to be awesome."

Uh-oh.

Tracy looked between us. "What club?"

"Um, you see . . ." This wasn't going to be good. "You know how I pretty much declared that all guys are scum?"

Tracy rolled her eyes. "Yeah."

"Well, I decided I'm not dating anymore."

"Penny —" Tracy interrupted.

"Tracy, can you just hear me out?" My patience was wearing thin. "I tried to tell you the other day, but you kept interrupting me."

Tracy closed her mouth and leaned back in her chair.

"I'm done dating. At least while I'm still here at this school and have to deal with these idiots. So I started calling myself The Lonely Hearts Club."

Tracy looked confused. "Is that a Beatles reference?"

"Yes, and if you ever listened to any of the music I've given you, you'd know that. ANYWAYS, I'm serious. I'm not dating anymore. And Diane's decided to join my ban."

Diane turned to Tracy. "You should join, too, Tracy. It could be fun."

Tracy looked at Diane with contempt. "Do you think I'm so pathetic I can't get a date?"

"Hey, that's not why —" I tried to interrupt.

"No, that's not what I meant. I . . ." Diane looked hurt.

Tracy glared at Diane. "Right — how long is your membership going to last? Like you could exist without being fawned over by the entire male population."

"Tracy, please," I said. "The Club is important to me."

Tracy groaned. "Be serious, Penny!"

My face became hot with anger. How could I have expected Tracy to understand the hurt that Diane and I were going through? Tracy had never had her heart crushed.

"You just don't get it!" I screamed. This was the first time I'd ever raised my voice to Tracy. The group of freshmen at the table next to us got up and left. "I know you don't understand what I'm going through, but this is what I need." My voice started to waver as I tried to fight back tears. "I thought it was over, but it isn't. He keeps sending me these texts."

"He what?" Tracy pursed her lips.

"He just . . ." I didn't have the energy to deal with Nate.

"Penny, I told you — he's such a jerk," Diane said softly. "You don't owe him anything."

Tracy turned to Diane. "You know about Nate?"

"Of course she knows. But I don't want to talk about Nate right now. This Club, not dating — this is what I want to do. And, even more important, it's what I *need* to do. Diane supports me. I wish you would, too."

Silence fell on the table. "Pen," Tracy said in a quiet voice. "I'm sorry if you think I'm not being supportive, but don't you see? She's just using you."

Diane flinched. "How can you say that? I'm not using Penny." She paused for a moment, took a deep breath, and looked directly at Tracy. "Why do you hate me so much?"

"I don't —"

"Yes, you do." Diane looked down at her half-eaten salad. "I don't know why, but you always have. I was hoping that the three of us could be friends, because I know how much you mean to Penny. There is no way I could be friends with Penny again without your . . . approval, I guess."

Tracy looked at Diane with complete incomprehension. I don't think she ever imagined Diane Monroe would look to her for anything, much less approval.

"I just . . ." Tracy looked upset. "I don't want you to take Penny away from me."

I looked at Tracy in horror. How could she think that? "Tracy, Diane isn't going to do that."

Diane hesitantly reached over and put her arm on Tracy's shoulder. "Do you think you could just give me a chance? *Please?*"

I reached over to Tracy. "You know I have to have you behind me."

Tracy shook her head. "I guess I could try . . . for Penny." Diane's face lit up. "But hold on a second." Tracy glared at Diane. "If you ever, I mean *ever*, pull that crap with Penny again, if you hurt her, you will not live long enough to regret it."

Diane nodded weakly. "I'd really like us to be friends, Tracy. I really would."

Tracy gave Diane an encouraging smile. "Yeah, well, knowing the history with my list, I guess it's only a matter of time before I join you guys on the dark side."

"Can I see your list?" Diane asked hesitantly.

Tracy paused a few seconds before she pulled it out of her bag. "Why not?"

"Oh, I know Paul Levine. He's a really nice guy," Diane offered.

I guessed this was as good a start as I could've hoped for in our new, three-way friendship.

Ten

AFTER FOUR YEARS OF BASICALLY ignoring each other, it surprised me how quickly Diane and I fell back into place. I assumed it would be awkward, but it wasn't. It was the Penny and Diane of old.

I was waiting for Diane at my locker at the end of the day when Ryan turned the corner, looking upset. He threw open his locker and started shoving books into his backpack with so much force I expected the strap to break.

I looked up and saw Diane approaching me with a smile on her face.

I kept looking between them. I knew they'd been speaking since the breakup, but I didn't want to find myself in the middle of it.

Ryan slammed his locker shut and nearly ran into me when he turned around.

"Sorry," he said.

"Um, that's okay," I replied. Diane was nearly at our lockers. "Um, everything okay?"

"Huh?" He looked agitated. "I didn't do well on my Chem Lab."

"Oh, okay." I didn't know what else to say to him. I'd never had trouble speaking with Ryan, but with Diane coming over, I felt like I was betraying her in a way.

"Hey, guys," Diane greeted us.

I noticed people in the hallways slowing down so they could watch Diane and Ryan.

Ryan and Diane noticed, too.

There was an awkward silence in our group as people were hovering, dissecting their every move. I just said the first thing that came to my mind. "Ryan didn't do well on his Chemistry Lab."

Ryan gave me a weird look.

"Sorry, I just . . ." I was embarrassed.

Diane rolled her eyes. "Like a B is hardly something to get bent out of shape about. Plus, aren't you getting extra credit or something for that student advisory thing?"

"What advisory thing?" I asked.

Ryan blushed. "It's nothing. Principal Braddock has asked some students to meet with him on a regular basis to give him a better sense of the concerns of the student body."

I was confused. "Isn't that what Student Council is for?"

Ryan shrugged. "I don't know. We've only met once, and all he wanted to talk to me about was football. I guess he just wants to relive his glory years."

Back in his day, Braddock was McKinley High's star athlete, and if one were to forget, there were a bunch of pictures of him in the trophy cases to remind us.

"Yeah, so much for —" Ryan was interrupted by a high, shrieking sound coming from the hallway. I nearly fell over when I saw that it was coming from Tracy.

She ran over with a look of pure excitement and ended up running me smack into my locker.

"Ow!"

Tracy put her hand over her mouth and tried to stifle her laughter. "Sorry! You're not going to believe what happened!"

I moved my shoulder to make sure it was still in its socket.

"Paul is having a party at his house on Saturday and asked me to come!"

"Paul Levine?" I asked.

"Yes, can you believe it? He's number three on the list."

"Wow, Tracy, that's great!" I looked over at Diane, who gave me a little wink.

Tracy was absolutely glowing, "So you're going to come with me, right? It's going to be so much fun. His parents are away and he's a senior, so there will probably be a ton of seniors there, probably even Kevin. You're going to be there, right, Diane?"

Diane looked shocked that Tracy was including her. "Of course."

"See, Pen, you have to go! Right, Diane?"

Diane laughed. "Come on, Penny!"

Just a few hours ago Tracy was at Diane's throat. And now Tracy was using Diane to bully me into going to a party.

"Of course, I'll go with you," I said. Ryan was looking at the three of us with a combined look of confusion and amusement.

I was a little nervous about attending a house party. Parkview was a pretty small town — only ten thousand people, and my parents knew most of them. If I was ever caught at a party where the parents weren't at home, I knew I'd be in so much trouble. My mother was a small woman, but she carried the wrath of God in her. I didn't like to make her angry. You wouldn't like her when she's angry.

It was just one more thing I was going to have to be careful about.

"What are you wearing to the party?" I asked Tracy, as we sat down in the football stands for the next night's game.

"What's *Diane* wearing?"

Tracy had been on her best behavior with Diane since Paul's invitation. I hoped it wasn't all an act.

"Maybe we'll get you a nice straitjacket to match your attitu — Ow!"

Tracy's fingers dug into my right arm. "Shh!" she said as she tried to subtly motion in front of us.

"Nuumb seev," Tracy mumbled.

"What?" I was convinced this was it. Tracy had finally lost her mind.

"Nuuummmb seeevvv." Tracy moved her head forward somewhat violently.

"Are you having a seizure?" I asked.

She looked over at me and held up seven fingers.

Seven? Seven what?

Clearly frustrated with me, she leaned in. "Steve is number seven on my list." She motioned to the row in front of us, where Steve Powell had sat down with some friends.

I rolled my eyes.

Tracy beamed. "This is the year the list is finally going to work. We have Paul tomorrow, and tonight . . ."

I was praying she was kidding. In the first few days of school, the list that consisted of eight guys at McKinley was already down to four. Mark Dowd was crossed off for talking to Kathy Ehrich too much in Trig, Eric Boyd had cut his hair too short, W. J. Ross had gotten a job at Tracy's least favorite fast-food restaurant, and Chris Miller committed the ultimate sin, dating Amy Gunderson over the summer. At this point, there wasn't going to even *be* a list by Homecoming.

"Say something." Tracy kept poking me. I was going to have a serious bruise.

"Um, okay. Do you know what Ryan's dad looks like?" I began to scan the crowd. I saw Ryan's mom, stepdad, and stepsister in the crowd, waving GO, RYAN! signs. I recognized all the parents around them; nobody looked like an older version of Ryan.

Tracy groaned. "What? Who cares? Say something to Steve — get his attention."

All of a sudden, she burst out in over-the-top laughter, complete with slapping her knee. As she doubled over, she moved her knee so it hit Steve's shoulder.

"Oh, I'm so sorry." Tracy leaned forward and put her hand where her knee had been.

Steve turned around and smiled. "Hey, Tracy, don't worry about it."

"So how are classes going so far?" Tracy began.

I looked on as Tracy worked her "magic" on Steve. I was impressed by the way it seemed so effortless, even though I knew it wasn't. Every once in a while, she'd touch his arm when she was making a point and she'd laugh at pretty much everything he said. I was so entertained by her and Steve that I wasn't even watching the game.

"Hey, so are you guys going to Paul's tomorrow night?" Steve asked.

Tracy smiled. "Of course. You?"

Steve nodded. "Hey, is Diane going to go with you guys? I see that you've been hanging out with her at lunch the last couple of days."

Tracy glared at Steve, bolted up in her seat, and headed toward the aisle.

Steve looked at me. "What's with her?"

I shrugged my shoulders as I got up to find her.

If I was keeping count correctly, there were now only three guys left on her list.

Eleven

I WAS ALMOST AFRAID TO LET Tracy drive the next night to Paul's house, for fear we'd be pulled over for Driving While Under the Influence of a Boy. She was looking in the rearview mirror so often to check her makeup that you would've thought she was driving backward, not forward.

When we finally pulled up outside Paul's house, there were already cars lining the entire left side of the street. We could hear music blaring from inside. I had a bad feeling about this.

"How do I look?" Tracy asked for the twelfth time. I looked out the window and saw a couple of sophomore girls wearing tight jeans and tiny pieces of fabric that I could only assume were supposed to be shirts. I glanced down at my long-sleeved top and tan cords, feeling more and more unsure about all of this by the minute.

We got out of the car and walked to the house. Suddenly, some guy burst out of the front door, startling both me and Tracy as he ran toward the bushes and threw up.

Paul appeared in the doorway. "Dude, that is so not cool." Then he started laughing and gesturing for people to come and watch.

Tracy cleared her throat, hoping that Paul would notice that she'd shown up.

It worked.

"Hey, guys!"

He motioned us to come inside, and I felt my heart start pounding. The odor of cigarette smoke stung my nose. My mom was going to kill me if she smelled cigarettes on me. And I didn't mean *kill* in a metaphoric way.

Paul grabbed a random plastic cup from the table in the hallway and took a swig. "Keg's in the kitchen. Help yourself," he instructed. Then he vanished among the mass of bodies in the next room.

I glanced at the door, hoping we could make a quick get-away. When I looked back, Tracy was already on her way toward the kitchen.

I hesitated, but began to follow her through the crowd of people. I scanned the room for familiar faces, but only recognized the standard football players and cheerleaders who Paul hung out with. Over in one corner were those two freshmen girls from the cafeteria, Missy and Ashley. Naturally, guys were all over them.

We reached the kitchen and saw the line for the keg. Tracy leaned in, and I couldn't make out what she was saying over the music blaring from the stereo in the living room. Then she screamed, "Are you going to drink?" I shook my head back and forth.

"Okay, good," she said.

I was glad to know Tracy still had some sense left in her.

"You can be the designated driver then."

On second thought . . .

My head started throbbing in time to the beat of the bass. As Tracy waited in line to get a beer, I tried to stand around like I belonged there, even though I felt so out of place, like I was on display.

"Woo! Who's gonna shotgun a beer with me?" Todd screamed as he entered the kitchen. "Margarita!" He came over and placed his arm around my shoulder. "My girl Margarita is here, all right! Time for the par-*tay* to start!" He started doing what was probably supposed to be the robot, but he'd obviously already had one too many to pull off any dance moves.

Ryan came into the kitchen and looked a little concerned when he saw Todd grabbing me. "Hey, Todd, I think there are some freshmen girls in there wanting to hear all about your interception that got us into the Regionals last year."

Todd ran over and gave Ryan a high five. "That's awesome! I don't want to disappoint the ladies." He left the kitchen as Ryan shook his head.

"Thought you needed some saving," he said to me.

"Thanks, he's, ah . . ."

"Wasted. I keep telling him that one of these days he's going to get caught. Coach Fredericks would kick us off the team if he caught any of us drinking."

I nodded, but couldn't help notice that Ryan was also holding a cup. Was I going to have to drive *everybody* home?

"I have to admit, I'm a little surprised that you ended up coming," he said.

"Why? Am I such a loser that I wouldn't come to some stupid keg party?" I was taken aback at how defensive I sounded.

"No, no, not at all." Ryan held his hands up. "I didn't really think this was your kind of crowd. To tell you the truth, I'm relieved to see you. At least there's someone here who can talk about something other than sports or drinking or . . . well, you know." I was sure he was referring to the breakup. He gave me a smile as he pointed to his cup, which was filled with a dark liquid. "I'm getting some more soda — do you want some?"

I nodded, thankful that I didn't have to do a keg stand to hang out with Ryan. He walked over to a counter and put some ice in a cup for me while Tracy returned from the keg line and started to drink.

"I can't believe how many girls are here," she said. "Well, wish me luck — I'm going to go find Paul." Before I could say anything, she had taken a deep breath and was out in the living room.

"Do you want to get away from the noise?" Ryan screamed over the music. I nodded, and we walked out to the far side of the backyard and sat under a big willow tree.

"Hey, I've been meaning to ask you — did that list ever work with your parents?" Ryan asked.

"What list?"

He ran his fingers through his hair. "Top Ten Reasons Penny Needs to Get a Car."

I couldn't believe he remembered that. "No, the list didn't work. Not even with such gems as number six: *Another venue to listen to Beatles music.*"

"So, how often do you work at your dad's dentist office? It seems like every time I have a checkup, you're there."

"Oh, not that often. Just a few days a week — extra pocket money." I started to shiver, wishing I'd worn a sweater.

He took off his letter jacket. "Here, wear this." I took the jacket and put it on — it was way too big for me, but warm.

"So, did you and Diane have fun the other night?" he asked.

I looked down at the ground. Talking to Ryan about Diane was making me uncomfortable. They seemed to talk a lot, but how was that possible? I usually pretended that any guy I had broken up with (or gotten dumped by) didn't exist anymore. Or, preferably, was dead.

"Yeah, um, is that weird for you?" I asked.

He studied me for a second. "I know that this might sound weird and I probably sound like a big loser, but Diane has been such a huge part of my life the last few years. I can't imagine never speaking to her again. As much as people can't seem to grasp the concept, we're still friends."

"You better be careful — you might make Todd jealous." I smiled at him.

He started to laugh. "Every year I keep thinking that Chesney will finally calm down, but he just keeps getting worse and worse." He shook his head. "You know, I probably shouldn't tell you this, but . . ."

"What?" I asked, curious about what kind of gossip Ryan would have about Todd.

"Have you heard of dibs? The guys on the team call dibs on girls they like so no other guy will go after her."

"Does the girl have any choice in this matter?" I asked. I guess it shouldn't have surprised me that guys did such a thing.

Ryan shook his head. "Hey, I'm still trying to figure all of this stuff out, too, you know."

"Uh-huh." I was so glad I didn't have to deal with this anymore.

"So, anyways, be careful with Todd."

"Why? You know, besides the usual harassment."

Ryan uncurled his long legs and stretched them out next to me. "Well, Todd has a major crush on you and called dibs. And he can kind of be persistent when he has his mind set on something."

Oh?

Oh.

Oh, no.

I stayed silent. Ryan looked at me expectantly. I tried to not look completely disgusted. This was the last thing I needed.

"Sorry," he said. "I probably shouldn't have told you that."

"No, that's okay," I assured him. "I guess I should've expected it. Are there even any girls left in our class that he hasn't dated?"

Ryan shook his head. "You sell yourself short, Bloom."

I groaned. "Please — this is Todd. He's just . . . Can we not talk about Todd?"

"Fair enough. What do you want to talk about?"

"Anything but Todd."

We continued talking about everything but Todd. He told funny stories involving his summer job lifeguarding at the beach. I shared my theory that my mother was going to leave her job to stalk Paul McCartney full-time. We both pondered where Michael Bergman hung out between classes, since neither of us ever saw him at his locker, which was between ours. I also discovered that Ryan got freaked out whenever he would see my dad, because he didn't want to get in trouble for not flossing. (I stored that one away for future teasing.)

And then Ryan ruined it all by defaming my character.

"You're out of your mind," I protested.

Ryan leaned his head back as he let out a laugh. "Oh, right — so you're going to deny that you're a Goody Two-shoes?"

"First off," I began, "only a Goody Two-shoes would use the expression 'Goody Two-shoes.'"

"Point taken," he replied. "But come on — don't think I didn't see what happened last year during locker inspections."

Oh, crap.

"I don't know what you're referring to," I lied.

Ryan sat up and leaned over so we were eye to eye. "You know."

I shrugged. "Really, Ryan. I mean, with a Goody Two-shoes like me . . ."

He bolted upright. "Okay, then answer me this: Were you or were you not concealing alcohol in your locker when Braddock came by for inspections last spring?"

So not fair.

"I technically wasn't hiding anything in my locker."

"Oh, really?"

"Really."

He stared me down with a smug look on his face. He knew he had me busted.

"Yes, technically *I* didn't hide it."

"But there was alcohol in your locker."

I nodded. "But only because Michael put his coat in my locker at the last minute."

"And why did he do that?"

"Because he had a bottle of vodka in his jacket."

"And . . ."

I looked at Ryan in confusion — that was pretty much it. We had a surprise locker inspection near spring break, and Michael freaked out and shoved his jacket into my locker. I didn't even have a chance to say anything, as Braddock was inspecting Michael's locker with intensity . . . and then pretty much passed mine by.

"Oh, wait . . ."

Ryan's eyes sparkled. "You see."

"Oh my God, people *do* think I'm a Goody Two-shoes."

"That's why he did it — he knew your locker would never get inspected." He started laughing as he playfully poked at my side.

"Yeah, but what about you?"

It was time for revenge.

"Oh, I'm a total badass." He couldn't even get the words out with a straight face.

"Right, I forgot. Exactly how many bad-a people are on Principal Braddock's kiss-up committee?"

Ryan's eyes narrowed. "Student Advisory Committee, thank you very much."

"Oh, I'm sorry — I know how hard it must have been for you to earn all those brownie points to get in."

He gasped dramatically. "My entire life's goal has been to get into that committee. Don't you dare belittle it."

"Oh, I wouldn't want to upset you. Hmmm . . ." I got up to start surveying the ground near where we were sitting.

"What are you looking for?" Ryan asked.

"Your purse."

He quickly stood up, and before I knew it he had me flung over his shoulders.

"Put me down!" I screamed.

He laughed while he twirled me around in response.

It was only when I was back down on the ground, giggling

while I regained my balance, that I saw Diane examining the scene before her.

"Hey, guys, um . . ." Diane looked awkward enough for the three of us. "Penny, I've been trying to find you for the past half hour. I didn't even see you come in. I think you may want to come inside — Tracy isn't feeling so hot."

Tracy!

I was a horrible friend. I had completely forgotten that she was inside drinking. I gave Ryan back his jacket as we followed Diane inside. She led me into a bathroom on the second floor where Tracy was lying on the tile floor, looking a light shade of green.

I bent down next to her and brushed her hair out of her face.

"What is she doing here?" Tracy pointed at Diane.

"Be nice." I started to help her off the floor.

"Wait." Ryan came in, washed out his cup, and filled it with water. "She's going to need this first."

Ryan, Diane, and I waited around in awkward silence for what seemed like ages while we forced Tracy to drink two cups of water. She stared at Diane the entire time.

"You aren't going to take her away from me," she slurred.

Diane began to reply but Ryan interrupted. "Okay, time to get you up and home."

"Stop!" Tracy pushed Ryan away. "I don't want Paul to know I'm a mess. I can walk out myself. I want to say good-bye first."

Diane gave me a weird look that I couldn't read. "I don't think that's a good idea, Tracy," she said. "Seriously — you should just make him wonder what happened to you. I might even let him know that you've had your share of guys hitting on you. . . ."

Tracy liked the thought of that and agreed to go quietly.

As we headed downstairs, we saw Todd standing on the couch, dancing with his shirt off.

"No way, Penny!" he called out. "You can't leave!" He stumbled over and nearly knocked me to the floor. Ryan grabbed Todd to steady him. Meanwhile, Diane was trying to hold Tracy up, but Tracy kept trying to push her away.

This was a nightmare.

"Margreeeeta," Todd was slurring. "Margreeeeta, where've you been?"

"She was out in the back talking to me," Ryan replied.

Todd pushed Ryan off of him. "God, Bauer! What, you need to . . . you need to . . . you can't . . ."

"I didn't *do* anything, Todd. Calm down." Ryan grabbed him again by the shoulders. "Penny and I are just friends. I'd never do anything with her. You should know me better than that."

Yeah, and I should've known better than to have gone to this party.

To make matters worse, Missy came running over. She threw her arms around Ryan and said, "Hey, sexy — I've been looking all over for you."

I took Tracy's hand and walked out to the car. Diane helped buckle her in as I adjusted the rearview mirror. Ryan came running over to the car (he somehow managed to escape from Missy's claws) and tapped on the window. I lowered it.

"Sorry about that. I didn't want to give him any reason to be more upset."

"It's fine." I started to fiddle with Tracy's radio.

"Are you mad?"

I took a deep breath. I didn't know what I was.

"No, I'm fine, really. This evening has been a complete disaster."

"Oh," he replied in a softer voice. "Well, I had fun."

"Well, good for you."

I turned on the engine and drove away.

Twelve

THINGS WERE A BIT AWKWARD the following morning. Tracy was hungover and miserable. Diane was coming over to talk, and I had a feeling it was about what she'd seen between me and Ryan.

"Hey, how's Tracy feeling?" Diane said as she entered my bedroom.

"Not so hot. She's in the shower now." I nodded toward the hallway. "There was no way I could've brought her home last night. I was able to sneak her in."

Diane was looking around. "Wow, I forgot how cool your room is." I looked around at the Beatles posters that lined my walls and the bulletin board full of old concert signs and ticket stubs. I guess it *was* pretty cool. Mostly it was just home.

"Well, I'm glad I have a few minutes alone with you, because there is something that I need to tell you." Diane sat on my bed and looked nervous.

"There's nothing going on between me and Ryan," I blurted out.

"What?" Diane replied.

I started pacing my room. "I was so miserable when I got to the party, and when he suggested going outside and getting away from it all, I just went along with it. I mean, he's a guy, the enemy. Not to mention the guy who broke your heart. I would never — and I mean *never* — do anything with him."

Diane shook her head. "I know that. I was a little surprised when I saw the two of you." She laughed. "It was a little uncomfortable, but you two have always been friends. What I really wanted to talk to you about was Tracy. You see . . . I saw Paul kissing someone else at the party."

Uh-oh.

"I got there with Audrey and Pam, and I needed to go to the bathroom. So I went upstairs, and I walked in on him . . ."

Tracy was *definitely* going to kill the messenger for this one.

I lay down on my bed. "This is going to be ugly," I warned Diane. "She was really hoping he was going to ask her out."

Diane shifted uncomfortably and started playing with the frayed end of one of my bed pillows.

"Much better!" Tracy came barging into my room with a towel on her head and collapsed onto the bed. "Okay, time to figure out what we're going to do about the complete ass I made out of myself. I don't think Paul is ever going to ask me out now."

Diane and I stared at each other, not sure what to say.

Tracy looked exhausted. "Okay, okay. I know, guys, and I'm so sorry."

What exactly did she know?

"First." She turned to Diane. "I'm sorry I was rude to you. I've been trying to be a good and understanding friend. And I know, I know . . . I shouldn't have had any beer but I gave into peer pressure. I've turned into a sad after-school special, blah, blah, blah . . ." Tracy covered her face with her hands. "Just please don't tell me that Paul ended up hooking up with one of those freshman girls."

Diane looked at me. "No, he didn't. . . ."

Tracy sat up a little too quickly, so she had to lie back down, curling up on her side and propping her head up with her hand. "That's great. I thought I really blew it. . . ."

Silence. I looked over at Diane and saw the look of pure panic in her face.

Tracy wrinkled her eyebrows. "Wait, what's going on?" She looked at the two of us. "What aren't you guys telling me? Did Paul hook up with somebody last night?"

Diane looked at me and I shrugged my shoulders. I wanted to know who it was. Especially since that girl needed to be put into protective custody once Tracy found out.

Before Diane could even say anything, Tracy rolled onto her stomach and put a pillow over her head. "I knew it! Why would he be interested in me?"

I yanked the pillow off her. "Tracy, that's ridiculous. I've told you time and time again that a guy would be lucky to have someone like you in his life."

She rolled her eyes. "What to the evs — I want Paul. Why doesn't he like me? Am I fat?"

"Tracy! Stop that!"

"What then?" I could see tears starting to form in the corners of her eyes. "Tell me what it is and I'll change it — my hair, my eye color, my clothes, my personality. What is it about me that he doesn't like?"

Diane hesitantly moved toward Tracy and put her hand on Tracy's shoulder. "It's none of those things. It's something you can't fix."

Tracy sniffled and turned around to face us. "What does that mean?"

"It means that you're not a guy," Diane said. "I walked in on him and Kevin Parker kissing."

Oh. My. God.

Tracy sat up and wiped the tears away.

"What?" She looked confused. "Who?"

Diane shifted uncomfortably. "Paul Levine and Kevin Parker."

Tracy stared at the ground. "You're telling me that numbers one and three on my list were making out? And that Kevin Parker, superstar jock who I've worshipped for years, is gay?"

Diane looked scared. "I only know what I saw."

"Well," Tracy started shaking her head. "Well, I guess that explains it."

I was confused. "Explains what?"

"That everybody in school has had a boyfriend, except for me. Even Kevin frickin' Parker has a boyfriend!" Tracy started to laugh. "Oh, this is so priceless. I mean, I'm running out of guys to even put on a list, let alone date!" Tracy's smile began to fade. "I'm such a freak."

I tried to protest, but Tracy cut me off. "Mike always has a girlfriend — he hooked up with some Michelle chick last weekend at some stupid freshman party and now they're dating. Michael and Michelle." She rolled her eyes again. "Puke."

"See, Tracy, this is exactly why I've given up boys entirely." I pretended to wipe my hands clean. "Done. Moving on. Not worth the trouble."

And as if Nate could tell I was trying to move on, my cell phone went off.

I peered at it with hesitation.

Tracy got up. "This is ridiculous." She flipped open my phone and read the text. "*I can't believe U R being so childish.* Is he serious? What a jerk."

Tracy's fingers started working my phone.

"What are you doing?" I asked in panic. "Just delete it."

"No — I'm telling him what's what."

My stomach dropped.

I got up and tried to grab the phone from Tracy, but she hit SEND and snapped it shut.

"Done. There's no harm in me telling him to go to hell, is there?"

My phone started to ring. Of course it was him. When it stopped ringing, Tracy opened it back up and started pressing buttons. "I'm changing his name to 'Jackass' and putting his ringer and indicator to silence. Maybe that will shut him up."

"Ah, thanks," I finally managed to get out. Why couldn't Tracy bounce back like that when guys treated *her* like crap?

Diane smiled. "See, Tracy — it's pretty obvious that dating guys gives you nothing but a headache. It's so stupid — I know a couple of girls in cheerleading that are dating guys just because they want to have a date for Homecoming." Diane looked up at me. "Hey, Penny, could we go to Homecoming together?"

"What?" I was still looking at my phone.

"Homecoming, you . . . me?"

"Oh. Oh! Hells, yeah!"

"Seriously," Tracy said as she got up and put my phone in my desk drawer. "I mean *seriously*, you guys are going to Homecoming together?"

I turned my attention back to the Club. "Of course!" I replied. "This is what the Club is all about. We don't need dates to have fun."

"Oh, I love it!" Diane got up and started doing her little cheerleaderly clap. "And, I'm totally going to buy you roses on Valentine's Day. I'm going to make all those stupid boys jealous!" She gave me a wink.

Tracy groaned and put her head underneath a pillow.

"Tracy, I'm really sorry about this, and I know you aren't happy with the Club, but try to see it my way."

Tracy emerged from the pillow. "No," she said, "I'm groaning because I'm totally giving in. Happy? Is your club ready for a third member?"

I hesitated. As much as I wanted her to be part of this, I wanted her to do it because she believed in it, not because she felt left out.

"Are you sure?"

She nodded. "Yes. I mean, hey, it isn't really going to change anything for me, when you think about it."

Diane gave Tracy a hug . . . and, surprisingly, Tracy didn't punch her in the face.

I guess this could've been considered a pretty good start.

"To The Lonely Hearts Club!" I stuck out my hand and Tracy and Diane followed.

"The Lonely Hearts Club!"

I ran over to my stereo and blasted the Beatles.

Tracy danced over to me. "So, if I have to pretend to be a Beatle, can I be Yoko?"

She knew how to egg me on so bad. I leaned over, grabbed a pillow from my bed, and threw it at her. It hit her perfectly in the face. "Hey!"

Tracy chased after me as I dodged her pillows. It took Diane a few minutes to decide what to do, so Tracy took advantage of her indecisiveness and landed a pillow blow right to her abdomen. Diane looked at Tracy in complete shock.

"Your little pom-poms aren't gonna do you any good here, Monroe," Tracy taunted. With that, Diane jumped over my desk chair and bombarded Tracy with an assault of cushions until my bedroom was destroyed.

When Diane finally caught her breath, she said, "You have to admit — this Club definitely isn't going to be boring."

Tracy rolled over on her stomach. "And we haven't even gotten to the sacrificing of live goats — and guys — yet!"

Thirteen

I TRIED TO GET MY BOOKS for Spanish class as quickly as possible on Monday morning, wondering how I'd be able to avoid Todd even though we were conversation partners.

"Chesney!" I heard Ryan call out.

Great.

I felt an arm wrap around my shoulders. I looked up to see Todd smiling. "Hey there, Margarita — how killer was Saturday night?"

I smiled weakly at him.

"You totally should've stayed longer."

"Oh, yeah," Ryan replied with a smirk. "What did she miss?"

Todd looked down at the floor as if he was genuinely trying to remember.

"That's what I thought." Ryan smiled and gave me a wink. "Good luck, Penny."

Ryan headed to class, shaking his head.

Todd still had his arm around my shoulder, and I picked up my stride to step out of it.

"Whoa, slow down!" Todd put his arm around my waist. "Your boy is still recovering from the weekend."

"Um, I actually have to talk to Señora Coles before class

starts about, um, something." I took his hand off my waist and practically ran to class.

I wondered if it would've been too subtle to wear a T-shirt that said THANK YOU FOR YOUR INTEREST, BUT I AM NO LONGER DATING.

I knew Todd wasn't a huge fan of reading, but he did like to stare at my shirts.

"I have sort of a weird question to ask," Morgan said to me as we walked to Bio.

"Um, okay?"

"Have you ever asked a guy out?"

"No, why?"

She slowed down. "Well, I'm interested in somebody, but he's a little shy, so I don't think he'd ever make the first move."

"Oh." So much for asking Morgan to join the Club. "I'm not really the best person to talk to about guys. I've sorta given them up after, well, you know . . ."

"Oh, right. Sorry." She bit her bottom lip.

"That's okay. Who's the guy?" I asked as we walked into class.

Morgan motioned to the boy sitting in the first row of the room.

I saw senior Tyson Bellamy hunched over his chair, his hair covering his face as he furiously wrote something in his notebook.

"Isn't he cute?" Morgan blushed. Tyson looked up toward the front of the room with an intense look on his face.

Even if I were interested in guys, Tyson really wasn't my type — long black hair, super skinny, vintage rock T-shirts. Basically, he had the whole mysterious rocker thing down to a science. Besides the fact that he was a pawn for the devil (being a guy and all), he seemed right for Morgan, who was a total punk-rock fanatic. She was one of my few friends who understood the cultural importance of the Beatles.

"Would you go to one of his concerts with me on Friday?"

I wasn't in the mood to play matchmaker, but after all the drama with Tracy at last week's football game, I didn't mind having an excuse to not go to this week's away game.

"Sure — but, Morgan, I'm not going to be a good wing girl."

She laughed. "But you're my concert buddy. You have to go with me. We don't even have to talk to any guys. Just listen to the music. Then we can leave."

Sounded like the perfect night to me.

"So, are we going to have rules for the anti-guy Club?" Tracy asked at lunch.

"It's called The Lonely Hearts Club," I reminded her.

"Uh-huh. And are we going to have to wear matching T-shirts or chastity belts or something? I can't wait to see *that* logo."

"Tracy —"

"I think having rules or guidelines or a mantra of some sort would be fun," Diane chimed in, interrupting what could've been the Club's first official fight.

Since the weather was still nice, we'd decided to eat outside. I leaned against a big oak tree as I ate my apple.

Tracy sat up. "Oh, please, let me write the rules. It'll be so much fun!"

"Fine," I said. "Do what you want . . ."

Tracy grabbed her notebook and started writing some suggestions. I leaned back against the trunk of the tree and closed my eyes.

"All right, I'll put together a draft and present it at our official meeting on Saturday night," Tracy yammered. "Sound good, boss?"

What had I gotten myself into?

"Hey, guys — what's going on?" Morgan asked as she and Kara joined us.

"It's our new Club," I said.

Kara looked at Tracy's notebook. "The Lonely Hearts Club?"

"The three of us have decided to not date the idiot boys at this school . . . or any school for that matter." I smiled.

Morgan's eyes got wide. "You weren't kidding about having a ban on boys?"

"Nope!"

"I don't get it," Kara said.

"There really isn't much to get," I explained. "I've just had it with guys. They've done nothing but cause me, and my friends, problems."

Diane and Tracy nodded.

"So you really aren't going to date, ever?"

"Not ever, just not while I'm here."

"Oh." Kara looked down at her water. With the way she'd been treated by guys like Todd in the past, you would've thought she'd understand.

Morgan stared at me. "Do you hate me for wanting to go to the concert?"

"No, not at all," I promised her. "I just meant that I wasn't the right person to encourage you to go on a date with anybody, since I'm pretty sure Tyson is probably the spawn of Satan."

"What's wrong with Tyson?" Morgan got defensive.

"Well, he's a *guy* . . ."

Tracy spoke up. "I think they get the point, Pen."

"Hey, Tracy," Jen Leonard called out from the next tree over. "What are you guys talking about? If you're bashing guys, I've got some stories for you."

Tracy motioned her over. "Join us, my friend. Let our leader Penny show you the way."

"Tracy . . ."

Jen and Amy Miller, both fellow juniors who I'd been friendly with since grade school, came over. They were inseparable best friends who on the surface seemed very different. Jen was the jock, captain of most of the girls teams, and could be a little intense, while Amy was very preppy and usually had a dress or blazer on, like she was going to work in an office instead of going to school.

Tracy excitedly filled them in on the details of the Club. Morgan and Kara just stayed silent the entire time. I'm sure they were probably wondering what they'd gotten themselves into.

"Wait," Amy asked. "I thought you mentioned today in Art that you're going shopping for Homecoming dresses. Who are you going to Homecoming with?"

"We're going with each other," I explained. "We figure it will be a lot more fun than going with guys who will ditch us to talk about whatever it is that guys talk about."

"Jock itch," Tracy offered with a smirk.

Both Amy and Jen looked at each other. Amy then looked at us and said, "That sounds cool to me . . . can I join?"

"Amy!" Jen protested. "Are you seriously going to decide to not date for the next two years, just like that?"

Amy flipped her long, wavy black hair. "Please, this is such an easy decision. I've had it with all these guys at school, especially after what Brian Reed did to me in seventh grade."

Tracy and I exchanged confused looks.

"What did Brian do?" I asked.

Amy's eyes widened. "You mean you don't remember?"

I shook my head.

She sighed. "Well, it was a while ago. But I always think about it because nothing has changed with guys since then. I mean, they're so juvenile."

"What happened?" Kara rejoined the conversation.

Amy sat up. "Well, Brian and I were dating — and I use the term *dating* loosely. He'd walk me home from school every once in a while, and then on Friday nights we'd go to the arcade where I watched him play video games. One day, out of the blue, he walks up to me at lunch and in front of *everybody*, he says, 'Roses are red. Violets are blue. Garbage gets dumped, and now so have you.' All of the stupid jerks at the jock table just sat there and laughed."

"Oh, wait, I *do* remember that," Diane said softly. "Brian can be such a jerk."

"I was traumatized all year. All the dumb jocks threw trash at me when I walked by. I still to this day have no idea what I did to deserve that. And then the other day, Brian had the nerve to talk to me, as if he hadn't completely humiliated me and ruined my entire seventh grade."

Jen rubbed Amy's shoulder. "I had no idea it still upset you so much."

"I was twelve — it totally traumatized me," Amy replied. "And believe me, I'm over it now. But that started my disastrous experiences with guys. The other stories aren't even worth repeating. I'm more than happy to banish these idiots from my memory."

Jen looked at Amy in shock. "But . . ."

Amy put her hand up to silence Jen. "Please — look at you! You've gotten screwed over more than I have."

"No, I —"

"Josh Fuller."

At the sound of Josh's name, Jen sank down on the lawn.

"Who's Josh Fuller?" Diane asked as she patted Jen's knee.

Jen ran her hands through her short blond hair. "He's the guy who broke my heart. We both coached basketball at park and rec this summer, and he . . ."

"He jerked her around," Amy finished. "He flirted with her constantly, led her on, even took her out on a date — and then he just stopped. He continued with the flirting, but there never was a second date. Instead, he would parade a different bimbo around the park every week, then tell Jen how hot she was. He just —"

"Enough," Jen said. "They get the point." She shook her head. "It's so stupid, but I hadn't really met a guy who I really clicked with before, and it all seemed to be there with him. It was too good to be true."

I nodded, knowing exactly how Jen felt.

I started to feel a surge of energy. "Come on, Jen, join us," I said. "We don't need them, do we?"

Jen smiled. "We sure as hell don't."

"Nice!" Diane nodded in approval. "We are up to five members. Kara? Morgan?"

Both Kara and Morgan had spent the last few minutes in silence.

"Um, I have a date to Homecoming . . ." Kara said, looking down at her uneaten lunch. "Ah . . ."

"That's okay . . ." Diane offered.

"And, ah." Morgan was clearly uncomfortable. "I'm sorry guys, I just need to . . ."

"No worries, seriously," I assured them. "I understand it's a lot. When you're ready, we'll be here."

Knowing the guys at our school, I didn't think it would take that long for them to decide to join us.

Fourteen

THANK GOD TODD CHESNEY sucked at Spanish.

He'd been trying to hit on me and ask me to Homecoming all week, but since his Spanish was so bad, I just looked at him, confused, and pretended that I didn't know what he was talking about. And since Todd was so bad in class, he believed me.

Just before the bell rang on Thursday morning, I started my usual routine of grabbing my books and running out of class.

"Whoa, hold up, Margarita." Todd grabbed my arm before I got a chance to dash into the hallway.

"Huh?" I tried to sound surprised.

"I need to talk with you." Todd followed me into the hallway. "So I was thinking . . ."

Oh, this was going to be bad.

". . . that you and I should, ya know, go to Homecoming together."

He stopped in the middle of the hallway and looked at me. Although he was a few inches taller than me and was who-knew-how-many-pounds bigger, he looked a little timid. It almost made me feel bad enough to say yes. *Almost.*

"Oh, wow, Todd, wow." I tried to sound surprised. "I actually have plans for Homecoming already."

"Who are you going with?" A hard edge seeped into his voice. "Bauer?"

"Ryan? No, why would you — never mind." That threw me off.

"Every chick in this school is waiting around for Bauer to ask her to Homecoming. He better ask someone ASAP." He folded his arms, looking impatient.

"Uh-huh. Well, see, I'm not going with a guy. I'm going with some friends, that's all."

"Why would you want to do that?" He looked confused. "You know what, Penny — if you don't want to go with me you should just say so."

"No, it's not that, I really am —"

"Whatever." Todd walked away.

Well, that went well.

Despite Todd's reaction, for the first time since I'd been in high school, I was looking forward to Homecoming. Anytime I got asked who I was going with, I'd tell the truth, not caring if people thought it was weird that a bunch of girls were going together.

"Hey there, stranger — have you forgotten where your locker is?" Ryan said to me after class.

"Yeah, well, I just . . ."

"It's okay. I understand."

I had no idea what he was supposed to be understanding. I'd been avoiding my locker so I wouldn't have to deal with Todd.

I got back to fishing my books out of my locker, but Ryan wasn't going anywhere. "So, Todd told me what happened."

I turned around and leaned my back against my locker. "How much does he hate me?"

Ryan moved so his head was leaning next to mine. "It's not that bad. I told him that you really are going with a bunch of girls. Sorry."

"Why should you be sorry?"

A smile spread across his face. "Well, I think he may start hitting on you again once Homecoming is over."

"Oh."

"Anyways, you should be the one apologizing to me."

"For what?"

Ryan opened his backpack and started putting things into his locker. He was pretending not to hear me.

"Hey." I kicked his leg gently. "What did I do? I mean, I can't imagine what it could be, since I'm such a Goody Two-shoes and all. . . ."

"It would've been nice to warn Chesney that you were off the market."

"Oh, nice, 'off the market.' I know Todd sees me as a piece of meat, but I expect a little more from you," I teased.

"I just can't believe I have to find out everything about you from Diane."

"What exactly did Diane tell you?"

He looked confused. "That you guys are going to Homecoming together. Is there something else?"

I shook my head. "No, nothing else. That's it."

Friday night I headed with Morgan to Tyson's concert. I'd never felt so out of place. I surveyed the room and all I saw were piercings, black eyeliner, and dirty hair. Everybody had a look on their face like they'd rather be somewhere else.

Well, I might've had one thing in common with them.

Morgan grabbed my arm. "I think we should go to the front, not too close, but close enough."

We maneuvered our way toward the front of the auto mechanic shop that was doubling as the concert venue. I didn't think we'd have a problem with Tyson seeing Morgan; there were only thirty other people there. Morgan reached in her purse and applied another coat of red lipstick.

There was movement toward the front as the band took the stage: Pete Vaughn sat behind the drum set and started twirling his sticks; Brian Silverman and Trent Riley stepped on stage with their respective instruments, guitar and bass; and Tyson came storming out with his guitar. Immediately, the band launched into The Clash's "London Calling." I was surprised at how Tyson, so shy in class, dominated the stage. He moved with the music, worked the crowd, and held himself like a seasoned pro. And the music wasn't half bad.

The song ended and everybody started to cheer.

"All right!" Tyson grabbed the microphone. "Enough with the covers. We got a new song we're gonna play for you tonight. So give it up!"

Those were the most words I had ever heard him speak.

"Oh, I can't wait to hear their new stuff — Tyson writes all of the songs." Morgan looked on like a lovesick puppy.

Tyson started playing a few power chords. His long hair was in his eyes as he bobbed his head back and forth. The rest of the band came in and I found myself now moving to the music. There was something intense about the beat. I looked around and saw everybody moving their heads to the bass.

As he sang his lyrics into the microphone, I was surprised at his voice — so clear, powerful, and, in a way, beautiful. The lyrics were a lot deeper than I would've guessed.

Tyson closed his eyes and reached out his hand to the crowd. *"You are the shadow that haunts me, the vision of who I want to be."*

Despite the fact that Tyson was a guy, I started to wonder if I'd had him wrong. Not the part about him being the scum of the earth because he was male. But besides his being a boy, I'd always been so quick to dismiss Tyson all these years. Had I allowed the way he looked and his timid behavior to over-shadow what was becoming increasingly obvious?

Tyson Bellamy wasn't a punk wannabe — he was a musical prodigy.

After the band finished its last song, Morgan turned to me and said, "A promise is a promise — we can leave."

We started to exit, but there was a cluster of people in front of us. I decided to maneuver over to the side of the stage to get to the exit, then tripped over an amp cord.

"Are you okay?" A hand grabbed me to steady my balance.

I looked up. "Yeah. Thanks, Tyson. Great show."

"Thanks, Penny," he said with a bit of a smile. "I was a little nervous when I saw you were here."

Really?

"Really?"

"Yeah." I could see him blushing behind his hair. "I mean, you're named after a song from *the* greatest rock band of all time."

"Oh." I laughed. "Um, you know Morgan, right?" I motioned to Morgan, who was trying to hide behind me. So much for me not being the wing girl.

"Yeah, hi," Tyson said and looked down at the floor.

"Hi," Morgan replied, also looking down.

"Um, so do you guys practice here?" I asked, trying to make things less awkward.

Tyson nodded his head, "Yeah, at night." He didn't look up.

"Uh-huh, well that's . . . interesting."

Morgan nudged me.

"Um, well, good talking to you . . ."

Tyson nodded his head and peeked up for just an instant to smile.

"I'm going to die!" Morgan screamed as we left the garage. "That was so embarrassing. Could he have shown any less interest in me?"

"He's just shy," I said, only half sure that was it.

Morgan opened the doors to her car and we got in. "Penny, do you know how long I've had a crush on Tyson?"

I shook my head.

"Since freshman year. Two years. And finally I decided that this year I would do something about it. He's a senior, so time is running out. But it's so obvious he doesn't care." Morgan put her head on the steering wheel. "I'm so embarrassed."

"You've nothing to be embarrassed about. You don't need Tyson to —"

I cut myself off. I didn't want to have a reenactment of our lunch from earlier in the week.

"I don't need to what?" Morgan looked at me expectedly.

"You don't need him."

Morgan nodded slowly. "You're right — I don't. I've already wasted so much time on him." She sighed. "Hey, got room for one more in your club?"

I smiled. "Of course. You free tomorrow night?"

Fifteen

"YOU GIRLS TRY TO BEHAVE yourselves tonight," Dad said as he put on his coat Saturday night. "Now, Penny Lane, we're only going to be gone for a couple hours. No boys."

I tried not to laugh. If only they knew.

My parents were on their way to dinner, while Tracy and I were in the middle of getting all of the important provisions ready for our first official Lonely Hearts Club meeting — potato chips, dip, soda, pizza, and a selection of cheesy comedy movies.

"Don't worry, Dr. Bloom — if Paul or Ringo stop by, we will be the perfect hostesses." Tracy loved the fact that my parents were so . . . not normal.

"Thank you, Tracy," Mom replied. "We know you will." She kissed me on the cheek before she headed out.

"Why do you encourage them?" I asked Tracy.

"Because it drives you crazy."

The doorbell rang — to the tune of "Love Me Do," of course.

"Let the festivities begin!" Tracy declared.

I'd been looking forward to this meeting all week. Just us girls, hanging out. But, part of me hoped that maybe, just maybe, it would end up being something bigger than that.

Once Tracy, Diane, Jen, Amy, Morgan, and I settled into the basement, got comfortable in the sofas, and started munching on chips, Tracy stood up and passed out a piece of paper to each of us.

I looked down and saw *The Official Guidelines of Penny Lane's Lonely Hearts Club*.

"Hey," I protested. "This isn't just MY Club . . ."

Tracy threw a chip at me. "Just read it, will you!"

The Official Guidelines of Penny Lane's Lonely Hearts Club

Heretofore are thy official rules for members of "Penny Lane's Lonely Hearts Club." All members must agree to such terms or thy membership shall be struck from thy record.

1) All members agree to stop dating men (or, if referring to the male population at McKinley High, "little boys") for the rest of thy high school existence. Whether or not said members want to date after high school, they choose to proceed at their own risk. Failure to adhere to this, the most sacred rule, will result in the highest punishment allowed by law — streaking through the halls at McKinley after lunch.

2) Members will attend all couple events together as a group, including, but not limited to, Homecoming, Prom, parties, and other couply events, despite possibly being labeled as freaks and getting jealous looks from guys who wish we were their hot dates, but instead have to settle for some lame wannabe.

3)   Saturday night is the official meeting night of Penny Lane's Lonely Hearts Club. Attendance is mandatory. Exceptions are for family emergencies and bad hair days only.

4)   Members must be supportive of their friends, despite bad choices in clothing, hair, and/or music.

Violators of the rules are subject to membership disqualification, public humiliation, vicious rumors, and possible beheading.

I loved it. Granted, it was a little melodramatic in places (typical Tracy), but, all in all, it worked.

Jen looked at the list and let out a sigh. "Ever since you told me about the Club, I've been thinking about all the drama that has happened in my life because of boys. I mean, I recently found out that last year three of the guys on the boys' basketball team had a bet on who could deflower me. How stupid is that?" Jen rolled her eyes.

"Yeah, unfortunately Jon Cart took that privilege away from me last year." Amy shook her head. "If only I could get those forty-five seconds of my life back."

"WHAT?!" Tracy practically screamed.

Amy covered her mouth. "Yeah, hate to break it to you, but losing it isn't that much fun."

Tracy looked disappointed. "Not that I'll ever get to know." She wrapped her arms around herself and pretended to sulk. "Stupid Club."

"Yeah, and in the continuing tradition of guys being total

jerks to me for no reason, literally the second after it was over, he completely lost interest in me."

"Typical," Jen agreed.

"Everything you see in the movies and on television is such crap. I did not see fireworks, and there was no sweeping symphony playing in my head." Amy glanced over at Diane. "Although I'm sure with you and Ryan, there was probably candlelight and rose petals."

Diane blushed. "Um, not exactly."

I wasn't really sure I wanted to hear this.

"Please tell me there were at least silk sheets?" Amy said.

Diane said something, but her voice was so low it wasn't really audible.

"Um, maybe we should change the subject?" I suggested.

Diane looked around at all of us and smiled. "It's okay. It's just that . . . I'm a virgin."

"YOU'RE A WHAT?" Tracy screamed and jumped off the couch. Diane just shrugged her shoulders.

No. Way.

She and Ryan were together for so long, they were practically married. Well, maybe those jokes about married people not having sex were true.

"Seriously!" Tracy screamed.

Diane nodded. "Seriously."

"Wow."

After an awkward pause, Diane got up and walked over to Tracy. "Thank you, Tracy," she said with a mischievous twinkle in her eye. "Thank you for thinking all this time that I was a huge slut."

Tracy shrugged her shoulders. "Hey, judging my friends is what I'm here for."

"Penny, can we please put some music on so we can drown her out?" Diane smiled at me.

"Yeah, like any speaker could do that," Tracy countered.

I couldn't have agreed with Diane more. I already knew the perfect song to blast.

What else?

"Come Together."

"You really don't have to worry about cleaning up," I said to Diane after everybody else had left. I washed out a few soda cans that needed to be recycled.

"Well, I wanted to ask you something."

I sat down at the kitchen table next to her.

She shifted uncomfortably. "Do you think it's weird?"

"The Club?"

"No, no. That Ryan and I never . . ."

"Um, well, I guess I just assumed . . ."

She looked down at the floor. "Yeah, I know. It's just . . . can I tell you something?"

I nodded.

"I've never told anybody this before, but we tried to once. Last New Year's we were going to — we had it all planned out. My parents were staying the night in the city, so we went back to my room after Todd's party, and we *did* have candles and he *did* buy me roses. . . ." Diane laughed. "I guess we were so predictable." Her smile slowly vanished, and she sat still for a while.

I nodded sympathetically. Thoughts of my embarrassing, disastrous evening with Nate started to flood back to me.

"I remember that I was so sure of Ryan, that we would be together forever. Everything was so romantic, so perfect, and then . . . I freaked out. We aren't talking a few nerves — I completely lost it. We didn't even get that far — most of our clothes were still on — but I just started crying. Ryan immediately sat up and turned the lights on. He looked so concerned, which made me feel worse.

"I still don't understand what happened. I guess I panicked. We spent that night just lying together, him holding me as I cried. After that night, things were different between us. I think Ryan was worried that he'd done something wrong, so he never tried going that far again. We were both so embarrassed that neither one of us ever talked about it. We hardly did anything the last couple months we dated. That's why it's been so easy for us to stay friends, because that's what we ended up being, in the end . . . just friends."

Diane looked sad for a moment, then looked up at me and smiled weakly. "Everybody wants to know what happened, why did the *perfect couple* break up? I think that evening was the beginning of the end for us. Not because we were going to have sex, but because I think we both realized that we were forcing ourselves to be something that neither of us wanted."

Diane looked at me and shrugged. "I'm tired of doing things for other people or because it's expected of me. I'm not going to do it any longer."

"Good for you."

Diane smiled at me. "There's something else I want you to know."

I leaned forward, wondering what could possibly come next.

"After football season, I'm quitting cheerleading."

This might have been even more of a surprise than the news about her and Ryan. "Really?"

"Yep, and I'm trying out for the basketball team. I'm doing this for *me*." Her face lit up and I could tell that she meant every word.

"Oh, Diane." I was practically speechless.

My head raced with all the information from the evening — this was only our first official meeting and already so many of us were changing and so many secrets had been revealed.

I was sure that over time only more would come out.

Maybe even a few secrets of my own.

Sixteen

OUR FIRST OFFICIAL CLUB OUTING was the following Saturday, to go Homecoming dress shopping together. I was extra excited because Rita was home from Northwestern and was going to be the excursion's honorary member.

But first we had to survive dinner with my parents on Friday night.

"Oh, it's so good to have my babies home," Mom kept saying.

I tried to ignore her, surveying the menu at our family's favorite restaurant, The Wilderness. (I never understood what was so wild about a family restaurant attached to a shopping center.)

The waiter came over to take our order, and I looked down so Rita could be the first one to order. She was always a lot braver with our parents than I was.

"Yes, I'll have the filet mignon with the garlic mashed potatoes," she said, looking directly at Mom, daring her.

"Rita . . ." Mom said with deep disapproval.

Rita took her napkin off her plate and put it on her lap. "Mother, young girls need their protein. Penny, what are you having?"

The waiter looked over at me, obviously confused. I just smiled as I ordered a cheeseburger — medium rare.

Mom started in, her big brown eyes, exactly like mine, narrowing as she locked in on Rita. "Rita . . . Penny Lane . . ." Oh, great, I was in trouble, too. "You know how we respect your decision to eat what you like, but I would really like for you to just try to understand where your father and I are coming from."

"See, Mom, I know where you're coming from." Rita made a grand gesture as she held out her hands. "I know what Paul would do in a situation like this, but I am not Paul McCartney. I'm Rita Bloom, and I choose meat. Lots of meat."

While most people become vegetarian for health or ethical reasons, Mom and Dad had done it simply because Paul McCartney led them there.

Sensing the tension at the table, Dad turned to me. "So, Penny Lane, what plans do you have with your big sister this weekend?"

I was about ready to tell him about the shopping trip when Rita interrupted with "I'm so excited because I get to meet Penny's club."

Uh-oh.

"You've joined a club, honey! That's great," Mom said as she took a sip of her water.

"Yes, what kind of club, kiddo?" Dad leaned in, interested.

"Well, um, it's not really an official club." I threw daggers at Rita with my eyes. This was so humiliating. What was I supposed to say? *See, Mom and Dad, I'm sick of boys because your best friend's son was an ass, so I decided to have my friends join together and forget about boys entirely.*

"Penny started it. It's called The Lonely Hearts Club," Rita chimed in.

"Oh, oh, Penny Lane, that's so, so wonderful!" Mom put her hand up to her chest, thrilled that I'd named something after the Beatles, although she had no idea what the Club stood for. I could've started a club called the Yellow Submariners that went out in the ocean and clubbed baby seals and they *still* would've been proud.

"Kiddo, it's so great you're taking an interest in your heritage. Goo goo g'joob!" Dad beamed.

My heritage? My great-grandfather on my father's side was from England, true, but nowhere near Liverpool. And Mom's family was from Germany.

"Do you even want to know what the club is about?" I said. "Some friends and I have decided to stop dating guys . . . at least until we're out of McKinley."

Dad's eyes lit up. "Penny Lane, that is the best idea for a club!"

Mom looked thoughtful for a minute before she said anything. "Penny Lane, is there a reason why you are doing this?"

My heart started beating quickly. She knew. I shook my head. "Not really. There were a lot of factors, I guess. But I'm just sick of my friends getting hurt . . ."

"Well, again, Penny Lane, this is just super." Dad reached across the table and grabbed my hand. "I want you to know that I'm more than willing to move more tables into the basement when this really takes off. To think that our baby girl has started a Beatles Club!"

"It's not a Beatles Club!" I pulled my hand away.

He winked at me. "Well, a father can dream, can't he?"

Mom sat silently at the table. I wasn't sure what she was making of all of this. But she didn't say a word when the food came and Rita and I dove into our red meat and enjoyed every bite.

It was strange. I'd been to countless dances and semiformal events since grade school. But this was the first time I'd been dress shopping with a group of friends. It really cemented the importance of the Club, and how much fun we could have without guys. I did think the salespeople were a little annoyed at having six teenage girls running around the dress section screaming at each other, but it didn't take long for Rita to take control.

"On a scale of hotness, you rate at scorching, baby!" she said to Amy as she walked out of the dressing room in a black dress.

As I watched, my sister grabbed her cell phone and started to mimic a cheesy game show host. "Next up, we have Amy Miller, wearing a black satin dress. Notice the beaded detail on the cap sleeve and the Empire waist to accentuate her ample bosom. . . ."

Amy blushed, did a little twirl, and curtsied.

The door opened to the dressing room next door. "Are you ready for me?" Tracy asked as she walked out for us to all admire her dress . . . whatever it was.

We all stared. Tracy was wearing what was best described as a smock — a hideous, floral smock that even my grandmother wouldn't have been caught dead wearing. Tracy strutted down the hallway to the three-way mirror. "Hey, Pen, I thought I would get the wardrobe ready for when we're old maids." She smiled as she took the smock off to reveal a red silk fitted dress with a red sequined belt underneath. She looked amazing. "Come on, Rita — what's my hotness rating?"

"Red hot all the way!"

Tracy did a little clap and jumped up and down. I noticed that she was behaving more and more like Diane every day.

She would've killed me if I'd told her that.

"Looks like you've all got your dresses," Rita said as we inspected one another's choices. Diane had found a pink flapper dress, Jen had a classic strapless black dress, and Morgan was wearing an Empire-waist red silk dress, while I'd chosen a black dress with a halter top and fitted lace skirt.

We lined up in front of the mirrors for a full view.

"You know," said Jen. "I like that I found a dress for me. It's always been about whether *he'll* like it enough —"

"Yeah," said Amy. "Like it enough to take it off."

Jen smiled. "I really feel like a weight has been lifted off my shoulders."

Diane nervously bit her lip. "I know, especially since I can concentrate on other things. Actually, that's where I need your help, Jen. I've decided to quit cheerleading after Homecoming . . . and try out for the basketball team."

There were a couple of gasps. Rita started applauding.

"Holy crap!" Tracy exclaimed. "Diane! You're . . ."

Diane blushed and looked down.

". . . going to completely kick ass!"

Diane lit up. "You think?"

"Hells, yeah! I can't wait until Principal Braddock hears the news. He'll die when he finds out one of his beloved cheerleaders is . . . um, switching teams, I guess."

Diane laughed. "I can only imagine the rumors that will be swirling around once I tell the girls."

"Do you mind me asking why you decided to join the team? It isn't as easy as it looks," Jen said.

"No, I don't think that at all. I've always loved basketball, and I would practice outside with my dad sometimes, I guess because he didn't have a son to play with. But I want to be part of a team. I want to try something different. Maybe I'm being selfish, but I'm sick of cheering for other people. I want someone cheering for me."

"Do you want to come over this week and run drills?" Jen offered.

Diane smiled. "That would be amazing. Ryan is already going through plays with me, and we've been practicing on the weekends."

"You have?" Tracy asked.

"Yeah!" Diane's expression quickly changed. "Wait — there isn't anything going on between us. I hope that's not what you think."

Tracy shrugged.

"He's been encouraging me for a while to do it, and I needed some practice to see if I was hopeless. But he seems to think I'll do well. Probably not start or anything, but that doesn't really matter to me. I just want to be on the team."

Jen nodded. "That's the spirit! And I'm sure you're going to be great."

"I don't know . . ."

We all erupted with words of encouragement. I could see Diane's confidence growing as she got the support from everybody.

Tracy put her hand out and we all stared at it for a second. "Come on . . ." she said.

I put my hand on top of hers, and one by one everyone else followed. There, in our new dresses, in front of mirror after mirror.

Tracy looked at me to say something.

"To our new members, our kick-ass Homecoming dresses, and Diane Monroe, basketball goddess!"

We cheered and hollered. The poor salesladies nearly keeled over at their registers.

Once we'd bought our dresses, Tracy suggested we "pig out so much we don't fit into them anymore." We did our best.

After we said good-bye to everyone, Tracy drove Rita and me home. Tracy popped a CD into her car stereo. "I have a surprise for you, Miss Penny Lane," she said. The Beatles began to fill the car.

"Wow, Tracy! I can't believe . . ."

"Yeah, well, I like to think that I can be full of surprises as well!" She winked at me.

Rita leaned forward between the driver and passenger seats. "You know, Pen, you guys are going to get more and more popular. Dad is going to have to build a new addition to the house to fit you all in."

I smiled. Maybe Rita was right. Maybe this was only the beginning.

Tracy turned up the volume and we all began to sing along.

"I've got to admit it's getting better . . ."

Seventeen

A WEEK LATER, THE TIME CAME for me to go to the dance, and it was a total and complete disaster.

What had I been thinking? My mind was racing. Why had I made such a big deal about us going to Homecoming? I couldn't be seen in public looking this way!

There was banging on my bathroom door. Diane. "Come on, Penny — what are you doing in there? We're all dying to see how you look."

I was pretty sure I was having a panic attack. "Uh, just a second . . ." I tried to adjust the dress for the millionth time, but it wasn't helping. There was no way I could go like this. I wanted to walk into that dance with my head held high. I swore this was not what I looked like at the store. I started feeling moisture form around my eyes. Great, not only did I look ridiculous, I was going to ruin the makeup Diane had spent so much time on.

"Penny Lane — get your butt out here now!" Diane howled, her fist banging more.

All right — these were my friends, and they'd have to be honest. I would just go out and see what they had to say. Maybe I was overreacting.

Or maybe I was going to be sick.

I opened the door. . . .

"Ta-dah!" I did my best to make a dramatic entrance, but didn't dare make any eye contact.

"Penny, you look beautiful." Diane beamed. "I'm so used to seeing you in T-shirts and jeans, but look at you!" She was jumping up and down. I had never known anybody to be more excited about going to a dance . . . with a bunch of girls.

Of course I knew Tracy would get down to business. "And look at your chest — who knew you had such a rack?"

Diane hit Tracy on the arm.

"I know," I said. "I'm so horrified. It didn't look like this when I tried it on. Maybe it's the bra." I looked down and all I could see was my cleavage.

"Please," Diane countered. "You have such a rockin' body, and you need to start showing it off."

"I know. It's sick," Morgan said. "Do you have any idea how lucky you are that you don't have to watch what you eat?"

Diane came over and started adjusting my hair. "Don't worry, you look great. Plus, it's really not as bad as you think. Look at all of you — not just your chest — in the mirror. You're beautiful."

As we arrived at school, we all double-checked our hair and makeup. I was becoming more confident in my outfit, and — I hated to admit it — there was a part of me that was dying to see what the reaction would be from some of the guys.

I could feel the music vibrating before we even opened the front door. I picked up the pace, suddenly wanting to get to the gym and get the entrance over with. I hurried inside, not sure what to expect. At least nobody was laughing or pointing at us.

Then I heard it — the high, screeching noise of teenage girls when they spot each other at formal events.

"AAAAMMMMYYYYYY — you look sooooo beautiful!"

"OHMYGODJEN, killer dress!"

"Look at YOU!"

"No, look at YOU!"

"Get out of here. I cannot *believe* you're wearing that color."

"No, YOU get out."

Kara, who had ended up going with a date, looked at the six of us and said, "So, you guys really are serious about the Club, huh?"

"We sure are," Diane said with so much enthusiasm, I thought that she was probably the most excited of all of us.

"Well . . . good for you." Kara wrapped a shawl around her thin frame. "I don't think I could ever do that, but good for you guys."

Diane grabbed my arm. "Come on, let's dance."

The six of us maneuvered onto the dance floor and started moving in time to the music. A few of our friends started to join us. The music was too loud to have a conversation, but I did find myself explaining the Club anytime a new person joined us.

I swung around and was surprised to see that our circle of six had doubled — Kara had joined us, along with a few other juniors and seniors.

After an hour of nonstop dancing, I took a break to go to the restroom and make sure I had some makeup left. I was having so much fun, I almost completely forgot about all the couples at the dance. I smiled at the thought of all the girls who were spending more time on the dance floor with us than with their dates.

Homecoming Queen Marisa Klein was with our group so much that her boyfriend, Homecoming King Larry Andrews, finally pulled her away so he could dance with her.

Jessica Chambers and her boyfriend got into a fight, since he felt she was ignoring him. In truth, they pretty much fought about anything — I didn't know him too well since he didn't go to school at McKinley, but I knew she could do much better.

"Guess we're the people to be seen with tonight," Tracy said with a laugh as we headed back in.

Then the DJ switched the music from pop to a ballad, and both Tracy and I froze, not sure what to do as couples started walking by us hand in hand.

"Ummm, anybody want to go grab a drink?" Tracy asked while the rest of our party came over to join us.

The six of us found refuge at a table where it felt nice to sit down and rest my feet.

"Oh my God, Diane," Tracy said, leaning across the table. "Did you see who Ryan is here with?"

WHO!?!

I casually shifted my line of vision to find Ryan. I'd been so wrapped up in the Club that I hadn't even noticed he was there.

"Relax," Diane said. *Relax?* Was she insane? "I knew he was bringing Missy, you guys. It's cool."

It was? Why was Diane being so calm about this? Finally something snapped into place.

"Wait a second — Missy Winston?" I said. "That freshman who spilled her drink on Kara? You've got to be kidding!"

"Seriously, Penny, it's no big deal. Apparently, Missy asked him out after the football game against Poynette. I think he was taken aback at how forward she was, but it seems the person he wanted to ask already had plans."

"Who was he going to ask?" For some reason, my heart was pounding.

"He wouldn't say. I told him that I'm not dating anymore, so I don't see why he thinks I would be upset."

Diane was way more mature than I would've been. I got up and decided it was time to make the rounds. Erin Fitzgerald was in the middle of telling me about the school play when I got a tap on my shoulder.

I turned around and almost couldn't catch my breath. Ryan was in a beautiful black suit with a light blue shirt and blue tie that made his eyes stand out even more.

"Hey, Penny, you look great."

"Hey."

I noticed him looking down at my chest and quickly glancing back up. His cheeks turned red and he cleared his throat.

"Yeah, so you guys seem to be having a great time tonight — I can see why you all decided to go as one another's dates." He leaned in and put his hand on my lower back. "Although between you and me, having the best girls in school all go to the dance together makes it really hard for us guys to get a good date."

Please. Just your typical empty flirting per usual, I told myself.

"Oh, you know . . . gotta make you men sweat a bit." I gave him a slight punch on the shoulder in a flirtatious way, but I ended up hitting him a lot harder than I thought.

"Ow!" Ryan exclaimed. "Jeez, Penny, who knew you were so strong?"

Well, this was going well.

We looked at each other in silence as the music changed again to a ballad.

Ryan ran his fingers through his hair. "Ah, so, Penny, do you think your dates would mind if you danced with me?"

Before I could respond, I heard that high-pitched nasal voice. "No, but YOUR date would mind."

Ryan was even more flustered than before. "Oh, hey, Missy. Wasn't sure when you'd be back. Um . . . you know Penny, right?"

Missy looked me up and down in a very disapproving way. What did she have to be mad at? She put her arms around Ryan's waist, and I tried not to smile as I saw Ryan squirm a little.

"Yeah, I've heard of you. Isn't your dad one of the Rolling Stones or something?"

You've got to be kidding.

"I'm named after a Beatles song — Penny Lane."

Missy stared at me like I was some sort of lunatic.

"Whatever," she said dismissively. "Ryan, I love this song — let's dance." She grabbed his hand and dragged him out onto the dance floor. For a five-foot stick figure with no soul, she certainly had the strength of a hundred linebackers.

Anger and resentment started bubbling up inside me. There was a part of me that wanted to cut in. Just to spite her.

But I wasn't playing that game anymore. I was with my girls.

Even if it seriously pissed me off that Missy had won this round.

Revolution

"We all want to change the world . . ."

Eighteen

I FIGURED THEY HAD DANCES ON Saturday nights so the drama could dissipate over Sunday and school could be normal on Monday.

Well, as soon as I opened the door to Tracy's car on Monday morning, I knew that wasn't going to be the case.

"Just shut up already!" she was shouting.

I cautiously pulled the handle, hoping that whatever was going on would stop once I got in.

"You are such a loser," Mike screamed at Tracy when I got in.

"Oh, YOU'RE such a freak," Tracy replied.

Nobody seemed to notice that I was in the car.

"Um, guys." I tried to get their attention, but it wasn't working.

"It's not MY fault your little girlfriend was having more fun with us," Tracy said as she pulled out into the street.

"Just stay away from me, and stay away from anybody I know. I'm so embarrassed that you're my sister."

Tracy slammed on the brakes. "Then get out!"

Mike opened the door and started to get out of the car in the middle of the street.

"Mike, don't . . ." I pleaded.

He got out, slammed the door shut, and started jogging on the sidewalk.

"Tracy, what on earth is going on? Go get him — he can't walk."

Tracy was gripping the wheel tightly. "No."

"He'll be late for school."

"Fine with me."

"All right, stop it. What on earth is going on?"

Tracy pulled back out into the street and stared forward while we passed Mike. "He freaked out at me yesterday simply because his stupid girlfriend spent most of Homecoming with us instead of him."

"Really? Which one was she?" I tried to go through all the girls who'd been dancing with us, but couldn't keep track.

"The petite brunette with that cute poofy lavender skirt."

"Oh! She's Mike's girlfriend?"

Tracy nodded as she pulled into the parking lot.

"Well, I don't see why you and Mike have to get into a huge fight over that."

"He was the one who started it. I knew he'd find a way to ruin what was an awesome evening." A smile spread across Tracy's face. "Seriously, we completely rocked that dance! Everybody kept saying their dates were such duds. Did you see one guy out there on the dance floor who was having a good time? No, they all just sat in a big group and talked about sports. . . ." She shifted into her best imitation of Mike. "Whatever, dude!"

When we got to school, I kept telling myself that this was just another normal week, nothing to be nervous about. But my stomach kept doing somersaults every time I thought about seeing Ryan at the dance in the clutches of that freshmonster. I decided to walk a lot slower than usual. Maybe he wouldn't be there. Maybe I could just pretend that I wasn't mad. Maybe . . .

As I turned the corner to my locker, I saw him taking off his jacket. I was very, very relieved to see there was no sign of She Who Would Not Be Named.

I started to fiddle with my combination and saw him turning around. We caught each other's eyes. He smiled, and started to say something —

"Um, Penny?" I was startled and nearly dropped my messenger bag. I turned around to see Eileen Vodak and Annette Ryan, both freshmen, hovering behind me.

"We, um, we really think you guys are so much fun, and we had a really great time, um, hanging out with you guys." Eileen blushed and started twirling her long auburn hair around her finger nervously.

Were they part of our group on Saturday?

"We just, um, really admire you. What you did was so cool."

"Thanks," I replied in a low voice, hoping Ryan wouldn't hear.

Annette nudged Eileen with her shoulder. "Um, yeah, we were wondering if your club was for juniors only, or if you would ever consider having freshmen involved. . . ."

I stared at Eileen for a few seconds while I tried to process what she was saying.

"I mean, I know we're underclassmen, but . . ."

My eyes grew wide as I realized what she was asking. "Of course. The more the merrier!"

Both Eileen's and Annette's faces lit up. "Oh, thanks so much, Penny! Just let us know what you need us to do."

I didn't even know what *I* was doing.

"Okay, will do."

I turned back to my locker as they left. Ryan closed his and leaned over. "Hey there."

"Hi," I replied. Now if I could only stop the urge to shake him and ask him what the hell he was thinking, going with that vile creature.

"Hey, Penny." I turned around as Jen and Amy came over.

I smiled at Ryan apologetically, but was relieved to have the distraction. He just nodded and headed off to class.

"A couple of the girls on the team who had dates called me to talk about the Club," Jen said. "Do you think we could add a few more members?"

As I walked to Spanish class, I couldn't help but notice how many girls were saying hi to me.

"*Hola*, Margarita," Todd greeted me as I sat down at my desk.

"*Hola*." I pulled out my Spanish book and opened to the new chapter.

Todd moved in closer to my desk. "Hey, Penny, what was up with your little chick parade on Saturday night?"

"Oh, well, _we_ had a lot of fun. I don't see what the big deal is." I was starting to feel a little defensive.

"And what the hell is this about Diane quitting cheerleading?" He started shaking his head. "There's just too much weird crap going on."

"It's not _that_ weird. Anyway, how was your night with . . ."

"Hilary," he said angrily.

"Oh, right, Hilary! She's really cool — you must have had fun." I tried to cheer Todd up a little, since it was strange to not have him goofing around.

"I wouldn't know — she spent most of her evening with you guys."

Oh, that's right.

Todd opened up his notebook and pretended to be really interested in his notes. This was not normal behavior at all.

I was sure he'd get over it soon. It really wasn't that big of a deal.

"Why do you care what Todd Chesney thinks?" Tracy asked as she and I headed to join Jen and Amy at our usual lunch table.

"It's not just him — I've been getting weird vibes from guys all day." I threw my lunch bag down on the table. "And all these girls have been coming up to me saying the nicest things."

"I know — isn't it great?" Tracy responded.

"Hey, guys, is it okay if Kara joins us?" Morgan asked, with Diane and Kara right behind her.

"Of course," Tracy said. "Good to have you back, Kara."

Kara blushed. "Well, you said I could come back when I was ready. . . ."

Tracy's eyes got wide. "Of course! Welcome to the dark side!" She laughed. "I guess we should probably move the other table over to make room."

Sure enough, Teresa Finer and Jessica Chambers asked to join us. Soon our table was packed with people talking about Homecoming. Teresa mentioned that her date was forty-five minutes late picking her up and the "fancy dinner" that Jessica's date had promised her ended up being a Burger King drive-thru. Kara's date spent the evening hitting on another girl.

"You guys were right." Kara shook her head and played with her apple stem.

"It's not about wrong or right — it's about being with people who appreciate you," Diane said. "I'm really glad you're here, Kara."

Kara smiled and took a bite of her apple.

"So basically, I had the best dates there," Tracy said.

While Diane, Jessica, and Jen discussed basketball plans for the weekend, I couldn't help but be impressed by how Diane showed absolutely no hesitation in discussing her big change. There wasn't any remorse or regret — she knew she was making the right decision, even if she didn't end up making the team.

It seemed like we had a team of our own now.

Nineteen

IT GOT TO THE POINT WHERE I had no idea how many girls would be meeting at my house on Saturday night. Sure, a lot of them had said they were coming. According to Tracy, Mike's girlfriend, Michelle, had even dumped him just so she could attend. He, in turn, was getting his own ride to school. I felt torn — I didn't want Mike's heart to be broken, but if Michelle was going to dump him over something like the Club, odds were that the relationship wasn't a keeper anyway.

"Is everything all right, kiddo?" Dad asked me, right before all the girls arrived. Mom had gone out without him since he was getting over a cold. "If you're worried that I'm going to get in your way, don't worry about a thing. I've got my tea and paper and I'll keep quiet in my room."

"I'm fine, Dad. I'm just a little worried about how many people are showing up tonight."

"Penny Lane, your mother and I are so proud of you, so don't worry about how many people show up. Marisa Klein was in for her cleaning today, and she was telling me what a hit you and your Beatles Club are at school."

"Dad, I keep —"

"I know, I know." He threw his hands up. "I'm still proud of you, kiddo."

The doorbell rang and I headed over to open the door. "You just go upstairs and feel better," I called after him as he headed toward the stairs.

Tracy and Diane were the first to arrive.

"Tonight is going to be so much fun!" Diane said.

I looked past them and saw a stream of cars pulling up. Jen and Amy brought Jessica Chambers and Teresa Finer with them. Maria Gonzales and Cyndi Alexander parked behind them in Maria's truck.

"Hey, guys — come on in."

We headed downstairs and the doorbell rang again — Hilary Jacobs, Christine Murphy, Meg Ross, and Karen Brown.

Then again — Jackie Memmott and Marisa Klein, with seniors Erin Fitzgerald and Laura Jaworski.

And again — Mike's now ex-girlfriend, Michelle, Eileen Vodak, and Annette Ryan — the freshmen contingent.

And again — Morgan and Kara, with Paula Goldberg rounding everything out.

I got to the basement and couldn't believe that there were over twenty girls from McKinley sitting there — freshmen, sophomores, juniors, and seniors.

Everybody was staring at me. It hit me. They were expecting me to say something. I'd thought we'd just watch a movie or something and eat pizza.

"All right, Penny!" Hilary shouted and started applauding. The whole room erupted. What had I started? I turned around expecting to see that some celebrity had walked into the room.

"Shhhh! Let Penny speak!"

Who said that? I had no idea what people were expecting. I opened my mouth and prayed for the best.

"Thanks, thanks for coming. Um, I'm a little surprised by the turnout. I'm not sure what everybody came here expecting, but . . ."

I looked at Diane and Tracy for help, and they were smiling at me. I could tell that they had faith in me. I wished I did.

"I really don't know why everybody decided to come this evening. I guess all I can tell you is why I'm here — well, except for the fact that I live here." Everybody laughed as I took a deep breath. "To be honest, I'm just tired of it all. The games . . . guys . . . everything. I doubt that there is a single girl among us who hasn't obsessed about whether that guy is going to call, or if we're going to have a date to go to a party. And because of the pressure to go to this and that with a guy, we settle for someone who isn't worth our time.

"And then when we *do* find someone we think is special, we forget about our friends." I tried not to look at Diane. "Or we change something about ourselves to please a guy instead of doing what makes us happy or what we know is right.

"Why do we do this? Why do we even bother?"

I felt my nerves subside as I saw every girl in the room nodding in agreement.

"I know some people will think that I'm being pessimistic — but seriously, let's examine the male population of McKinley, shall we?" Laughter filled the room. "It's not like we have a huge wealth of decent guys to choose from!"

A few people cheered, "Hear! Hear!"

"Now, I'm not saying that we have to give up guys for the rest of our lives. I'm not *that* crazy. But I feel that we shouldn't settle, that I want to spend the last two years at McKinley having fun with my friends. Guys can only mess with that.

"If you look around you, you'll see that there is an amazing group of people here tonight, a perfect support system. We can do anything if we stick together. We just have to believe in ourselves. And we deserve whatever we want. If one of us needs help with a test, we should be there for that person. If one of us wants to pursue our dreams, no matter what anybody else seems to think of it" — I winked at Diane — "we will be there for that person.

"So all we're asking is that members put themselves and their friends before some guy. Every Saturday night, we have a standing date with one another. We need to be here for one another to remind ourselves how special we are.

"And the best part? We don't have to put up with any more crap from guys!"

Amy stood up. "To Penny!"

"No," I protested. "This isn't about me, it's about *us*. To The Lonely Hearts Club!"

The room went up in loud cheers. Diane went over to the stereo and put on the only guys allowed at the meeting: the Beatles.

"You know, Penny," Diane said to me over the music. "Had I known that getting dumped would be such a positive influence on everyone else, I would've had Ryan dump me a long time ago."

I started laughing. I had no idea if it was the high I was on from the Club, the music, or just Diane's sense of humor, but for some reason that was the funniest thing I had ever heard.

"What are you two dying over?" Tracy asked, rocking her hips back and forth to the music. She smacked her hips into mine, and I almost fell over. "Do you have any idea what you've started, Miss Penny Lane? We've single-handedly changed the social structure at McKinley High. You know what this means?"

I'd never thought about it that way. "What?"

She smiled. "Well, if we thought guys were jerks before this, you can guarantee they will be staying *miles* away from us now."

The three of us looked at each other before we started laughing again.

If this was what it was going to be like being single for the rest of my high school existence, I wasn't going to mind at all.

Twenty

"HEY, PENNY — IT'S RYAN."

I stared at the number on my phone — why was Ryan calling me? It was Tuesday night, and I'd just seen him at school a few hours before. The fact that we'd been having surface-level conversations ever since the dance made it even stranger to hear his voice now.

"Hello? Penny?"

Speak! Say something.

"Ah, yeah — hey, Ryan, what's up?"

"Not much. I had a question about History. I think I wrote down the wrong chapter we were supposed to read. Is it chapter twelve?"

"Hold on, let me check. . . ." I had to run over to my desk to grab my book.

"Crap!" A surge of pain shot up my left toe as it slammed into the leg of my chair. This was just great. "Yep, chapter twelve."

There was a pause on the other end of the phone. "Are you okay?"

Apparently I was not okay. "Yeah, I'm fine — stubbed my toe. . . ."

"Okay, thanks, Penny." Another long pause. "Actually there's something else I wanted to ask. . . . Ah, my parents got tickets to see this Beatles tribute band at the Civic Center in a few weeks, but realized they have to leave town early to attend this wedding, so they were going to see if any of their friends wanted them, but I thought it would be kinda fun to go to . . . if you're interested."

Ryan was talking really fast for him, so it took me a second to comprehend what he was asking.

He wasn't asking me on a date, was he?

Of course he wasn't. That was stupid. He was dating that short, curly-haired *thing*.

I was his friend. His Beatles-named friend, no less. It made sense for him to ask me out on a non-date to see a Beatles-ish band.

"Hello? Penny?"

Oops.

"Um, sounds great."

I could still be friends with guys. Ryan and I had always been friends, and there was no way he would see me as anything else. What had he said at Paul's party? *"I'd never do anything with her."*

"Awesome," he said now. "Diane told me your parents are against tribute bands or something, but she thought you might get a kick out of it."

Diane knew! Why hadn't she given me a heads-up that Ryan was going to ask me . . . on . . . some sort of social outing.

I cleared my throat. "I think it'd be fun. Thanks for think-ing of me."

"Of course! I think it'd be cool to go to a tribute band with none other than Penny Lane herself."

Ugh.

"So I guess we can figure out the details later, but I figure we can head into the city early and grab a bite before the show. Does that sound okay?"

"That sounds great, Ryan. See you tomorrow."

I hung up the phone and just stared at it.

Then it hit me. I had agreed to go to a Beatles tribute band concert with Ryan Bauer. Now I had to tell the one person who was going to absolutely hate this idea.

"Oh, Penny Lane, no, no, no. I'm so disappointed in you. How could you?"

This was going to be harder than I thought.

I sat down at our kitchen table. "Come on, Mom, it's not that big of a deal."

Mom set her coffee mug down and looked at me like I had a second head. "Penny Lane, I just thought your father and I raised you better than to go to some complete *rip-off* band. It's just . . . Dave, help me out!"

Dad stopped hiding behind his paper and set it down. "Now, Becky, I don't think it's necessarily a bad thing. At least she's interested in learning about her heritage. And I think we should trust Penny Lane to know that what she will be hearing is nothing compared to the real thing. Remember how embarrassed she was with the massacre at Lucy's graduation?"

Yes, I'd been mortified at Lucy's graduation, but unfortunately it was my parents who'd been the weapons of mass humiliation. Some poor graduate sang a not very flattering rendition of "Yesterday" and my parents almost walked out of the auditorium. They even refused to clap. It wouldn't have been so bad if the guy's parents hadn't been sitting right next to us, recording the whole thing. I'm sure they appreciated watching the video with my parents' commentary track: "Ewww, all wrong. . . . Why do people feel it necessary to tamper with a classic. . . . There is only one Paul McCartney and you, child, are no Paul."

"Ah, yeah, Dad, it was awful." I got up and started unloading the dishwasher. I thought that maybe that would help get Mom in a better mood.

"What do you say, Becs?" Dad reached across the table and squeezed my mother's hand.

"Oh, okay . . ." Mom looked defeated.

I tried not to laugh as I opened the top cabinet to put the glasses back in place.

"Oh, cheer up. Remember, we have guests coming in a few weeks!" Dad tried to get Mom to smile.

"That's right! Penny Lane, we forgot to tell you — we have some wonderful news. The Taylors are going to spend Thanksgiving with us. Isn't that —"

I tried to blink a few times to regain focus as I felt the glass slip from my hand. There was a crash on the floor. I looked up and saw a shocked look on my parents' faces.

They hadn't just said . . .

"Oh, Penny!" Mom got up and grabbed the broom and dustpan from the pantry. I just stood there while she started to clean up around me. "What has gotten into you?"

I couldn't even begin to explain.

This was a nightmare.

Twenty-one

I WAS STILL IN SHOCK THE following morning. I sat in a daze outside while I waited for Tracy to come pick me up. After the horrific news from the previous night, I needed my best friend more than ever.

Tracy's car turned on Ashland, and I practically ran out into the street. The car didn't even make a complete stop as I opened the door and got in the passenger seat.

"Wow, someone is excited to get to school," Tracy observed.

"You're not going to believe what happened last night!" My voice was quivering, on the verge of a full-on breakdown.

"Whoa, what on earth is going on, Pen? With everything that has happened the past couple of weeks, I'm sure it can't be that bad."

"Oh, really, really, really, I think you might want to pull over for this."

Tracy pulled the car over and I told her the news. The words felt like they'd been festering inside of me for weeks instead of hours.

"WHAT?!!! How come you didn't call me?"

"I left about fourteen messages."

Tracy reached into her purse and started swearing as she turned on her phone.

I went on. "I just, I just . . . It's so awful. I don't want to see him again. What am I supposed to do?" Tears were starting to form behind my eyes.

"You mean besides kill him? What exactly did your parents say, and did you tell them that that creep is not welcome in your house?"

I shook my head. "Of course I didn't say that. You know my parents have no idea what happened this summer with Nate. Sometimes I swear that they're so clueless."

"Okay, give me the outline of what happened, and then I'm going to call an emergency meeting of The Lonely Hearts Club at lunch so we can come together and help you out."

Not only was I having the worst morning of my life, but I was also going to flunk out of school.

Luckily, Tyson had been assigned to be my lab partner for our fetal pig dissection, and he seemed to know biology as well as he knew punk rock. I must've been in a state, because even he picked up on my mood.

"Hey, is everything all right?" he asked, looking up from the syllabus.

I nodded weakly.

"So, do you think we should name it?"

I had no idea what he was talking about. "What?"

A smile crept on his face. I was surprised to find he had nice teeth. "You know, do you think we should name it?" He gestured down to the fetal pig resting in the dissection pan.

"Oh, sure."

"Well." Tyson leaned over and started to examine the pig. "I was thinking of either Babe or Wilbur."

I looked at him in surprise.

"What? Do you think I would want to name him something like Slash or Killer?"

I couldn't help but laugh. That was exactly what I was thinking.

"I like Wilbur." I looked down at the poor pickled pig.

"Wilbur, it is." Tyson took a marker and wrote the name on the pan.

When the period ended, I immediately collected my books and practically ran out of the room, knocking over half the class. The hallway was a blur of people talking and lockers slamming as I ran down the corridor to the cafeteria.

When I got there, I saw Jen and Tracy rearranging tables in the back corner.

"I think we're going to have a big showing today," Tracy said, pulling over a few chairs. We now had even more people at our table than the jock/cheerleader contingent.

All the members started to file in quickly. Everyone gave me a smile or a hug before they sat down.

After a few minutes, the table went silent, and I noticed everybody was looking at me with encouraging smiles.

"Well, I guess I should start." I put down my sandwich and leaned in so everybody could hear me.

"First off, thanks so much for being here for me. I really

need all the help I can get." I looked around at the faces of my friends — old and new. I took a deep breath before giving the state of my disunion. "Um, I think some of you might remember Nate . . . ?"

Apparently they did remember, as I heard a lot of groaning from the tables and I caught the words *pig*, *jackass*, and *jerk*.

"Well, last night my parents dropped the bomb that Nate is coming with his family to spend Thanksgiving with us. Boom!"

Hilary raised her hand.

"Um . . . Hilary?"

"Why don't you tell your parents what happened? They probably would completely understand and then uninvite the loser and his parents."

"I thought of that, but Mr. Taylor is one of my dad's oldest friends. I don't want him to know that his friend's son is a complete and utter ass."

Jackie Memmott raised her hand next.

"Guys," I said, "we aren't in class. You don't have to raise your hands."

Jackie's hand shot down as she looked really embarrassed.

"Sorry, Jackie — you wanted to say something?"

"You can spend Thanksgiving with my family if you want, Penny."

A chorus of "me, too!" came out from the group. This was all the proof I needed that no matter what happened, I'd be fine.

"Thanks so much, all of you. I think I might be slightly overreacting. It probably will be good for me to see him — I never really had closure with him. I basically fled anytime he was in the vicinity of our house."

"Hey, Pen," Tracy said. "I'd be more than happy to help you with the closure. That is, if by *closure* you mean *kick his ass.*"

I started to relax. Plus, maybe Tracy was onto something. I wouldn't be violent, but I wasn't going to pass on an opportunity to set things straight with him.

"All right, enough about me! Anybody else have any issues — boy-related or otherwise?"

Jen shot up from her seat. "Actually, we do!" She gestured to Jessica and Diane.

"As a lot of you may know, the girls' basketball team is in desperate need of new uniforms. And since it seems that the entire athletic fund always goes to the guys' sports, we need to do some sort of fund-raiser. We wanted to do something different this year instead of a car wash or the gross candy drive. So what do you all think of doing a karaoke night to raise money?"

Erin Fitzgerald screamed, "I love that idea, Jen — brilliant!"

No one was surprised by Erin's reaction, since everybody in school knew that Erin had the best voice at McKinley and loved any chance she could get to show it off.

"Thanks, but do you think people would actually do it?" Jen asked. "Pay a cover charge and one dollar per song to sing in front of people?" Erin raised her hand. "People besides Erin?"

"Could we go in groups?" Amy asked.

"I don't see why not." The crowd started to talk amongst themselves, and there was mostly nodding and excitement as people started discussing songs.

Jen looked hopeful. "Okay, we're going to do it. Just promise me that you guys will help kick it off if people are chicken."

Erin stood up. "I promise you I'll be the first person in line. I can't wait!"

"So, Diane, how's practice going?" Amy asked.

Diane smiled. "Well, people have been looking at me a little differently the last couple of days, because . . ." She sighed as she got up and put her foot on the table.

Tracy gasped. "Diane, are you wearing *sneakers*?"

"Yep! I'm officially in pain and unable to wear heels. I think it's hysterical that you guys didn't notice. I'm only about four inches shorter!"

"I knew there was something different!" Tracy shouted.

"Oh, that isn't the only thing." Diane got a mischievous look on her face as she opened her lunch bag and pulled out a large piece of bread. "I'm eating complex carbs!"

"Holy crap!" Tracy's eyes were huge. "It's like you're an entirely different person."

Diane threw a napkin at Tracy. "No, I'm just hungry from all the workouts. It's amazing guys — I'm so excited."

"She's totally going to get a spot on the team," Jen proclaimed. "Meg, you need to do a feature on our newest player."

Meg Ross smiled. "Well, I do have something I wanted to discuss with all of you on Saturday, but I've got deadlines, so no time like the present. As some of you know, I'm the Life-Styles editor at the *McKinley Monitor*, and, well, I'd like to do an article on The Lonely Hearts Club."

Oh, dear God, no. I wasn't sure I could handle any more drama in my life. The school paper?

Meg continued, "Word about the Club is starting to spread and there are a lot of people out there who aren't truly understanding what this Club is all about. I think it's important for us to get our side of the story out. What do you guys think?"

Meg looked directly at me when she asked the question, and I could tell that there could only be one answer.

The Lonely Hearts Club was about to go public in a big way.

"So, are your parents okay with the concert?" Ryan asked at the end of the day.

"Well, as much as my parents can be *okay.*" He smiled at me and I felt my heart sink. I really needed to get over whatever it was that was making me so nervous before our outing.

"Hey, guys. Ryan, ready for our run?" Diane approached us with her workout gear.

"Yep, I just have to drop off some student advisor stuff to Braddock," Ryan responded.

"Okay, seriously, what is the deal with that?"

Ryan shrugged. "Hey, as soon as I figure it out, I'll let you know. We now have gone from talking football to talking about the upcoming basketball season. I'm starting to get annoyed that I'm losing out on study hall once a week."

Diane rolled her eyes. "Oh, poor you."

He grimaced at her before heading to the office.

They seemed rather friendly . . . although I knew better than anybody that they were just friends.

"At last, we're alone." Diane smiled at me. "So the jig is up!"

I stopped dead in my tracks. "What are you even talking about?"

"So when exactly were you going to mention to me that you and Ryan are going to a concert?"

My heart stopped. "Oh, Diane, I'm so sorry. It's just everything with Nate happened and it sort of slipped my mind. I was planning on telling you and the Club, but I didn't want anybody to think it was a date or something. I mean, I was going to say no, but Ryan made it seem like it was almost your idea so I didn't think you would mind —"

Diane just started to laugh. "Jeez, relax, will ya, Pen! I'm not upset. I was just waiting for you to say something. Are you worried what the Club will think?"

"Honestly? I haven't thought much about it. He called last night, and then before I knew it, my parents dropped the Nate bomb on me. So . . ." This was so awkward. "What exactly did Ryan tell you?"

Diane's smile just widened. "Not much. He asked me if I thought you'd be interested in going with him to the concert. He was afraid that he might offend you."

"Why?"

Diane curled a long, blond strand of hair with her finger. "He just thought that you'd be a true Beatle fan and not want to hear some cheesy tribute band. I know how your parents feel about it."

"Yes, my parents don't understand why people remake anything — even movies. They are very traditional, although the term *traditional* is probably the last word people would use when thinking of my parents."

Diane smiled at me. "Well, I'm sure you guys will have a great time."

"Diane, are you really okay that I'm going?"

She nodded. "Of course. You two are the most important people in my life. Why would I be upset?"

I paused for a moment. "No reason."

"Well, I'm going to warm up — can you tell Ryan I'll meet him at the track?"

"Sure." I instantly felt uncomfortable with the thought of having to deal with Ryan alone.

He came back a few minutes later.

"Diane said she'd meet you at the track."

"Okay, thanks."

I started to walk to Tracy's locker.

"Hey, Penny," Ryan called after me.

"Yeah."

I turned around and saw him smiling at me. "I'm really glad you agreed to go with me to the concert. It will be nice to spend some time together outside of school."

I just stared at him.

"See you tomorrow," he said to me. As he jogged by, he reached out and gently squeezed my arm.

There was no way this was going to end well.

Twenty-two

MEG SPENT THAT SATURDAY interviewing the Club members for her article. But she wanted to interview me, Tracy, and Diane separately.

While I was one hundred percent behind the Club and couldn't have been happier about our success, the timing for this interview couldn't have been any worse. The looks we all had been getting from the male population at McKinley High and girl nonmembers had become more and more awkward. Todd had stopped talking to me all together.

"So do you consider yourself a feminist?" Meg asked after I'd given her the background.

"Um, I guess?"

Nice answer.

I knew I had to start focusing on the interview. The Club was too important to me not to, and I really wanted it to be portrayed as something positive.

"You better only be saying nice things about me," Tracy interrupted as she walked into the room. "Is it my turn yet?"

Meg shut off the tape recorder. "I just need to grab another tape. I'll be right back."

For over a week I'd been avoiding telling Tracy about the upcoming whatever-it-was with Ryan. With Meg out of the room, it seemed as good a time as any.

After I was done, I asked, "So how do you feel about that?"

"Sounds like fun, Pen. This isn't a date or anything, is it?"

"Are you kidding me? No, Tracy. It's just a concert. No big deal."

"Yeah, I've always liked Ryan. I'm surprised he hasn't started dating someone new."

"Well, he went to Homecoming with Missy —"

"Penny, he's not *dating* her — he just took her to Homecoming. He is one hundred percent single and available." My heart stopped. "Man, I should talk to Meg about writing some sort of gossip column for the *Monitor*. I would hate to think where you'd be without my knowledge of the goings-on of the student body. Anyways, you're not going to believe what those little brats did to me last night while I was babysitting. . . ."

And like that, the conversation was over. I had nothing to worry about. It was just going to be an evening with two classmates catching a concert. Nothing more.

Diane looked like she was going to be sick.

"Everything is going to be okay," I did my best to reassure her.

"Oh God, oh God, oh God." She paced the hallway, her hands rolled up in tight fists.

Tracy and I exchanged worried looks.

Diane slouched down on the floor. "What was I thinking?"

I sat down next to her. Tracy moved a few feet away with Jen to give us privacy.

"Diane." I put my arm around her. "I can't get over how much you've changed the past few weeks — you should be proud. No matter what happens."

We looked up to see Coach Ramsey open the gymnasium doors and slowly walk toward the bulletin board. A group of girls opened up a narrow passage for her and quickly closed up once she'd posted a single sheet of paper.

"Do you want me to look?" I asked.

Diane looked up as several girls started jumping up and down, cheering. Tracy walked over and scanned the list. Coach Ramsey walked past us on her way back to the gym, paused, and turned around.

"Welcome to the team, Monroe."

Diane's eyes widened. "You mean . . ."

"Of course you made the team!" Tracy could no longer contain herself. "You made the flippin' *varsity* squad, Diane!"

Diane jumped up and rushed over to the bulletin board and studied the team list.

"I . . . I . . ." She turned back toward us. "I did it! Holy crap, I did it!" She rushed over and engulfed me in a giant hug.

"Congratulations, we all knew you could do it!" I was practically screaming, I was so excited for her. "All right, guys, you can come over now!"

A screaming mob with "Congratulations, Diane" signs came rushing from around the corner.

"What's going on?" Diane said in shock.

"You didn't want there to be a big scene in case you didn't make the team, but of course everybody wanted to be here for you."

Laura proudly displayed her "Way to Go, Diane" sign and quickly flipped it over to reveal another option: "Screw 'em, they don't know what they're missing." Laura winked at Diane. "Hey, a girl's gotta be prepared!"

Diane was swarmed by well-wishers, including the rest of her team members.

Tracy put her arm around me. "Our little baby is all grown up! Did you ever imagine this could've happened?" Tracy asked.

I shook my head.

Not even in my wildest dreams.

"Extra! Extra! Read all about us!" Meg greeted me at my locker between classes on Monday and handed me a copy of the *McKinley Monitor*.

I grabbed the paper, and my eyes went straight to the headline about the Club and a picture of us that was on the *front* page.

"Oh, I didn't realize it was so big," I remarked as I tried to not have a panic attack.

I raced to the girls' bathroom, checked the stalls to make sure I was alone, and sat down. It was all pretty much the

standard story that I felt was already getting pretty old . . .
until we got to the end.

> Rumors about the Club have been swirling the last
> few weeks, especially among the males at McKinley.
>
> "All that estrogen in one place can't be good," said
> junior Todd Chesney. "I just think all this no-dating
> stuff is a bunch of crap."
>
> "I really haven't seen too much of a change in the
> chicks at school, except that they are a little too busy to
> hang," adds senior Derek Simpson.
>
> Despite some concerns of the male population at
> McKinley, The Lonely Hearts Club doesn't appear to be
> slowing down anytime soon.
>
> "I'm really excited to see what happens next,"
> said Bloom. "There really doesn't seem to be an end
> in sight."
>
> One thing is for sure. This reporter looks forward to
> her standing date every Saturday night, thanks to Penny
> Bloom and her lonely heart.

I just stared at the last words:
Penny Bloom and her lonely heart.
My stomach tightened as the realization sank in that the
entire school was going to read this. *The entire school.*
What were people going to think of me after this got
around?

Twenty-three

I FELT LIKE I'D BEEN CUT open. I was exposed. So I guess it was fitting to be in Bio class, dissecting our pig, when my quiet punk-rock lab partner Tyson said, "Um . . . Penny. There's something, um, I wanted to talk to you about." He leaned back on the chair and stared at his hands. "Um, I read about that club of yours in the paper. Is it true that you can't date anybody if you're in it?"

"Well, yes, but there's more to the Club than that," I replied.

For the first time ever, Tyson looked me directly in the eyes. "You know, not every guy in this school is a jerk."

I was taken aback. "I don't think . . ."

He tucked his hair behind his ears. "Maybe some of us deserve a chance."

I began to nod slowly.

"You know, it's really hard for a guy to get up the courage to ask a girl out."

I looked down at the table, not sure what to say next.

"I was finally going to do it — and then I read the article. Now it's useless, because Morgan can't even go on a date."

My jaw dropped open, and I turned around to where Morgan and her lab partner were reading from the syllabus.

"Don't look!" Tyson said sharply, sinking down in his seat.

Oh. My. God.

Tyson liked Morgan! Why couldn't he have admitted it earlier?

"Just forget that I said anything." He opened up his notebook and started to vigorously write something down. I peeked over his hunched shoulder and saw that all over the paper were words — most likely lyrics. I wanted to grab the notebook out of his hands and read it. I'd noticed him writing things down before — I just thought he was doodling or writing down his band's name over and over again. Little did I know that he was pouring his heart onto the page.

I walked to the cafeteria in a daze. While I was waiting in line, debating between the pizza and chicken nuggets, I heard that awful high-pitched voice.

"Ohmygod! How pathetic!"

Missy was standing next to me with a couple of Missy wannabes.

I grabbed a slice of pizza and a bottle of water and headed to the cash register. She followed closely behind me.

"Guys, ohmygod look, it's *lonely* Penny. Where's your group of followers, Penny?" Missy whipped her head from side to side dramatically, looking around the cafeteria. Then she got in my face, her herd giggling behind her. "Do you only let pathetic people into your club?"

I rolled my eyes and tried to move around her, but she moved to block me.

"Are you even being serious?" I asked back. "What exactly is your problem?" More people were watching now.

Missy opened her eyes wide, trying to look all innocent. "Problem? *Moi?* No, no, I just think it's so sad that you're so *lonely.*" The Missy-lites high-fived each other.

"This is ridiculous. . . ."

I tried to turn around, but Missy grabbed my elbow. "What? I can't join your club? Oh, wait — I can't, because guys actually *want* to date me."

A voice came from behind me. "You can't join because we only allow people who have an IQ." Missy dropped her grip, and I turned around and saw Diane standing there with her arms folded across her chest. "And, we usually prefer people who have their own sense of self. Nice top, Missy." Diane motioned toward Missy's scoop-neck sweater with a tie at the waist. "That is so me, two years ago."

I thought that would be it, but then Diane leaned in to Missy and said, "You can try to be me all you want. He'll never date you."

If humanly possible, I bet smoke would've come from Missy's ears. I was enjoying the moment so much I was a little startled when Diane linked her arm in mine and said, "Let's not waste any more of our time, Pen."

We got a round of applause when we reached our group of tables. Diane curtsied.

"Hey, guys!" A loud voice silenced the group. I looked over my shoulder to see Rosanna Shaw, a senior, with her lunch tray. She put it down in the small space between me and Tracy. "Do you mind moving over?" she said to Tracy.

Tracy shifted over and Rosanna sat down. "I absolutely loved, LOVED the article, guys. What's going on?" Rosanne asked, as if there was something important she was missing.

I shrugged my shoulders. "Nothing, we were just talking about our days —"

"Anyways, you aren't going to believe what happened to me this morning when I was getting ready for school . . ." Rosanna started telling this overly long story that I think had something to do with her losing the hot water in her shower, but it was getting so drawn out I had to stop paying attention. I looked around the table and saw everybody looking down.

Kara leaned in to say something to Morgan.

"Wait, I'm not finished yet!" Rosanna exploded.

"Um, actually," Diane said, "people are allowed to talk amongst themselves at lunch."

A few people at the table laughed.

"Oh, I'm sorry. Guess I'll have to catch up on the rules later. I just think it's *rude* to interrupt people."

Rosanna continued to talk for the rest of lunch. Not surprisingly, most people left the table early.

"Ugh, Penny, we seriously need to develop some kind of process to join," Tracy said on the way to my locker. "After the article, more people are going to want to become members, and I don't necessarily think for the right reasons. You can't seriously think that Rosanna Shaw is for female bonding. She just wants a bigger audience for her lame stories."

I hesitated. "I know she can be annoying, but I think we should at least give her a chance."

"I guess. Hey — aren't you impressed I didn't yell at her or anything? I think this Club is mellowing me out!"

I was shaking my head as I retrieved my books for the rest of the afternoon.

"Hey." Ryan started to go through his locker. "That article in the paper was really great."

"Thanks." This could really only last a day, right?

"So," Ryan leaned against the lockers and started playing with the corner of his Physics book. "Are we still on for next week?"

"Yeah, why?" I asked him.

"Oh, nothing. . . ." He put his hand on my shoulder and I felt a jolt of electricity. "Since you're technically a celebrity now, you might need some security." He held out his arm. "May I escort you to your next class?"

I hesitantly began to reach for his arm. My nerves were completely on edge.

"Jesus Christ, you have got to be kidding me," Todd said as he approached Ryan. "Don't you start encouraging Eleanor Rigby."

Ryan dropped his arm. "Todd —"

"Whatever, Ryan. Are we going to class or not?" Todd wouldn't even look in my direction. Before Ryan could say anything, I told him that I had to go and headed down the hallway.

"Oh, Penny, are you lonely?" I heard a voice — not Todd's — call out from behind me, along with laughter. I just stared down at the floor, wanting to get to class as quickly as possible.

I continued to hear laughter and my name as I walked down the hall.

You've Got to Hide Your Love Away

"How can I even try?
I can never win . . ."

Twenty-four

BEING AT SCHOOL WAS UNBEARABLE after the article came out. The looks, the stares, the sudden focus on the Club. I was overjoyed when Saturday night finally arrived.

Right before I headed downstairs, I checked my e-mail one last time and there was a message from Nate with the subject:

PLEASE READ.

I hesitated before I clicked it open.

Pen,

I really hope you will give me a chance by just reading this, although you probably won't. And you have every reason to be mad at me. I am so sorry that I hurt you. I've been miserable since I came back home. I miss you so much. You mean everything to me and what I did, what I said, all of it was wrong. I'm an idiot. A jerk. A loser.

I'm so sorry, Pen. If there was something I could do to make what I did go away and erase any hurt I've caused you, I would do it. I would do anything for you. I need you in my life and I'm lost without you.

I miss talking to you. I miss seeing you. I miss YOU.

When my parents told me about Thanksgiving I was so happy at the thought of seeing you. Until I realized that you wouldn't feel the same way. Do you think you can see it in your beautiful, kind heart to at least hear me out at Thanksgiving? There is so much I want you to know, so much I want to tell you. You are everything to me, Pen. I want you back and I'm willing to do whatever it takes to earn your trust back.

Please talk to me.

Love,

Big Dumb Idiot

The mouse hovered over the DELETE button, but I couldn't get myself to delete it.

The doorbell rang and I jumped up. I had to run away from my computer and push his e-mail from my mind.

"Are you okay?" Tracy asked when she saw me.

I nodded. "I think it is going to be a big meeting. We should start getting things ready."

Diane and Tracy exchanged worried looks. I pretended not to notice.

A half hour later, the meeting was pure chaos.

I stopped counting the number of people in the basement at forty. This kind of turnout should've made me excited, but I kept wondering who was there because they believed in The Lonely Hearts Club and who was there because we were the "It" thing of the moment at McKinley.

"All right, what're we doing?" Rosanna screamed from the arm of an already-packed couch.

The entire room looked my way.

"I have a feeling my nasty side may come out this evening," Tracy whispered to me.

"Just give her a chance," I begged. I couldn't deal with any more drama, especially after that e-mail from Nate. Although I had to admit, Rosanna seemed to not entirely grasp what the Club was about.

"Um, okay everybody." I raised my voice to get everybody to quiet down. "We've got a packed house this evening."

Rosanna raised her hand. "I've got a question for you."

I tried to not look annoyed. "Um, yes."

"I thought we weren't supposed to date?"

"Um, well, *members* of the club" — I made sure she realized that she wasn't an official member yet — "know that this is much more than just not —"

"Yeah, but aren't you going on a date with Ryan Bauer?" Rosanna said, the smug look on her narrow face coming through loud and clear.

All eyes were on me. The "original crew" — as Tracy, Diane, and I had been referring to the six of us — knew all about my outing with Ryan. And nobody seemed to think anything of it. Because there *wasn't* anything to it.

"Not really. We're going to a concert. Ryan and I have been friends for years, so it isn't a big deal."

"Uh-huh. So you aren't interested in Ryan?"

Diane glared at Rosanna. "Actually, that is none of your business."

"Well," Rosanna got up and flipped her thin, blond-highlighted hair, "you're asking me to give up dating guys, so I want to make sure our *leader* is staying true to the Club." She wasn't even trying to hide her sarcasm anymore.

"I'm not going on a date with Ryan," I repeated.

Diane got up from the floor. "Okay, all of you new to the Club join me upstairs. There are a few rules we need to go through to make sure people are here" — Diane looked directly at Rosanna — "for the right reasons."

Nearly twenty people went upstairs with Diane.

"What have we gotten ourselves into?" Jen asked. I was a little surprised. She held her hands up. "No, no, not the Club — I mean about Rosanna and the other girls here for their fifteen minutes of fame."

Oddly enough, I *was* thinking about the Club.

The school week went by so fast, Thursday was here before I knew it. I hadn't responded to Nate's e-mail, and he hadn't e-mailed again. I hated the fact that he'd said all the right things. I didn't want to deal with it, so I tried not to think about it. That meant not even telling my friends about it. That would make it more real. And I had enough to deal with already — not only with defending my non-date with Ryan, but also figuring out what a girl should wear on a non-date.

I just kept staring at my closet hoping the answer would present itself. At first I thought vintage Beatles T-shirt and jeans, but realized that would be too corny, plus I was pretty sure the entire fiftysomething-year-old crowd was going to be wearing that. I heard the doorbell ring and quickly grabbed my white fitted tee and navy blue corduroy blazer.

I ran downstairs just in time to hear Dad tell Ryan, "You know, I think it's good that bands want to keep the music alive, but the audience shouldn't kid themselves —"

"Here I am!" I interrupted. I was afraid that Ryan would bolt out the door if my parents kept this up. I gave my parents a wave as I reached for the door. I quickly glanced at Ryan and tried not to notice how particularly fine he looked in khakis and a blue shirt — Rita and I had joked that guys always wore that on a first date while girls always wore jeans and a black top. Since I wasn't wearing a black top, this was clearly not a date.

"Wait a second, Penny Lane." Dad was giving me a very weird look. *Please don't lecture me, please don't lecture me.* "Honey, you look great! Is that *makeup* you're wearing?"

Dear God, why, why now?

I looked over at Ryan, and he had the most wonderful smile on his face; he was clearly amused by my parents, most people were — except for their children.

I could feel my cheeks burning with embarrassment. "Dad . . ."

"Oh, leave her alone, dear." For once, it was Mom to the rescue. "Have a fabulous time, Penny. You, too, Ryan. And, Penny, you *do* look beautiful. I can't believe how fast you're growing up. Why, it seems like it was only yesterday . . ."

"Yesterday . . ." my dad began to sing.

Maybe, I thought, *I should just run back into my bedroom and hide . . . until I turn eighteen.* But instead, I dug up the one ounce of dignity I had left. "If you're done embarrassing me, I think we'll be on our way."

"Well, Ryan," I said once we were free, "now you can see why I'm looking at colleges in Europe."

Ryan laughed and shook his head. "I think parents feel that it's their right to humiliate their children, probably as a way of getting back at their own parents. I'm sure you'll do the same."

Well, I could say one thing — I certainly was going to give my children normal names.

We approached the car, and Ryan opened up the passenger door for me. That certainly fit under the "date" category.

"Plus," Ryan said as he got in his seat, "your parents are only telling you the truth. You do look very beautiful tonight."

My mind was swirling as he pulled away from the curb.

Can someone please explain to me exactly what's going on?

The car ride was spent talking mostly about school and basic gossip about teachers, but only one thought kept racing through my mind: *Ryan Bauer called me beautiful. Ryan Bauer thinks I'm beautiful.*

Or maybe he was just being polite.

I looked across the booth at the restaurant and saw him studying the menu. His black wavy hair was still slightly damp from the shower he'd no doubt taken after practice. He looked up and caught me staring. "See anything that looks good to you?"

You have no idea.

I debated over what to eat. Rita always ordered salads on first dates, but I wasn't on a first date. Although I did wonder if Ryan was expecting me to eat light. But I was really hungry . . .

"What can I get you, sweetie?" Our middle-aged waitress looked down and smiled at me in an encouraging way, probably sensing we were on a . . . whatever we were on.

I opted for a club sandwich with fries and a soda. I hated salads, and I would never approve of someone who gave up their identity for a guy, even a guy who was just a friend. I wasn't going to pretend to be someone that I wasn't. Although I was hoping that Ryan would order something similar.

"And what about you?" The waitress looked Ryan up and down, clearly impressed. I knew most girls would probably be offended by another woman checking out her date, or in this case, pseudo date, but I thought it was a compliment. Plus, she was like twenty years older than us.

"I'd like the green salad," Ryan began. My head started pounding. *No, no, no, for the love of all that is pure, you can't be ordering a salad, you're a sixteen-year-old boy!* ". . . with ranch dressing to start, then a double cheeseburger, fries, and a chocolate shake."

That's my boy.

Well, not technically my *boy.*

"So, Penny, I'm sort of surprised you agreed to come out with me."

"Why would you say that?"

He shrugged. "I don't know — to be honest, I was a little frightened your group of girls were going to tie me down when they found out we were doing something together."

"You know, the things Todd says about the Club aren't true." I felt my cheeks begin to burn.

"I know. . . ." He started playing with his straw wrapper. "I guess I sometimes don't know what to believe. But none of that matters, because you're here with me now."

I stared at him in silence, not sure what to say next.

"Anyways, I've really been looking forward to this evening." He looked up and smiled at me.

Me, too, I thought to myself. *Maybe too much.*

A few moments of silence passed between us. I found it hard to break away from his gaze.

"Ah, so, anyways." Ryan looked away and ran his hand through his hair. "Um, I hope you don't think less of me when I tell you this, but I don't know a lot about the Beatles. I probably only know a couple songs."

"What? You can*not* be serious!" I practically screamed, forgetting that I was in a restaurant.

"Whoa, sorry! This is one of the reasons I wanted to come, to see what the big deal is about."

"What the big deal is about?" It was nice to know that Ryan had a flaw — and it was a major one. "The Beatles are the greatest band of all time. They . . . they . . ." I put my head in my hands.

"What?"

"Nothing. I just started to remind myself of my parents, and it was very, very scary."

"Aw, come on." Ryan took my chin and lifted it away from my hands. "I think it's cute."

"Yeah, cute in a demented way. Like a drunk puppy."

He shook his head, but kept his hand on my chin. "No, I mean cute in a completely irresistible way."

The smile on his face diminished as he started to slowly lean forward. . . .

"Which one of you ordered the salad?"

Ryan sat back up as our food was delivered. I looked down at the food and tried to collect myself. I could practically feel Ryan's eyes on me.

He wasn't going to . . .

Last Saturday night with Rosanna flashed in my head. If he . . . The Lonely Hearts Club would be ruined.

But I was being silly. Ryan was just leaning in. He was just being friendly. He had always been friendly. I was clearly misinterpreting him.

I started to pick at my fries, wishing that I could escape to call Rita on my cell phone.

This was a major emergency.

❤ ❤ ❤

"You can't be serious!"

Ryan rolled his eyes at me. "Just drop it already."

He handed me my ticket as we went through the entrance of the Civic Center. I noticed that the envelope from the ticket agent was addressed to Ryan, not his mom or stepdad, although they were supposedly the ones who'd gotten the tickets.

A shiver rippled through me as Ryan put his hand on the small of my back to guide us to our seats.

"Okay, then, be difficult." I sat down and crossed my arms.

Ryan laughed. "Oh, *I'm* the one being difficult, huh? Seriously, Penny, I didn't know you were the stubborn type."

"Oh, yeah, I totally am." I tried to keep my face straight. "Besides, I'm not the one being completely unreasonable."

Ryan put his arm around the back of my chair and leaned in. "Oh, really?" His voice was filled with amusement. "I don't think there's a single person here who'd take your side in this argument."

I slouched down in my seat and sighed exaggeratedly.

"Okay, don't believe me." He smirked at me. He started surveying the crowd of older people in the audience. "Excuse me, miss?" Ryan tapped the woman in front of us on her shoulder.

"What are you doing?" I asked in shock.

He turned back to me. "I'm proving a point."

A woman in her fifties — with a Beatles T-shirt on, no less — turned around and looked surprised to see someone like Ryan here among the Baby Boomers.

"Sorry to bother you, ma'am." Ryan flashed his best smile to the woman, who didn't seem bothered by him one bit. "I'm hoping you could help me with a small disagreement I'm having with my date."

Did he just say date*?*

He continued, "You see, I like to think that chivalry is indeed not dead, so I'm trying to do the gentlemanly thing this evening." The woman nodded excitedly at Ryan. I could already tell that he was going to win this one. "Now, I've seemed to upset this beautiful woman that I'm seated next to, who just happens to be named after a Beatles song." Ryan motioned toward me, and I did my best to smile and wave at the nice woman instead of hit my gentleman companion. "To be honest, I think she is being unfair. I invited her out this evening, so it's only fair that I pay, but she isn't cooperating."

Ryan looked back at me and winked. I moved my foot over so my heel could dig into his left foot.

"Ow!" He moved his foot over and cleared his throat. "In your opinion, don't you think she should just say thank you instead of trying to throw money at me?"

The woman patted Ryan's knee. "Of course, it's very sweet of you. I can tell that you're an excellent boyfriend."

I opened my mouth to protest, but Ryan looked up, beaming at the woman. "Why, thank you, miss!"

The woman blushed slightly, enjoying the attention from Ryan. She leaned in. "First date?"

I held my breath.

He smiled. "Yes, and what chance do you think I'd have with a second date if I made her pay?"

Blackness swallowed me. For a quick moment I hoped that I was having some sort of seizure. I kept blinking, but the darkness wouldn't go away. Then my ears were filled with screams and my pulse was quickening. A fitting punishment for going on a date.

Light burst a few hundred feet away as four guys dressed in black suits took the stage.

The concert. I shook my head as I got back to the present. Ryan stood up with the rest of the crowd as the Faux Four began with "I Want to Hold Your Hand." I needed to use the support of the armrest to stand up — there was too much confusion swirling around in my head.

I looked over at Ryan, who smiled at me and put his arms gently around my waist.

I am on a date with Ryan Bauer.

My stomach did a somersault and I tried to catch my breath. *Crap, I'm on a date with Ryan Bauer. I'm not supposed to be on a date!* Not only that, I'd declared in front of the entire Lonely Hearts Club that I wasn't going on a date.

I focused on the music. The words to every song flowed through me like memories — good and bad — as the set list continued.

Okay, Penny — you can handle this.

The lights dimmed as a guitar started to play, and my heart dropped. I could feel the tears begin to well up in my eyes, and I fought them back with every ounce of strength I had. I tried to block the words out of my head, but I couldn't. I wasn't going to be okay; this whole situation was wrong. And of course, leave it up to John, Paul, George, and Ringo — even fake ones — to put things in perspective.

I started swaying to the music and closed my eyes. I sang along to the lyrics about hopelessness, yearning, and being foolish about love. Basically, everything I was feeling at that moment.

I was a complete hypocrite. Even though I had kept telling everybody that this wasn't a date, a big part of me had wanted it to be. I realized that now.

This felt right. Ryan had never been anything but kind to me. He was a good person.

But I'd thought the same thing about Nate. Nate was nice to me, he was a good person. And then he lied and broke my heart.

I'd made a promise to myself to never let that happen again.

Big Dumb Idiot.

That's what Nate had called himself.

I didn't want to be a Big Dumb Idiot, too.

As much as I wanted to fool myself into thinking that things would be different with Ryan, they wouldn't. I wasn't going to fall for it. I knew better.

As the song ended, I knew what I had to do. It had to end — the flirting, the longing, everything. It wasn't just about what I wanted, it was about what was best for the group, my friends.

Face the music, Penny. You've got to hide your love away. You can't just hide your feelings. You have to destroy them. Kill them before they kill you.

The lights went up and Ryan looked at me excitedly. "That was awesome ... although don't tell your parents I said that, okay?"

I gave him a quick smile then started to exit the aisle. I remained quiet for most of our way home, only answering Ryan's Beatles questions. As he turned the corner to my house, I knew I needed a quick exit strategy, one that would guarantee that there wouldn't be a second date. And knowing me, it wasn't going to be graceful.

He pulled into the driveway. "I'm really glad you came out with me tonight, Penny. I had a great time."

I jumped out of the car before he had a chance to shut off the engine. I turned around with the door open and saw a stunned Ryan. "Yeah, thanks. 'Bye," I said. I slammed the door and ran up to the front door, trying desperately to get in before I burst into tears.

I am doing the right thing.

That's what I was going to keep telling myself.

Twenty-five

"SO HOW'D LAST NIGHT GO?" Tracy asked when I got into the car the next morning.

Horrible.

"The concert was good. . . ." I replied as I started to dig through my bag, not sure what I was looking for.

"Yeah, so did Ryan hit on you?"

I stared at Tracy like she had lost her mind.

"Hey, I wouldn't blame a guy for trying. You're a hottie!"

I ignored her and continued to go through my bag.

"Oh, Pen, I'm just teasing you. Ryan is a cool guy. If there is one guy that I'd break the rules for, it would be him."

My bag fell on the floor.

"Crap! Sorry!" I started to pick up my books and pens.

"Are you okay?"

No, not at all.

"Yep."

Diane was waiting for us by the front doors.

"Hey, Penny, how was last night?"

"Fine."

Diane seemed confused. "It was fine?"

I started to dig in my bag as we walked. "Oh, it was fun, the band was great. Of course, they didn't play all the songs I was hoping to hear, but it's the Beatles, after all, and they do have a lot of classics. Did you know that they have more number one singles than any other artist in history?"

Tracy just shook her head. Clearly she was used to me just spouting out random Beatles facts. Diane started to say something, and I found that I couldn't stop talking about Beatles history. Tracy headed to her locker, but Diane continued following me.

"Penny." She put her hand on my arm, probably trying to steady my nerves. "Is there something you want to talk —"

"Oh, I forgot something. Gotta go!" I headed in the opposite direction of my locker and my first class. Anywhere would've been better than having a conversation about Ryan with Diane.

It was going to be a long day.

"Do you mind making the incision? My hand is killing me." Tyson kept flexing his right hand and wincing.

"Sure." I grabbed the scalpel from him. "What did you do?"

"Oh, I've just been overrehearsing, I guess." He looked a little worried.

"Big gig coming up?"

"You could call it that." He looked down at the floor. When I didn't respond, he looked back up at me. "I have an audition."

But he already had a band. I guess he wanted to move on to bigger and better things.

"What's the audition for?"

"Juilliard." He looked back down.

"Juilliard? *The* Juilliard?" My voice started to rise. "The music school?"

Tyson's face instantly turned red as he nodded. He looked around, hoping nobody had heard me. "Yeah, I guess I've been practicing too much. I just really want to nail it."

I was in shock. Juilliard was probably the most prestigious music school in the country.

"What are you playing?" This was fascinating. Every time I thought I had him figured out, he totally surprised me.

Just like Ryan, who turned out to be a wonderful surprise.

But then my voice of reason kicked in. *Nate surprised you, too. And that started out wonderful, didn't it?*

"Well, first I'm playing Beethoven's Sonata in C Minor, and then I'm doing an original composition on the guitar."

"You play the piano?"

He nodded. "Since I was four."

I just shook my head in pure awe.

"Seriously, Penny, how big of a loser do you think I am?"

I didn't think Tyson was a loser. Actually, I thought he was a good guy. Yes, a good guy — I thought that was an oxymoron, but maybe I was wrong . . . about Tyson.

Tyson wasn't Nate.

Tyson wasn't Ryan.

I had a gut feeling that he'd be good to Morgan. And Morgan deserved to have a good guy.

I looked at him. "You should ask Morgan out."

"What?"

I leaned in. "I think you should ask Morgan out."

"But . . . I thought . . ."

"Forget about The Lonely Hearts Club. I'll take care of it."

There was a look of pure panic on his face. "But how do I know if she'll even say yes?"

"Because she likes you. She has for a very, very long time."

Tyson smiled so widely it looked as if he was about to burst. "Okay, I will. But after auditions. I'm nervous enough already."

"Great!"

I figured at least one member of The Lonely Hearts Club should get what she wanted.

"Hey, so I think I may have done something bad," I confessed to Tracy after lunch.

"Did you kiss Ryan?" she asked, practically jumping up and down.

"No — what? This has nothing to do with Ryan."

I told Tracy all about Morgan and Tyson, and she nodded as she processed everything I was telling her. "I don't see what the big deal would be if Morgan went on a date with him," I said. "As long as she attends the meetings on Saturday night and still eats lunch with us, what's the big deal? The second she starts to lose her identity, we can bring her back."

"You do realize that this is going to change things with the Club?"

I nodded. "I know, but there's no harm in talking about it on Saturday."

I started to pace, contemplating for the first time in my high school existence that skipping class probably was the best option. So far, I had been able to avoid Ryan, but that wasn't going to last. When I turned the corner into World History, I saw him out of the corner of my eye. I immediately went up to Jackie Memmott, who sat two rows behind us, and started to make small talk about the Club. I pretended to be in deep conversation, but I could see that Ryan was leaning over to the right side of his desk, near where I sat.

"Miss Bloom, can I start class?" Ms. Barnes asked, tapping her chalk impatiently at the side of her desk.

Okay, maybe I wasn't being very stealth about it. I got to my desk and gave Ryan a weak smile as I sat down. I was going to focus on the class and take notes and buckle down and study. I was not going to let him distract me. I saw him writing in his notebook. It looked like he wasn't having any problems concentrating.

There was a tap on my left hand, and I nearly jumped out of my seat. Ryan moved his notebook so I could see what he had written. I tried to ignore him, but he pushed his notebook so far off his desk that it was practically in my lap.

Is everything okay?

I just looked straight ahead and nodded.

He started to write in his notebook again as Ms. Barnes droned on and on about the financial ramifications of World War II.

Ryan tapped my hand again. I looked over.

Had a lot of fun last night.

A smile crept over my face thinking about how much fun I'd had. Ryan lit up and sat back in his desk, clearly satisfied with my response.

Why did I have to smile, and why was he making this so hard on me? Putting Ryan Bauer out of my mind was going to be a lot harder than I thought.

When the bell rang, I jumped out of my seat and headed to the door as fast as possible. I felt a tug and my body slammed against the cold, hard tile floor. I tried to make sense of what had happened as a small crowd gathered around me. I got to my feet and unraveled my messenger bag strap, which was caught on a chair.

"Whoa, Penny, are you okay?" Ryan asked, hurrying over.

"I'm *fine*." The words came out harsher than I intended, but maybe that was a good thing. He tried to help me up off the floor, but I pushed his arm out of the way. "I'm fine. I'm sort of in a rush . . ."

"Yeah, I gathered that." His tone surprised me; he was no longer amused by the situation. We both looked at each other in silence, until we heard an announcement over the intercom.

"Penny Bloom, please come to the principal's office. Penny Bloom."

I finished collecting my things as Todd started making an "*ooh*" noise. "Looks like little Miss *Thang* is in trouble."

"Shut up, Todd," Ryan and I said in unison.

Ryan gave me one last hurtful look before he walked out of the door.

I headed to the principal's office as I tried to think about what I could've possibly done wrong. I saw my parents waiting there, looking concerned. I ran the rest of the way.

Twenty-six

"WHAT'S WRONG?" I SAID THE SECOND I got inside the office.

"You tell us," Mom replied. "Mr. Braddock called us in and said that it's important. Your father had to cancel a few appointments to make this."

I was confused. I stared at my parents and could tell they were mad. "I don't know." I hadn't cheated. I hadn't been late to class. My grades, which had always been good, had been getting even better this year. . . .

The door to the principal's office opened and Principal Braddock stepped out and motioned for us to come in. Braddock was a big, stocky bald man, who looked like a nice guy until he opened his mouth. As we walked into his faux-wood-paneled office covered in photos and trophies from his glory days at McKinley thirty-plus years ago, I felt my pulse start to race.

"My apologies for calling you both in on such short notice." He motioned to my parents. "But we're having a problem with Penny that's starting to get out of hand. I'm not sure if you're aware of this little *club* that Penny has started."

WHAT?

"Of course we are," Dad said. "They meet at our house every Saturday night. Great bunch of girls."

Principal Braddock shifted in his seat. "Well, it's causing some problems at school."

It is?

"It is?" Mom asked. "What kind of problems?"

Principal Braddock straightened his tie. "Dr. and Mrs. Bloom, the problem is that Penny is using her unfortunate experiences to turn the rest of the female population against the males at this school."

I was dumbfounded. "The Club isn't about that!"

Principal Braddock put his hand up to silence me.

"Now, I'm sorry that Penny can't find a boyfriend —"

"Excuse me!" Mom protested.

Principal Braddock held up his hands again. "My apologies. I meant to say that I don't really think it's appropriate for Penny to be pushing her ideals on the rest of the female student body, especially the impressionable freshman class."

"Hold on," Mom started. "Penny Lane has created an amazing group of friends. There is no hidden agenda except to spend time with her friends without the pressures of dating. Mr. Braddock, you know how messy high school romances can get. I'm surprised you aren't *encouraging* this." I looked at my mom and saw that her cheeks were flushed. This was going to be good.

"Mrs. Bloom, I am not going to sit here and allow one girl to start running the school. Penny is getting way too much power at this school. Her influence with the female population is getting a little out of control."

Mom started to tap her foot impatiently. "And I suppose you don't have a problem with the fact that, just because some jock can throw a ball far, the entire male population worships him? Let me ask you a question, Mr. Braddock. Have any of the Club members gotten in trouble for anything?"

"Well, technically no. But her little club is unsanctioned by the school, therefore —"

"Therefore," Mom cut him off, "it really isn't any of your business."

Principal Braddock cleared his throat. "*Therefore*, you can understand the problem, that something not authorized by the school should not be encouraged by the school. I cannot allow this to continue."

Mom crossed her legs. "Excuse me, Mr. Braddock, but have Penny Lane's grades slipped at all?"

"No . . ."

"In fact, her grades have actually improved last semester, haven't they?"

He started to flip through my thin file. "I guess."

"So, Penny Lane has done nothing wrong, the Club is not affecting her grades, and the Club is meeting off school grounds. Am I correct?"

"Technically —"

"Well, then I don't see what the problem is."

"The problem is, Mrs. Bloom" — Principal Braddock's face was explosive — "that after that article came out in the *Monitor*, a lot of the males at this school have been complaining.

Not only that, but I've received some troubling reports from my Student Advisory Committee."

Wait, Ryan wouldn't . . .

"Nothing has happened yet, but that doesn't mean that it won't. This spells trouble — T-R-O-U-B-L-E."

Mom got up. "Well, I don't really give an S-H —"

"Becky." Dad finally spoke. He got up and put his hand on her shoulder. Mr. Braddock relaxed considerably, probably hoping that my dad would agree with him.

"Thank you, Dr. Bloom."

"Penny Lane," Dad said, "we're leaving, let's go. And, Mr. Braddock, I'm sure you won't argue that we're going to take Penny with us, as I really don't think it's fair for her to have to stay here today after the way you insulted her."

Dad grabbed his coat. I just stared at him.

"And, Mr. Braddock, as Penny's parents, we encourage this, as you call it, 'little' club. What she has done is wonderful, and you should be putting her picture on the wall instead of chastising her. We couldn't be prouder."

Dad hugged me and kissed me on the forehead. "Let's go, kiddo. Grab your stuff."

Twenty-seven

WORD OF MY QUICK DEPARTURE from school spread like wildfire around school. Non–Club members thought I was expelled. Todd even told people that the police had to escort me out of the building. Of course, I texted Tracy and Diane the truth on my way home, and they spread the word to the rest of The Lonely Hearts Club members. They all thought I was a hero.

Everybody at our next meeting was ecstatic. It was as if Braddock's condemnation of the Club somehow validated us.

I hoped this made it a good time for an announcement.

Diane and Tracy joined me in the front of the room. I looked over and saw Morgan was blushing. She had been thrilled when she'd found out that Tyson liked her, but thankfully didn't want to drop out of the Club.

"All right, I want everybody to hear us out before you make up your minds or jump to conclusions." I looked at Rosanna when I said this. "I started this club because I was sick of guys. But as the Club has grown, I've noticed that it's more about focusing on ourselves, and that we're really good at that. So now I think maybe our focus shouldn't be on *never* dating a guy, but on keeping true to your friends. If one of us wants to go —"

"I knew it!" Rosanna got out of her seat. "I knew it! You want to date Ryan!" She pointed at me like I was a convicted felon.

"If you just wait and hear —"

"Oh, this is just great. Some leader *you* are," she replied.

I noticed that the entire room was glaring at Rosanna. "This isn't about me," I replied.

"Oh, really?" Rosanna rolled her eyes dramatically. "How *convenient* that you decide to change the rules after you go on a date with the hottest guy in school." Jealousy was oozing out of her voice. "Maybe it shouldn't be called The Lonely Hearts Club — maybe you should call it The Rules Will Change When Convenient For Penny Club."

"Oh, just shut it already!" Tracy screamed at Rosanna. "Sit your skinny ass down and listen to what Penny has to say or get the hell out. I can tell you no tears will be shed if you leave."

It was good to have the old Tracy back.

Rosanna sat back down like a spoiled six-year-old who had just been told she couldn't have a pony for Christmas.

"Thank you, Tracy," I said.

"You're welcome, our divine leader." Tracy smiled at me.

"This isn't about me. This is actually about Morgan." The entire room turned toward Morgan, who shrunk from embarrassment. "I'm sorry, Morgan, for having to single you out, but everybody is going to find out eventually. See, the guy that Morgan has had a crush on for years also likes her. And the thing is, Tyson is a really great guy, probably one of the few at McKinley, and I don't want to be the one responsible for denying them the chance to see what could happen.

"So, Tracy, Diane, and I have sat down with Morgan and have agreed that as long as she still attends Saturday meetings, group events, and remains the Morgan we all love, there's no reason she can't give it a try."

Morgan stood up. "Consider me the lab rat. Plus, this may all be premature, since he hasn't even asked me out yet . . ."

He better, I thought. Tyson had *no idea* how much trouble he was causing.

I walked over to Morgan and put my hand on her shoulder. "And I, for one, will be so excited to hear all the details about your date at our next meeting."

Rosanna started to laugh. "You've got to be joking. And when are we going to hear about *your* date?"

That was it. I'd had it with Rosanna.

"Let me make something perfectly clear to you and to everybody else." I was practically shaking I was so mad. "I have absolutely zero interest in Ryan Bauer and I never will. So to clarify to anybody who may be confused, I will never, *never* date Ryan."

The room had gone silent. Tracy and Diane had horrified expressions on their faces.

What had I done?

Twenty-eight

WHILE I FULLY ENJOYED TRACY'S rules for the Club, there was a very important one she missed. *What happens in The Lonely Hearts Club, stays in The Lonely Hearts Club.*

I'd thought that was a given.

If you couldn't trust a member of the Club, who could you trust?

But I hadn't counted on one very shootworthy messenger.

Tracy, Diane, and I were walking into school together on Monday morning, talking about Morgan and Tyson, hoping his audition had gone well and he was ready to ask her out. We were just rounding the corner when Diane's expression fell.

"Oh, no," she said. Both Tracy and I followed her gaze and saw Rosanna talking to Ryan at his locker with a smug look on her face.

This couldn't have been good.

Diane quickened her pace, and Ryan spotted the three of us walking over. He gave me a hurt look before slamming his locker and walking away.

"Let me talk to him." Diane headed after him.

I could tell Tracy was about ready to go after Rosanna, but she stopped when she noticed the panicked expression on my face. "It's okay, Penny," she said. "She's a jerk."

I nodded slowly. A numbness had spread over my body.

"That's it, she's out of the Club," Tracy went on. "I'll tell her." Tracy guided me to my locker and opened it up for me. All I could do was stare straight ahead.

"No, I'll tell her," I said. "At lunch." I could hardly get the words out.

"Okay." Tracy got my books for me. "Do you need anything else?"

Yes, I needed to know why, if I didn't have any feelings for Ryan, I felt so demolished.

Diane filled me in right before lunch. "Rosanna told Ryan that basically you declared in front of the entire Club that you think he's pathetic, that you don't even like him as a friend, and that you would never go on a date with him."

"That's not what I said!" I protested.

Well, not the first two parts.

"That's what I told him, but he's still pretty upset. I don't think he liked the fact that you would talk about him to the Club."

"All right," Tracy chimed in. "Let's slow down for a second and catch our breath." She put her arm around me and looked me in the eye. "Are you sure you want to do this now?"

I couldn't believe that at a time like this Tracy had decided to be the voice of reason. Even Diane looked at her like she was mental. Of course I wanted to do this.

Right.

Now.

"Yes."

I marched into the cafeteria like a soldier off to battle, with Diane and Tracy right behind me. Rosanna was at the end of the table talking poor Eileen's and Annette's ears off. She jumped a bit when I slammed down my books next to her. The entire table went silent.

"I have something I need to say." I was looking at Rosanna, but said it loud enough for everyone to hear. "There are certain people who are here for the wrong reasons. Certain people who aren't here because of friendship. People who are manipulative and wouldn't know how to be a good friend even if their bony ass depended on it. They're here because they want to be popular. Well, you know what? I've been used far too much in my life to stand here and let it happen to me again. It's bad enough that I've been screwed around by boys. But to be screwed around by a girl . . . a supposed friend . . . is even worse. Underminers are not welcome in The Lonely Hearts Club any longer."

Rosanna continued to eat her banana, while looking around as if I couldn't possibly be speaking about her.

"Apparently, I'm not making myself clear." I leaned over so I was face-to-face with her. "Rosanna Shaw, you've taken advantage of me, of the Club, of our trust. You took something I said when I thought I was among friends, and you twisted it into a hurtful lie. You're no longer welcome in the Club, in my house, or at this table. Do you understand?"

She squinted at me. "Are you seriously going to kick me out?"

"I just did!" My voice started to rise. "Get out of here, you backstabbing, two-faced wench."

"Yes!" Tracy got up and clapped, followed by Diane, then Morgan and Kara and Jen. Soon the entire table was up, cheering me on.

Rosanna quickly got up and started to leave. Adrenaline was pumping through my entire body as I sat down. I examined the happy faces around me. I was so glad to have the old, supportive Club back.

I turned around to see the entire cafeteria was looking in our direction. A few other tables even joined in the celebration of Rosanna's departure.

I caught Ryan's eye at the other end of the room and gave him a smile, but he looked away.

The camaraderie within The Lonely Hearts Club was better than ever all week. We were stronger, more united. Maybe it was Braddock's threats, or Rosanna's interference, but all the Club members seemed to have become more invested in the Club and one another.

We all came out in full force to support Diane's debut as a member of the McKinley Ravens basketball team. With only two minutes left, Diane had yet to be put in the game.

"Coach Ramsey has to let Diane in — we're up by nineteen points," Tracy said.

I kept stealing glances over by Diane's parents, where Ryan was sitting. I guessed there was no way Todd, or any of the guys, would've come to support Diane, despite how many times she had cheered them on. I had tried to talk to Ryan since Monday's debacle with Rosanna, but he wouldn't even look at me. Anytime I tried to approach him, he walked away. He had to have heard the conversation in the cafeteria; it was all anybody had been talking about the last four days.

The junior varsity cheerleading squad took the floor. They didn't even try to display any enthusiasm for the game, like they were being punished by having to cheer for the girls' team.

"Ugh, this is painful. I could do a better job," Tracy said as the cheerleaders anemically asked if we had spirit.

The buzzer sounded and the teams got back to the court. Diane sat patiently at the end of the bench, her knee visibly shaking with nerves.

Jen threw the ball from out-of-bounds to Britney Stewart, who was immediately fouled by a desperate member of the Springfield team. The team lined up at the free-throw line, and Britney easily scored two extra points for the team.

"Oh, come on, Coach!" Tracy screamed. "Put Diane in!"

All five Ravens players sprinted down to the other end of the court. Jen easily recovered a failed attempt from Springfield to score a basket. She grabbed the ball fiercely and began to dribble it down the court. A tall brunette player from Springfield ran up alongside her and pushed her down with a swift motion of her hips.

The whistle blew as the referees conferred.

"That *so* better be a technical foul," Tracy hissed.

The team congregated near the bench to be briefed by Coach Ramsey. As the coach talked to the team and went over the next play, Diane looked on intently, then she bit her lip, and headed into the game.

The entire Club section stood up and started cheering. Signs were hoisted, and chants of "Diane" started filling the gymnasium.

Diane's eyes narrowed as she lined up at the foul line and watched Jen miss her two free throws. Then, when the action resumed, she ran full force to Springfield's end of the court. She was squatting down and staying low as the guard from the other team approached her. Diane stayed with the guard the entire time, focused on the player's torso, a trick Ryan taught her.

The ball was thrown to a tall blonde who missed the basket. Jen recovered the ball and threw it to Diane.

Diane dribbled the length of the court, every ounce of her attention on the basket before her.

"Come on, Diane!" Tracy and I screamed in unison. Tracy grabbed my hand as we watched Diane approach the basket for a layup and . . . miss.

"It's okay, Diane!" Kara screamed next to me. We all continued to clap as Springfield called another time-out.

"Can you believe them?" Tracy motioned down to the front, where the cheerleading team had decided to take a break. "They sat down the second Diane took to the court. So pathetic."

The cheerleaders were sitting on the first bench. Missy was texting someone on her phone, while the rest of them were doing everything they could to ignore the game.

"Oh, they make me so mad. A few weeks ago, all those girls were kissing Diane's ass and now they can't even cheer for the team . . . it's their job!"

I nodded, annoyed at how shallow they were being.

"I've had it." Tracy stood up.

"Tracy, don't cause any . . ."

Before I could finish my sentence, Tracy stood up on our bench, turned around to face the people behind us, and screamed at the top of her lungs, "GIVE ME A *D*!"

Our section quieted down as everybody stared at Tracy.

She looked exasperated. "Come on, people, I *said* GIVE ME A *D*!"

Oh my God. Is Tracy . . . cheerleading?

"*D!*" Morgan, Kara, and Amy shouted.

"GIVE ME AN *I*!" Tracy continued.

"*I!*" The Lonely Hearts Club started to roar.

"That's more like it! GIVE ME AN *A*!" Tracy started to clap and bounce on the balls of her feet.

The cheerleaders from below turned around, mouths opened in shock as the Ravens side of the gymnasium gave Tracy an *"N!"*

"GIVE ME AN *E*!"

The gymnasium echoed with a loud *"E!"*

"What's that spell?" Tracy made her way down to the front of the bleachers.

"DIANE!"

She was now at the space occupied a few moments earlier by the cheerleading squad. "I CAN'T HEAR YOU!" She placed her hand up toward her ear.

"DIANE!" the crowd cheered back.

The buzzer sounded and everybody was on their feet cheering. Tracy looked over at Missy and company and gave them a little smirk, letting them know they were no longer the ones in control of the crowd.

Diane got back on the court, determination sketched on her face. Less than fifteen seconds was left on the clock. Springfield took possession of the ball, and the guard slowly made her way down the court. Their team was going to lose, so why would they let us score any more points.

"TEN . . ." — the crowd started to count down with the clock.

Diane's eyes zeroed in on the approaching player.

"NINE . . ."

She started to shuffle back and forth.

"EIGHT . . ."

The guard tried to make a quick break to the left, but it was too late.

"SEVEN . . ."

Diane stole the ball and dribbled at a sprint down the court . . .

"SIX . . ."

. . . while the entire Springfield team rushed after her.

"FIVE . . ."

Diane focused on the net ahead and . . .

"FOUR . . ."

. . . went in for the layup.

"THREE . . ."

The ball bounced off the rim and hit the backboard . . .

"TWO . . ."

. . . and went right into the net.

The buzzer was muffled by the cheers erupting from the crowd. Diane was swarmed by her teammates. The cheerleaders rushed out of the auditorium with disgusted looks on their faces. The Springfield side was clearly confused about the celebration before them.

I thought back to the Diane who sat across from me at the diner less than two months ago. I looked around at all of the Club members to whom Diane had been such an inspiration. She had shown us all that it could be done.

Twenty-nine

I<small>T WASN'T LOST ON ME THAT</small> there was a correlation between the demise of my friendship with Ryan and the growth of the bond within the Club.

Every time the Club moved forward (Diane's basketball triumph last night), Ryan and I took a step back (he never showed up at his locker that day).

While that was upsetting, there was another problem that I needed to face.

Nate.

There was another e-mail waiting for me when I got home. This one entitled

FRIENDS?

I sat down and clicked it open.

Pen,

I've been thinking about us a lot lately. Actually, you're all I think about. I know I'm not going to hear from you. I know you hate me. I know you will never feel for me the way I feel for you. I deserve this. But I just need to ask you one question, and I want you to think about it (if you're even reading this) before I see you in a couple weeks. Do you think we could at least be friends? I need you in my life. And I'll take you whatever way I can.

I am going to do everything possible to get you back in my life.

Love,

Loser

Friends? He wanted us to be friends? Could I be friends with Nate after everything that happened?

Ryan and Diane were friends, but Ryan didn't cheat on Diane. Ryan was . . .

I couldn't handle thinking about how wonderful Ryan was. Or being friends with Ryan, since he clearly had no interest in even talking to me.

Maybe the best thing would be just to tell Nate we could be friends and move on.

But I knew: I was fooling myself if I thought that I would be able to do that.

After brooding about it for a week, I decided to ask Diane for advice over dinner. "How can you be friends with Ryan?" I blurted out before we even ordered.

Diane was surprised. "He's been in my life for so long."

"But so has Nate . . . for me," I replied.

Diane looked concerned. "Yeah, but Ryan never . . ."

I sank back in my chair.

"What is this about?" Diane bit her lip.

I filled her in on the e-mails and Nate's plea for us to be friends.

She shook her head. "Penny, do you want to be friends with Nate?"

"No — I never want to see Nate again. But that isn't going to happen."

She sighed. "I really think you need to come clean to your parents."

"No way."

Diane set down her menu and grabbed my hand. "Is everything okay? You've been really quiet all week."

I shrugged.

"You know," Diane offered, "it wasn't easy at first, being friends with Ryan. I had to get in a new routine with him, but now he's one of my best friends. And so are you." She hesitated. "And I wish that my two closest friends could forgive each other."

"What?" My mouth dropped open. "Forgive each other? Diane, he won't even look at me. I've tried to apologize to him, but he doesn't even acknowledge my existence."

"I know. He's just upset."

"Upset?" I was so frustrated. "What Rosanna said was a blatant lie. He knows that, right?"

Diane nodded.

"So, what's his problem? We've been friends for a long time and then he doesn't want to talk to me? Why? Because people thought we went on a date."

Diane shifted uncomfortably in her chair. "Penny, *Ryan* thought it was a date."

"Diane, he knew about The Lonely Hearts Club. He knew I couldn't date."

She shrugged.

"You know," I said, "maybe Nate and Ryan aren't that different after all."

Diane looked shocked. "How can you say that?"

"Come on, Diane." My face was flushed. "So, fine, Ryan thought it was a date. So because I wouldn't be . . ." I wanted to say "his little girlfriend" but didn't want to offend her. "Because I wouldn't go on a date with him, he doesn't even want to be my friend? Is all he wants from me, I don't know, to get laid?"

Diane pursed her lips. "You know he's not like that."

"Do I?"

I started to get upset. I knew I'd crossed the line. I knew that Ryan wasn't like Nate — but I missed Ryan. I missed talking to him, hanging out with him between classes. And he just dumped on me. Just like Nate did. So was he any different?

"I'm just saying that my opinion on guys hasn't changed," I said.

I was sure I was right to not get involved with Ryan. He would've just hurt me in the end. Just like he'd already hurt me.

Tracy came up to me the next day after class. "Hey, I need to talk to you for a minute." She looked serious.

We walked over to the benches that lined the hallway near the cafeteria.

"There's some stuff going on with the Club that I need to let you in on."

"The Club?" I thought everything was great. But I'd been so distracted lately, it didn't surprise me that I may have missed something.

"Yeah, Kara is going to miss the next two meetings."

"Oh?"

Tracy looked around. "Yeah, I didn't say anything to you or Diane because I swore I wouldn't tell anybody."

"What's going on?"

"She's going in for counseling."

"Counseling?"

Tracy sighed. "Oh, come on, Pen. We've all kept quiet the last couple of years while we watched her waste away. I don't know what prompted her, but she started talking to me and Morgan at the last meeting about wanting to get back in control."

"That's great." I was so happy for Kara. Happy and concerned.

"So, anyways," Tracy continued. "The program she is going to is all weekend long."

"Of course, it's fine." I felt bad that I didn't know about it or hadn't been there for Kara.

Ryan came walking toward his locker. It was the first time I had seen him outside of World History in a week.

"Hey, Ryan," Tracy said.

He looked up from his locker. "Hey, Tracy."

He, once again, didn't even look at me. He quickly grabbed his things and left.

Tracy looked between me and Ryan, who was walking out the door. "What's going on with you two, anyways?"

"Nothing."

And that was the truth. There was absolutely, positively nothing going on.

I decided I was going to use the week before Thanksgiving break to focus back on the Club. I'd had enough of stressing over Ryan's coldness and Nate's desire to be friends.

"Okay, spill it!" Tracy said to Morgan as she sat down at our meeting on Saturday. "We want details."

Morgan blushed as the entire group awaited the details of her first date with Tyson.

"Well, Tyson picked me up in his mom's station wagon."

"He did not!" Erin exclaimed. "That is so not what I pictured."

"I know." Morgan smiled. "I thought he would've had some rock-star car, but it was really sweet. We went to the Mexicana Grill and had the greatest meal — they have the best guacamole. Then we went to the garage, and I got to hear their band rehearse, and he sang a song for me." Morgan blushed at the memory.

"An original song?" Teresa asked.

As Morgan continued the story of her night, I looked around at the group. Everybody was interested in Morgan's date and happy for her. I couldn't help but smile.

These were the kinds of friends that I needed. Supportive ones. Not Nate, who'd betrayed me. And not Ryan, who was so quick to dismiss me.

"Did he kiss you or not? I said details," Tracy teased.

Morgan blushed and looked down.

A chorus of "wooo" filled the room as Morgan put her hands up to her face. "Penny, you've got to help me," she begged.

"All right, all right. Let the girl have some amount of privacy." I laughed.

I went through a list of movies we could watch and let the debate start between an eighties teen comedy or a horror flick.

"Hey, Penny." Teresa Finer came up to me. "Would it be okay if Maria and I went upstairs to study?"

"Study? It's a Saturday night, guys."

Maria Gonzales took out her Advanced Calculus textbook. "I know, but there's a big test on Monday we need to go over."

Teresa leaned in. "I failed the last exam, and if my grade drops any lower I'm going to lose my volleyball scholarship at UW."

"Oh, of course!" I motioned for them to follow me as I walked them up to my room. "It will be quiet here. Let me know if you need anything."

"Thanks," Teresa said as she sat down on my floor.

When I headed downstairs, I saw I had a text from Nate. Tracy had shut off his ringer, but that didn't mean he couldn't get through.

I flipped open the phone and burst out laughing.

"What's going on?" Tracy was in the kitchen with Diane getting more food.

I kept laughing. "Oh, it's this text from Nate . . ."

Tracy ran over and grabbed the phone. "What? I don't get it."

"What's it say?" Diane asked.

"Milk was a bad choice," Tracy read. I burst out laughing again.

"It's . . ." I kept giggling. "It's from *Anchorman.* We saw it this summer on TV, and we kept quoting lines from it all the time. See, it was really hot out . . ."

Tracy and Diane were both horrified.

"Penny, have you lost your mind?"

"What? It's a funny movie."

"You don't see what he's doing?"

What *was* he doing?

Tracy hit the DELETE button. "I'm keeping this tonight." She put my phone in her pocket. "Let's go back downstairs. Maybe being around the group will remind you why we're here."

I followed Tracy downstairs. But I had a smile on my face, remembering laughing so hard with Nate that I had tears running down my face. Good tears.

I had almost forgotten that there were good times with Nate.

❤ ❤ ❤

I kept getting texts all week. And I hated to admit that I was beginning to look forward to them. Just like I used to look forward to going to my locker and talking to Ryan.

I told Tracy that they'd stopped, because she was demanding possession of my cell phone. And it wasn't like a few funny lines were going to make me forget about what he'd done.

I just needed to laugh.

I raced back to my locker to pack up before Thanksgiving break. I checked my phone and began laughing at his newest quote.

"Hey, what's so funny?"

I almost didn't recognize the voice.

Ryan. He was smiling at me.

"Oh." I hadn't talked to him in weeks. I had been waiting for this moment, but didn't know what to do. "Oh, I just got a funny text."

"Well, it's good to see you smile again, Bloom."

I didn't know how to take that. "Um . . ." It was good to be talking to him again. If only I could've figured out what to say. I decided to be honest. "I guess I could say the same thing to you."

He laughed. "Yeah, you're right. Been a tough few weeks, huh?"

I just nodded. Where had this come from?

"Well." He shut his locker. "Have a great Thanksgiving. I'll see you when we get back." He touched my shoulder as he walked off. My heart sank.

Right then I got another text from Nate, but I deleted it without looking. Funny quotes were all well and good, but that's not what I wanted.

It scared me that that brief encounter with Ryan meant so much to me.

I closed my eyes. I was thankful for the Club. For not dating.

Because there was no way Ryan Bauer could do anything but break my heart.

Thirty

"PENNY LANE, YOU AREN'T GOING to wear that are you?" Mom asked when I walked down to the kitchen on Thanksgiving morning.

I looked down and inspected my outfit — a nice pair of jeans and a long-sleeved tee. "Ah . . . yes. This is standard Bloom holiday wear."

She was busy wiping down the kitchen counter and looked more stressed than usual.

"I know, but we have guests this year."

"Oh, I'm sorry I didn't realize the Queen of England was stopping by."

"Penny Lane!" Mom snapped at me. I had forgotten how much entertaining took out of her. Rita and I had been doing our best to help her, peeling potatoes and cutting up vegetables. I had the cuts on my hand to prove it.

Dad walked in with the newspaper rolled up in his hand. "Penny Lane, please change for your mother, will you? She's a little upset that Lucy isn't coming home this weekend."

This was the first holiday our whole family wasn't together. Lucy was spending Thanksgiving with her fiancé's family in Boston.

Mom wiped the sweat off her brow. "I know she'll be spending a whole week at Christmas, but that's going to be spent getting ready for the wedding . . ."

Rita entered the room in jeans and a T-shirt.

"Girls, change right this instant!"

As we walked upstairs Rita asked, "What did I miss?" I just shook my head. *Happy Thanksgiving to me.* Rita could tell that I was a nervous wreck.

"Penny, it's going to be fine," she said. "You've got to be the bigger person. You don't want him to have any power."

The Taylors were going to arrive in less than an hour, and I still had no idea what I was going to say to Nate. To be honest, I didn't even know what I was going to feel like when I saw him. Angry? Sad? E-mails and texts were one thing, but what would I feel when I looked in his eyes? That was going to reveal a lot. I just hoped I would be able to stay strong. He wasn't going to get to me. I had moved on.

I went to my room and found the white halter top Diane had lent me after Homecoming, when she told me that I needed to accentuate "what your mama gave you." So I put that on with black-and-white pinstripe pants and black heels. I headed downstairs thinking that I looked a lot better . . . maybe a little too good for my father.

"Uh, is that top new, Penny Lane?" Dad said, as he nervously looked at my outfit.

"Oh, Dave, relax," Mom said. "She's filled out nicely."

The doorbell rang, and I tried to take a few deep breaths. Rita grabbed my hand and whispered, "Don't let him win."

Win? What was there to win?

The door opened and there was an explosion of activity — my parents embracing Mr. and Mrs. Taylor and exchanges of cheerful greetings.

Mrs. Taylor turned to me. "Oh, Penny, look at you!" She hugged me tightly. "Oh, sweetie, you look fantastic." She let go of me and I turned around.

And there he was. With a look on his face — I couldn't tell whether it was shy or smug.

"Hey, Penny."

I opened my mouth and tried to say something, anything. But it was hard. I thought about what Diane had said about Ryan being in her life for so long. Here was Nate in front of me, Nate whom I had always known. I thought that maybe my last memory of him would drown out the others, but they didn't. Seeing each other was such a routine, and even though we'd always say "Hey, Penny" and "Hey, Nate" like it was no big deal, we usually said it like we shared a secret between us. Because we did. And now it was bigger than before.

I hated seeing him. I hated him being here. Because I hated what I was feeling. As much as I wanted to scream and run away, I could hardly breathe. I felt the same excitement that I would always feel when I saw him.

This was going to be harder than I had ever imagined.

"Here." Rita shoved the Taylors' coats in my arms. "Penny will hang these up."

I gave Rita a grateful look as I darted to the closet. I spent more time than necessary hanging up the coats. The entire time I sensed Nate's eyes on my back. And I enjoyed it.

"So, what can I get you to drink?" I asked the second the last of the jackets was on a hanger.

"I've got it, sweetie." Dad began to take drink orders.

"No, Dad," Rita protested. "Let me and Penny help."

I turned to head to the kitchen, when I felt a tug on my arm.

"Penny," Nate said as he enveloped me in a hug. "I missed you so much."

"Aww," Nate's mom cooed. "He's been talking about nothing but seeing you again, sweetie."

I just stood there with Nate's arms around me.

"Come on, Penny." Rita came over and Nate quickly loosened his grasp. "We've got to go to the kitchen." She turned to Nate. "You know, the room with all the sharp knives."

As he backed away, I examined him for the first time since he'd completely crushed me. And it was strange, because he wasn't the same as my memory of him. Had I not noticed before how flat his face was? And he had these tiny, pale, lifeless eyes.

I was starting to breathe a little easier.

I hung out in the kitchen with Rita and Mom, helping to get ready while Mrs. Taylor grilled us with questions about school. Fortunately, the guys were downstairs watching the football game. It was the first time that this sexist tradition didn't bother me.

I went into the dining room to pour water in the glasses and noticed that Mom had put me right next to Nate. There was no way I would be able to avoid a conversation with him.

There wasn't enough time to switch places — everyone was already coming in for dinner. As I grabbed a plate, I realized that Mom had certainly outdone herself this year with food. I could hardly fit everything on my plate the first go-round, although I did skip the cranberry sauce as I was afraid it would stain my shirt. The cranberry sauce and the tofurkey. My parents weren't going to let tradition get in the way of their beliefs, so I'd gotten used to filling myself up on salad, mashed potatoes, wild rice, and sweet potatoes.

Nate followed me in line at the counter. He reached across me to grab a roll, then placed his other hand on the bare part of my back and moved his thumb back and forth. I stayed there, unable to move.

"I missed you," he murmured.

For a moment, I almost whispered back *I missed you, too.* I was so used to this exchange between us. This time, I tried to refuse it. I'd spent months blocking out his touch, his words. I knew where this always led for him.

I couldn't force myself to look at him. I just walked back to the table.

Then, as we sat down, Nate took a long look at my chest.

And I thought, *Wait a second.*

Mr. Taylor turned to me. "So, Penny, what's this Club of yours I keep hearing about?"

I almost choked on my mashed potatoes. How did he know about it?

Mrs. Taylor chimed in next. "Yes, your mother sent us the link to the article in the school paper." If Mom thought I was going to help her with the dishes, she had another thing coming. "It sounds like so much fun. I wish I had had something like that when I was your age!"

That meant Nate knew about the Club. I couldn't bear to look at his reaction. Instead, I smiled and cheerfully replied, "Yes, it's so much fun!"

I could feel my hand start to shake. I looked at Rita, who was giving me an encouraging smile.

"It's really great," she said, glaring at Nate. "Especially since you wouldn't believe *the complete losers* who've asked Penny out. She's much better off."

Mr. Taylor smiled and nodded. "Well, that's just great, Penny."

The conversation shifted to politics. I couldn't resist looking at Nate. He was shoving food into his mouth. A speck of tofurkey dangled from his chin.

This was the guy that I would dream about every summer? *This* was the guy who broke my heart? *Him?*

After dinner and dishes, I went upstairs to my room to call Tracy. Before I could dial, Nate knocked on my door and asked to come in.

The thought of being alone with him made me a little sick, but I figured I couldn't keep ignoring him any longer.

He sat down on the corner of my bed. "Come here," he said, tapping the place next to him.

"No, thank you." I stayed at my desk.

Nate got up. "Aw, come on, Penny. I meant every word in my e-mails. You can't still be mad at me, can you?" He came over and placed his hands on my shoulders.

It used to be that his touch was all I wanted. It used to be that I would've happily spelled out my life in moments like this — the two of us alone together, the two of us in secret. It used to be that my unwritten boyfriend list had only one name on it. It used to be that my love for him could make him beautiful no matter how he acted, no matter what he did.

"Tell me what I can do to make it better," he whispered, leaning in to rub my shoulders.

"Well," I said, "you can start by getting your hands off me."

He kept going. "You used to like it when I did this."

I stood up and pushed him away from me. "Yeah, I used to like a lot of stupid things."

He looked genuinely hurt. "Don't say that, Penny. I know things didn't end well with us, but it wasn't all that bad."

"You have *got* to be kidding me." I didn't even bother controlling my voice.

I heard loud footsteps on the stairs, and in a few seconds Rita was in my room. "So help me, jerkwad — get away from my sister."

I turned toward Rita. "Actually, Rita, close the door." She put her hand on the door. "No, I mean, leave." Rita closed the door behind her.

Nate looked triumphant. "See, this is more like it." He crossed the room, but I held out my hand.

"Stop."

"Why do you always have to be such a tease?" He winked at me.

I felt hotness rise in my face. I was trying to do everything I possibly could to not punch him.

"How can you stand there and think that after everything you did to me that I would just forgive you? A few e-mails and funny texts aren't going to change that."

Something came over Nate then. This strange calm, as if the answer was the most obvious one in the world, at least to him.

"I figured you'd forgive me because I love you," he said.

And he believed it. He was a fake, a cheat, a liar, a scum. But at that very moment, I couldn't sense any faking, cheating, lying, or scumming. He truly believed it, if only for the second he needed it to be true.

"Nate," I said, "you're not allowed to do that. You're not allowed to say that. You lied to me."

I could start to taste bile in my throat.

"Nate, you lied to me."

"I told you what you wanted to hear," he said, regaining his defensiveness.

"Well, did you think that maybe what I wanted to hear was the truth?"

I could see what was happening. The minute I challenged him, that *"I love you"* was gone. "You know what, Pen. No, I didn't think that, because you didn't want to hear the truth. You built up some stupid fairy tale about us since we were little, so yeah, I did what I thought you wanted."

"You used me."

Nate threw his hands up. "It's not like I got very far!"

My body started to shake. "You got far enough."

"Whatever. I think you at least owe me a thank-you."

"What?" I must have heard him wrong.

A smile spread across his face. "The Lonely Hearts Club? You obviously started it because of me."

My mouth practically dropped to the floor. He thought that I should *thank* him.

"Aw, come on — you needed to get over me, so you started the club. To be honest, I'm a little flattered, babe."

I looked at him in complete shock.

I tried to remember what Rita had said about being a bigger person. I could either calmly tell him that he was mistaken or let him have it. I could be the bigger person or I could be like any normal sixteen-year-old.

Like there really was a choice.

"First off, you ever call me a babe again and no medical team on earth will be able to tell that you were once a guy."

I was only sixteen after all.

The smile quickly vanished from his face.

"Seriously, I don't know what I ever saw in you. You're a completely selfish human being. Not only that, you're not nearly as good-looking as you think you are and add as much to a conversation as a bag of rocks. I believe in people learning from mistakes, and let me tell you something — you were a *huge* mistake.

"Not only am I never going to make a mistake like that again, I'm never going to have to put up with you again."

I went over to where he was sitting and got in his face.

"You're going to get a job next summer back at home and stay with someone there. You're not going to spend any more summers with us. Do you understand?"

"You can't make me do anything." He crossed his arms.

"Oh, really? Okay, fine." I grabbed his arm. "We're going downstairs and we're going to tell my mother exactly everything that happened this summer — and I mean *everything*."

Nate stopped in his tracks.

"Come on, Nate — you don't think you did anything wrong, so what's the big deal? I think my mom would love to hear what you did to me, especially since you were doing a whole lot more with a bunch of other people at the same time. God, maybe I'll get lucky and be able to be there when my mom tells *your* mom about it. Honestly, I'm sick of keeping it a secret from them. True, my mom will be disappointed in me for my poor choices and for giving in to a pig, but for some reason, I think she'll have a few more . . . ah, words for you."

Nate removed my grip from his arm. "Penny, stop it."

"Stop what? You can't possibly be scared of my mother?"

I couldn't believe I was able to say that with a straight face.

"You know what," I went on. "Something good *did* come from this summer. I deserve so much better than you. I always have. So I guess I should thank you for being a complete and utter jerk so I would wake up and see what I'm worth. But in the end, the people who matter the most to me are my friends, not someone like you. You mean absolutely nothing to me. Yes, in a way your actions are responsible for the Club, which is the best thing that ever happened to me. But I owe you nothing."

I turned around and started to leave my room, but had a second thought.

"And, Nate? You kiss like a slobbering dog, you have bad breath, and you wouldn't know how to push the right buttons on a girl if we came with manuals. Happy Thanksgiving, Jackass."

All right, I am going to be a bigger person starting right now.

Thirty-one

"NO YOU DIDN'T!" TRACY WAS screaming on the phone after I gave her the details.

"Can you believe it? I think I may have gone a little overboard in the end, but I just feel this incredible weight lifted off my shoulders." I was lying in bed with my pajamas on, feeling so giddy. The Taylors had left, and Rita had brought me a big piece of pumpkin pie before heading out for the evening. Life was grand.

"Seriously, next meeting I want you to do a complete reenactment for the Club. I'll be more than happy to play the part of Nate. I'll just grunt a lot and shove food in my face. Priceless! Who else knows?"

"Just you and Rita. She thinks I'm a goddess!"

"You have got to call the Club. Everybody's dying to know what happened."

"I will — I just can't believe that seeing him was a good thing; I don't know what I was thinking. He changed so much."

"Penny, it wasn't Nate who changed, it was you. You know that I've never liked him. I always told you that you could do better, but you didn't listen and now you know the truth. Pretty sweet, huh?"

Very sweet indeed.

I fell into bed exhausted after calling Diane, Jen, Amy, and Morgan.

I had done it. I had stood up to Nate.

I went over to my desk and picked up my old journal and went to the last entry. The one that had broken my heart so many times in the past. I ran my finger along the indentations the pen left. There was so much pain in those words. But now I knew that everything would be okay.

I grabbed a pen off my desk and wrote below my "Yesterday" entry. I wasn't rewriting history, I was just reminding myself that I could get over heartbreak if it happened another time.

. . . I'll be back again.

Yes, I would be back. I could take chances with my heart and I would be able to bounce back, and anything that might hurt me would just make me stronger in the end.

And I did deserve everything I wanted — somebody who would appreciate me, someone I could trust, someone who liked me for me.

My heart sank as I thought of Ryan.

Thirty-two

"NOW, PENNY LANE, THIS IS our little secret, pinky swear."
Dad held out his pinky and I locked mine with his. "Your
mother would kill me if she knew we did this with all of the
leftovers still in the house."

Dad and I were on our own for Saturday dinner, and neither of us had been able to stand looking at the leftover
tofurkey . . . so we'd thrown it down the garbage disposal.
Mom was never going to buy the story that I'd helped him
finish it off.

"So what's the Club up to tonight?" Dad asked.

"We're going to catch a movie so you guys don't have to
worry about a zillion screaming girls in the house."

Dad smiled. "Well, that's a relief. No karaoke planning?"

Ugh, that was the purpose of us going to a movie — to try
to distract Jen from the following weekend's party. She had
been totally stressing out. Not only had I promised to sing a
solo, I had also agreed to lead the Club in a rendition of "Sgt.
Pepper's Lonely Hearts Club Band."

The phone rang and Dad went over and picked it up. "Oh,
hello, Ryan," he said after listening for a moment.

It can't be . . .

I looked over and saw that my dad's forehead was creasing.

"No, no, you did the right thing. I'll be in my office in five minutes. Meet me there."

Medical emergency. "Is everything all right?"

"No, actually that was Ryan Bauer — his sister fell and hit her mouth against a table and is bleeding. I need to get over to the office." He grabbed his jacket. "Actually, Penny Lane, can you come with me? I might need an extra set of hands."

"Umm . . ."

"Plus," he added, "Ryan seems a little shaken up. It might be good for him to have a friend there."

Before I could protest, Dad threw my jacket at me and was out the door.

Ryan was waiting for us when we pulled up. He was holding his eight-year-old stepsister, Katie, in his arms, her long black hair covering her face. Dad ran over to him and reached out to touch Katie's head. "Sweetie," he told her, "it's going to be okay." He handed me his keys. "Penny Lane, open up the office, get the lights on in my exam room, turn everything on, and get a clean set of instruments." Ryan looked at me, noticing that I was with my father, and I saw that his eyes were filled with panic.

I nervously reached for the keys and sprinted into the office. I flipped on the overhead lights and then ran in the back to my dad's main exam room. Like an automatic reflex, I turned on all of the equipment, grabbed a fresh set of instruments, and placed them down on the counter.

Katie's sobs were getting louder as my dad and Ryan

approached the room. "I was upstairs getting dinner ready, and then I heard a crash. I guess she was jumping around and . . . fell," Ryan was explaining to my dad.

He set Katie in the chair and Dad gently removed the towel that was covering her face. All I could see was blood.

"Oh, no!" Ryan exclaimed, and he put his hands over his head and started to pace.

"Everything's going to be fine," Dad said. I couldn't tell if he was talking to Katie or Ryan.

I ran into my dad's office, grabbed Abbey the Walrus, and ran back. Dad was examining Katie, who was now crying even harder. "Here, sweetie." I went over and gave her the stuffed animal that I used to play with when I was about her age. Katie hesitantly took the walrus and then held on to it for dear life.

"All right, some of the teeth are a little loose, but everything is going to be fine. I'm just going to clean up the wound and then see about stabilizing the teeth." Dad looked over at Ryan, who seemed like he was about to faint.

"Penny Lane, why don't you take Ryan to the lobby," Dad went on, even as Ryan began to protest. "Ryan, I think it's best for you to wait there. You've done all you can."

I walked out the door and Ryan followed me. Before I could even think about it, I placed my hand on his shoulder.

He plunked down on the couch in the reception area and put his hands over his face. "My mother's going to kill me."

I sat down next to him and put my arm around him. "Ryan, you didn't do anything wrong."

"There's so much blood," he protested.

"But that's just because the blood is mixed with the saliva, so it just looks worse than it actually is," I assured him.

He jerked his head up. "Why are you even here?" I couldn't tell if he was angry or embarrassed.

"My dad, he, um, thought he might need help . . . and that you might need a friend." I reached for his hand and gave it a squeeze.

Ryan's cell phone rang and he jumped. "Hey, Mom. . . . no, I got ahold of Dr. Bloom. . . . Yes . . . okay . . . okay . . . I will . . . 'bye."

"You have to know this isn't your fault," I said after he'd hung up. He just stared straight ahead. "Um, when I was two, Lucy was supposed to be watching me. She was only ten at the time, so that was probably pretty irresponsible of my parents, but she left me on the top bunk bed in her room and, well, the next thing you know, I fell off the bunk bed and onto the floor. And you know, I turned out seminormal." I bumped my knee against his. "Or maybe not. . . ."

He smiled. "I know she'll be okay, but my mom sounded like I really let her down, and Cole is so overprotective of Katie. It's just . . . do you have any idea how frickin' exhausting it is to be me sometimes?"

I stared at him in disbelief.

"Ryan," I said, "nobody expects you to be perfect."

"Right, tell that to the coaches and my parents."

I'd never really thought about that. I'd just always assumed that Ryan *was* perfect.

"It's my own fault," he continued. "I kill myself to live up to people's expectations. Just once I'd like to skip class, drink at a party, not always say the right thing. I can already hear my parents, 'You should have been watching her, Ryan,' 'What were you thinking, Ryan,' 'How irresponsible, Ryan,' 'We are so disappointed, Ryan.' That's the worst, when they tell me that they're disappointed in me, like I'm not allowed to mess up once in a while. I'm just thankful my dad doesn't need to know about this."

It was the first time Ryan had mentioned his father since he hadn't shown up at the game earlier in the year. "If I have to hear from him one more time that an A-minus is the same as a B-minus and that no decent college is going to let me in unless I get nothing but straight As . . . like I want to follow his path to being a self-absorbed prick."

My mouth dropped open.

He looked horrified. "I'm sorry . . . I shouldn't have . . . I didn't mean . . ."

"It's okay." I rubbed his arm. "You're just really stressed about Katie, that's all. There's just . . . a lot going on right now."

He turned to me, looking so tired. "I know you think I'm overreacting, but I spend so much time doing things to not disappoint people. . . . What about what I want?"

"What *do* you want?" I asked.

"Does it even matter?" he replied as he leaned his head against the wall.

"Yes, it does, if it's important to you."

"Well, I can't have it, so what's the point?"

This was such a different side to Ryan — he was so vulnerable. It made me like him even more. I reached out and held his hand again. "Ryan, you're an amazing person and you do deserve whatever you want."

He looked down at my hand in his. "I'm not stupid, so I'm willing to settle."

I was confused; I had no idea what he was talking about. He reached out his free hand and cupped my chin. "I know things have been weird, but can we please have things go back to normal between us?"

I didn't know if that was even possible. What was normal anymore?

I nodded. "I'm really sorry for everything. Rosanna was just . . ."

"I know," he said as he put his hand back down and took his other hand away from mine. I had the urge to grab it again, but resisted.

"Well." I hit him on the knee. "Leave it to you. You come in here with your sister and you end up making *me* feel better."

"Yeah, well, leave it to Mr. Perfect . . ."

I laughed. "Hardly. Don't forget I overheard you singing at the concert and you, mister, have a little problem with pitch. I say you're far from perfect."

He shook his head and we sat in silence. I started to hum along to the Muzak playing in the background.

"Oh my God," I said.

Ryan looked up. "What's wrong?"

I shook my head, "Nothing, it's just . . ." I went over to the front desk and turned up the volume. "Seems to be appropriate, don't you think?" I started to sing along to the music playing.

Won't you please, please help me.

"You have no idea." He breathed what appeared to be a sigh of relief.

Dad came out a few minutes later, holding Katie's hand. Her mouth looked a lot better, besides the gauze that Dad affixed to help slow the bleeding. Ryan jumped out of his chair and was on his knees hugging her.

"Dr. Bloom, thank you so much. I'm so sorry for having to call you at home — I just didn't know what to do."

My dad shook Ryan's hand. "No worries — you did the right thing."

Katie came over to me and extended Abbey in her small arms. I bent down. "You know, I think you might need Abbey more than me." Her face lit up and she ran over to Ryan and grabbed his leg.

"Well," he said, "I guess we should go. Thanks again, Dr. Bloom." He walked over to me, saying "Thanks, Penny" as he gave me a hug. Then he leaned down and kissed me on the cheek.

I saw the surprised look on my dad's face. As we let them out the front door, he looked at me. "So . . . that Ryan. Great guy, huh?"

You have no idea, I thought.

With a Little Help From My Friends

"I get by with a little help from my friends . . ."

Thirty-three

USUALLY AFTER A BREAK, I dreaded going back to school. But I couldn't wait to see Ryan, to see if things were really okay between us.

We fell quickly back in place, and I practically ran to my locker between classes. Instead of dread, I started to look forward to my between-class teasing session. Usually I told him how many ways he wasn't perfect, and he commented on the unfortunate shape of my head from my bunk bed trauma.

"Come to think of it, I never see you wear hats — is that because of the, you know, *accident*." He tugged on my scarf as I was buttoning up my wool coat.

"Gee, let me think. I've never seen you play a musical instrument — is that maybe because you're completely inept at anything related to music?"

I wrapped my scarf around my neck so it smacked him in the head every time it circled around.

"Oh, excuse me . . ."

"Penny!" I heard someone cry from across the hall. I saw Jen running toward me, with Tracy following quickly behind her.

This couldn't be good.

Tracy broke the news. "Principal Braddock told her that we can't have the karaoke night in the gymnasium anymore."

"What?" I screamed. "It's four days away!"

Jen took a deep breath. "He said that he feels it's turned into a Lonely Hearts Club event and that it can't be on school grounds."

"That doesn't make any sense," I protested. "We're raising money for the basketball team. We're just helping because you're our friend. Everybody's invited."

Jen put her head in her hands. "I just don't know what we're going to do. We've all worked so hard."

Tracy sat down and put her hand around Jen's shaking body. "It's okay, we'll just have to postpone it until . . ."

"The hell we are!" I proclaimed. Both Tracy and Jen looked up at me in shock. "We're going to have this party and raise so much flippin' money that the basketball team is going to have the best uniforms in the school's history."

Tracy looked at me like I had gone insane. "But, Pen, we can't use the school."

"Then we'll find somewhere else to have it. I am so sick of all the drama. Seriously, what's the point of having the Club if we can't find a way to overcome these little obstacles?"

"But all of the flyers have been put up. . . ." Jen argued.

"So we'll make new ones. Screw Principal Braddock — let's show him how much power we really have." Now even I was a little surprised by myself. "Let's go to my house — we've got some phone calls to make."

In less than an hour, all thirty members of The Lonely Hearts Club were at my house, ready to step into action. My parents had ordered pizza for the group as we analyzed our options.

"I still say all the parents need to get together and talk to Braddock," Dad said, opening up a pizza box and helping himself to another slice.

I shook my head. "No, we need to do this on our own and show him that we can stand on our own two feet. We can handle whatever he's going to throw at us."

Dad nodded while he chewed, looking around the room, clearly happy to be in the middle of all the excitement.

"All right, here's the deal," Eileen Vodak said as she came into the basement. "My uncle will let us use the event space at the Bowlarama for free, but since it's a Saturday night and he'll have to turn away paying customers, he asks that we don't bring in any food but have people buy sodas and snacks. Or, if we give him $5 a person, they will cater the event for us with soda and chips and stuff."

"But that's going to cut into the profit," Jen replied as she sat nervously on the floor.

"Exactly how many people are you expecting?" Dad asked.

Jen picked at her uneaten slice of pepperoni, "I have no idea — fifty?"

"But fifty hardly covers the Club and the basketball team," Diane reminded us.

"Wow, you're right. I guess a hundred or a hundred and fifty." Jen started writing figures down in her notepad.

Dad looked over Jen's shoulder at her writing. "Come to

think of it, Jen, I don't think the Bloom Dental Office has made a donation to the team this year. How about this — you guys pull this off and I'll pay for the refreshments?"

Jen looked up at my dad with her big blue eyes, and for the first time all night she smiled. "Dr. Bloom, thank you so much." She got up and threw her arms around him. "I promise to start flossing every day!"

Dad laughed. "Well, that's just great."

I think that might have made his day more than saving the basketball team.

"Okay." Jen nervously bit her lip. "I guess all we need to do now is to let everybody know about the location change. We've got flyers. . . . I guess that will be enough." She didn't seem convinced.

"We should make an announcement over the PA system," Tracy said, drawing a microphone on poster board. "Like Braddock would ever let that happen. I just wish I could find a way to get in there and do it."

"You can't," Diane told her.

"Well, I know that. I was just joking," Tracy responded.

Diane stood up. "No, I'm just saying that *you* can't, but *I* can."

I stared nervously at the clock before homeroom and took a deep breath to calm down. I hoped Diane could pull this off and that she wouldn't be suspended for it.

Since Diane was the president of the student council, she was responsible for the Friday morning announcements.

Usually, she just edited the announcements that all the clubs had submitted for the week and let other members read them over the PA.

Not this time.

Hilary Jacobs and I exchanged glances as the bell rang and everybody started to take their seats.

We had been distributing the new flyers all week in the school parking lot. We had to take different shifts to make sure we didn't get caught. One girl hung outside the school office with cell phone in hand, while two others monitored the exit closest to the parking lot. The rest of us were each assigned a row in the parking lot to hand out flyers. Another group came in later to make sure that nobody had littered so there wasn't any evidence.

To my knowledge, Principal Braddock had no idea that we were even still having the karaoke fund-raiser. I couldn't wait to see the look on his face when Jen presented him with the money on Monday.

The buzz of the intercom sounded. "Good morning, everybody, and happy Friday," Diane announced. "The following are your announcements for the week. The Key Club's annual flower drive begins next week. Carnations are a dollar, and you can get . . ."

I could hardly concentrate on the announcements as I was too nervous for Diane. I prayed that Principal Braddock wasn't too close by and that she would have enough time to do it.

"And, finally, please note that the girls' basketball karaoke fund-raiser on Saturday night at seven P.M. has been switched from the gymnasium to the Bowlarama on Cook Street." There was a noise in the background, but Diane sounded as calm as ever. "The entrance fee is five dollars, which includes food and drinks. We look forward to seeing you all Saturday night at the Bowl —"

The intercom went dead.

"You're my hero, Diane," Jen said as we headed into the Bowlarama. She was beaming as we bought tickets. "There are so many people here already! I've got to go check on the sign-in sheet for the songs. Remember, you guys aren't off the hook yet."

I didn't want to be reminded.

Diane smiled at her as she handed over her admission fee. "Hey, I took one for the team. Anybody would've done it."

I don't know how many people would've taken getting suspended from playing at Tuesday's basketball game and having her announcement duties revoked in such stride, but Diane was glowing.

We walked into the back room, and it was packed — there had to be easily over one hundred and fifty people already there. The room was dark with white lights hanging down from the ceiling. It was sort of pretty, for a bowling alley.

I saw the stage up front with a big spotlight on it and a monitor to display the words to the songs. As we headed there, Jen ran over. "This is a total disaster!"

"Everything is great and look at the turnout — what could possibly be wrong?" I asked.

"Erin is sick — her voice is shot."

Wow, Jen really needed to chill out. With all of the drama the past few weeks, I really didn't see one person being sick as a disaster. "Jen, there are plenty of people who will sing, don't worry about it."

"But who will be the first person? Everybody who has signed up has refused to go first. Please, Penny, you need to help me."

I looked around and noticed that Tracy had made a quick getaway.

"Really, Jen, you don't want my help. If I'm the first person to start, the room will be cleared out."

"Please, Penny. Everybody looks up to you. If you do it, I'm sure the whole Club will, too."

Okay, I was wrong. This *was* a disaster.

"Fine."

"Thank you, thank you. I totally owe you."

No kidding. I wasn't going to forget this anytime soon.

I walked over to the Club's five front tables. "All right, guys, I'm going first. Who wants to go up with me?"

You could hear a pin drop. For the first time since The Lonely Hearts Club started, nobody would look me in the eye. "Seriously, guys, if we all go up in a group together, it won't be so bad." *Please, oh, please, somebody has got to go up with me.* "Anybody?"

Tracy was playing around with her bag of chips, refusing to make eye contact.

Et tu, Tracy?

This was ridiculous. It was just singing a song.

Jen was looking around anxiously. If I didn't act soon, she was going to snap.

"Okay, Jen, let's get this over with! What song am I singing?"

A look of relief spread over her face. "Any song you want. Remember — I've got Beatles songs!"

Although I loved the Beatles, I felt a little silly singing one of their songs in front of everybody. As Ryan had learned, there were only four people who could ever do those songs justice, and I was not one of them.

I nervously started flipping through the binder — nothing seemed to be calling out to me. I needed something that wouldn't be difficult to sing and maybe something people would want to join in on. Nothing was looking right, so I figured I might as well go to the old standby. I flipped to the B section of the songs and started going through the Beatles, when I spotted it.

Perfect.

Okay, so I was no Paul, John, or George, but maybe, just maybe, I could be Ringo.

I reluctantly got up on the stage, and as the Club began to cheer, I gave them all a glare. *Traitors.* My hands were shaking as I scanned the crowd — it seemed like the entire school was here. Toward the back I saw Ryan clapping for me. I began to smile until I noticed who was standing right next to him — Missy. How could he be around her after everything that had happened?

And, more important, what on earth was I doing up onstage?

Jen grabbed the microphone. "Thank you all so much for coming to this fund-raiser for the team. All the profits from tonight's event will help pay for our new uniforms. So don't be shy, and come up and request your songs. Kicking off tonight's festivities is none other than Miss Penny Lane Bloom!"

I heard cheering, but stared at the monitor, trying to control my breathing. I didn't need the lyrics to this song, but I couldn't stand to look out to the audience. There was hardly an introduction to the song, and before I knew it I was singing, asking everyone what they would do if I sang out of tune — would they stand up and walk out on me?

So far, no.

Although if I kept singing, that most certainly would happen and, really, would that have necessarily been a bad thing?

I closed my eyes and just moved back and forth as I sang the song. I looked out to the front row, *Please help me*. I was not only begging, I was actually singing for help. The audience started to clap along.

I strutted over to the side where Tracy and Diane were sitting and cheering me on. I pointed to them as I continued to sing about getting by with a little help from my friends. I motioned for them to join me on the stage.

Diane got the hint and got up and dragged Tracy along. Morgan and Amy followed, and even Erin came up onstage — never one to turn down a spotlight.

We all gathered around the microphone, and the rest of the Club members got on their feet and clapped in time with the song. I grabbed the other microphone and headed out into the audience. I started dancing around with the other girls. They all started taking turns singing.

And yes, I somehow got by with a little help from my friends.

The song ended and a roar erupted from the crowd. I joined everybody back onstage and we high-fived each other. Jen was jumping up and down as a line started to form for people to request songs.

We heard everything from girls singing along to boy-band pop to the football team doing a very off-key rendition of "We Are the Champions." Even Morgan and Tyson did a cute duet. The Club couldn't get enough. But most important, Jen was raking in the money.

Morgan, Eileen, Meg, and Kara finished singing "We Are Family," and we were on our feet again.

I sat down next to Tracy and stole a chip from her bag. "Oh my God, Penny," she said.

"Relax, Tracy, it's just a chip."

She pointed to the stage. I saw Ryan standing up there by himself. I started to laugh — was he trying to prove to the whole school how completely imperfect he was? He looked down at me and winked.

"What's the big deal?" I asked.

Tracy looked at me with wide eyes. "Did you see the song he picked?"

The music started and my heart dropped.

I recognized the song instantly.

How could I not?

I was named after it.

The entire Club looked over at me as Ryan started singing "Penny Lane." Incredibly off-key. I wanted to feel embarrassed for him as he struggled with the first verse, but I was trying to control the emotion on my face as the entire room kept switching their stares from Ryan to me.

I had to concentrate on breathing. I was so overwhelmed and touched. I couldn't believe this was happening, that Ryan would do this in front of the entire school.

He liked me. He really, really liked me.

And I liked him. I really, really liked him.

I could no longer deny my feelings and tell myself that I couldn't risk the Club. How could I not want to be with someone like Ryan? How much longer was I going to fight it? How much longer was I going to lie to myself?

The first verse ended and Ryan stepped back, looking like he knew what a mistake he'd made. It was heartbreaking in so many ways. Diane suddenly popped out of her seat to help him. A second later Tracy joined him, followed by the majority of The Lonely Hearts Club. Ryan looked instantly relieved to have the backup help. I knew exactly how he felt.

I also knew that there were going to be so many rumors after this.

But at that moment, I didn't care. This was the single best thing a guy had ever done for me.

Granted, "Penny Lane" wasn't a grand love song, but to me it was the most romantic gesture a person could make. The song ended, and I gave the group a standing ovation. Looking at everybody, except Ryan, I had a slight panic attack. What was I supposed to do now? Maybe since the entire Club had joined in, people wouldn't focus on me and Ryan?

Highly unlikely.

Ryan got off the stage and headed over to me. "If you couldn't guess," he said, "that song was for you."

I smiled, not knowing what exactly to say to him.

"All right, there is only time for one last song," Jen announced. "Penny?"

"I've, uh, got to go," I said, but squeezed Ryan's hand before I headed up.

The last song kicked in and the entire Club was up onstage singing "Sgt. Pepper's Lonely Hearts Club Band."

We hope that you enjoyed the show.

Thirty-four

TRACY, DIANE, JEN, LAURA, AND I walked out to the parking lot with a feeling of success.

"You guys, we raised over three thousand dollars! People were actually giving me more money so they could move up in the line," Jen said as she held on to the envelope of cash with all her might.

"That's fantastic, Jen — congratulations!" Diane said.

"Well, look who it is. Miss Penny God Damn Street!" We turned to see Todd, with the standard coupling of Brian and Pam, Don and Audrey. Ryan was right behind him. Missy was there, too. But it was unclear whether she was with Ryan or Todd . . . or just hanging on.

Ryan tried to grab Todd's shoulder, but he shrugged it off.

"Todd, are you drunk?" Diane said, unimpressed.

"Get bent, Diane." Todd was *clearly* drunk, weaving between the cars. I hadn't seen him for most of the evening. I was sure I would've heard his booing during my song . . . and Ryan's.

Ryan, once again, tried to bring Todd back to the car, and this time Todd pushed him. "Ryan, you're so pathetic."

"Oh, sure, he's the pathetic one." It took me a second to realize that came from me. Todd was suddenly in my face.

"Stay out of it, Bauer. This is between me and the dyke."

I tried to pull my face away from Todd's horrible breath. "What are you even talking about, Todd?" I asked. Ryan came over and I just snapped. "I can handle myself, Ryan." He backed away, but kept his hands in fists as if he was ready to go into action at any moment.

Todd just kept staring at me. "You know, just because you're so pathetic that no guy in his right mind would want to go out with you, doesn't mean you have to taint the rest of the chicks in the school."

"Really, if I recall correctly, there was a time when you wanted to go out with me, but I seem to have a brain that prevented it from happening. If it makes you happy, go ahead and blame me for why no girls want to go out with you." I started to back away from him, but Todd took another step.

"Seriously, Todd, you better leave her alone," Diane said as she walked over with Tracy, Jen, and Laura right behind her.

"Oooh." He swayed in their direction and threw his arms up in mock horror. "I'm soooo scared of a bunch of girls."

"Actually, we prefer to be called women," I said, then bit my lip. I couldn't help it, but I knew that I was only making it worse.

Behind his shoulder, Missy was watching with a look of pure satisfaction.

Todd just kept swaying. "Look here —"

"No, you look here, Todd —" I'd had enough of his childish behavior, and I wasn't going to let him ruin our night.

"Maybe the reason why you haven't had a date in a while is because no girl in her right mind would want to date a guy with the intellect of a four-year-old."

He leaned into me. "Well, maybe the reason why guys keep cheating on you is because you're a self-centered bitch." He laughed as I winced.

"You know what? Maybe the reason why all the girls in the school are in this Club is because all of you guys are complete jerks. We'd rather hang out with each other than go out with any of you." I realized I was making a generalization that included Ryan. "You're such a little boy, Todd. Why don't you go back to the football field where you belong, chasing after a little ball instead of trying to chase after girls who are ten times smarter than you."

That set Todd off completely. "You little bitch!" He grabbed my wrist hard. I felt a surge of pain as he squeezed and twisted my arm.

I screamed out in pain as Brian and Don pulled Todd off me.

Brian pulled Todd by the waist. "She's not worth it, man. She's totally not worth it. Come on, come on . . ."

Todd shrugged Brian off and stood up straight. He gave me the finger as he walked back to his group of friends. Missy gave him a standing ovation as he returned.

And *I* was the bitch?

Ryan walked over to me. "Are you okay? I didn't realize he was that gone." I was shaking, and my wrist was throbbing, but besides that everything was just great! I meekly nodded as the girls came over to make sure I was fine.

Diane walked over to him. "Seriously, how can you be friends with him, with any of them?"

He just shrugged. "You know he's not always like that."

"Ryan, Todd just assaulted Penny and you're just going to go back there and pretend that everything is okay?" Diane shook her head.

Ryan looked back at his supposed friends. "All right, let's not overreact," he countered.

"You have got to be kidding me." I looked at Ryan in complete disbelief. "You're going to stand up for him?"

You're on my side, I thought. *You sang to me, right?*

"No, of course not. It's just . . ."

All my frustration from the last few weeks had built up. I was so pissed, I could barely see straight.

I turned to Ryan, heat rising in my cheeks. I could taste the acid on my tongue. He was supposed to be a friend of mine, but he was going to stand there and allow this to happen. He didn't want to create waves with his idiot best friend and disgusting teammates.

"Wow, Ryan, how *disappointing*. You wouldn't want to have to stand up for yourself, now would you?"

Ryan looked at me like I'd stabbed him. We both just stared at each other.

I instantly regretted it.

"I didn't mean . . ." I sputtered.

He turned away and left me standing there, with a look of pure horror on my face.

How could I say that to him in front of everybody?

Tracy put her arm around me and led me to her car. "Pen, he's such a jerk, don't pay attention to anything he said."

"But Ryan . . ."

Tracy looked confused. "I'm not talking about Ryan. I'm talking about Todd."

Oh, right, Todd.

I kept replaying the conversation over and over in my head.

"Here, put this on your wrist. I'll take care of the bed." Tracy handed me a bag of ice, took the sheet from my hand, and started to make up the air mattress on my bedroom floor. "Penny, stop beating yourself up over it. He's an idiot."

I looked up at her. "Do you really think we've upset that many people at the school by starting the Club? First Principal Braddock and now . . ."

She shook out the sheet as it fell onto the bed. "Sit down." She sat on my bed and patted the cushion next to her. "Penny, the Club is one of the most important things that either of us has ever done. Todd Chesney is an idiot, end of story. Don't let it ruin the success of the evening."

I looked down at my flannel pajamas and put my knees up so my chin was resting on them. "I just don't want to be responsible for making anyone upset."

"Do you know what you're responsible for?"

I shrugged my shoulders. I didn't know what to think anymore. Every time I thought I could handle the Club and being friends with Ryan, everything fell apart.

Tracy grabbed my shoulder so I was forced to look at her. "You're responsible for Kara being comfortable enough to talk to people about her eating disorder."

Kara's transformation had been remarkable. Gone were the baggy sweats, pictures of stick-thin models in her locker, and her lunch routine of picking at a salad with no dressing. Now she wore more flattering clothes, had pictures of her friends up in her locker instead of waif models, and ate with the group. She still had a long way to go, but it was a start.

"You're responsible for the fact that Teresa kept her volleyball scholarship to UW."

Teresa ended up acing her Calculus exam, thanks to Maria.

"You're responsible for the fact that, for the first time in her life, Diane Monroe has her own identity. Remember what she was like at the beginning of school?"

I pictured Diane at the diner, clearly miserable, but trying to pretend that everything was fine.

"And now anytime you see her she's so happy to be in the Club and to have girlfriends. She's really surprised me."

Tracy wasn't the only person Diane had surprised. I still couldn't believe that she risked her standing with Braddock to help the Club, or that she stood up to Todd tonight . . . or to Missy after the article came out.

I felt my chest restrict and my eyes were starting to burn. "Those things didn't happen because of me. I can't take responsibility for them."

Tracy got up and took my hands. "You were the one to open our eyes. You're the one that's the strongest of us all."

My bottom lip started to quiver. "Yeah, I'm so strong."

"Stop it, Penny. Don't sell yourself short. You're the leader of the group because everybody respects you, because you're there for people, and because you're one of the greatest people I've ever known. I'm so happy to have you as my best friend. How many times do I have to tell you that?"

Tracy hugged me, and I held her tightly.

"Plus," she continued, "everybody is pretty much scared of me when they first meet me and Diane comes off as Little Miss Perfect, so I guess you were the lesser of three evils."

I let go of my grasp as Tracy started to laugh. "Sorry, you know I can't help it. This is exactly why we all need you so much!"

I sat back down on my bed and realized how tired I was. Tracy lay down on her mattress and threw the covers over herself. "Enough drama for today. I'm out."

I turned off the lamp on my nightstand and pulled my duvet cover over me. Laughter came from below.

"What is it?"

Tracy giggled. "I just wish we could see Todd tomorrow morning. He is going to be *so* sick. Let's hope he got sick on Missy! I'd pay to see that!"

I laughed for a second before I thought of Ryan. I had to figure out a way to make everything right between the two of us — *again*.

How was it that I could be part of a big group of girls, but couldn't seem to stop causing problems with one guy?

I winced as I remembered the look on his face.

I closed my eyes and pushed the thought away. I would deal with that tomorrow. Tonight I was going to enjoy the success of the evening. It was a great night, except for Todd yelling at me and me yelling at Ryan.

As I lay awake in the dark, I tried to visualize all the good things that happened tonight — Jen raising all the money for the team, Kara's killer rendition of "I Will Survive," Diane and Tracy joining me in my song. . . .

But each time I started to feel happy, Ryan's hurt face popped into my head.

"Ow!" I exclaimed as I hit my head a little too hard, hoping that I could shake the thought loose.

"Penny," Tracy said groggily, "are you okay?"

No, no I'm not.

"Yes, I'm fine. Good night."

I really had to stop lying to my best friend.

And myself.

Thirty-five

THE CLOCK WASN'T MOVING FAST ENOUGH. I had been pacing in front of my locker for what seemed liked an eternity. Granted, I was at school a lot earlier than normal. I had asked my mom to drop me off this morning so I could be this early. My stomach tightened up — Ryan would be here any minute.

He rounded the corner and took off his wool hat, making his hair a mess. He started to run his fingers through it to calm it, then looked up and saw me. He stopped for a second and then looked down as he approached his locker.

"Hey . . ." I said to him.

He just nodded as he took off his puffy black winter coat.

I knew I deserved that.

"Ryan, I am really, really sorry about what I said. You know I didn't mean it."

He put his backpack in his locker and started to take out his books. I wondered how long it would be before he looked at me again.

"I know you didn't mean it," he said in a low voice, still not making eye contact. "The problem is you said it because you knew it would hurt me. Well, mission accomplished." He shook his head. "Out of everybody at the school, I thought you would be the last person to stoop so low."

He slammed his locker shut and started to walk away. He paused and turned to me. "You know what I've been doing every morning for the last few weeks? I drive to school wondering which Penny I'm going to see at my locker today. Will it be the sweet, warm, and funny Penny or the cold and distant Penny? I practically hold my breath to see how you're going to react to me and then try to figure out what I did to deserve your behavior. That's why I didn't talk to you for those couple of weeks. I was hurt."

I stared at him. I couldn't deny what he was saying. I knew that I'd been erratic around him, and I couldn't tell him the real reason why.

He shook his head. "I just never know where I stand with you." He began to walk away.

"Wait." I ran to get in front of him. "I know what I said is unforgivable — I really am so sorry. So much has happened the last couple months and, yes, I've taken some stuff out on you."

"Why?" He looked at me intensely.

"I . . ." I reached in my bag. "I . . . I wanted to give you this."

I held out my hand and gave Ryan the only thing I could think of to let him know how I really felt.

He reached out and examined the CD case. He opened it up and his expression changed as his finger traced the songs. "You made me this?" He looked up at me.

"Yes."

He studied the inside and read the inscription aloud. *"From me to you . . ."*

"It's from one of the songs — this one." I took the case and pointed out one of the tracks. I didn't dare write the entire lyrics out — it would just say too much. He'd have to listen to it to understand everything.

He kept studying the case.

"I know it seems silly, but it's the only thing I could think of." I started to feel the desperation in my voice and the tears starting to form. Everything in my life, except the Club, seemed to be crashing around me — the stares from the guys at school, Todd yelling at me, Principal Braddock being on my case — I just couldn't handle it if Ryan hated me, too.

Ryan heard my voice crack and looked up again. "I love it. Thank you."

"It's just a stupid CD." I walked over to the wall, trying to control the tears that had now started trickling down my face. What was I thinking? That a Beatles mix would make everything better? If only he knew what these songs meant to me. This wasn't just a mix CD, it was my heart and soul. I was giving it to him, I was letting him in. I just wished he could see that.

Ryan walked over and leaned in, knowing that in doing so he was blocking my tears from the flood of students now entering the hall. His closeness gave me a sense of comfort rather than unease.

"Penny, this means so much, coming from you. Please don't be upset." He placed his hand around my neck and leaned in farther so his chin was resting on my forehead.

"I'm sorry, I'm just . . ." I tried to calm myself down. "It's been a long few weeks."

He held on. "Yes, it has."

More tears ran down my face. I tried to compose myself as the hallways filled. "Great. All I need is more rumors about me. I'm getting so sick of people talking behind my back, and I'm sure this will just give them more fodder."

He bent down and wiped my tears away with his hand. I looked into his blue eyes and wished all the obstacles would just go away.

"You know, you being nice and all isn't helping," I said to him.

Ryan stared at me intensely for a few seconds before a smile crept over his face.

"Okay, stop your blubbering, woman. You're being a big tear whore."

"What?" I screamed in surprise. I couldn't help but laugh. "What the hell was that?"

He shrugged. "Well, you needed a good laugh."

"Yeah, but 'tear whore'?"

"I was under pressure — it was all I could think of."

He leaned in one last time to wipe the tears from my face. He smiled warmly at me. "All better?"

As I nodded, something caught my eye in the hallway. I saw Tracy staring at us with her mouth open. She walked away quickly when she knew she'd been spotted.

"Look, we've got two weeks left before break. Let's make a pact to not let anything get in the way of our . . . friendship again," he said to me.

I smiled at him. "That would be great."

"All right, let's get back to our lockers before we're late for first period." He put his arm around me and led me to my locker. A wave of relief started to come over me as I grabbed my books.

Crap. I had completely forgotten that my first class was Spanish with Todd. Crap.

Or, more appropriately, *caca*.

There was no way I was going to pass Spanish. I kept copying everything Señora Coles was writing on the blackboard, but I couldn't concentrate. Todd came in a few minutes late to class with a pass, and I was too scared to look over at him.

"All right, just a reminder that your final is next Thursday. That's it for today. Now it's time for your conversations. *En Español, por favor,*" Señora Coles said to the class as she walked to her desk in the back of the room.

I turned around to face Todd and found him staring at my wrist. I wore a long-sleeved sweater to cover up the bruise, but you could still see some of the brown and blue. I opened my mouth to speak, but couldn't think of what to say.

Todd said something, but his voice was so low, I couldn't hear him.

"*¿Qué?*" I asked.

Todd looked over at me. "*Lo siento, Margarita. Lo siento.*"

He looked exhausted. Before I could say anything, the bell rang. I started to collect my books. When I walked out of the class Todd was waiting for me.

"I really meant it, Penny. I'm sorry." His face was red, and he was slouching up against the lockers right outside of class.

"Thanks, Todd."

He gave me a weak smile before he headed to his next class. Todd just didn't seem like Todd unless he was making a joke or goofing around. I felt a little sad — how much else could possibly change? I could hardly keep up as it was.

By lunch the entire school knew that not only had Todd gotten drunk on Saturday night, but his parents had caught him, and this morning they'd met with Principal Braddock, who'd had no choice but to suspend Todd from the basketball team for three games.

Now I understood why Todd was so upset. Even though it was his own fault.

"So . . ." Jen said as Morgan sat down. "Where did you and Tyson run off to after the party?"

Morgan blushed.

"Nice!" Jen laughed. "I see it was a successful evening all around."

"Oh, leave her alone," Diane said.

"Actually, this is sort of what I wanted to talk about," Tracy said.

Morgan looked horrified.

"No," Tracy shook her head. "I meant about the Club." She started to hand everybody a sheet of paper.

My heart jumped when it got to me. I was a little hurt that this was the first I was seeing of it. I knew we talked about it, but still . . .

The New and Improved Rules of The Lonely Hearts Club

Heretofore are thy official rules for members of "The Lonely Hearts Club." All members must agree to such terms or thy membership shall be struck from thy record.

1) Members are allowed to date, but must never, ever forget that their friends come first and foremost.

2) Members are not allowed to date jerks, tools, liars, scum of the earth, or basically anybody who doesn't treat them well.

3) Members are required to attend all Club meetings on Saturday nights. No member shall wuss out on attending due to a date with a boy. Exceptions are still for family emergencies and bad hair days only.

4) Members will attend all couple events together as a group, including, but not limited to, Homecoming, Prom, parties, and other couply events. Members may choose to bring a boy with them, but said male attends event at his own risk.

5)   Members must first and foremost be supportive of their friends, no matter what choices they make. What matters most is for us to stick together.

6)   And most of all, under no circumstances, shall anybody take what is said in the Club and use it against someone. You all know what I'm referring to.

Violators of the rules are subject to membership disqualification, public humiliation, vicious rumors, and possible beheading.

As people started reading, there was a lot of head nodding and verbal support for the new rules. I looked over and saw that Tracy was waiting for a reaction from me. "What do you say, boss lady?"

"Let's make this a group vote. All in favor of the new rules?"

All the hands at the table shot up.

"Thank God!" Tracy exclaimed. "Michelle, can you please start dating my brother again so he'll talk to me?"

Michelle started to blush.

"Here, invite him to the party." Amy started passing out envelopes. "There is one for each of you, but feel free to bring a guest. Even male ones." She winked at Morgan.

Amy handed me mine, which had "Penny Lane, Fearless Leader" written neatly on the front. She was throwing a big holiday party for the Club after our final exams.

We all started talking about the party, and I looked over at Tracy again. She hadn't mentioned a word to me about what she'd seen between me and Ryan. And I didn't feel like bringing any more drama into my life. I just needed to survive my finals.

"Hey, Teresa," I yelled across the table. "You took Spanish Three last year, right?"

"*Sí*," Teresa responded.

A lightbulb went off in my head.

"Hey, guys." I stood up and everybody stopped talking. "Maybe we should use the next couple meetings to do study groups for finals." I heard some groans. "I know, I know, but think for a second. We can all help one another with our finals, especially members who have been in classes the year before."

I wanted to get even better grades this semester, just to prove Principal Braddock wrong. And, of course, I wanted everybody in the Club to ace their exams. When Jen had gone to the office that morning to give Braddock the money, he'd just grunted while he counted the bills.

Could anything make that man happy?

Thirty-six

IT WAS WEIRD, BECAUSE EVEN though I was a believer in Club secrecy, I wanted someone to let Ryan know the new rules. And at the same time, I still wasn't sure I was ready to date again, to take the risk that it wouldn't work out. It was so unfair: The more I liked Ryan, the more I knew he could break my heart.

I decided a study session was a safe non-date. So I invited Ryan over to review World History. He seemed a little surprised by the invitation, but didn't hesitate to say yes.

"So exactly how do you know all this inside information?" Ryan asked me, as we went over notes in my basement.

"Oh, I've got my resources." I took out a map of Nazi-occupied Europe during World War II.

During Saturday's meeting, I'd found out that Ms. Barnes had asked a lot about World War II last year. I knew teachers didn't use the same exams, but it was good to get the scoop on what they had done before.

Plus, I didn't consider it cheating, as we weren't given any answers, just information on what happened the past year. I took anything I could get.

"Oh, hello, Ryan," Mom said, coming downstairs. "Do you want to stay for dinner?"

Ryan looked at me and I shrugged. "That would be great. Thanks, Mrs. Bloom."

Mom looked at both of us with a big smile on her face. It wasn't like we were up to anything — there were textbooks spread across the floor, and Ryan and I were at least a few feet apart. I kept looking at her, waiting for her to say something, but she was just staring at us.

"Mom . . ."

"Oh, sorry." She headed back upstairs.

Could that woman, for once in her life, just try, *try* to not embarrass me?

Although I was pretty impressed with myself, both Ryan and I had been able to be friends for nearly two weeks without any drama. That seemed to be our agreement. I did sometimes think about him in non-appropriate friend ways, but I was only human.

"Any big plans during the break?" Ryan got up and stretched. I looked at the clock, surprised that we had been studying for two hours straight.

"Wedding dress shopping." I unfolded my legs and tried to get feeling back in my left foot.

"So who's the lucky guy?" He winked at me.

I rolled my eyes. "Not for me, for Lucy. She's coming home for Christmas and she, Rita, and I are going to look for brides-maid dresses." Rita had made it very clear to Lucy that we needed to be involved because she refused to look "like a pink taffeta nightmare."

I lay down on the floor and stared up at the ceiling. "I cannot wait for them both to be home. I just wish finals were over already."

"Just one more day," he reminded me as he sat back down. "Hey, I'm really looking forward to Amy's party tomorrow night."

I jerked my head up so fast that I felt a little faint. "What? You're going?"

Ryan's eyes widened. "Yes, is that a bad thing?"

"No, no, I just didn't know that Amy invited you."

He shook his head. "Well, I obviously wasn't going to get an invitation from you." He threw his folder at me.

"Oh, sorry . . ." Why hadn't I invited Ryan?

"But Amy wasn't the one who invited me."

Of course, Diane. How stupid of me to have thought that she wouldn't have invited him.

"Tracy asked me out."

Tracy? *My* Tracy?

Asked him out?

I tried to comprehend that not only had Tracy invited Ryan to the party, but that she hadn't told me. She usually told me everything.

I was the one who kept secrets.

My stomach tightened up. Oh my God. I knew exactly what this meant.

Ryan had finally made it onto Tracy's list.

That was ridiculous. Tracy had never once expressed an interest in him before. Maybe this was why she didn't mention seeing us near our lockers that one time. But hadn't she said earlier in the year that he and I would've made a good couple?

Of course, the last thing I'd said about the issue was when I was proclaiming that I'd never go out with Ryan in a million years. And it wasn't like I'd told Tracy what I was feeling. No.

I looked across and saw Ryan copying down some notes.

I couldn't really blame her.

I'd had weeks — months! — to ask him out.

But I had stayed silent.

And Tracy's hadn't.

Tracy wanted Ryan.

And I wanted to curl up in a ball and die.

Thirty-seven

I HAD BEEN DREADING THE PARTY since I'd discovered that Tracy had asked Ryan out. I'd been waiting for her to bring it up, but she hadn't said a word. And I wasn't about to bring it up. Not even now, as we were getting ready.

I took the cap off of some shimmer and started applying it to my face. "Don't forget your chest," Diane said as she pointed to my maroon V-necked tank. I paired the top with a new pair of dark blue jeans, a sparkly silver belt, and high-heel boots. I took a step back to look in the mirror, satisfied with the results.

"Oh, let me try," Tracy said as she grabbed the shimmer from me and started applying it. Tracy was wearing a black lace fitted top with black pinstripe flare pants. She looked so beautiful tonight with her hair down — she usually wore it up in a ponytail. It was obvious she was pulling out all the stops for Ryan.

"All right, I think we're ready," Diane said as we all gave one another a once-over in my bathroom mirror. Diane, as always, looked perfect. She was wearing a black A-line skirt and an aqua-blue sheer turtleneck with matching tank underneath.

We walked into my bedroom to grab our coats, but Diane sat down on my bed and opened her matching aqua purse. "I have something for the two of you," she said as she removed two small boxes wrapped in silver paper with a red ribbon and handed them to me and Tracy. "I wanted to let you know how much I appreciate everything you did for me this year."

"Diane, you didn't have to," I protested.

She simply shook her head and nodded toward the package.

I pulled off the red ribbon and tried to be careful to not tear the delicate silver paper. I gasped when I saw a blue Tiffany's box.

"Diane!" I could hardly believe it. I looked over to make sure Tracy wasn't ahead of me. She gave me a nod and we both opened our boxes.

Inside the box was a matching blue bag. I opened it to find a silver chain bracelet with a heart at the clasp.

"It's beautiful," both Tracy and I said in unison.

"Read the inscription," Diane said as she walked over to me and held up the heart. One side read LHC while the other said my name. She reached over and put the bracelet on my wrist.

"Diane, it's too much. You shouldn't have," I said.

"Yeah, Diane — I mean, Tiffany's." Tracy fiddled with the clasp.

Diane walked over to help Tracy. "You guys have done so much for me this year and this is just a small way to say thank you. Plus . . ." Diane held up her left arm and pulled her sleeve up to show that she was wearing a matching bracelet. "You don't think it's too corny, do you?"

I couldn't take my eyes off the bracelet. It was the nicest thing anybody had ever given to me.

"No, it's not at all." Both Tracy and I embraced Diane in a group hug.

"And there's one other thing I wanted to tell you guys." Diane looked nervous. "I know things are changing with the Club and that you guys will probably start dating soon . . . and I just wanted you to know" — she looked up at me — "that I'll support you, whoever it is you date."

She knew.

Diane knew about Tracy.

Tracy rubbed her back. "Thank you, Diane. You know we'll always be there for you as well."

They started walking out of the room. "Tonight is going to be so much fun," Tracy said.

Yeah, right.

It seemed that we were nearly the last people to arrive at Amy's. We had to park around the block.

The three of us linked arms as we rang the doorbell. We heard the noise die down from inside as Amy opened the door wearing a beautiful red knee-length dress.

"Welcome." She stepped aside so we could see everybody gathered inside the living room and spilling into the adjacent kitchen.

"Happy Holidays!" everybody said at once and started applauding.

"Wow, you guys must be sick of that by now," Tracy said.

It took the three of us a while to figure out that this was for us. All of the members of the Club were on their feet cheering for us. I spotted Ryan, Tyson, and Tracy's brother over in the corner doing the same thing.

"What's going on?" Diane asked Amy.

"We just wanted to give you three the welcome you deserve." She ushered us in and took our coats.

The cheering died down, but we realized that everybody was looking in our direction with smiles on their faces. I looked over at Jen and Morgan to see if I could get a hint from them. Both of them just smiled at me.

"So," Amy said to the crowd, "we all just wanted to let the three of you know how much you have meant to all of us."

Tracy grabbed my hand and squeezed it. I guess she was right after all. The three of us had really created something here. Something positive, something worth doing. Regardless of what any of the other guys in school, or Braddock, thought.

"We just wanted to give you something to say thanks." Amy grabbed three presents from under the Christmas tree by the bay window.

"Jen and I were reminiscing about the first time we joined the Club and everything we were talking about. Little did we know back then that under the tree in front of school, something this big was starting." Amy gestured toward the packed room.

Diane, Tracy, and I unwrapped our presents, but I was starting to get nervous as I heard giggling in the room. I fumbled with the wrapping, so Tracy was the first person to open her box.

"It's brilliant!" she exclaimed. I looked over and saw her hold up a white T-shirt with pink three-quarter-length sleeves. She showed me the shirt and on the front it said LHC and on the back LARSON.

I started laughing as Amy continued. "Well, we all figured it was time we finally got T-shirts." Everybody in the room held up matching T-shirts. "Now, what do you think Principal Braddock would do if we all walked into school the first day back wearing them?"

"Hey, I don't want to be responsible for putting a man in the hospital." Tracy went over to the table that had the drinks on it, grabbed three glasses of apple cider, and handed one each to Diane and me.

"Penny, I think we should do a toast," she said to me.

I raised my glass. "To The Lonely Hearts Club!"

Everybody in the room raised their glasses. "The Lonely Hearts Club!"

"And," Tracy continued, "to all of the people who have supported us." She motioned to the corner in the room that held her brother, Tyson, and Ryan, and then looked back at me. She grabbed my hand. "Come on, let's socialize."

We made the rounds and said thanks and Happy Holidays to everybody. All of the members were in high spirits and looked amazing. I couldn't have imagined my life without them.

"Hey, let's go over there." Tracy started dragging me over to the corner where Ryan was talking to Mike and Michelle.

Please, I didn't want to be the conduit for the two of them. I'd rather not be there to witness it. I didn't think my heart could take it.

"Happy Holidays," Tracy said. She pushed me so hard I accidentally fell into Ryan.

"Whoa there, what's in your glass?" He nodded toward my apple cider.

I blushed, suddenly full of all this nervous energy inside me. It was probably from the all the excitement of the evening. Or the twelve pieces of fudge I ate.

"So we did it. We survived." Ryan clinked his glass against mine.

I smiled. I didn't say anything, waiting for Tracy to jump right in and start working her charm on Ryan. I turned to Tracy and noticed she was gone. Michael and Michelle were gone, too. It was just me and Ryan.

"Hey, there." He put his hand on the small of my back. "Everything okay? Did your brain implode from all the exams?" He started to play with my hair.

I slapped his hand away. "Careful, this takes a really long time to do, you know. Especially with a big ol' dent in my head."

He started laughing. "Oh, okay."

I smirked. "Let's see how you like it." I reached up and did what I had always wanted to do. Tousle his hair. And it was as soft as I had always imagined it.

I let out a huge laugh. I noticed that everybody was staring, then quickly looked away the second I looked over.

Right. I shouldn't have been doing that with the guy Tracy had a crush on.

I moved away from Ryan so we were no longer touching.

Maybe I shouldn't have been so self-conscious. Everybody knew that we were friends. I was sure I was imagining it.

But just to be safe, I took another step back.

I couldn't believe how much I ate, but I figured I might as well have one last piece of fudge. I popped the last piece on the plate into my mouth as I started clearing the table.

The party was starting to wind down and there were only about a dozen people left. I had taken off my boots when I started to gather all of the trash that was lying around.

Tracy came over, linked her elbow with mine, and brought me toward the front hallway. "Good lord," she said. "I thought that if I invited him you would finally do something, but I guess not. You can be so frustrating sometimes."

What?

"Just go out with him already, you're driving me crazy!"

What?

I just stared at her. Tracy groaned, "Pen, I've been your best friend for years. Do you think I didn't know what was going on with you and Ryan?"

What?

"Listen, Penny — I know you've been worried about

dating with the Club. But the rules have changed, remember? Stop denying yourself." She started to smile. "Plus, you're really annoying when you have to hide your feelings, so just go in there and ask him out."

"Wait." I was in shock. "You invited Ryan for me?"

Tracy groaned. "Of course I did! Why else would I?"

Holy crap.

I started shaking my head. "I can't . . ."

Oh God.

I looked over and saw Ryan talking to Morgan and Tyson. I had never asked out anybody in my life, and what if he said no?

"He's not going to say no."

How did she . . . ?

"Well, what about Diane?" I asked, hoping that I could put this off for a few more days or months or years.

"Were you not paying attention to what she said earlier?"

I looked at Tracy in disbelief.

"She was talking to me. . . ."

"Seriously, Penny. Diane and I have already discussed this —"

"Wait a second, *you and Diane have discussed this?*"

"Pen, the guy only sang to you in front of the whole school. It's pretty much the only thing The Lonely Hearts Club talks about when you're not around."

Great, the Club knows. So people really *were* staring! I was so embarrassed. This couldn't have been happening.

"Plus, you and Ryan are Diane's closest friends. She wants you both to be happy."

"Well, I should talk to her first . . ."

Tracy smiled. "She already left. She didn't want to make you more uncomfortable. She wanted me to tell you to call her tomorrow so you can plan your outfit for your date."

Diane had left. But . . . But . . .

Tracy just shook her head. "Sometimes I really wonder about you. Go for it, girl."

Before I could even catch my breath, Tracy yelled out, "Hey, Ryan, do you have a second?"

Oh. My. God. Not now, I can't do this right now.

Ryan excused himself and walked over, seeming a little confused.

"What's up, Tracy?"

Tracy just smiled and pulled Ryan over so he was standing directly in front of me. "I don't have enough room in my car — can you give Penny a ride home?"

"Of course," he said.

"Great! Especially since Penny needs to ask you something." Tracy turned her back and started to walk away.

I was completely horrified.

"Oh, and one more thing." Tracy turned around and pointed above us. "You're standing under the mistletoe. 'Bye!"

Both Ryan and I looked up and saw mistletoe directly above us.

I looked back and saw Tracy scooting the few remaining people into the kitchen.

I was going to kill her.

I turned back and flinched as I found Ryan leaning in to kiss me.

He saw my reaction and stepped back. "Sorry, it's just . . . a holiday tradition." He pointed above our heads. "I guess I shouldn't have." He stepped farther away.

"No, no, it's okay. I just . . ."

How was I supposed to do this?

"You had something you wanted to ask me?" He folded his arms, a look of amusement flickering across his face.

"Um, yes. See . . ."

I was hopeless.

"So, funny story . . ." *Here goes, you can do this.* "It seems that things have changed a bit for the Club."

"Did I miss something? Did they kick you out?"

"Ha, not yet." I took a deep breath. "Well, you know we couldn't, um . . . we didn't . . ."

Ryan straightened up and his smile faded a bit. "You can't have a boyfriend."

"Well, yeah. But we've decided that maybe that wasn't very fair for people. . . ."

"I see. And now?"

I started to shift back and forth. Why would Tracy do this to me? I wasn't prepared for this at all.

"Now . . . I'd like to . . . try to . . ." I hadn't given guys enough credit all these years — this was torture.

"Penny, would you like to go on a date with me?"

Wow, that was easy.

Thankfully Ryan could take a hint.

"Yes, that would be great."

We smiled at each other, and he stepped forward and put his arm around my waist. Then I realized something.

"Wait! We can't go out on Saturday nights. Those nights are for the Club."

"No worries. There are six other days in the week."

He was making this way too easy. Maybe this dating thing wasn't going to be so hard after all.

"Oh! And I eat lunch with my friends, and if you want to do something, you have to give me advance notice because I will not change plans with any of my friends just because you come calling."

Ryan nodded. "Okay, anything else?"

"Umm, well, I'll have to look over the new rules. I just want to make sure —"

Ryan grabbed my hand and leaned in. "Penny, I'm not going to take you away from your friends. Do you think we can go on a few dates first before we start making too many rules for us?"

I blushed. I needed to take it down a notch before I started making decisions about our china pattern.

"We can do that."

"All right. Let's go say good-bye to everybody and I'll take you home."

He started to head to the kitchen.

"Wait!" I called after him. I pointed at the mistletoe that was still over my head. "It would be wrong to break a holiday tradition."

Ryan smiled at me and walked over to where I stood. My heart was beating fast as he cradled my head with his hands. He leaned in, but instead of freezing or running away, I leaned in toward him as he kissed me.

We pulled our lips away and he hovered an inch from my face. "I've been waiting all year to do that," he told me.

"What took you so long?" I asked him.

"Do I really need to remind you?" We both smiled.

As we walked into the kitchen, the entire room went silent.

It wasn't hard to figure out what they were talking about.

As we said good-bye to everybody, Tracy came over to give me a hug. "So. . . ." She studied my face and I was sure she could tell what had happened.

Tracy bit her lip and tried to hide her smile. I started giggling. I was happy my friend was so supportive of me. Ryan walked over and held my coat open for me.

"Hey, Tracy, thanks for inviting me," he said to her.

Tracy jumped up and gave Ryan a huge hug. "Thank *you*."

As we walked out, she mouthed, "Call me!"

Here Comes the Sun

"Little darling, it's been a long cold lonely winter . . ."

Thirty-eight

THE WINTER AIR GAVE ME A shock as we left Amy's house. I started to shiver as we walked to Ryan's car and he put his arm around me.

I suddenly didn't feel cold anymore.

Ryan opened the door for me to get in. I sat down and put my seat belt on as Ryan got in the other side. He turned on his engine and his stereo started blaring. He started to blush.

"Nice CD," I commented.

"Thanks, I really like it."

"Me, too," I said, no longer talking about the music.

I leaned back in the passenger seat and laid my head on the headrest. It had taken us a while, but we were finally here.

I reached over and turned up the volume and sang along to the last song on the CD I had made him.

Because even though it was the middle of the night, I could still sing "Here Comes the Sun" and mean every word, every emotion.

Especially the part about it being all right.

It was more than all right.

It was perfect.

Acknowledgments

There are numerous people to whom I owe a huge debt of gratitude for their help with this book.

First and foremost, my brilliant editor, David Levithan, for his guidance, patience, and support. I am extremely lucky to have my book in such great hands. And I really didn't mean it about guys with names with D being the devil.

My wonderful agent, Jodi Reamer, who spent years getting me to this point. I am truly thankful for everything that you have done for me. You were right, you were right, you were right (and you now have that in writing to taunt me with).

Thanks to everybody at Scholastic who has worked so hard on this book. Special thanks to Karen Brooks for her copyedit expertise and Becky Terhune for the most adorbs cover and book design an author could hope for.

My dear friend Stephenie Meyer for being my biggest cheerleader, especially when I needed it the most. Your enthusiasm for this book has meant the world to me and I am so grateful for all your positive advice and support. I owe you one. Oh, wait . . .

I had wonderful readers throughout these many drafts who provided me with invaluable feedback: Anamika Bhatnagar, my first reader (I still cringe when I think back on that first draft — sorry about that); (the real) Jennifer Leonard; Heidi Shannon; Tina McIntyre; Natalie Thrasher; Genevieve Gagne-Hawes, and Bethany Strout.

My friends and the loser tools we've dated, who have provided me with many ideas for The Lonely Hearts Club. Especially Alexis Burling, who lent me her "Roses are red . . ." story, and Tara McWilliams Coombs, who worked her styling magic for my author photo. May we all find the one who is worth it.

And, of course, John, Paul, George, and Ringo, my constant inspiration from the very beginning.

About the Author

Elizabeth Eulberg was born and raised in Wisconsin before heading off to college in Syracuse and making a career in the New York City book biz. She lives outside of Manhattan with her three guitars, two keyboards, and one drumstick. In researching this book, she tried swearing off boys forever. It didn't work.

It is a truth universally acknowledged,
that a single girl of high standing at
Longbourn Academy must be
in want of a prom date.

ELIZABETH EULBERG

Author of The Lonely Hearts Club

From Elizabeth Eulberg, a very funny,
completely stylish delight for any season!

To Do List:
Read all the Point books!

Point
www.thisispoint.com

i

INTRODUCTION

Is your phone ringing?

CONTENTS

— PASTOR RAY JOHNSTON, for being a
steadfast friend and spiritual mentor. My
sincere appreciation for teaching me to trust in
God's power, promises, and possibilities.

— ELEANOR DUGAN, for the ability to transform my
gibberish into coherent thought. This book would have
been impossible without your talent and commitment.

— MARK AND CELESTE CUELLAR, dear friends who
have brought love, laughter, and healing to our family.

— PATTY LAUTERJUNG, whose intellect, insight, and
quick wit were a great support in the birth of this book.

— OVER 4,000 AUDIENCES, who have given me
the unique privilege of sharing my message.

— AND ABOVE ALL, TO GOD for His never-
ending grace, amazing love, and humbling
acceptance of a flawed human being like me.
You are the Creator of all possibilities!

ACKNOWLEDGEMENTS

Although this is a book about possibilities, it is impossible to adequately acknowledge the inspiration and influence I have received from others. With heartfelt gratitude I would like to thank:

— MY AMAZING WIFE KATHRYN, who taught me that unconditional love is truly possible. I thank God every day for the blessing of you!

— OUR CHILDREN, who patiently endured my "motivational minute" around the breakfast table as you went off to school. I pray that you will enjoy a life brimming with abundant possibilities.

— MY COLLEAGUES IN SPEAKERS ROUNDTABLE. You all have been so unselfish with your knowledge and so generous with your encouragement. Thank you for walking with me during the challenges and celebrating the great joys. I cherish each and every one of you!

Acknowledgements continue on reverse...

THINK AGAIN

Thrive Publications
P.O. BOX 2336
Granite Bay, CA 95746
PHONE: (800) 311-3344, (916) 773-4455
FAX: (916) 797-3038
WEB: www.rogercrawford.com

Crawford, Roger;
2. Possibilities; 3. Tennis players - United States-Biography;
4. Physically handicapped-United States-Biography.

Cover: David Durham; Interior: Tim Chambers

Printed in the United States of America

ISBN 0-9779306-3-7

THINK AGAIN

*Discover Possibilities
Hidden in Plain Sight*

Roger Crawford

Thrive Publications
P.O. BOX 2336
Granite Bay, CA 95746
(800) 311-3344

OTHER BOOKS BY ROGER CRAWFORD

Playing from the Heart

How High Can You Bounce?

THINK AGAIN

Discover Possibilities
Hidden in Plain Sight

I love ringing phones! You never know who will be on the other end. That day in June 2005, it was an unfamiliar female voice. "Roger, this is Nancy Baker. I'm the executive producer for *Larry King Live*. We'd like to have you on the show."

She explained that the theme was people who have done the "impossible" – who have overcome some seemingly insurmountable challenges and realized amazing opportunities. I felt honored that Larry King thought my story would serve as an inspiration.

I began life with what some would call a disability or handicap. My perspective is that I have an "inconvenience." Prior to my birth there was no indication that something might be wrong. When my parents held me for the first time, they were understandably shocked at my appearance. My arms are shorter than normal, and I have two fingers on my left hand and one on my right. When my daughter Alexa was very young, she described my hands this way: "Dad, you have a 'peace sign' on one hand and a 'thumbs up' on the other." It is the result of a rare genetic condition called ectrodactylism. My parents have no signs of this anomaly. In addition, my right leg is missing the fibula, and the foot has three toes. This is my "good leg." My left leg was twisted at the knee so severely I was unable to walk and navigated stairs as if I was participating in a bobsled race!

It was at this point in my life that my parents showed me the life-transforming power of *Thinking Again* about life's possibilities. Doctor after doctor told my parents that I would never walk, and a wheelchair or crutches seemed to be my only option. "It is out of the realm of possibility" they heard over and over. Yet, they turned discouragement into determination and expanded the realm of what was possible. This attitude led them to a doctor at Shrines Hospital in Chicago. After examining me, he informed my parents that by amputating my left leg and reconstructing my knee, potentially I might walk! That's all they needed to hear.

Whenever we choose to pursue potential possibilities, if rewards are significant then risk is present. I often wonder how different my life would be if my parents had chosen to focus on the obstacle instead of the opportunity. At the age of six, the surgery was successful, and I was able to run and play like other children. Today, with the stability of a prosthesis, I am able to walk without a noticeable limp.

My *thinking again* led to becoming an avid athlete. I played football, basketball, and found my passion when I stepped on a tennis court. My athletic possibilities were realized when I played Division I college tennis at Loyola Marymount University. You might be thinking, "Hey, you have one leg, half a foot, and a total of three fingers. How well do you play tennis?" In addition to being a fully-certified instructor with the United States Professional Tennis Association, I had the opportunity to play against John McEnroe. Please don't be overly impressed. What I learned from this match was that a positive attitude doesn't work every time… he beat me!

Now back to the show. The big evening at CNN came. Larry King was ill, but Nancy Grace from *Court TV* filled in. Her interview style was crisp and to the point. She immediately asked about my birth defect, and I described the challenges I faced growing up and how my parents insisted I see possibilities instead of limitations. They refused to let me feel sorry for myself. "I'm a lousy piano player," I admitted. "I had to accept that at a young age. But accepting the real impossibilities allowed me to focus on the possibilities instead of the problems."

For example, when I began playing tennis, I faced an obstacle. Because of my lack of fingers, I was unable to serve in the conventional way. Some well-meaning people suggested I abandon my dream of becoming a tennis player and try something more "realistic." But what a person sees as attainable is subjective and viewed through their prism of possibility. My coach said I could toss the ball up with two fingers, quickly grasp the racket with both hands, and swing through my serve. Initially I thought 'No way!' but my coach helped me *think again* about what was possible! My serve improved as I stayed inspired by focusing on it being possible! Today I have the best two-handed tennis serve in the world—I decided to overlook any impossibility that I might have the *only* two-handed serve in the world.

I said to Nancy, "My dad used to say, don't ask '*Am* I gifted?' Instead, continually ask, '*How* am I gifted?' I learned that I wasn't going to be the fastest or the most powerful tennis player because it wasn't in my strength zone. But I did possess the gift of patience. Therefore, if I hit the ball over the net one more time than my opponent, consistency could overcome power and speed and I'd win the point." Sharing my story on CNN was a blessing.

The morning after the interview, I started my workday as usual, turning on the computer to check e-mail. My mailbox was full! There were more than a hundred responses to my appearance, most of them from people eagerly telling me their own stories about how they too had done something that they had once thought impossible. The message their stories communicated was truly inspiring... they did what some said was impossible! *You can too!*

How do *you* respond to the ring of a telephone? Do you feel a little rush of exhilaration, wondering what is going to happen next? Or do you check caller ID to be sure it is someone you want to talk to? Or screen your calls with an answering machine? Or have someone else take messages so you're not bothered?

Think of a ringing phone as a metaphor for how eagerly you greet new and unexpected possibilities. Sure, it could be an annoying telemarketer, a bill collector, a tedious relative, a wrong number, or even an offensive caller. And, of course, you don't have to answer every time the phone rings, or agree to everything asked of you! But do you cut yourself off because you doubt your ability to deal with these possibilities? Do you fear that responding will just add another stressful demand to your already full plate? Is your life so closed that you've ruled out the possibility of something good at the other end of the line?

Of course, a metaphor comparing life's infinite possibilities with a ringing telephone can be carried only so far. No one should be a slave to interruptions and distractions. Life can be frittered away by jumping at every opportunity and leaping to accept every challenge without a clear vision of what's important to you.

I have read that a number of legendary VIPs have astonished callers by answering their own phones. They believe this immediate, direct contact creates more possibilities than the "protection" of an obstacle course of secretaries and assistants. And these same VIPs share another eccentricity: they have often achieved the impossible.

WHAT'S AHEAD?

So, one day you enthusiastically share a dream that you're passionate about. And your trusted listener smiles skeptically and says, "But is that possible?" Or they stridently say, "Who do you think you are?" These words can be discouraging and create self-doubt. My question for you: Is that negative mindset temporary? Do you rethink your objectives and decide your dream was just an idle fantasy?

Or do you marshal your inner resources and recommit yourself to your possibilities? That's why I wrote this book – to rekindle your motivation and expand your realm of possibility.

PREMISE:

> You have greater possibilities in your
> life than you may imagine.

STRATEGY:

> Uncover these possibilities by *thinking
> again* or thinking differently about
> your abilities and opportunities.

STEPS:

- Clarify Your Purpose

- Identify Your Pessimism

- Amplify Your Potential

- Multiply Your Possibilities

- Quantify Your Progress

I was on a radio program with author Jack Canfield, discussing the success of his *Chicken Soup for the Soul* books. He was asked, "How did you react when others said you couldn't make this happen?" Jack replied, "When everyone said it was impossible, I decided I needed to give myself a little extra time."

His story reminded me that we can achieve remarkable possibilities despite "impossible" circumstances. It requires perspective, purpose, and perseverance! And to *think again!*

1

CLARIFY YOUR PURPOSE

What's impossible?

DEFINE THE IMPOSSIBLE

For various reasons, I will never be King of England, Miss America, or a Tsumo wrestler. You probably won't either. However, there are endless possibilities of what we *can* be! One of the best ways to open ourselves up to possibilities is to eliminate the truly impossible. That includes both things we really *can't* do and also things we really *don't want* to do. It is important to separate the two. If you have absolutely no interest in something, it doesn't matter how much talent you may have. Passion is crucial for achieving the impossible.

Let's start by deciding what's truly impossible. The maxim of the famous fictional detective Sherlock Holmes was that when you have excluded the impossible, whatever remains, however improbable, must be possible. Every one of us has thought something was impossible at some point and then done it. When I was a young boy, I thought tying my shoes was impossible because of having three fingers and shorter than normal arms. But a teacher inspired me to believe in possibilities by saying, "Failure only happens when you quit, Roger." I desperately needed this encouragement, and although it took me sixteen years, I finally tied my shoes. My feeling of accomplishment dulled when a new fashion trend appeared at school... Velcro shoes!

When it comes to speaking, it's impossible for me not to sweat. I was so nervous during my first paid speech that

I perspired through my suit. The audience members must have thought they were in the splash zone of an amusement park. Was it possible to overcome my nerves and stop sweating? No, and I still get nervous, so if you're in my audience, it may be best to sit near the back! A fellow speaker encouraged me to focus more on the audience and less on myself. When I embraced this mindset, accepted what was unchangeable, amazing possibilities opened up before me. Today it is crystal clear to me that my purpose is to encourage others.

The fact is, some things *are* impossible. Currently, time travel and living forever would be on that list, though new discoveries are being made all the time. Ending world hunger and curing cancer are vastly multifaceted tasks that probably require the efforts of more than one person. Thankfully, possibility thinkers inspired by a passionate purpose continue to pursue these and other lofty ambitions. Their achievements will change our world and help others *think again* about their possibilities.

What items are on *your* impossible list? Some people defeat themselves before they even try, based on their *perception* of their own possibilities. Perception can be a powerful dream-killer. Have you heard about the traditional elephant trainer's technique? Each baby elephant has a heavy chain put on its leg. No matter how hard it tugs, it can't escape. By the time the elephant is an adult, just a thin string serves the same purpose. The imprisoning chain is in the elephant's mind; its perception is that it can't escape. How many chains of impossibility do you have in your mind? How many are real, and how many are imagined?

To do the seemingly impossible, start by making a list of impossible things that you wish you could do. Get a sheet of paper and write down at least twenty things that you'd like to do but absolutely can't do. Once you get past the usual silly ideas like "give birth to a Porsche" and "fly to Mars without a spaceship," you'll notice that your answers start getting closer to home and to your heart. As your imagination soars, so will your awareness, until items start appearing on the paper that make you stop and *think again*. I'm willing to bet that you'll stare at some of the things you've written and realize that they are *not* impossible. With some ingenuity and effort, you will make them possible!

I can answer you in two words – im possible.

    — SAMUEL GOLDWYN
    HOLLYWOOD PRODUCER

FIVE CLICHÉ QUESTIONS

Before you can set out to see what's possible, you're going to need a direction, an intention, a *purpose*. The reason is "where we look determines where we end up." Here are some questions to help identify and clarify your purpose. You've heard some or all of them before, perhaps so often that they have become clichés. I'm going to ask you to consider them again – and then to answer some questions about your answers.

QUESTION 1. WHAT DO YOU WANT WRITTEN ON YOUR TOMBSTONE?

Does your answer indicate your definition of true success? Or is it someone else's?

This question usually evokes some emotion, as well as witticisms. Mine would say, "I'd rather be speaking!" A serious answer can help clarify our purpose. Powerful questions are what give our purpose power. When we think about the end of our lives, our legacy and hoped-for contributions come into focus. Did we realize our potential? Use our gifts? Do our best? Follow our dreams?

An interview I once read asked a similar question of people who had lived to be over a hundred: "How do you want to be remembered?" Their collective wisdom about what

23

they hoped they had achieved was both insightful and in spirational. Their answers reminded me that understanding is not derived from experience alone. Wisdom is *experience evaluated*, a life examined.

The interviewer then asked them, "What would you have done differently if you could live those hundred years over again? What do you think you have not achieved?" Remarkably, most of their answers fell into four categories:

- "Give more."

- "Love more."

- "Risk more."

- "Be more."

What terrific philosophy for finding our purpose and realizing our possibilities! These are all passionate answers, and when passion aligns with purpose, it is easy to achieve the "impossible." An influential book of recent times is *The Purpose-Driven Life* by Pastor Rick Warren. I believe people respond so strongly to his ideas because we all want to live purposefully—to live a life that has meaning, significance, and substance. Too many people are led to believe that the purpose of life is to achieve prominence, which they translate as fame (or notoriety), wealth, and status. Yet, if they do achieve such prominence, they discover that it doesn't fulfill them. They are still hungry for meaning and contentment. They are forced to *think again*.

QUESTION 2. WHAT WOULD YOU DO IF MONEY WERE NO OBJECT?

Do your answers describe what gives you joy? Or do some of them also address the things that give your life purpose? Do you see any connection between what gives you joy and what gives you purpose?

The news agent across the street from my friend's office has a big digital sign flashing the amount of the current lottery prize. Twice a week the number jumps if no one has won, and on those days more and more of her colleagues drift over to the window to check out the latest figure. When the amount tops $100 million, some slip out to buy tickets, either individually or as part of a pool. Then talk turns to what they'd do if they won the money. Being highly-educated, highly-paid professionals, their first thoughts are often of tax shelters and investments.

Then they discuss how their lives would be different. Here are some actual examples of their answers. (You might want to speculate on how successful you think each of these people would actually be in bettering their lives and achieving something meaningful).

- Austin would expand his lifestyle with material possessions, starting with a $1.3 million custom car. He has it all picked out. "A car says a lot about who you are," he says. (I don't know about you, but I have trouble visualizing where I would drive such a car without security guards jogging along beside each wheel, rather like the Presidential motorcade.) He's not sure $100 million would be enough money to maintain him for the rest of his life.

- Jack has always worked, while planning to be an independent entrepreneur like his dad. He's already parlayed a smart real estate investment and lots of sweat equity into a half-million dollars. "I'd like to start a luxury car dealership with my son and take my wife's side business national by selling franchises." He'd quit his job and put his lottery winnings into advancing his business plans more quickly.

- Jennifer would be happy winning a pool share of even a half-million dollars. "I'd reduce my lifestyle and take as much time off as possible to write novels full-time." She has already written several, all unpublished. If her winnings were sufficient, she'd like to live modestly in the south of France. She loves the process of writing more than she loves her current work, and she wouldn't mind being famous someday.

- Phillip says, "I'd use the money to fund orphanages back home in the Philippines, feed and educate poor children, and end poverty there." Typically, Filipinos send massive amounts of money home when working in the States. According to the website www.remithome.com this is one of the major sources of income in the Philippines. Think of the possibilities it is creating for others less fortunate.

- Maggie would pay for "college educations for my children, nieces, and nephews, then set each of them up with trust funds so they wouldn't have to work." She would continue to work because

she looks forward to the intellectual stimulation
and daily contact with her colleagues.

What would *you* do with a huge windfall? Would the tremendous responsibility be a blessing or a burden? How would you guard the money so it wouldn't slip away from you? How would you respond to the hundreds of people—friends, relatives, strangers, legitimate business people, and scurrilous con men—who would swarm all over you, so that you didn't dare answer the phone or step outside your house? What would change for the better in your life? And what would change for the worse? It's an interesting mental exercise.

The reality is that follow-up reports on people who have suddenly acquired a great deal of money indicate that few lived the life they had hoped for. The vast majority found their relationships with family and friends severely disrupted. Many subsequently divorced or were alienated from loved ones. They often abused drugs or alcohol and—ironically—went bankrupt. They weren't able to use the money to create their ideal lives or to fulfill long-held dreams. And they weren't able to enjoy what they won because they had no confidence thinking they would lose it all just as capriciously and be unable to regain it.

Think about this whenever you put your dreams and ambitions on hold, awaiting some stroke of luck. It may not take a huge windfall to finance a desired business project, educate yourself or your children, travel, improve your living situation, or fund a cause you care about. It may only require imagination, planning, enlisting the help of others, or a bit of patience. If you aren't waiting for someone or something outside of you to magically fulfill your needs and desires, you open yourself to noticing and creating possibilities that let you fulfill them *yourself*. And once you've created your own opportunities, then you believe you can do it again.

A common characteristic of people who await a huge stroke of luck to make their lives better is that, right or wrong, they don't see a direct connection between their efforts and their results. They reason that no matter how hard they work and how smart they are, they'll never get anywhere. They firmly believe that the only way to succeed is through the magic of a sudden bonanza. Enchanting fairytales of "pots of gold" are perfect illustrations of unexpected wealth. These stories led to the novels of the last century where the destitute hero or heroine was usually discovered to be the lost heir to a fortune. But in the twenty-first century, it is not a fairytale. The reality is most of us have the capacity and opportunities to make our own luck, shape our destinies, and create our *possibilities*.

In case you doubt the dangers of fantasizing about winning the lottery, people argue about the possibilities! Some employees have created pools to buy blocks of lottery tickets with the stipulation that all members would share the winnings equally. But what would happen if a pool member also bought a separate ticket that won? Would he or she also have to share those winnings? And what if someone who usually buys into a pool was out sick and didn't put any money in? Would the winners still give that person a share? What if someone lends someone else the money that buys a winning ticket? Would the lender then rate a percentage of that winner's share? These thorny questions have been raised and argued over, with people expending time and energy, taking sides until they quarrel. And all about imaginary money that no one has won!

QUESTION 3. WHAT WOULD YOU ATTEMPT IF YOU KNEW YOU COULD NOT FAIL?

Who would benefit if you did succeed? Is your project truly impossible right now—like "visit other galaxies?" If you could overcome doubt and fear, does your purpose suggest a course of action you could start right now?

British actor Harvey Jason was thinking about retiring after forty years as a character actor in movies and television but knew he'd need something to occupy his creative brain. While playing a dinosaur hunter in Steven Spielberg's *The Lost World: Jurassic Park*, he was inspired by a visit to a local bookstore in Eureka, California. As Jason was paying for his selections, the director himself wandered in. "Steven," Jason told him, "I've decided to open a bookstore!"

Jason didn't want to take unnecessary risks with his retirement money—and small general-interest bookstores are notoriously hazardous in the age of mega-stores and the Internet. Therefore, he decided to focus on the always popular mysteries and crime. Back in Los Angeles, he opened Mystery Pier Books. He soon added a section devoted to books that have been made into films, thus combining his twin passions. Jason's show-business connections brought many customers, and the shop has thrived for nearly a decade. Side by side you can find original editions of *The Postman Always Rings Twice*, *The Great Gatsby*, *East of Eden*, and a $40,000 set of *Harry Potter* books signed by J.K. Rowling. "Mystery Pier Books is like the most wonderful museum," says actor Michael Caine, "except that you get to keep the exhibits."

Of course, Harvey Jason took a risk, and he could have failed. Happily, he didn't. Success is never guaranteed, but sometimes we need to act as if it were.

QUESTION 4. WHAT IS YOUR GREATEST INSPIRATION?

What motivates you? Who or what sets your
goals? What sparks your passion? And does
your passion support your current goals?

It was twenty years ago, and there I was, about to listen to someone who had greatly influenced my life–Dr. Norman Vincent Peale. In my youth, a family friend had given me his book, *The Power of Positive Thinking*, and it inpacted my thinking about life's possibilities in a profound way. To share the speaking platform with this legend was one of the highlights of my speaking career.

Dr. Peale was in his nineties. His gait was unsteady, and he had difficulty walking up the stairs to the lectern. My initial concern was that perhaps he would not be able to finish his speech. Boy, was I wrong. All he needed was to grip the podium, steady himself, raise his right arm, and the magic began. It was as if he had found the Fountain of Youth as he mesmerized the audience with stories and uncommon wisdom.

"Positive thinking," he said, "is how you *think* about a problem. Enthusiasm is how you *feel* about a problem. The two together determine what you *do* about a problem."

Wow! Isn't that true of possibilities as well? If you *think* optimistically about a possibility and you *feel* passionately about that possibility, imagine what you can *do* about it. Think back to a time in your life when you felt most alive, most engaged, when you were *inspired*. Wouldn't you like to be able to re-experience that now?

Whether you think, in general, optimistically or pessimistically determines how you *think* about your possibilities. Your passion determines what you *feel* about your possibilities. Combine intellect and passion, and you'll discover what you can *do* with the possibilities all around you.

QUESTION 5. WHAT WOULD YOUR "PERFECT LIFE" LOOK LIKE?

What does your answer tell you about your values, your vision, and your relationships? How close are you now to perfection? What could you do to get closer to your ideal? What would you be willing to do to get closer to your ideal?

Recently, a TV talk-show host told viewers about her "Life List" of seven things she wanted to accomplish: "Be more patient. Take tennis lessons. Learn Spanish. Do more to help New Orleans. Learn to use a computer. Visit Amsterdam. Go to Africa." She invited viewers to create and act upon their own lists, an admirable activity for her and them.

I'm going to ask you to make a "Perfect Life List." When was the last time that you stopped to think about what *you* really want to do and be doing? What would you want to achieve if your life were perfect? Our planning time and energy are eaten up with figuring out the exhausting everyday intricacies of *living*, leaving little time for *life*. We're consumed with balancing work, family, bills, insurance, social obligations, education, money, schedules, and deadlines. If we manage to get 75 percent of all that done correctly, it is a triumph.

But every once in a while, we need to stop and think about the possible and the impossible. We need to make new mental connections and look for new directions. It's not that we can't do amazing things. It's just that often it doesn't occur to us to stop and take inventory of the amazing things we really want to do and then figure out a way to do them. Many people spend more time thinking about what to have for lunch than what to have for life. Make a regular date with yourself to plan a Perfect Life.

So, what do you think of your *answers* to these five questions? Do they reveal anything about your *purpose* in life? The possibilities you choose to notice and seize will be determined by how you see your future and your purpose.

It is not our abilities that show what we truly are... it is our choices.

— DUMBLEDORE
HARRY POTTER AND THE
CHAMBER OF SECRETS
J.K. ROWLING

WHO CAN DO THE IMPOSSIBLE?

Over the years, I've discovered that people who can do the impossible – whatever their talents, skills, or backgrounds – have one thing in common: They all concentrate on what they *can* do instead of what they *can't* do. They focus on *possibilities* instead of problems.

Many of the recent leaps in technology have been achieved by mavericks who didn't believe in "impossible." Who would have been able to conceive of the enormous cultural influence of ideas like Craig's List, Google, Amazon. com, or eBay until someone risked the impossible? For example, what about the idea of being able to watch any movie you want, at any time you want, right in the comfort of your home? Impossible – or is it?

Some of you are old enough to remember when movies could be seen only in movie theatres, a time before video and DVDs. In the 1980s, new technology allowed home viewing, generating chains of rental stores, as well as late fees and occasional disappointment that the film you wanted to see was not in stock.

Then along came Reed Hastings, a former math major, Peace Corps volunteer, and software exec with a highly improbable idea. In 1998, he started an on-line video rental business called Netflix. It followed the traditional pay-per-rental model that included postage charges and late fees. The next year, Netflix started a monthly subscription concept. Then, with the introduction of lightweight DVDs, it became economically feasible to include postage in the fee. Since then, Netflix has built its reputation on having no due dates, late fees, shipping or handling fees, or per-title rental fees. It now offers more than 65,000 film and TV titles, and it had almost five million subscribers in 2006. What's next for Reed Hastings? Well, he'd like to send you *any* movie you want *whenever* you want it, using the Internet! The technological problems and legal complications will be enormous, and his rivals are all working as hard as they can to beat him to it. Many are saying his goal is impossible. But then, he's heard that before.

What about you? What prospects could you be overlooking? Between birth and adulthood, we use feedback from our culture, experiences, and those around us to build a mental image of our own capabilities and possibilities. This carefully-erected belief structure represents our place in society. It is our fortress and strength, the image we present to the world, but it can also become our prison. We operate within barriers that we've built ourselves, sometimes blocking access to exciting opportunities and possibilities.

To look past our protective structures and norms requires real bravery. *Possibilities* can be frightening. *Potential* means uncertainty, which is always uncomfortable. It is *so* much easier and more comfortable to go with the status quo, to do what is expected of us. It is so much trouble to have to *think again*.

Do you remember sitting in a math class, working out a problem written on the board? You were sure you had figured out the right answer. The teacher looked around the room, eyes moving from student to student, and then she called on *you*. What a great moment! Suppressing your excitement, you gave the answer. There was a pause while you waited for her congratulatory smile. Then you realized the teacher was shaking her head. "No, not quite right," she said encouragingly. "You can do it. Think again."

Peak performers stick up their hand, determined to try, even if they are wrong. And they carry that encouraging teacher with them every day, urging them to keep trying. Whenever they hear a voice muttering, "That's not possible – you'll never succeed – don't bother trying – better safe than sorry," they change the channel. They tune in a new voice, loud and clear, telling them over and over, "Think again!"

Do you need to change the voice inside your head? I guarantee the change will open up possibilities that lead to the "impossible."

The more you try, the more you triumph.

WHAT'S YOUR PHILOSOPHY ABOUT POSSIBILITIES?

I was traveling to a speaking engagement and suddenly broke my artificial leg. In half! I'm known as someone who has experience in overcoming adversity, but doing the bunny hop in front of 400 executives wasn't going to be pretty. The local 7-Eleven was out of limbs, so I phoned home to get a spare leg shipped to me. No answer. I phoned my neighbor Jerry, and as we were speaking, Dave, our neighborhood FedEx guy, rang Jerry's doorbell. As soon as Dave heard about my predicament, he went into action. Jerry used my spare key to retrieve a spare leg, and a few minutes later Dave had it boxed and on its way to me, 3,000 miles away. It absolutely, positively had to be there overnight and it *was*, arriving just in time for my 11 AM speech.

That's the power of being possibility-focused rather than problem-focused. And the power of building a business's reputation on doing the seemingly impossible. Imagine the thinking that went into figuring out how to get packages anywhere within the continental U.S. overnight – making the impossible possible.

You find what you look for. If you look for problems, boy, you find them! If you look for possibilities, there they are too. Every morning when we wake up, we have these two choices:

OPTION 1
> *"Life is a series of problems. We are either confront-*
> *ing one, going through one, or coming out of one."*

Of course, we all face difficulties. Big ones, little ones, funny ones, and really tragic ones. That's a given. However, there is another way to look at things.

OPTION 2
> *"Life is a series of possibilities. We are either approaching*
> *one, embracing and benefiting from one, or pursuing one."*

Which philosophy do you choose? Are you going to devote your energy to noticing your problems or your possibilities?

Let's start with how you would like to *feel*. Wouldn't you agree that being inspired by possibilities makes you feel energized, optimistic, and hopeful? And during the times when you lack hope, you tend to feel lethargic, disheartened, and unmotivated? In other words, when your perception of possibilities is positive, your self-esteem and performance are sky-high, but when your *perception* is pessimistic, they suffer.

Possibilities are rarely limited by our lack of talent, time, or training. It is our *perception* of our own limitations that holds us back. It is not aptitude or ability, but our *attitude* about our aptitude or ability that sabotages us. The greatest limits on what we can do, be, or achieve are the barriers we create ourselves. These barriers are incredibly powerful despite the fact that they are both invisible and imaginary. Our possibilities are constructed or destructed by our thoughts and attitudes.

Someone I consider a true possibility thinker is noted Christian author Chuck Swindoll. His philosophy on possibilities is well expressed in the following quote:

> *The longer I live, the more I realize the impact of attitude on life. The remarkable thing is we have a choice every day regarding the attitude we will embrace for the day. I am convinced that life is ten percent what happens to me and 90 percent how I react to it. And so it is with you... we are in charge of our attitudes.*

If you want to change your possibilities, *think again* about any erroneous beliefs you have about your abilities. All too often, we accept negative beliefs, even if we have little or no evidence to support this pessimistic view. Many people underestimate themselves and simultaneously overestimate others. Mistakenly, we feel that if others seem to be doing better than we are, they must be better than we are. We accept the false belief that we are incompetent, inadequate, or incapable of achieving greatness. How often do you perform better than you expect to? It almost never happens because you don't believe you can do any better. To unlock your possibilities, change the way you *think*.

If an elderly, but distinguished scientist says that something is possible, he is almost certainly right; but, if he says that it is impossible, he is very probably wrong.

— ARTHUR C. CLARKE
BRITISH AUTHOR, INVENTOR

TIVO

When I was a young man, the thought of shaking hands with people nearly paralyzed me with anxiety. Because I have one finger on my right hand, I anticipated they would respond negatively. In my anxiety, I visualized people being visibly startled when they saw my hands, and I replayed this mental recording over and over. I TiVoed it.

Fortunately, my tennis coach, a very wise man, took me aside one day. "Roger," he told me, "you can never reach higher if you keep your hands in your pockets." He refocused my thoughts on possibilities instead of a perceived problem, giving me a whole new video to watch.

Both fear and possibility are strong motivators. When you are gripped by anxiety, you are anticipating a negative event. A good way to feed and reinforce this fearful mind-set is to TiVo your past failures, hurts, and disappointments. TiVo is an amazing technology that lets you record, replay, and even skip commercials while watching TV. Our mental TiVo works the same way, letting us re-experience a rejection, discouragement, or fear over and over again. When we decide to view new programming and uncover new possibilities, we may still hit the negative rewind button out of force of habit. Then, we end up reliving past negativity, thus creating a vicious cycle that sabotages access to new possibilities.

To break the cycle, use your mental TiVo to replay your past *successes* rather than your negative experiences. As you do, your courage will grow and your hope for your future will increase. You might ask, "Don't people who succeed have negative events in their past?" Of course, but they realize that they can live in anxiety or they can live in hope, based on what they choose to dwell on. They anticipate that their efforts will probably produce positive outcomes. They inspire and energize themselves with positive scenarios.

Have you ever stopped short of pursuing future possibilities because of a past experience? It's interesting that what sometimes discourages us from attempting the extraordinary can be something unchangeable in the past. Everything bright and wonderful that the future holds is shot down because of a long-ago disappointment. Let's *think again* about our history and reevaluate the meaning we place on it.

Here is a mental image that you may find empowering. Our past experiences are like a closet of old home movies—images filled with joys and jolts, hurts and heights. We all have a choice about which movies we choose to take out and rerun. If we dwell on the ones about failure, our energy wanes, negative expectations begin to dominate, and possibilities fade. If we replay the images about joy and courage, our confidence soars.

Of course, one of the intriguing things about looking at old images is how much our perspective has changed. The tree that seemed so huge is actually a tiny sapling. The same is true of disasters. Some events remain true tragedies, offering important life lessons and wisdom, but others now seem trivial, irrelevant, and even funny. Your past is defined by what you choose to dwell on. Don't let old negative images define your future!

Changing what you choose to focus on diminishes anxiety. Fear is hungry and needs food in the form of negative thoughts. Have you ever noticed that if you try to increase your energy and motivate yourself by using anxiety, you spend more time thinking about what can go wrong rather than how things can go right? Dwelling on potential pitfalls makes you act defensively. You expect the worst and over-react at any sign of failure. Concentrating on avoiding what you fear almost guarantees that it will happen. It's like someone telling you, "Be sure you don't drop that." Immediately, you're all thumbs.

People are either encouraged or discouraged by what they chose to dwell on from their past. They look for evidence to support their current mind-set. As they look into the future, they may glance back at past failures and use it as a template for future failures. However, the people who realize possibilities are those who identify possibilities in their past and use that experience as the framework for future possibilities. In the movie *Pee-wee's Big Adventure*, Pee-wee counsels a waitress who has "always wanted to visit France, but..." and she tells him all the reasons why this is impossible. "Everyone has a big 'but,'" he warns, and persuades her to follow her dream.

Remember the opening sequence of the classic Dick Van Dyke Show? Every episode, behind the credits, he'd walk in his front door as the lively theme song played. Half the time he would fall kersplat over the ottoman, and half the time he'd spot it and nimbly dance around it. You never knew which version you were going to see.

Now imagine running your *own* disaster on your TiVo, taking a huge pratfall over an obstacle. Then, switch the tape and see yourself stepping around it at the last minute, giving a big, triumphant grin like Dick Van Dyke did. Choose to run that new tape, not the old one, and see yourself not failing but *succeeding*. Don't let your past hold you back. TiVo your successes and watch your possibilities grow!

Is a big "but" holding you back? Exercise your imagination to reduce your but.

SEVEN POSSIBILITY-BUSTING BELIEFS

While you're choosing a philosophy and a way to describe your life, start choosing to challenge some of the common negative beliefs that can keep you from seeing your possibilities. Seven beliefs that can definitely inhibit your success in life are:

1. *Accentuate the negative*. You may remember the old Harold Arlen/Johnny Mercer song, "Ac-Cent-Tchu-Ate the Positive, E-Lim-Mi-Nate the Negative." Our possibilities are infinite when we accentuate the positive, but very limited when we dwell on the negative. To counteract negative thought habits, identify a pessimistic viewpoint. Then gather evidence to support a contrary positive view. (If you need help, Chapter 2 describes a special kind of friend who can provide that positive perspective.)

2. *Blame yourself.* Here is a thought to embrace. We are not responsible for everything that happens. However, we *are* responsible for how we respond to everything that happens. Possibility thinkers are clear about what they can control and what they can't control. Why devote energy to things you absolutely cannot control or change? Focus on facts, not fault.

3. *Be inflexible*. "If I keep an open mind, my brain might fall out!" If we are rigid in our thinking, we limit our potential. Have you ever said, "Why didn't *I* think of that?" Perhaps those who did have developed the habit of searching for new and different ways of thinking and doing things. They identify exciting new options and are not limited by a fear of failure.

4. *Be your own severest critic*. Remember the schoolyard chant, "Sticks and stones may break my bones, but names will never hurt me"? I don't buy that. Negative names break your spirit and decrease your possibilities. And far worse than the bully down the street is your own inner persecutor who can really defeat you. If you hear a voice saying "Boy, you blew it again," or "You're the biggest idiot in the world," *think again!* Dr. Robert Shuller says, "Do not put yourself down; there are plenty of other people happy to do that for you."

5. *Believe things won't change*. When I was in high school, the song that everyone wanted to slow-dance to was "Always and Forever." It's a beautiful song, but the lyrics are just wishful thinking. Nothing stays the same. Yet, I have met people who crush their possibilities with the belief that "I'll always be this bad," or "Things will never get better," or "Everything always goes wrong," or "Nothing ever goes right." The truth is that everything changes. Life can be very different today and tomorrow than it was yesterday, so why can't it be a lot better?

6. *Use Blue-Light Special thinking.* One discount store uses a flashing blue light to signify a big discount. Some people discount their own abilities and accomplishments with similar emphasis, talking themselves down while exaggerating their liabilities and flaws. The negative is given priority over the positive. A typical response to an impressive achievement is dismissive: "It was plain luck. Anyone could have done it. Right place, right time." That's a sure way to limit possibilities. Put this advertising razzle-dazzle into promoting, not demeaning.

7. *Predict a negative outcome.* Have you met people who are convinced they can predict negative events in their lives? "Why try?" they ask. "I'll fall flat on my face again." Their pessimistic predictions rarely extend to foreseeing exciting possibilities and positive outcomes. Yet, no one is omnipotent. Baseball manager Yogi Berra used to say, "Predicting is hard, especially when it comes to the future." So, get rid of cracked and cloudy crystal balls. Instead, anticipate a positive outcome. This is the first step in achieving possibilities.

I've always believed that you can think positive just as well as you can think negative.

— JAMES A. BALDWIN
AUTHOR

WATCH YOUR MOUTH

"If thought corrupts language," wrote noted novelist George Orwell, "language can also corrupt thought." Words are more powerful than armies. There are lots of words that society uses to label actions in an attempt to influence behavior; words like *polite, civilized, manly, ladylike, honorable, high class,* and also their negative counterparts.

We can influence our own actions, positively and negatively, by how we refer to things and how we talk to ourselves. Here are some words and phrases to avoid. Stop yourself if you start to use them.

POSSIBILITY-SABOTAGING WORDS AND PHRASES:

Should: I should have done better.
    I should be smarter than that.

Must: I must not make a mistake.
    I must be an idiot.

Always: That stuff always happens.
    It's always going to be this way.

Never: I never get it right.
    I could never do that.

Now, reframe your words. The language of possibilities is encouraging and fortifies our perseverance.

POSSIBILITY-SUPPORTING WORDS AND PHRASES:

Could: I could try that.
That could be a solution.

Might: This might work.
I might win.

Often: Things often turn out okay.
I'm often on target.

Sometimes: That sometimes happens.
Sometimes I don't get it right.

When you catch yourself TiVo-ing a negative phrase, try restating it in more positive language. If this seems too uncomfortable and unfamiliar, consider at least setting a "statute of limitations" on old negativity. I got this idea from an organizational consultant who came to my office to help me be more organized, and therefore more effective. One thing the consultant advised was setting a "statute of limitations" on unread books, magazines, brochures, and catalogues, and all those old clippings I had intended to follow up on.

Wow, what an idea! Why not also put a "statute of limitations" on your worries and anxieties?

I remember thinking, "If I get rid of everything that I haven't gotten around to doing, will I have anything left to do?" Hanging on to old worries involves a similar lack of logic. People are afraid to let go of their worries, wondering, "Will I have anything else to think about?"

Let's say that someone close to you didn't approve of your choice when you started on some venture. Perhaps they felt it was too risky for you, or they were jealous or fearful that you might surpass them. Since then, you've done very well, but you continue to feel bad about that lack of support. Is it somehow disloyal to really succeed? Or, alternatively, will the negative prediction prove to be right and you'll soon crash and fall on your face? This double-pronged worry occupies your mind, sapping your energy and enthusiasm, while keeping you from noticing exciting new possibilities right under your nose!

Declare a moratorium. After a certain point, these worries are past their "sell-by" date. Just like other obsolete stuff cluttering your closet, pack them up and get rid of them. If that's too uncomfortable at first, set aside one minute every day to focus on that obsolete worry. You'll still have 1,439 minutes left in the day to *think again* about possibilities!

Man does not live by words alone, despite the fact that sometimes he has to eat them.

— ADLAI STEVENSON
AMERICAN POLITICIAN

51

IDENTIFY YOUR POSSIBILITY ZONE

"Hey, Dad, you're phat!" The first time I heard my kids say that, I wanted to ground them for life. I sucked in my gut, straightened my shoulders, and held my breath. As soon as I had regained consciousness, I noticed their laughter was mixed with admiring looks. They explained that "phat" refers to fab, not flab.

So here's a thought. Are your possibilities phat? Do they stir your passion and challenge your talents and abilities? Are they just within your perceived realm of possibility? Are you expanding that realm? "Good enough" gets in the way of great possibilities. Of course, we all need goals that are attainable, measurable, and achievable. They build strength, confidence, and positive expectations. But extraordinary possibilities require lofty thinking and imagination.

What about *you?* Are you starting to see a pattern of how to use your resources, talents, and passions to achieve the possible and attempt the "impossible"?

POSSIBLE-SELF EXERCISE NO. 1:

- What are your favorite things to do? What do you do best? (They're not necessarily the same things.)

- What do you dislike doing or
  usually procrastinate about?

- What are you so bad at, that when you try, it
  is often a disaster? (Are you really that bad, or
  have you decided to prove to others that you
  can't do this so they won't expect you to?)

- What do *other* people see as your greatest
  strengths? As your greatest weaknesses?

- Is there something specific you'd like to
  attempt? What will it take to achieve it?

- What do you already have? What are you missing?

- Can you leverage your weaknesses to turn them
  into strengths? Can you subcontract the missing
  factors? Can you involve others in supplying
  what's absent? Can you redesign your strategy to
  eliminate the need for anything you can't deliver?

Fantasizing about your "possible self" can help you identify the qualities that you'd be willing to defend, those you'd like to develop, and those you'd like to get rid of. The images you create as you do this can clarify your values and provide powerful stores of resilience. Most of all, you'll start to notice more options.

What is your ideal "possible self?" In an experiment at the University of Texas, 173 adults, aged 18 to 86, were asked to describe their hoped-for possible self (for example, *glamor-*

ous, powerful, esteemed) and also their feared possible self (*unwanted, out-of-shape, lacking control*). As expected, researchers Susan Cross and Hazel Markus found big expectation differences between those who had previously scored high in rating their life satisfaction and those who had low scores. There were also differences by age group.

POSSIBLE-SELF EXERCISE NO. 2:

Relax and think of the self you'd like to *be*. Jot down your description. Then do the opposite, concentrating on the negativity and listing what you fear becoming. Did this exercise offer you clearer ideas about what you want to accomplish?

Shakespeare has Hamlet say, "There is nothing either good or bad, but thinking makes it so." Concentrate on how your life is and how it could be. If you waste time looking back at what it wasn't, you're not noticing the new opportunities all around you. It's an extraordinarily simple concept but extraordinarily difficult for some people to act on.

What in life have you achieved by accident? Yes, there are wonderful instances of serendipity – stumbling across something delightful and unexpected. That's what makes each day a joyous adventure. However, whatever your objectives have been – learning to walk, read, drive a car, or use the newest digital device – chances are that you saw yourself achieving them, you intended to achieve, and you were willing to put time and effort into these goals.

So, once again, *identify your possibility zone*. Work within your strengths. There is a difference between your talents and your strengths. Talents are your inborn gifts and abilities – *what* you do well. Strengths are qualities like courage, hope, resilience, and integrity—*how* you do well. Talents without strengths are like rocket ships without fuel; they won't get off the ground and soar.

Where you aim determines what you hit; as the popular saying goes, "shoot for the moon." Then, if you miss, the stars aren't bad as a backup. Even if you end up hitting your own foot (as I often do), at least you've activated your launch equipment.

Your focus is most often dictated by your beliefs and opinions of yourself. The importance of your perceptions of your own courage and competence cannot be underestimated. Faulty judgment can stop you before you start. What you see in yourself is what you get out of yourself! Focus on your unique skills and interests, and don't settle for anything less than the best possible you.

Decide how. Do it now.

SHOOTING MOSQUITOES

I will never forget the day I learned that my mother-in-law, Judy Allen Young, is a Hall of Fame member. Not for science or baseball or rock-and-roll. She is in the National Skeet Shooting Hall of Fame for her remarkable accuracy with a shotgun.

Now, I don't want you to have any misconceptions about the significance of this honor. Skeet shooting is not a casual gun sport like the shooting gallery at a county fair. It requires some serious shooting ability. I once asked Judy what she did to perfect her marksmanship.

She kiddingly replied, "We used to shoot mosquitoes for target practice." With her answer in mind, I understood just how skilled she was with a firearm. Let me put it another way: Since that day, I have not uttered another mother-in-law joke.

I was intrigued by her champion achievement and asked Judy to share some of her techniques of sporting excellence with me. Her response came to her with familiar ease, as though she were introducing me to an old friend. Her answers held remarkable insight as principles for life, whether on or off the skeet field. Here is what she said:

- Be ready when you call for your target. (Be
  fully prepared and focused. Then, just do it!)

- You can't shoot two targets at once. (Give it your
  full attention. Multi-tasking is much overrated.)

- Keep your cheek to the stock and follow
  through. (Stay steady and stay with it!
  Otherwise, none of the rest of it will work.)

So, the moral of the story? You can do lots of wonderful
things in life. But if you don't fully *prepare*, keep your *focus*,
and *follow through*, nothing great is likely to happen.

Here are some more thoughts on Judy's techniques:

Preparation: Success happens when extraordinary
preparation meets extraordinary possibility. Have you
ever heard someone say, "It was a good opportunity,
but I wasn't ready"? The fact is that we are always
prepared—either we're prepared to succeed or we're
prepared to fail. Some convince themselves that they
are unworthy or incapable of achieving their best.
Then, when possibility presents itself, their mental
conditioning prepares them for failure.

Focus: Here's an example of focus. It happened during
a five-man-team skeet shooting competition in
Bakersfield, California. The championship team
was nearly finished with their event when they
heard a roar go up from the crowd. Did they pause?
No! Despite this noisy distraction, they pressed
on, focusing intently on each target as it was called
for and successfully broken. They continued their

concentration, one target at a time. Then, as the team finished their event, they were surrounded by an exuberant crowd of spectators. The officials informed them that even before they were finished, it had become obvious they were probably going to win – not only the competition, but a new world record. Imagine if their concentration had wavered, and they had missed some of those shots.

Follow Through: All the preparation and focus in the world won't let us achieve our goals unless we actually follow through with our plans. We can have super skills, fine training, great ideas, and a clear vision of where we want to end up. However, if we don't take the necessary steps to get there – whether it's just a short-term project or a day-in, day-out marathon effort towards a long-term goal – then we will never be able to turn our possibilities into reality. There is a saying tennis coaches use to emphasize the importance of finishing your stroke. "Failure follows those who fail to follow through." True on the court as well as off.

I am convinced that possibilities are available to everyone. However, the people who realize possibilities are ready when they identify their "target." They are prepared mentally, physically, and perhaps spiritually when they pull the trigger. They focus, and they *follow through*.

Success in our own personal world-records is much like this. Stay focused on the target, and ignore the distractions. Great things will happen if you can just hit and break the next target, then the next. That's how a possibility life is. We achieve our purpose one target at a time.

If you aim for nothing, you'll hit it every time.

— AUTHOR UNKNOWN

THE DAY MY FINGER GOT STUCK

The passion that totally changed my life was tennis. It wasn't an obvious choice. In all likelihood my parents could never have predicted I had any potential in sports, given my physical challenges.

When I was twelve, my family moved from Ohio to northern California. By chance, our new home was across the street from the Greenbrook Racquet Club. The first summer we were there, I spent many hours sitting on a hill above the courts, watching people play tennis. There was something exhilarating about watching that ball thwack against their racquets and soar over the net.

One day I was in the garage and came across my Dad's old wooden tennis racquet. It was heavy and cumbersome, and I had a hard time holding onto it. Undaunted, I bought some tennis balls and began trying to hit them against the large, green backboard at the end of the courts. I experimented with several ways to hold the racquet before I found a technique that worked for me; the same way I hold it today. I'd pin the grip of the racquet to my right elbow with my left hand. However, I couldn't always hold the heavy wooden neck of the racquet with my right hand. When I swung hard, the racquet sometimes went flying. That explains why I had very few doubles partners back in those early days.

Then one day the local tennis shop got a shipment of the new Wilson T-2000 metal racquets. Two parallel bars connected the face of the racquet with the handle. I picked one up, and my finger accidentally slipped down between the two bars and got stuck. Instinctively, I tried to pull the racquet off, but it was snugly stuck to my finger. "I can hold this racquet!" I shouted, swinging it harder and harder. The racquet didn't budge.

My life had changed forever. I went on to become an athlete, a four-year high school letterman in tennis with a 47-win/6-loss record. At Loyola Marymount University in Los Angeles, I competed in NCAA Division I and earned full certification as a tennis coach through the United States Professional Tennis Association. My passion became my profession, and it opened a whole new world for me. Anything became possible!

Our passion determines what and how we feel about our own potential. Our ability to perceive possibilities expands enormously when we can identify both the value and *fun* of our objectives. *Value* is an intellectual concept. *Fun* is an emotion – a burst of child-like wonder and joy. The combination results in *passion*, an infinite energy source that can inspire us to tackle any obstacle in our path.

Think about the last time you felt totally fulfilled, when you knew that life just couldn't get any better. What were you doing? Probably it was something you are passionate about, something that you could and should incorporate into your life plan.

Passion + Purpose = Potential

NO LEGS TO STAND ON

Here's something you don't see every day. Two kids in an amusement park, running happily through the crowd, while holding ice cream cones, stuffed animals, and a pair of adult-size prosthetic legs. It was one of those zany events that regularly enliven the lives of people who discover possibilities – and everyone around them.

Dan Adragna was a high-level electrician foreman in Aptos, California, and an active single dad with two teenagers. One Christmas eve, he felt flu-like symptoms that grew so intense that he began to lose consciousness. He was rushed to Dominican Hospital in Santa Cruz, where he went into a coma. Dan had developed *septicemia* (blood poisoning), possibly from all the small wire cuts he routinely sustained on his job. The bacteria attacked his limbs. He lost parts of his fingers, and eventually his legs were amputated at the knee to stop the spread of gangrene. In the coming weeks, his heart flat-lined twice, and his family prepared for the worst. The next time he opened his eyes, it was February 10. He now weighed 85 pounds and was unrecognizable to his friends.

Dan spent the next four months enduring agonizing rehab. In the past he had been able to run with his kids. Now he was in a manual wheelchair. Almost a year after his near-death experience, Dan finally took his first step on two prosthetic legs. His mode of transportation was upgraded from wheelchair to an automobile with hand controls. He couldn't return to his former profession because he'd lost his dexterity and balance. You might be thinking that his potential was now limited. *Think again.*

Dan decided he now had the opportunity to help others discover their own possibilities in spite of their obstacles. One thing he did was volunteer to work with the teen ministry at his church. The teenagers' boundless energy inspired him, and the kids related to his strong sense of humor. Sure, he walked with a rolling gait, but they assumed he was just "strutting his stuff." Most were unaware of Dan's prosthetic legs – until the group trip to Great America.

The big day dawned, the buses pulled up, and several dozen excited kids exploded through the gates of the San Jose amusement park with chaperone Dan in hot pursuit. The students soon made a beeline to Invertigo, a double-inverted sidewinder, regarded as the mother of all roller coasters – ninety seconds of sheer hell, and thus irresistible. The kids nicknamed it "Barf-igo," because its high-speed loops and steep plunges sometimes have riders upside-down 138 feet up in the air. Each seat holds two, and some of the teens later claimed temporary hearing loss due to the hysterical screaming of their partners.

Dan courageously volunteered to go on the ride. He counted off the group and calculated that his partner in terror would be a shy 13-year-old girl. When it was Dan's turn to be strapped into a seat, he discovered, to his horror, that there were no leg supports. His legs just dangled. What would a G-force of five gravities do to his prosthetic legs? He didn't have time to wonder long. The ride took off!

The initial 138-foot lift and drop was completed without incident, and Dan breathed a sigh of relief. Then the inverted sidewinders began. Dan grabbed his knees, but his strength was no match for the G-force. The first leg to break free was the right one. But instead of flying off, the prosthesis started spinning like a shot-putter winding up before a launch, its toe rotating within inches of his partner's face. Alarmed, he reached over to protect her and loosened the grip on his left leg. It joined the first in rapid rotation.

The right leg reached launch speed and shot off like a rocket, sailing over the crowd below and vanishing. Seconds later, it was followed by the left leg. Dan glanced over at his 13-year-old friend, fearing she would be terrified. Instead, he saw her laughing uncontrollably. As the G-force continued, her face acquired the wrinkled look of one of those Shar-Pei dogs, and his own must have too, because she kept pointing at his face and laughing even harder.

A number of the students had witnessed the blastoff. As soon as the ride stopped, they scattered on a mission to find Dan's legs. Dan suddenly realized that he was stuck. He couldn't leave the ride without his legs. He suddenly had a terrifying vision of himself riding Barf-igo over and over until the park closed. Then he saw one of the most welcome sights he'd ever experienced. Two members of his youth group were running toward him, holding those cones, stuffed animals – and his precious legs. Everyone, including Dan, cheered!

Dan continues his quest to inspire others to uncover possibilities. Today, he is a key leader in Wheels for the World, an organization that finds wheelchairs for disadvantaged people throughout the world. He has traveled to many countrics, encouraging others to see what's possible. When I told him about the concept of this book, he smiled. "When someone can go from crawling, or being carried, to the independence of a wheelchair," he explained, "they are transformed instantly. Independent mobility changes a person's thinking. It changes what's possible and that reveals new purpose."

The people Dan meets through his new job aren't the only ones who find new purpose. It was through attending a function to publicize Wheels of the World that Dan met, fell in love with, and married his wife Melinda. Their lives have never been the same and their future filled with endless possibilities.

Dan has made an unforgettable impact on my life! Some people love to show off their new outfit; Dan and I enjoy showing off our new legs. He inspires me to embrace my possibilities and live life to the fullest. The greatest lesson his life has taught me is problems don't reduce potential, they *reveal* potential.

Problems are only opportunities in work clothes.

— HENRY J. KAISER
KNOWN AS THE FATHER OF MODERN
AMERICAN SHIPBUILDING

2

IDENTIFY YOUR PESSIMISM

Why is it impossible?

DOING THE TURKEY TROT

One Thanksgiving, my daughter Alexa thought it would be a fabulous idea to run a 10K fund-raising race called the Turkey Trot. The proceeds provided meals for low-income families. I embraced the idea enthusiastically, and we both signed up. To ensure that I would not be the last turkey to finish the race, I started training daily. But after a couple of weeks, my bright self-image as a tireless young champion athlete began to fade a bit. My motivation began to lapse as I visualized the effort it was going to take.

Finally, I explained to my daughter that my schedule was so busy that perhaps we should delay our trot until the following year. Alexa, then eleven, gave me one of those reproachful daughter looks. "Dad," she chided, "you're focusing on the obstacles instead of the objective."

Huh? That sounded familiar. I'd been telling audiences that for years! There I was, dwelling on the daunting task ahead, instead of the exultation of crossing the finish line with my darling daughter.

I'm not suggesting that you discount the effort or difficulties involved as you pursue your possibilities. Don't kid yourself that an ambitious goal won't be tough. That's delusional thinking, and you'll soon lose momentum. Acknowledge up front how much work it's going to be, and you'll *increase* your possibilities instead of decreasing them. Anyone who makes it to the top (or to the finish line) understands the effort required to achieve desired possibilities.

A realistic assessment of the challenges ahead is not an adequate reason to abandon the race. Some people focus on the barriers they may face and abandon possibilities before they even begin. Those who make it—who even achieve greatness—are those who decide to take the first step anyway. And then the next... and the next!

Of *course*, there will still be disappointment, difficulty, and discouragement. How do we counteract that? My friend Jeff Salz, an accomplished rock climber, tells me that when his arms tire, he immediately thinks of the potential view awaiting him at the top. How about you? Have you thought of what your view will look like?

I am happy to report that I did not finish last in the Turkey Trot race. There was one person behind me, nipping at my heels: an athletic-looking young man, perhaps twenty-five years old. He was driving a golf cart, weaving back and forth to pick up the orange cones that outlined the racecourse!

The reality is that in the pursuit of ambitious possibilities, we are likely to fail or finish last. To stay optimistic we must *think again* about these experiences. Some people see setbacks as absolute failures, while others view them as important information gathering. If you are reluctant to attempt something because you fear negative results, here is a compelling thought:

Who really loses? The person finishing last or the one who never entered the race?

POOH'S VIEW OF POSSIBILITIES

The stories we read as children – and read to our children – often contain powerful messages about possibilities. Remember *The Little Engine That Could?* What a great parable about determination. How about Dr. Seuss's *Oh, the Places You'll Go!*, a story that rejoices in the potential everyone has to fulfill their wildest dreams? It's too bad this childhood wisdom sometimes fades as we age and become "terminally adult."

One classic character who lives a life filled with possibilities is A.A. Milne's Winnie-the-Pooh. What a great role model! Now, you may scoff and think, "What can I possibly learn from a storybook bear who loves honey?" Here's what.

Pooh is someone who refuses to become discouraged, despite dire circumstances and some pessimistic friends. In addition to level-headed Christopher Robin and bouncy Tigger, Pooh also has some fairly dispiriting pals. There's Eeyore, the dismal donkey, who walks around in a cloud of perpetual gloom and melancholy. And then there's worried little Piglet, always asking, "What if we're lost?" or "What if we fail?" It is up to Pooh to provide a positive alternate view.

One day, Pooh and Piglet are walking through the forest in a heavy wind that turns into a roaring gale. Piglet, as usual, becomes alarmed at the negative possibilities. "Supposing a tree fell down when we were underneath it?" Pooh thinks carefully. "Supposing it didn't?" he replies.

Pooh is always asking questions that challenge Piglet to think about circumstances from a different perspective. Pooh is helping Piglet to *think again.*

No matter who we are or what we have achieved, we all have a little Pooh and a little Piglet in us. People who are open to possibilities are focusing on their Pooh side. When we keep a little Pooh in our outlook, our possibilities multiply. If you constantly interpret situations and facts in Piglet mode, stop and consider the Pooh view. To be our best we all need to be full of Pooh. (Happily, people are constantly telling me that I am full of it.)

Have you noticed that many worries tend to fall into two categories—those that are unlikely and those that are unimportant? If paralyzing worry is blocking possibilities, try asking yourself these three questions:

QUESTION 1: HOW LIKELY IS THIS TO HAPPEN?

The reality is that almost anything *can* happen, but what are the *actual* chances? Like Pooh, question the probability of a negative outcome by considering facts. Facts build fortitude.

Some people seek out or invent drama to energize themselves. However, if catastrophizing has the opposite effect—if the imaginary possibilities for disaster distract you from the real possibilities for opportunity—go Pooh. Examine the facts, re-evaluate your thinking, and consider adopting an optimistic perspective.

Sometimes people come up to talk to me after my presentations. Occasionally, some tell me how they wish they could have my attitude, but it's just not possible. I am humbled by their comments, but in reality my life is not very different from theirs. We all face challenges and we all have choices. As we chat, it usually becomes clear that what's getting them down hasn't happened yet. In fact, there is often overwhelming evidence that it will probably never happen. They've been blinded by their personal viewpoint and haven't examined the evidence from an alternate perspective.

If you are stuck in Piglet mode, surrounded by alarming consequences that are blocking your way, seek out a Pooh. Not someone who offers empty platitudes of reassurance, but someone who can help you evaluate whether your thinking fits the facts. Maybe you're right. Maybe something *is* really wrong that needs to be confronted. Or maybe you're wrong. The French essayist Montaigne said, "My life has been a series of catastrophes – most of which never happened."

QUESTION 2: IF IT HAPPENS, IS IT REALLY IMPORTANT?

The main problem with focusing on problems is that they distract you from noticing and pursuing opportunities. One common piece of advice about unproductive worrying is: "You won't remember this worry in a hundred years." Hey, I think; I can't remember what I had for *lunch*, and I'm still at the table staring at my empty plate!

My late friend Richard Carlson wrote the book *Don't Sweat the Small Stuff*. What a profound life principle – to live positively and conserve your mental energy for possibilities instead of problems. As an objective self-observer, I realize that I have given disproportionate significance to the small stuff. Have you ever lain awake at night, worrying about something that *might* happen? The next morning you wake up and, momentarily, you've forgotten all about it. Then it comes back to you, and you say to yourself, "Time to start worrying again."

I find it fascinating that many people cope more effectively with the big stuff than the small stuff. Then they proceed to let little irritants assume insurmountable importance.

QUESTION 3: WHAT'S THE BEST THING THAT COULD HAPPEN?

Many self-help books advise the following way to increase your courage in tough situations: "Just imagine the *worst* that could possibly happen." The underlying logic is that this will strengthen you for whatever is to come. However, whenever I mention this strategy to people who are discouraged, they tell me they've already rehearsed and anticipated all the negative events so thoroughly that they can recite every tiny detail as if it had already happened.

Instead, my suggestion is to rehearse and imagine the *best* that can happen. Here's a positive strategy. Let's say you are considering pursuing a possibility that seems a bit daunting. Therefore, to prepare for the great possibilities that are going to require extra stamina and courage:

> *Relive past successes.* Make a list, mental or on paper, of the times you've tried and succeeded. Here is a powerful mental image: Braid a rope of past achievements to hang on to, both in good times and challenging ones.

> *Release past disappointments.* Make another list of disappointments, and then tear it up, literally or

figuratively. Shred it, set fire to it, flush it, and toss it in the waste basket. Gone!

Rehearse future possibilities. Produce, direct, and star in a mental movie of yourself exploring this wonderful possibility. See yourself meeting the challenges, bouncing back from any setbacks, and continuing on with energy and determination.

When you go all-out pursuing potential possibilities, your attitude becomes more positive, your energy increases, and your courage strengthens. Even if things don't turn out exactly as you had hoped, you've permanently boosted your attitude and resilience, keeping yourself open to new possibilities in the future.

If you start with the belief that possibilities are abundant and within your grasp, you will begin to see all the new opportunities available to you. If your belief is negative, you will see barriers instead. We all want to feel our opinions are correct. Therefore, if your opinion is that you have the ability to achieve great things, great things appear. But if you are convinced you're mediocre, you will only notice the average. To further support this diminishing belief in yourself, you will actually *ignore* the extraordinary abilities you have and focus your attention solely on your average attributes! It's time to take on a "poohsitive" attitude and *think again!*

Accept the challenges so that you can feel the exhilaration of victory.

— GEORGE S. PATTON

FEAR VERSUS ANXIETY

The famous actor Laurence Olivier was so afraid of driving that whenever his car approached a red light, he'd step on the gas. He reasoned that the sooner he passed through "danger," the better. It's amazing he survived to win four Oscars and eleven Oscar nominations.

Putting aside such an irrational response, fear is fundamentally a useful and practical emotion. It alerts us to potential dangers so we can take adequate precautions to avoid them. Fear is usually inspired by some real likelihood. Facts indicate we will face a bad outcome unless we keep our brakes fixed, child-proof our homes when we have little ones, change the batteries in our smoke detectors, and practice good health habits.

Fear can also be a good indicator that we are stretching, growing, and challenging ourselves. It keeps us alert and focused. Great possibilities are rarely realized through comfortable circumstances. Great possibilities require risks, and taking risks generates fear. Adequately addressed, such fear doesn't have to hold us back.

Anxiety, on the other hand, is an entirely useless emotion. It is a product of our imagination. Anxiety anticipates a negative event, even a remote or impossible one, with such intensity that we can be immobilized. Anxiety is a disabling roadblock to possibilities. It distorts our vision and disrupts momentum, distracting and discouraging us. When we are gripped by anxiety, we focus on everything that could possibly go wrong. There's no energy left to think about what can, might, or must go right.

Have you ever felt as if a huge boulder was on your chest? Have you felt weighed down by a sense of impending doom? This was most likely anxiety. Now, think about the last time you tried something new or different. How did you feel? Would you agree that every time you have achieved something extraordinary you were nervous or a bit scared? Going for a job interview, asking someone for a date, making a speech – most people experience a little bit of fear, but did you also feel anxiety? Was it a useful emotion?

The word *fear* comes from the Old English word *faer*, meaning sudden danger. Today, we see fear as an emotional reaction to real danger. Here is my own definition with a more positive view: "Fear is an emotional response to real possibilities."

Anxiety comes from the Latin word *anxius*, which means to be troubled in the mind by an uncertain event. Another definition is to press tightly or strangle. The key words are "troubled" and "mind." The provoking thought is neither identifiable nor reality based. Here is my own definition: "Anxiety is anything that suffocates your possibilities." Anxiety is an emotional barrier because it causes us to resist possibilities.

Fear heightens alertness, which can serve as a catalyst to propel us towards exciting new possibilities. Use it to your advantage to accomplish remarkable things!

If we all did the things we are capable of
doing, we would literally astound ourselves.

— THOMAS EDISON

THE "GO!" TECHNIQUE

There's a popular behavior-modification technique called "thought-interruption." The idea is that whenever a negative idea pops into your head, you shout, "Stop!" or imagine a big stop sign. This strategy is supposed to help people interrupt their worry/anxiety cycle before it gains momentum.

However, this system of thought-interruption violates one of the principles of possibility language, which is to use *positive* terms only. Saying "Stop" causes a negative reaction and is a bit like telling someone, "Don't think about elephants." They're going to think about elephants! I'd like to suggest a more positive "possibility" approach, one that my audiences have responded to with great enthusiasm.

Whenever you catch yourself indulging in unproductive anxieties, visualize a red light changing to a huge green one. Shout, "Go!" and step on the gas, leaving your anxious thoughts behind. Put yourself in the driver's seat and take the anxiety-free, "possibility" road.

Some people engage in a sort of backwards magical thinking: "If I vividly visualize failure, then it won't actually occur." It's like the tradition in some societies of demeaning everything precious so the gods won't be jealous and take the good things away. ("Oh, *this* old thing!") But here's the news. Anticipating a negative outcome from our efforts does *not* prevent bad things from happening. It may actually help to bring them about. It's like "rehearsing" doom, creating a self-fulfilling prophesy.

But what about doing this instead? Rather than visualizing disaster, dedicate all that effort and energy to believing your intentions are possible. Your chances for achieving them are much greater.

If you're still not convinced, analyze your anxiety-producing thoughts. How are they beneficial? What are the payoffs? How uncomfortable would you be if you decided to dump them? If you're like me, this exercise will show that anxiety produces only new problems, not new possibilities.

In my book *How High Can You Bounce?* I explain how "motion affects emotion." When you're feeling stalled or stymied, the best way to jump-start yourself is literally to get moving. Working your muscles, getting your blood pumping, and inhaling oxygen all stimulate your brain to produce the chemicals it needs to function happily and efficiently.

Interestingly, "emotion affects motion" is also true. Motion—your energy level and stamina—is profoundly influenced by emotions. When you are inspired by possibilities, your body and brain get a continuous jolt of chemical signals that keep them functioning at peak level. Athletes describe this as being "in the zone." Just the thought of what you might be able to achieve propels you out of bed, eager for whatever's ahead. The boring, tedious things we all face daily, even stress, become insignificant because you see the big picture. When your possibilities are compelling, and attitude positive, most of your hours are lived with zest, enthusiasm, and joy. You notice options and openings, that you would have been blind to, because you're *looking* for them. Ready, set...

CLEAN YOUR CLOSETS

Have you ever had a closet full of nothing to wear? That was my dilemma. I wear an odd size. Because I have very short arms and legs, I am not an off-the-rack kind of guy. Let's put it this way... the only one who wears the same size as me is a dachshund!

This has been a continual challenge, especially with my hectic travel schedule. In my profession I have to be presentable, so my solution was to buy anything that sort of fit and make do. If something actually fit, I'd wear it until it fell to pieces. If nothing fit, I'd go out and buy something new. Eventually, the closets were bursting. Yet, the more clothes I had, the harder it was to get dressed.

One day, my wife Kathryn had had enough. She insisted I get rid of everything worn-out, outdated, or that didn't fit. Furthermore, following this radical purge, I could not go right out and buy more clothes. "You'll find you have everything you need and more," she assured me.

Very reluctantly, I began to sort, and it was just amazing. Clothes kept appearing, like clowns from one of those clown cars, and I kept saying, "Now, where did *that* come from?" And an astonishing thing happened. After the Big Clear-Out, it was as if I had a whole new wardrobe of clothes I couldn't remember buying. Kathryn was right (as always). My clothing struggle of finding something acceptable to wear was over, until I wore out all the "new" clothes I had rediscovered. Only then was I found at the store.

When you get rid of the useless stuff, you often discover that you already have most or all of what you really need. Here's how that applies to possibilities. As you analyze your past and present, think about what you can let go of so you can find something new. Do you have beliefs that are worn or outdated? Perhaps you are clothing yourself in actions and attitudes that no longer fit. Have you outgrown low expectations of yourself?

Here are some outmoded thinking habits you may not need anymore:

"I've been dealt a bad hand, so why bother?"

"I tried, but I don't have what it takes."

"People like me can only dream about that."

"Other people get all the breaks."

Dump obsolete beliefs. Here are new thinking habits to help generate possibilities:

"I'm starting with a new deck."

"I've learned a lot for my next try."

"Dreaming is just the beginning."

"My unique perspectives give me the edge."

Maybe it's time to get rid of old thinking that may be obscuring your possibilities and limiting your potential. Time to *think again*, clothed in a new wardrobe.

You don't have to have more or be more
before anything can happen.

THE LANGUAGE OF POSSIBILITIES

One of the most possibility-limiting words in the English language is "improbable." It is like a big, black wall, effectively blocking any further effort or consideration. While some may say it can't be done because of the obstacles, peak performers move towards their goals regardless of the barriers. When faced with inevitable obstacles, possibility-seekers use a different vocabulary – a "language of possibilities" – to describe options and opportunities." If someone says, "That's really not likely" or "This would be much safer," the minds of possibility-seekers *think again*. "*Why* isn't it likely?" "What would happen if...?" "Could I try it *this* way instead?" They develop a unique questioning style, a powerful tool for expanding possibilities.

Extreme language portrays things as black and white with no tantalizing in-between. It can discourage possibility thinking with either/or words like "never" and "always," "must" and "mustn't," "mandatory" and "forbidden." Here are a few examples.

NON-POSSIBILITY LANGUAGE	POSSIBILITY LANGUAGE
Never	Maybe – could be
Always	Sometimes
Forever	Temporarily
Absolutely	Perhaps

Forbidden	Reconsidered
Compulsory	Optional
Discouraged	Encouraged
Behave	Struggle
Suitable	Imaginative
Normal	Exceptional
Acceptance	Exploration
Respectful	Questioning
Respectable	Provocative
Staid	Inspirational
Customary	Creative
Traditional	Innovative
Disaster	Opportunity
Success	Opportunity
An end	A beginning
Destiny, fate	Common sense, curiosity
That's just how it is.	Why?
No one's ever done that.	Why not?

Language is the power tool of possibilities. It's not just the words we use, but how we *frame* ideas so they inspire us to see possibilities in new ways.

There's the classic story of the time Steve Jobs was trying to talk John Sculley, a top executive at Pepsi-Cola, into becoming the CEO of Apple Computer. Jobs flew from Silicon Valley in California to New York and sat in Sculley's Manhattan office with its breathtaking view. Sculley was not enthusiastic. He had a list of demands that included a huge salary, huge bonus, and a huge severance package. Not only that, he wouldn't leave New York. He'd be a consultant for Apple from his New York office.

How did Steve Jobs convince John Sculley to take the position and to move from New York City to California? He helped him *think again* and see the extraordinary possibilities with a simple word picture: *"Do you want to sell sugar water for the rest of your life, or do you want to change the world?"*

Dwell in possibility.

— EMILY DICKINSON
POET

BLUE GENES

Psychologists have a saying: "We have *traits* (inborn) and we have *states* (chosen)." Depression can be both. The negative feelings, physical and emotional, that arise from depression and negativity are champion opportunity blockers. For example, when choosing what socks to wear is overwhelming, making positive decisions about significant life choices is impossible. Fortunately, medical science is making huge advances in treating debilitating disorders. And one of the best re-discoveries made is that our thoughts have a tremendous impact on our feelings.

People aren't optimistic *because* they have recognized possibilities. They recognize possibilities *because* they are *optimistic*. Maybe you've heard someone say, "I was born pessimistic. That's how my brain works." The implication is that they were born to think negatively. They are convinced it's genetically programmed into their DNA. "I came into this world with curly hair, brown eyes, and a negative attitude." If this is your belief, *think again*. A negative mind-set is definitely a big barrier to seeing new possibilities.

Just like everyone else, I was born with some unchangeable physical characteristics. And just like everyone, at times I struggle to remain positive and accept what I can't change. However, a major turning point in my life took place when I discovered I had the power to be a "super hero." No, I couldn't leap tall buildings with a single bound, and the only bird I was ever mistaken for was a stork! But I do have X-ray vision; I can see through the brick walls of negativity that well-meaning people build in my path. You can have that same powerful vision.

Being born with an unchangeable physical challenge forced me to look *within* for something that *was* changeable, for something I *could* control. Suddenly, I realized what it was! The greatest obstacle to my success was not my hands or legs. It was how I *viewed* them. Real power happens when we take complete control over our *perspective.*

When you take control over the attitudes and beliefs that are holding you back, you accept responsibility for your choices. You choose whether to notice and evaluate possibilities. You can choose which opportunities to jump at and which to reject because they are not in line with your values and goals. You become an active driver, rather than passive passenger, of your life.

When I was a kid, busy making excuses to get out of things I didn't want to do, I'd play the "physically-challenged" card. I thought of it as my ace in the hole. Oh, was I good! What I never seemed to learn was that my father was playing a different game, and he held the trump card. He wanted me to succeed on the world's terms, and that didn't leave any room for "poor me-ism." He'd confront my negativity with a comment like, "Move out of pity city!" His admonition was he wanted me to look *inside* myself, to look at my state of mind, instead of in the mirror at my physical traits. Yes, the shape of my hands and legs, and my cranium pattern baldness (darn!), are predetermined genetic traits. My choice to become excited about possibilities and explore them is not.

I choose to *think again* and live in the powerful state of possibility. How about you?!

A POSSIBILITY IN A TRAFFIC JAM

It is a very humbling experience to have a career as a motivational speaker and to parent teenagers. I wish you could be a guest around our dinner table as we discuss family issues. If one of the kids is struggling with something, I've been known to launch into my best podium material, words that have inspired the applause of hundreds of thousands of people. "Challenges are inevitable," I'll proclaim in my most persuasive tones. "Defeat is optional." And three pairs of eyes give me blank looks followed by deep sighs and mutterings of, "Whatever."

Recently, I was in the car with my three teenagers. As we drove along, I was grumbling to myself about the near-gridlock traffic and how tremendously important it was that we not be late. I was leaning so close to the steering wheel that I considered taking a bite out of it to relieve my stress. My complaining escalated until one of my kids said, "Sounds like Dad needs to pull over and read his own book."

Oh, they had a hearty laugh, and I was reminded to ask myself, "Will the world come to an end if we're late?" The truth is that no real damage would be done. It would be an inconvenience but not important in the long run. I was wasting an excellent opportunity to chat with my kids and notice the scenery. I was overlooking an invaluable possibility: the chance to build our relationship, and maybe even create a moment that they – and I – might remember all our lives.

A note on roadblocks. As you pursue possibilities, you will invariably encounter traffic jams. It is inevitable. An important thinking strategy is to be *ready* for them. "Aha," you might be saying, "but that's contrary to what you said about not anticipating negative outcomes." It's vital, however, to *acknowledge* that you're going to run into roadblocks (and overcome them) as a basic principle of staying optimistic. You'll maintain a buoyant attitude because you are seldom surprised by setbacks. You accept that they are an inescapable reality of life.

The ability to hang in there in spite of obstacles is essential if we are to realize our possibilities. Whenever you hit a wall and feel like quitting, *think again*. Even the best planning and forethought will not prevent all unexpected obstacles. When you encounter roadblocks, your initial response may be to floor it – in reverse. But if you anticipate barriers, you can respond positively by slowing down and deciding whether the best course of action is to go around it, through it, or over it.

Choice, not chance, determines your possibilities.

FINDING A PARKING SPACE

I once knew a man named Dave Martin who boasted that he could always find a parking spot, no matter how difficult the situation. I watched him, and by golly, he invariably did! He confided that he'd paid a psychic to enhance this ability.

Had he actually acquired some supernatural or extrasensory power? Or was it that his belief in the possibility tuned him into signals that others would overlook? A man striding down the street with his hand in his pocket might be reaching for his car keys. A woman passing between parked cars while carrying packages might be about to the put them in a trunk and drive off. However, if Dave had convinced himself that his lot in life was to circle the block endlessly, he would have ignored any clues that a space was opening up.

It's the chicken-and-egg paradox. Which comes first? When you're aware of possibilities, you throw your mind, body, and soul into pursuing them. You work in your "zest zone," feeling invigorated instead of exhausted. Awareness helps you see a future filled with hope, confidence, and optimism – a future full of possibilities.

We all visualize the outcome of our efforts. The difference is that some people see what they *don't* want. Others have a vivid picture of what they want and see it happening. They believe it *can* happen. Visualization is a power tool for possibilities. When you project your mind forward and see a clear picture of your possibilities being realized, it's an amazing force that moves you toward them. Achieving possibilities begins with an "inside job" instead of external actions.

Using this technique of mental "rehearsal," you can make current possibilities into future achievements. Actors, speakers, and athletes rehearse what they plan to do until it comes automatically and effortlessly. You can do the same. Here are some guidelines for effective possibility-visualization.

> *Relax.* Take a deep breath and begin to release any tension you may be experiencing. Breathe deeply until your body and mind are calm. Something I find helpful is to identify my doubts and, as I am exhaling, to visualize the doubts being blown away. I have witnessed many successful athletes use this relaxation exercise to reprogram their minds and prepare for victory.

> *Recall.* Take a moment to identify a previously successful experience that clearly shows your competence and self-confidence. Resist recalling past hurts or disappointments so you can fortify your resolve. As you do this, start to affirm yourself by making sure your thoughts are positive, personal, and embrace possibilities.

> *Rehearse.* Have you ever said, "I knew that would happen"? Most likely you were visualizing—either negatively or positively. Focus on the positive. Imagine you actually doing and saying exactly what is needed for success. Before important events, I

visualize right before I go to sleep. I see a positive outcome and then I "sleep on it." It is amazing how much better you sleep when you look forward to the next day with excitement rather than dread.

Now go out and find those front-row parking spots that have your name on them.

TASTING THE HOT DOGS

It was a baseball fan's dream: to be in the stands on the historic day when Cal Ripken of the Baltimore Orioles would break Lou Gehrig's record for consecutive games played. The 1996 game was completely sold out, and dignitaries from all over the world were competing for seats. However, my friend Phil Hempfing was undaunted.

Phil had hired me to speak when he was a school superintendent in Hanover, Pennsylvania. He was an avid baseball fan, and attending this game was a dream come true! Phil was able to secure tickets through a friend, and at five o'clock he stood in line at will call. But when his turn came, the ticket agent said Phil's name wasn't on the list. You can imagine how he felt. A one-time event in the history of baseball, and his name wasn't on the list!

But Phil was determined to realize his possibilities... He politely suggested that the agent recheck her records. He waited as the rest of the people in line passed inside. The ticket agent returned and said she was sorry, but they had no record of a Phil Hempfing. It was now 6:20 PM, and the game would start at 7:00.

Many human reactions are possible at such a moment, some negative and unproductive. Phil chose the positive approach, pleading with her to search again. "I had visualized being there so strongly," Phil told me later, "that

I could even taste the hot dogs. I hadn't come this far to give up now."

Did Phil's perseverance pay off? As he was standing at the ticket counter, a representative from the Orioles overheard his conversation. He was clearly impressed with Phil's tenacity and, more importantly, his optimistic attitude. He handed Phil a ticket and said, "Enjoy the game." Phil told me he was overwhelmed with emotion as he took his seat, in the front row! Well, if you've ever seen the famous picture of Cal Ripken facing the Oriole dugout with the fans cheering wildly, then you've seen Phil Hempfing. He was seated near President Bill Clinton, Tom Hanks, and other world-renowned celebrities.

You see, sometimes possibilities often happen if you just hang in there and never give up. When someone asks me what is the first step to success, I simply say, "Show up and stay up!" In other words, make a decision to take action and remain possibility focused no matter what resistance you face. It may be your priceless ticket to success!

Let me tell you the secret that has led to my goal: My strength lies solely in my tenacity.

— LOUIS PASTEUR
CHEMIST KNOWN FOR HIS
LIFE-SAVING WORK

CHARIOTS AND TRUMPETS

When the ancient Romans wanted to make Julius Caesar a god, he ordered a servant to ride just behind him in the chariot during triumphal processions. The crowds cheered their heads off, trumpets blew, and beautiful women swooned as he was pelted with flower petals. Yet, through it all, the servant, on Caesar's order, kept repeating in his ear: "You are only a man. You are only a man..."

It's far too easy to get an exaggerated idea of our own importance. Sometimes I come home from an especially successful presentation. With applause and praise ringing in my ears, I turn into the driveway and wonder why a red carpet hasn't been rolled out for me. No trumpets, no rose petals. My wife and kids soon return my ego to normal size.

I always fall for this one! Someone will call and ask, "Hey Roger, do you believe in free speech?" My reply was, "Of course I believe in free speech." "Happy to hear that. How about giving a free one to my group?!"

I had placed on my calendar a freebie, speaking before an audience of 500 physically-challenged adults. By the way, I only speak to groups of disabled people. Isn't it true we all have "handicaps"? Some you can see, many you cannot. Soon after confirming the engagement, a corporate client (paying) called and requested the same day. I had a dilemma: should I call my free speech audience and cancel? The fact was, the month was lasting longer than my money, and I needed an extra date on the calendar! I thought, "Of course these people have an idea of who I am – a big-cheese corporate speaker. They will understand I am one important dude, and if they are not aware of this, all they have to do is ask me!" My self-aggrandizement became so intense I stood outside feeling I might burst and mess up my office!

Then, thankfully, I stopped and *thought again*. My career was built by speaking in front of audiences for no fee. I would temporarily increase my bank account but permanently damage my reputation and character.

I swallowed my dangerously inflated ego and went. They turned out to be one of the most memorable audiences I have ever had, teaching me more about possibilities than I was able to teach them. It was a humbling reality check and much-needed reminder of my early days in the speaking business. When I started out talking to school kids and other audiences, they didn't care how important I thought *I* was. They only cared how important I could make *them* feel. It was true then, and it's twice as true today.

On my way home I thought, "Okay Roger, you could be staying in a luxury resort being pampered and eating your favorite... swordfish." Did I really miss it? Nah. I went and had a fish sandwich at McDonalds.

Don't let ego and a lack of humility deprive you of possibilities. What does "humility" mean? And why should you care? You may wonder why I stop so often to analyze the origins of the words we use every day. It's because this background can provide unexpected insight and understanding. But I have to admit that before I wrote this book, I did not have the humility to explore the meaning of the word "humility." It is a nice word, a concept that is thought of favorably, but somewhat difficult to define. It's one of those "I know it when I see it" kind of words.

We'd be unlikely to make a connection between "humility" and "possibility," but, as I've learned more about the people and organizations who exemplify possibility thinking, the characteristics of humility have become evident. Humility is a positive value in all our lives, but it is even more than that. The practice of humility can lead us to even greater possibilities.

Let's look first at what humility is *not*. It means the quality of being humble, not arrogant. It comes from the same Latin root, but is not synonymous with "humiliated." Humility doesn't imply that you are powerless and pitiful. It does not have to include an attitude of meekness or victimhood.

There is a popular flippant statement that clearly shows a lack of humility: "Been there, done that." This implies that you've gotten all you need from an experience and have no need to learn more. However, one of the paradoxes of life is that the more you know, the more you realize how much you *don't* know. A truth I've learned from the examples in this book is that possibilities are realized by continuing to grow and expand my awareness, no matter what I have already learned or accomplished.

Humility, as I define it, is a sincere interest in others, knowing that everyone has something to teach us. It is also an open-minded approach to life that encourages the flexible thinking that sparks possibilities. Those lacking humility are so self-focused that they rarely have time to learn from others. Remember the old joke of the egocentric celebrity who says, "But enough about me. How do *you* feel about me?"

Yet, being humble does not eliminate self assuredness or self-confidence. In fact, both are important characteristics of humble people.

One word you rarely associate with humility is "greed." However, humble people are usually greedy – voracious to learn from the viewpoints and wisdom of others. They possess a child-like fascination with the world around them. Far from being a contradiction, "ambition" is also an essential component of humility, making us eager to spot and pursue possibilities.

Humility is not only an attitude, but also a way of being. Do you remember the best selling book, *I'm OK, You're OK*, by Thomas A. Harris? I like to paraphrase that title: "I'm not always OK, nobody is always OK, and that's OK." The fact is, I am no better or no worse a person than anyone else. Accept, with humility and pride, the reality that you have your own unique resources, talents, and passions. Then *think again* with confidence about the unlimited possibilities available to the unique you.

There's nothing so becomes a man as modest stillness and humility.

— WILLIAM SHAKESPEARE

THE PHANTOM GARAGE DOOR

Our neighbor was having trouble with his automatic garage-door opener. The door would open at unexpected times, both day and night. Sometimes he would come home to find it open and his dogs out relandscaping the neighbors' yards. Late at night, he would hear the gears grinding. He'd run downstairs to find the door open, but no one in sight.

First, he called the manufacturer. They told him that he had one of the first models on the market, the granddaddy of all openers, and that his remote signal could not be changed or reprogrammed. However, they agreed to check out his system. A repairman came and studied the door. It might be interference from a police scanner or radio station, the repairman decided. He also confirmed that the opener could not be reprogrammed and advised my neighbor to buy a newer model.

Being frugal and highly suspicious that this advice was just a sales pitch, my neighbor determined to find a solution short of buying a whole new mechanism. He spent several months looking for a pattern in the unexpected garage-door openings, but there were none.

Still, he absolutely refused to buy a new opener. (Did I mention he was frugal?) Finally, he disconnected the opening device. I would drive by and see him pulling into his driveway, stopping the car, and climbing out to yank on the handle and haul the door up with an angry grunt. After pulling in and shutting off the car, he would repeat the operation and, with a whoosh of air, the door would slam down and smack against the pavement. Rain or shine, he had to get out of his car and pull the door open. The process didn't seem to be doing much for his blood pressure or the door. He could have purchased a new garage-door opener, but he refused to do so on principle. After three years of raising and lowering the garage door by hand, he put his house up for sale and moved away.

The new owner wondered why the automatic garage-door opener wasn't working and quickly discovered it was unplugged. He located the remotes, reconnected the opener, and felt proud that he had solved the first problem with his new house. Except that within a week, the door creaked open while he was enjoying dinner. The next time it opened itself was late at night. He and his wife thought they were being robbed. The third time, he was retrieving his newspaper early in the morning and noticed the door eerily swing open. And no one was in sight up or down the street.

Again, our new neighbor sought out an expert, a "garage-door electronics specialist" from San Francisco. The specialist was standing in the driveway with my neighbor, diagnosing the problem, when I drove past the house after an early morning tennis match. My usual routine is to turn the corner onto my street and press my automatic door remote to open my garage. My house is second from the corner, and by the time I reach it, my garage door is open, and I pull right in. As usual, I depressed the button on my remote and then waved to my new neighbor. As I drove into my garage, I glanced in my rearview mirror and noticed the two men running toward my house. They raced up to me in the garage. "Hand over your clicker!" they shouted.

Their faces were flushed, they were panting, and I thought it best to obey and ask questions later. They grabbed the remote and raced back to my neighbor's front yard. I curiously followed them. The specialist held my remote in his right hand and extended his arm, pointing the remote at my neighbor's garage door. Click. The door rattled open.

Laughter echoed down the street, and my new neighbor's laughter was the loudest. He could barely catch his breath. Because of a jog in the road and the positions of our houses, I had never been able to see that my remote was also opening a second garage door down the street. And by the time my neighbor ran out, I would already be inside my garage with the door closed, striding into my kitchen.

Normally, one might be able to figure this out because of the schedule of the neighbor with the rogue remote. However, I keep no set schedule. I leave for the airport at all hours of the day, often returning in the middle of the night. Thus, there had never been any pattern to the ghostly openings.

My neighbor and I were both happy that the mystery had been solved. Riddled with undeserved guilt and kicking myself that I had never made the possible connection, I reprogrammed my remote (easy to do with my model) and ended the problem.

This incident made me realize how often we overlook what is right under our noses and look outside our own capabilities, hoping that an "expert" can solve our problems and point us in the right direction. Often we *do* need outside help, but sometimes the real expertise is as close as Dorothy's ruby slippers were to her getting home on her own. We often have the potential and expertise within ourselves, if we just *think again* and ask the right questions.

The problems of the world cannot possibly be solved by skeptics or cynics whose horizons are limited by the obvious realities. We need men who can dream of things that never were.

— PRESIDENT JOHN F. KENNEDY

3

AMPLIFY YOUR POTENTIAL

What are your assets?

THE PARABLE OF THE TALENTS

In ancient times, a talent was a weight, sometimes used to measure silver. It came to signify a monetary unit or something of great value. The *Bible* offers the Parable of the Talents in Matthew 25:15-40, using the silver variety of talent as a metaphor. It explains the behavior needed to achieve heaven, but it is easy to apply the parable's message to the more intangible kind of talents we possess and how we use them here on earth.

The story starts, "For the kingdom of heaven is as a man traveling into a far country, who called his own servants, and delivered unto them his goods." This traveler entrusts his fortune to his three servants to guard while he is gone. To the first servant he gives five talents (a lot of money); to the second, he gives two; and to the third, the one he trusts least, he gives only one talent. The first two risk the money by investing it. Fortunately, they are successful and able to hand their master double on his return, which makes him very happy: "Well done, good and faithful servant," he tells both of them.

The third servant is so concerned about not losing his master's money that he buries his coin. Thus, when the master returns, the money is safe, but there is still only the single talent. Is the master content? Hardly. He cries, "Thou wicked and slothful servant" and throws the man out. The message is that it's wrong to have talents and not use them. We must invest and multiply them.

An important point of the parable is that everyone is given talents in different amounts. What really matters is not what talents we have, but what we *do* with them. What if the servant with five talents had risked and lost them all? Would the master have been as happy? Would he have forgiven him? We'll never know for sure. What if the first two servants had lost everything, and the master returned to find that his entire remaining wealth consisted only of the single buried talent? Then servant number three would have been the *hero* of the story. Once again, we'll never know for sure. Parables are stories designed to teach, so the intended message is we must *risk* using our talents, win or lose.

No doubt you can think of a few individuals who have experienced great success in life with just a single talent, sometimes even a modest one. They combined this talent with their resources and passions to achieve great things. They took a risk and made it possible.

You, I, and nearly everyone else have a variety of talents—useful ones, important ones, even silly ones like being able to wiggle your ears. Composer Noël Coward wrote a poignant lyric about a singer who laments, "The most I've had is just a talent to amuse." But even so, singing is a wonderful talent and one that makes the world much richer. In fact, Coward chose the phrase as the title for one of his autobiographies. He recognized the importance in his own life of using one's talents.

EXERCISE:

Get out a piece of paper and write a list of the things you are really good at. As you expand your possibility thinking, you may find yourself covering both sides of the sheet; keep going. If it helps, start with the big categories: marketing, managing, designing, abstract thinking, leadership, etc. But don't stop there and don't disparage your talents if you're not at the top of your field. Keep going. Your potential is still there, waiting for you to make connections.

Do you make a great pot of chili? Are you skilled at parallel parking? Balancing your checkbook? Keeping a hula-hoop going? Remembering names? Planning a trip? Making people feel good in stressful situations? Growing things? Fixing things? Recognizing bird calls? What separate skills and natural abilities – what *talents* – go into these activities? How can you combine and connect them to achieve your goals and your ideal life?

When I stand before God at the end of my life, I would hope that I would not have a single bit of talent left, and could say, "I used everything you gave me."

— ERMA BOMBECK

WHAT ARE YOU REALLY BAD AT?

What are you gifted at? The popular wisdom is that we must struggle to improve the areas in which we are weakest – that we should always be pushing our boundaries, no pain-no gain, etc. *Think again!*

Instead, figure out what you are really good at and then go for it! Figure out what you are *really* bad at – separating *real* from *imaginary* – and then figure a way around it. Either eliminate that skill from your job/life description or, more positively, find skilled people or professional services that will fill in the gap and take up the slack. You don't have to do everything perfectly.

Everyone has talents. We choose how we see them, and we choose how we use them. Does great training help to build on those talents and achieve possibilities? Without a doubt. Training is a valuable ingredient in achievement, influencing *what* we can become, but not *who* we can become. In fact, exceptional talent plus exceptional training does not *guarantee* exceptional possibilities. You still need to do exceptional thinking.

Are some people born hardwired to achieve greatness? Well, of course. There are the prodigies of the world, and then there are the rest of us. Fortunately, the rest of us have almost limitless possibilities to choose from. However, some individuals have decided they have been preprogrammed to fail. They wear the label "Born Loser" like a badge of honor. They figure their lot in life has been predetermined, so why fight it?

Here is a great philosophy for possibility living. Your potential will rise to the level of your expectations. I have often wondered how successful underachievers could be if they worked as hard on their expectations as they do on their excuses. Far too often, audience members will approach me after one of my presentations and tell me all the reasons they have for not realizing their possibilities. Many times, their stories are so creative that, if they put their words to music, they'd have a hit country-western song.

My hope is that, after they get home, they'll *think again* about their potential and come up with new possibility-oriented lyrics. In other words, that they'll play their current song backwards. There's an old joke that goes, "What do you get when you play a country-western recording backwards? You get your wife back, you get your truck back, and you get your dog back."

What lies behind us and what lies before us
are small matters to what lies within us.

— RALPH WALDO EMERSON
AMERICAN ESSAYIST AND POET

IT'S CURTAINS

For weeks, my daughter Monica had been rehearsing for the big holiday concert. It was to be a gala evening with several different youth choirs and orchestras performing. The big night finally came, and the audience was full of proud parents. First, there was the junior choir performance, followed by a violin and piano duet, and then an orchestral recital and another choral performance.

Between each segment, the huge velvet curtain glided shut and an announcer would introduce the next group. Monica's turn came at last, and her choir sang beautifully. As any impartial parents would, of course, Kathryn and I were just sure we could hear Monica's voice clearly among all the other voices. The curtain closed, the choir exited the stage, and the next group, a concert band, took their place behind the closed curtain. Their musical selections were introduced, and the audience applauded expectantly.

But the curtain didn't open. It was stuck. Hurried whispers, some rushing about back stage, murmuring parents, and a rustling of young feet behind the thick velvet. A long pause. Still nothing.

Finally, Mrs. Leighton, my daughter's choir teacher, announced that the technician had been sent for, but could not arrive for at least twenty minutes. Making the best of the situation, she called for volunteers to help by holding the curtain up as far as possible, so the concert could continue. Willing parents and tuxedo-clad choir members trooped up on stage and hoisted the heavy velvet, groaning under its weight. Finally, an arched opening was made. We could see *all* of the band members in the exact center of the stage; then the headless bodies of those immediately left and right of center; then just the waists and legs of those further out; then their neighbors from the knees down; and finally, only the shoes of those near the ends of the rows. The unlucky lads and lasses on the extreme outer edges of the rows were invisible. At a signal from the director, the gallant band began to play, its sound slightly muffled by the velvet, as we gazed mostly at their uniformed legs and feet.

Finally, a shout went up backstage. A helpful parent had quietly located a tall ladder, scaled the behind-the-scenes equipment, and somehow figured out how to get the curtain machinery moving again. There was some clanking, the curtain shuddered, and then it slowly separated to reveal the full band, flushed and triumphant.

All the parents agreed that the kids looked fabulous and performed beautifully that evening, but the stars—the ones who got the loudest applause of the night—were Mrs. Leighton and the parents and students who had so gallantly improvised a way for the concert to continue.

Since I am a big fan of felines, I have reworded a popular statement. "There is more than one way to skin someone who does not like cats!"

There is more than one path towards possibilities. The key is to find your own path and keep an eye out for detours. We all have an opportunity to march to the beat of a different drummer. Do you hear possibility playing your song?

THE DEVIL MADE ME SAY IT

Have you ever heard the saying "Talk is cheap"? Think again about that statement. Talk can be very costly.

One afternoon, my wife and I were visiting with a mutual friend when he gave her a wonderful compliment. "Kathryn," he said, "you are like Ruth from the Bible – steadfast, kind, faithful, and loving." I smiled with appreciation, thinking how I had "out-married" myself. My facial expression must have communicated that I hoped he would identify some Biblical figure that I emulated. He got the hint.

"And Roger, *you* are like Boaz: strong, kind, and committed – a man of character."

After we parted, I reminisced about our conversation. I felt so blessed to have a wife like Ruth. Also, *I* was like… what was his name? All I remembered was that it started with a "B."

Several weeks later, Kathryn and I attended a party where we knew only a few people. The topic of conversation turned to the best qualities of our spouses. When my turn came, I said that my wife reminded me of Ruth in the Bible. I explained that a friend had pointed this out to me, and I agreed wholeheartedly. "And did he say anything about you?" someone asked. I smiled modestly; a little embarrassed to admit that my friend had also compared me to a well-respected Biblical figure.

"He said I was like... uhhh..." and I frantically tried to recall the "B" name "...*Beelzebub!*"

My wife blushed and was clearly overwhelmed. Well, when you're married to a person whose character is like that of a Biblical figure, it *is* a bit awe-inspiring.

"Roger," she said quietly, "I don't think you mean that."

"I certainly *do*," I replied confidently. Then I looked around the room. I had not seen expressions like that since the time I told 1,000 people at a national sales meeting to "Enjoy great success this year," but it had come out as "Enjoy great sex this year."

By now, Kathryn was desperate to save me from myself and salvage our reputations. "He means '*Boaz*,'" she hastily announced to the group, a few of whom looked unconvinced. Then, in a fierce whisper to me, she said: "Roger, Beelzebub is the *devil!*"

My wife and I have known each other since we were twelve years old. This shared history is precious to us, filled with wonderful memories. That day we added another memory, one that I will never forget – nor live down. I'm also unlikely to forget the names of Boaz and Beelzebub ever again.

I'll also never forget the saying "The devil is in the details" meaning the details can cause failure. However, when it comes to possibilities, I believe the devil is in the *delay!* Failure to *think again* can lead to procrastination, and we miss an opportunity to succeed. Instead, we need to zip the lip, run like the devil, and race towards possibilities.

THE FUTURE FARMERS
TEACH ME ENGLISH

Kids have a keen "baloney detector." If you ever want to reduce an inflated ego or get a firm reality-check, try talking to them. They'll tune out at the slightest hint of disingenuousness or lack of authenticity.

During the past twenty-five years, I've been privileged to speak before hundreds of high school audiences. It's amazing how your exaggerated self-importance shrinks when you watch them plug in their iPods and listen to their favorite music as you are introduced. Standing before more than a thousand kids in a stuffy gym, with a poor sound system, during the last period of the day, on Friday afternoon, and getting their attention – now, that's really good speaking!

So, there I was, addressing the California Future Farmers of America at the Fresno Convention Center and looking into the faces of 4,000 of the liveliest teenagers I had ever seen. The energy in that crowd reminded me of grade school the day after Halloween, when everyone is on a sugar high.

I loved the enthusiasm of this audience! I matched their energy with mine, and I *hope* they related to my life – maybe not the actual experiences, but the *feelings* we've all had about our experiences. I *willed* those iPods back in their pockets as I made them laugh and, hopefully, *think again*. There were 8,000 eyes following my every move, and when I was through, their applause made the podium vibrate.

After my talk, a young man came on stage and presented me with an FFA sweatshirt. "Mr. Crawford showed us some mad skills today," he told the audience. The students erupted into applause as I smiled and acknowledged the gift. I remember thinking, "*Mad?* Does he mean 'angry' or 'mentally unstable'?" I hoped I hadn't communicated either.

As we walked backstage, I thanked the chairperson and my student hosts for the honor of being part of their conference. Then I risked asking, "What is a 'mad skill'?"

The kids chuckled at my terminal adultness. One explained, "It's what you're good at! Like if you're a good dancer, singer, mathematician, or athlete–it's your 'mad skill.' Mr. Crawford, you *kill* (impress) as a speaker, and you are *down with* (good at) tennis. You've got *mad* skills!"

I may not have spoken the language of these kids, but hopefully I had come across as someone they could relate to–a real person with struggles who could teach them something. And I learned from them that if you build your *downness*, you'll *kill* yourself with your own *mad* possibilities. Your potential is determined by discovering your "mad skills."

Language is the dress of thought.

— SAMUEL JOHNSON
  CONSIDERED THE FINEST CRITIC
  OF ENGLISH LITERATURE

EAGLES AND SLOTHS

I have no doubt you've had conversations like this. Our family was enjoying dinner together one night, and the question was posed, "What animal are you most like? What characteristics do you possess that suggest this animal?" We decided that we'd each state our choice, and then the others would debate how on-target we were.

The kids were intrigued and enthusiastically volunteered their wild kingdom identities. Christopher told us that he would be a bat. When he saw our puzzlement, he explained that bats are stealthy, agile, and have unseen abilities like supersonic hearing. Monica preferred a cat because they are graceful and you must earn their respect. Alexa's choice was a giraffe because she is tall and likes looking over the crowd.

Then it was my turn. Without hesitation, I blurted out that I was a sloth.

"A what?" everyone exclaimed.

"A three-toed sloth," I said. They looked bewildered.

I explained that since my foot was narrow and had only three toes, it resembled the foot of a sloth with its three claws. When I was a child, we had been studying pictures of animals in school. The teacher showed a photo of a sloth, and some of the kids started saying that I had a sloth foot. The less-than-flattering nickname stuck: "Super Sloth."

"Roger," my somewhat biased wife objected, "I disagree. Your physical challenge reminds *me* of an animal that you often emulate – an *eagle!* An eagle has three talons. You're strong and determined, and when you grab hold of something, you never let go."

It must be obvious by now that I firmly believe the greatest results can come out of working around a deficiency. Always remember that Michelangelo carved his masterpiece "David" from a block of marble that no other sculptor wanted. Even with all your weaknesses and defects, you still have the potential to be a masterpiece yourself.

EXERCISE:

Make a list of things that you believe are unique about you – useful things, admirable things, and irrelevant and silly things. Use your possibility thinking to fill a sheet of paper; keep going. Are you beginning to see how unique you are? No one else on earth has the same combination of abilities and experiences.

What talents do you already possess that make you great? What kinds of possibilities are within your reach now, and how can you obtain them? No one can do everything superbly, but all of us can do some things better than anyone else. What is *your* combination of abilities, limitations, enthusiasms, accomplishments, experiences, and aspirations that makes you unique? The truth is there has never been anyone exactly like you, and there never will be again. Even if you have an identical twin, just the things you've done and thought give you a unique take on the world around you.

Yes, you are an exciting tangle of incredible strengths and weaknesses, brilliance and blind spots. Opportunities open up when you leverage these wildly different components into a powerful whole. What tapestry of possibilities will your life create?

OUR DEEPEST FEAR

"Our deepest fear is not that we are inadequate. Our deepest fear is that we are powerful beyond measure. It is our light, not our darkness that most frightens us. We ask ourselves, Who am I to be brilliant, gorgeous, talented, fabulous? Actually, who are you not to be? You are a child of God. Your playing small does not serve the world. There is nothing enlightened about shrinking so that other people won't feel insecure around you. We are all meant to shine, as children do. We were born to make manifest the glory of God that is within us. It's not just in some of us; it's in everyone. And as we let our own light shine, we unconsciously give other people permission to do the same. As we are liberated from our own fear, our presence automatically liberates others."

— MARIANNE WILLIAMSON
AUTHOR

SISTERS CUTTING THE MUSTARD

Here I was in Portland, Oregon, seated at a banquet table prior to my speech. As the wait staff served the salads, I noticed something unusual. Instead of using the provided dressing, the audience members were opening jars sitting on their tables and slathering a yellow sauce over their greens. They also were putting a dollop on their plate and dipping their bread in it. As I watched my table mates ooh and ah over this obvious delight, I had to ask my seatmate what it was.

"Monastery Mustard," he replied. "It's the best in the world." He suggested I speak with Sister Terrie who had provided the samples for the group. As I approached her, she extended her arms in an enthusiastic embrace and said, "I am praying for you."

Taking this as a blessing rather than a warning, I asked her to tell me about Monastery Mustard. Her face lit up as she told me the history. Ten years earlier, the Benedictine Sisters of Mt. Angel had been facing two challenges. For eight decades, the Sisters had operated Mt. Angel Academy, Mt. Angel College, and other schools in the Willamette Valley. They also founded the nationally recognized Benedictine Nursing Center.

But now their retirement fund was not sufficient to support the more than 40 sisters in the Queen of Angels Monastery. In addition, they ran St. Joseph's Shelter which provided housing for homeless families and individuals. They dis cussed the traditional ways to raise money, the raffle ticket and bake-sale avenue, but they wanted to find something different and more effective. "Let's *think again*," they said.

One of their lay volunteers said, "I have this amazing mustard recipe passed down through my family. You could make it and sell it." The sisters thought it over and decided this had possibilities. They gathered the ingredients, experimented, and decided to give it a try. Between 4:00 and 5:30 AM each morning, a dozen sisters would prepare the day's supply, finishing just in time for morning prayers. At midmorning, another team of nuns would package the mustard in glass jars. The final inspection was done by the Mother Superior who blessed each jar as she sealed it.

The nuns began distributing their delicious mustard at farmers' markets throughout the Portland area. It was there that they met the Three Amigos, three teenaged boys who roasted Jalapeño peppers and sold them at the markets. The nuns noticed that customers were buying both products, dipping the peppers in the mustard. The sisters tried blending the peppers into their mustard, and, hallelujah–Hallelujah Jalapeño Mustard was born.

Other new flavors followed. The mustard is now offered in seven flavors including Glorious Garlic, Angelic Honey Garlic, Heavenly Honey, Devoutly Dill, Jubilant Blueberry, and Divinely Original. Their label shows a 1912 picture of the Monastery and a sister in the habit of their order. Because none of the actual sisters are depicted, they have named her Sister Generica.

Word began to spread beyond Oregon, and soon Monastery Mustard developed a national following. Specialty food stores started placing orders, and business boomed. A devoted fan nominated the mustard for the Mustard Hall of Fame. Monastery Mustard was inducted in 2003. Today, Monastery Mustard is distributed worldwide. But it is still made the same way, right before morning prayers, and is still sealed with a blessing.

I left the meeting hoping that I would see Sister Terrie again and that my wife could get the mustard stain out of my tie!

I tell you the truth, if you have faith as small as a mustard seed, you can say to this mountain, "Move from here to there" and it will move.

— JESUS CHRIST

WHAT'S BEHIND A NAME?

In 2006, Gary Johnson needed a new name for the business systems company he had just bought. He'd worked for this company as a salesman since 1990 and now wanted the name to reflect the new direction he planned to take. He had a dynamic organization that was experiencing tremendous growth in the copying, printing, and imaging business. He came up with a doozy.

"How did you come up with such a great name," I asked, "when the names of your competitors lack your creativity and are easily forgotten?" I assumed he'd say what I've heard numerous times: "Our advertising company chose it."

Instead, Gary said, "I was looking for something relevant to our industry, something that would be remembered for its uniqueness. One day I was walking around my office, thinking, when I focused on one of our products, a copy machine. When I saw the button labeled 'Zoom,' I had it!"

That's how Zoom Imaging Solutions got its name.

Nike, Rolex, and Starbucks are company names you recognize. Like Zoom Imaging Solutions, they were not named after a person. Disney, Ford, and Hewlett Packard are companies that carry the founder's name. Mental images appear when you think of these recognized companies.

Here's a question that is sure to conger up some interesting mental images. What would be the possibilities if you combined the rugged sport of football with women's under-garments? Could you "slip" by your defender? Have spaghetti strap shoulder pads? Wear a jersey that looked like a bustier? (And would former New York Jets quarterback, Joe Namath model it on TV?) But before you start making plans to watch the Chicago "Bares" in the Lingerie Bowl, *think again!*

Bennie Russell was an Alabama University football player in 1926. Practice after practice in the sweltering heat of the South, he and his teammates would sweat and chafe profusely while they wore the regulation wool jerseys. To say the least, this was an uncomfortable problem to have, but Bennie saw possibilities.

His father, Ben, owned Russell Manufacturing located in the small Alabama town of Alexander City. Their core business was manufacturing ladies undergarments. Benny watched his father making women's long johns and he saw a possibility. What if his dad made the teams' jerseys out of the thick, absorbent cotton used in the long johns? It would be cooler, more comfortable, and of course lighter weight.

Since the purpose of this product revolved around sweat, a mill worker came up with a name that has become an American icon...the sweatshirt. The company who originated the sweatshirt is now called Russell Athletic. So the next time you're relaxing in your favorite sweatshirt, thank a possibility thinker named Bennie Russell. The Einstein of sweat!

So many people say, "Oh, I could never be creative like that. If only I were smarter, better, more competent..." As kids, they came up with a hundred new ideas and solutions every hour, but somehow they lost touch with that inquiring, imaginative spirit. That spirit is your creativity. Bring it out of hiding.

Think like a child. Literally get down on all fours or up on a chair to consider a spatial problem. Turn things upside down and inside out, mentally and physically, to expand options. Imagine things happening backwards. Be silly if need be. It's amazing the solutions you can come up with.

Think "outside the box." This expression grew out of a connect-the-dots problem that can be solved only by extending the joining lines outside the grid of dots. Reconsider the "rules." Are they limiting your possible options? Can you rewrite them? Reverse them? Get around them?

Think again. What is the actual problem? Negotiators often find that people in conflict spend their time disagreeing about the specific route to their goal, when, in fact, a very different route to the same goal is available and mutually agreeable. Clarify the results you want, and then try redefining the steps necessary to achieve them.

What was the founder of a company thinking about when she started her business making chocolate-covered strawberries? Probably about customers like me who love chocolate and love strawberries.

I'll never forget the day refreshments were served prior to one of my speeches, and someone handed me a chocolate-covered strawberry that I eagerly accepted. It was challenging for me to hang on to the little green stem, and, as I bit into it, the berry exploded and dropped onto my shirt. Splat! The stain looked as if I had been shot on the way to the podium But there was no time to clean up or change. I was on.

My opening line of explanation was, "I got hit by a drive-by berry." It got a good laugh and motivated an audience member to introduce me to Shari Fitzpatrick, founder of Shari's Berries, maker of the irresistible confections.

Shari also loves chocolate and berries. When she was a banker, she used to make up homemade gift baskets of her dipped berries for her mortgage business customers. Her tactic worked. People remembered her, and they remembered her berry baskets.

Shari thought, "Wouldn't it be wonderful if I could market my gift baskets?" But, of course, people told her it would be impossible. Berries are seasonal and perishable, even covered in gourmet chocolate. Shari loves problem-solving almost as much as cooking. With a chorus of people telling her it was impossible, she did her homework and devised a way.

Shari opened her first store in Sacramento, California in 1989. She soon acquired three more nearby locations. Then she worked with packaging engineers to develop a foolproof method of shipping. When we met in 2005, Shari's Berries was dipping two million berries in more than sixty tons of toppings a year and shipping them throughout the world.

"How did you do it?" I had to ask.

Her smiling response was, "Just see possibilities before they become obvious to everyone else."

That's one of the powers of passion. Your passions open you to options and opportunities that no one else has spotted, yet.

We can't solve problems by using the same kind of thinking we used when we created them.

— ALBERT EINSTEIN
PHYSICIST

ASK, CONNECT, PERSIST

There are three basic techniques that amplify our potential:

- Asking questions no one else has asked

- Making connections no one else has made

- Overcoming "impossible" obstacles

Asking questions no one else has asked: The right question can be more important than the right answer because it opens up all kinds of possibilities. Helen Keller's teacher, Anne Sullivan, changed the life of her blind and deaf student by changing the question. Others were asking, "What can we do with Helen?" Sullivan asked, "What can I do *for* Helen?" Sullivan's answer was to introduce the child to language, first by spelling words into her hand and then through reading Braille. Helen Keller went on to speak, graduate with honors from Radcliffe College, master several languages besides English, and write eloquent books and articles. Her many friends included kings, presidents, and Mark Twain. She changed forever the public image of physically-challenged people. Yet, she might have remained mute and uneducated if Anne hadn't asked the right question.

Making connections: In the 1988 film *Working Girl*, Melanie Griffith plays a secretary who puts together a multimillion dollar deal in her boss's absence. The boss returns and claims credit for the innovative concept. However, Griffith ultimately triumphs, demonstrating how she came up with the idea by melding a society page item with a clipping from the business section and a knowledge of current trade law. And, to clinch her claim to connection-making possibility thinking, she saves the huge merger from disaster at the last minute by pointing out a gossip column item in the morning paper. Historian James Burke has produced several lively PBS TV series about people who have connected apparently unrelated ideas to come up with world-changing devices and strategies – most of the wonders of the modern world. His title? *Connections.*

Overcoming "impossible" obstacles: In 1997, David Baldacci was just like thousands of other rather anonymous Washington, D.C. lawyers. Then, overnight, he became a best-selling author. His book *Absolute Power* got the highest advance ever for a first novel, and within days he had sold the movie rights for $1 million. The next year, *People* magazine proclaimed Baldacci one of the fifty sexiest people in the world.

David wrote his novel while working full-time as an associate at a Washington law firm and with a new baby at home. Few knew about his spare-time activity. But this *wasn't* his first novel. He had had numerous almost-deals in the past. His "instant" success took years of rejections and tantalizing near-breakthroughs. He knew people, had connections, but couldn't quite get things sold. He must have had close friends telling him, "Concentrate on your legal career" – "What about your new baby and family?" – "You've come so close over and over, it's obvious this isn't going to work!"

At a book signing, he told me that being a writer is like a "war of attrition" – a constant battle against the slow abrasion of discouragement and the exhausting demands of everyday life. "There are hundreds of other people who have the potential and could do the same thing, but most of them just can't keep slogging at it after work, day after day, and they drop out." Baldacci didn't. He did the impossible by never giving in to discouragement or the demands of life.

Never give in. Never give in. Never, never, never, never – in nothing, great or small, large or petty--never give in, except to convictions of honor and good sense.

— WINSTON CHURCHILL
PRIME MINISTER OF BRITAIN

SIX DEGREES OF SEPARATION

"It's not what you know, it's *who* you know" – and what *they* know. With about five billion people on the planet, that's a lot of possibilities. Someone came up with the idea of "six degrees of separation," suggesting that everyone on earth can now connect with any other specific individual in a meaningful way through a maximum of up to six varied relationships. For example, your brother has a French client, who went to school with a Brazilian, whose uncle is an archeologist, who knows the inhabitants of a remote Mongolian village. Thus, you have a way to secure an introduction to someone in that village and obtain some information or support you may want. Actually, I think six is an exaggeration. Often, such a connection can be done with three.

For example, Tony Thornton is the editor of eight magazines in Cumbria, England. He wanted to publish an interesting article about the early twentieth-century American composer Harry Woods ("Try a Little Tenderness," "When the Moon Comes Over the Mountain") – but he had no illustrations. He e-mailed one of his American contributors, Eleanor Knowles in San Francisco. She replied that, though she'd never heard of the composer, she did know a man who was very knowledgeable about American popular music. She phoned Bob Grimes who has nearly 80,000 pieces of late nineteenth-/early twentieth-century sheet music, an extensive library of reference books, and a reputation for total recall of everything in his collection.

And did he have a photo of Harry Woods?

"No," replied Grimes thoughtfully. "...I've never seen a photograph of him. Would an *engraved portrait* do?"

Within an hour, that engraved portrait and several beautifully-designed sheet music covers for songs composed by Woods had been scanned and e-mailed directly to England. This "connection" allowed Tony Thornton to illustrate his article lavishly and go to press the next morning.

Don't dismiss your ability to find the information and support you need to pursue your possibilities. An amazing number of people are willing, and even eager, to help others who share their interests and passions. There are five billion potential possibility partners out there, and many are just a few degrees of separation away.

There is nothing on this earth more to
be prized than true friendship.

— SAINT THOMAS AQUINAS

144

4 MULTIPLY YOUR POSSIBILITIES

Who will help you?

WHAT IS A POSSIBILITY PARTNER?

Even the Lone Ranger was not alone. I find it fascinating that an American icon who was revered for courage and justice found strength in partnership. The name "Lone Ranger" suggests a solitary existence. However, his partner, Tonto, was an integral part of his success. We all need to have Tontos and *be* Tontos. We all need *possibility partners*.

I love the Japanese proverb, "No one of us is as smart as all of us." Isn't that true? No single person knows everything. We need others to accelerate our learning curve so that we can rise above our current level of performance. Many successful people I've met tell me they have achieved what they previously thought was impossible by finding, developing, or creating possibility partners. These advisers allow them to access new wisdom, new perspectives, and new *possibilities*.

Peak performers quickly acknowledge that their own thinking may not be enough. If we are to excel, we need others to exchange ideas with, people who encourage our vision, excite our thinking, challenge us, and equip us with tools. These wonderful people can provide much needed support and encouragement as we strive to achieve our purpose.

Encouragers can inspire us to act boldly in spite of our circumstances. They remind us that setbacks are temporary and future possibilities are within our grasp. They provide reality checks without destroying dreams.

Who are these encouragers, these possibility partners? They are all around us. A possibility partner doesn't have to be a CEO, a celebrity, or a person of great power or wealth. They very likely can be someone who others regard as "ordinary" and therefore over-looked. Potential possibility partners could be:

- Friends and family

- Someone we work with

- Someone who does what we do (for fun or for a living)

- Someone whose interests interconnect in some way with our own

- Teachers

- Role models

- Mentors

- Mentorees

- Experts

- Acquaintances

- Anyone we regularly interact with (bus drivers, store clerks, delivery people)

- Friends of friends

- Total strangers

Possibility partners encourage and guide us in achieving our goals. They try to expand our options by helping us look beyond our current vision. Goals can be calculated and unemotional, but dreaming about them isn't, and it's the dreaming that fuels our possibilities. It is invaluable to have others kindle this passion by encouraging us to see what could be. My own life changed the day I *finally* realized a principle was absolutely true that someone had reminded me of: we can all learn something from everyone!

So, what can possibility partners do for you? Well, they have the potential to:

- Guide you through difficulties.

- Provide encouragement when discouragement sets in.

- Help define and redefine purpose, potential, and possibilities.

- Keep you focused on what's important.

- Motivate you to face anxiety and break through self-imposed barriers.

- Create synergy that will accelerate growth.

- Add new thoughts and new resources.

How do you cultivate "possibility partners"? Here are some guidelines that have proven useful in my life when I needed encouragement.

> *Go where your partner might be.* Fish rarely jump in the boat. It takes some planning and research. Some possibility partners *do* appear serendipitously, but don't count on it. Be proactive. Establish a deliberate course of action to find a suitable partner. Be sure to look for a person who exemplifies your own values.

> *Seek guidance instead of answers.* Possibility partners can offer a different perspective and offer encouragement, walking alongside you. Consider the example of the Sherpa guides who assist visiting mountain climbers on Mt. Everest. They provide direction, tactics, motivation, and, if necessary, oxygen. However, ultimately it is up to the climber to reach the pinnacle. We all need a possibility Sherpa!

> *Be clear.* Identify your challenges and future desires for your potential possibility partner. Most likely, he or she is busy. Be clear about who you are and where you want to be. It gives the relationship a head start.

> *Think win/win.* The most powerful possibility partner relationship is one where *both* develop talents and awareness. Both should benefit from this relationship. To paraphrase President John F. Kennedy, "Don't just ask what they can do for you; ask also what you can do for them."

Of course, some common sense and knowledge of human nature should be used in the selection process. Occasionally, a potential partner will not take the relationship seriously and instead use it as an opportunity to play a practical joke! I recall someone starting out in the speaking business asked the advice of a more experienced speaker (a humorist). He was told he would grab the attention of meeting planners if he bleeped some words in the opening minute of his demo tape, making it appear that he used profanity in his presentations! Ironically, this created unexpected possibilities. He did not enjoy much success as a speaker; however, he became a wildly-successful rap star!

Possibility partners usually fall into three general categories, each useful for multiplying your effectiveness and securing the information and support you need to achieve your possibilities.

Mentors: Those who will support, inspire, and guide you, sharing their expertise. These people can be colleagues, superiors, *and* subordinates.

Mentorees: Those *you* can support, inspire, and guide, sharing your own expertise. You mentor others while learning from them in return.

Subcontractors: Those who will do the parts of the job you can't do or can't do well. This frees you up to do what you do best.

We're going to explore all three categories in this chapter. You are probably already familiar with mentoring and being mentored, a highly rewarding two-way street. There's a saying, "Good teachers learn from their students." When I go to speak to a group, sharing my "wisdom" with them, I nearly always come away with new insights and understanding. What an education I'm getting!

Sharing life experiences allows others to learn from mistakes, without making them, and to evaluate actions, without taking them. A Tonto helps others see possibilities and multiply possibilities that were previously invisible.

If one advances confidently in the direction of his dreams, and endeavors to live the life which he imagined, he will meet with a success unexpected in common hours. He will pass an invincible boundary; new, universal, and more liberal laws will begin to establish themselves around and within him...and he will live with the license of a higher order of beings.

— HENRY DAVID THOREAU

FAMILY AND FRIENDS: A RUNNING START

Do you remember the first day you rode a bike without training wheels? A friend or family member was most likely there to assist and encourage. They were hanging on to you, and you were hanging on to the bike, and something wonderful was happening. Your mind probably raced with different possibilities. If you're like me, the potential outcomes ranged from popping a wheelie that would be the envy of all the kids to taking a header and having an asphalt sandwich for lunch. At the same time you were learning a valuable lesson about depending on others, you were also experiencing an incredible sense of freedom.

Who doesn't remember the thrill of pedaling a bike for the first time, all by themselves? Remember the scene in the movie *E.T.* where the kids are trying to rescue the alien, and as they are being pursued, their bikes leave the ground and fly through the air? That's how it felt when I was able to ride my bike for the first time. If we are going to multiply our possibilities, we need the people closest to us to "hang on," "cheer us on," and let us soar with a new-found freedom.

Childhood memories, in addition to reminding us of the importance of persistence (and how we can learn from our skinned knees), also remind us of how important emotional and physical support is from others. People closest to you when you were young can become possibility partners. That vital support from family and friends is still available to us as adults; it's often just as important to us now, as we try new things and work through new and exciting challenges. Sharing childhood memories with your possibility partner can also be a lot of fun, so seek out those closest to you!

Our families are a remarkable resource – one that we can all draw on. And here's the really intriguing thing. Not everyone comes from a great family. If you grew up in a negative one, or even had no family at all, it is *still* a resource. Here's why.

Psychologists have long noted that people can have a very negative experience and still retain a positive self-image and outlook for the future. They call this "framing." Two people may have an identical experience but interpret it very differently, drawing diverse conclusions. One "frames" it positively, the other negatively. Thus, a child who has had very poor parenting could decide, "Obviously, I am worthless and undeserving of love," or "People hurt me and cannot be trusted." Alternatively, that child could use positive framing and decide, "My parents were deeply flawed people who taught me what *not* to do in life. Because of them, I am a stronger, more compassionate, resilient person."

A British researcher, David B.P. Sims, analyzed the autobiographies of five successful industrial managers to see if he could identify any common childhood experiences. His unexpected finding was that these five managers had very different backgrounds and shared only one characteristic: all had chosen careers in areas that had little relation to the cultures they had grown up in. Each believed that it was this *discrepancy* that increased his awareness of, and sensitivity to, the lessons learned as a child. All agreed that their early experiences, so different from their later lives, had prepared them for the company, industry, or culture in which they became successful.

I have heard numerous stories that fall into a similar pattern. Two male siblings grew up in the same household but had completely different adult experiences. Their parents were unethical, unloving, and unreliable.

One brother follows the exact path his parents had modeled. Falling short of his potential, he is unsuccessful both personally and professionally. His life is one problem after another.

The other brother uses positive framing and decides *not* to model after his parents. He excels both socially and academically. He lives a life of success and significance, enjoying a loving home life. His life is filled with one possibility after another.

When these two siblings were asked why their lives turned out this way, ironically they gave the same answer. "How could I be any different with parents like mine?"

How your life turns out is not the result of the family you were born into or the experiences you shared. It's what you *learn* from your family that determines whether or not you'll be open to opportunities to multiply your possibilities.

A successful man is one who can lay a firm foundation with the bricks others have thrown at him.

— DAVID BRINKLEY
AMERICAN TV NEWSCASTER

WATT'S UP?

If you doubt the power of possibility, consider what turning on the lights can do.

Let me start by saying that I am a die-hard Cleveland sports fan. If you don't follow professional sports, you wouldn't know that Cleveland has not had a world championship in any sport since 1960. Nevertheless, their stadiums sell out, and their citizens still believe the team will win. I grew up there and have had the privilege of sitting in the "dog pound" at the stadium during a Cleveland Browns game. Let me set the scene: fans drinking beer, temperature below zero, and everyone donning dog masks and yelping for their beloved Browns. It was culture shock to attend a San Francisco 49ers game where no one barked and, instead of beer and brats, there was chardonnay and paté.

Cleveland is a city that has recently realized its possibilities and now enjoys a renaissance some thought impossible. For years, this city suffered the fate of others in the "rust belt." Many factories shut down. Dilapidated buildings and antiquated infrastructure caused a population shift to the suburbs. The city became a ghost town after 5 PM.

Today, Cleveland is thriving again, with new construction and a bustling downtown. It has been transformed from the "mistake" on the lake to "magnificence" on the lake. How did this happen?

On one of my trips there, I had the privilege of speaking before the Cleveland Rotary Club. When I saw the brand-new warehouse district, baseball stadium, football stadium, sparkling hotels, and the Rock-and-Roll Hall of Fame, I was astounded! I assumed this had all been a masterful plan executed by an expert in city revitalization.

Remarkably, when I asked how this amazing turnaround had been engineered, everyone gave the same answer: "They turned on the lights."

"What lights?" I asked.

"Terminal Tower," they said.

The Terminal Tower building is the *grande dame* of the Cleveland skyline. During the decline of the city, the lights were dimmed at night and eventually turned off. What had once been a beacon of activity now communicated the message that no one was home. The Cleveland Rotarians shared with me that, once the lights were turned on again, everyone's attitude changed dramatically. People were intrigued. What was happening in the city? They wanted to go see. Of course, there were plans for renewal that followed, but if you ask anyone in Cleveland what the *tipping point* was, most would say, "When they lit up the Tower."

Symbols have enormous power. Seeing the Tower lit up made people begin to *think again* that renewal and change were possible. This intriguing sense of possibility motivated many to come together to achieve the "impossible." Possibilities are the foundation of motivation because they give us the reason to act!

We all have periods in our lives when our possibilities need a little revitalization. How do we accomplish this and in turn create more possibilities? Resist getting bogged down in the problems and instead dwell on the possibilities. In other words, focus on the "light" instead of the dark.

A friend of mine recently retired after 40 years as a classroom teacher. I asked him what kept the spark alive to inspire possibilities for himself and others. His answer was simply, "I was a first year teacher 40 times!" Now that's an example of someone who "flipped the switch" on his possibilities.

As a mentor, your job is to *turn on the lights*. Showing you believe in possibilities changes attitudes and helps those possibilities happen. Go ahead and "light up" a life!

For any of us to be truly free-if we are to learn to soar in this changing world-we must first be willing to be responsible for our lives. We can learn to soar only in direct proportion to our determination to rise above the doubts and transcend the limitations. We cannot become what we need to be by remaining what we are.

— MAX DePREE
AUTHOR ON LEADERSHIP

BANK ON YOUR POSSIBILITIES

Did you know there's a prize for lending money? Well, not exactly, but Bangladesh economist Muhammad Yunus won the 2006 Nobel Peace Prize for his pioneering work in making small loans to millions of poor people. "He proved the impossible: that the poor were bankable," says Jonathan J. Morduch, an economics professor at New York University. Yunus' loans have been given to destitute widows and abandoned wives, landless laborers and rickshaw drivers, sweepers and beggars.

The Nobel Committee praised Mr. Yunus and the Grameen Bank for making *microcredit*, as the loans are called, a practical solution to combating rural poverty in Bangladesh and for inspiring similar ventures across the developing world. When the committee announced the prize, they stated, "Microcredit has proven to be an important liberating force in societies where women, in particular, have to struggle against repressive social and economic conditions."

Mr. Yunus is a long-time champion of the idea that even the most impoverished people have the drive and creativity to build small businesses if they can get the resources—sometimes a loan as small as $12. The borrowers use the money to buy milk-giving cows, or bamboo to craft stools, or yarn to weave into stoles, or incense to sell in stalls—all modest money-making ideas by American standards, but life-changing for the entrepreneurs.

In 1976, Yunus was teaching "elegant theories of economics" at Chittagong University when he reached into his own pocket to make his first loan of $27 to 42 villagers living nearby. The borrowers had no collateral and signed nothing, but they invested the money and repaid him in full. "If you can make so many people that happy with such a small amount of money, why shouldn't you do more of it?" he said.

Yunus' new model of banking for the poor had several unusual features. For example, the Grameen Bank lent only to groups of five people. Thus, peer pressure helped to make sure that each member repaid his or her share. The bank also required borrowers to repay their loans in manageable weekly installments. The average loan from Grameen Bank was $130.

While microcredit loans are hardly a total cure for the misery and hardship of poverty, the Nobel committee noted that "Yunus' long-term vision is to eliminate poverty in the world. That vision cannot be realized by means of microcredit alone. But Muhammad Yunus and Grameen Bank have shown that, in the continuing effort to achieve a cure, microcredit must play a major part." Since Yunus' first loan, microcredit has become one of the most popular antipoverty strategies in the world. According to Microcredit Summit, a nonprofit advocacy group based in Washington. D.C. that Yunus helped found, last year more than 100 million people received small loans from more than 3,100 institutions in 130 countries.

Muhammad Yunus is a mentor on a world scale, starting with a seemingly "impossible dream," and making it come true for millions of people. It is so easy to assume that huge, complex problems require huge, complex solutions. It is exciting when one person comes along with a simple, workable plan that achieves so much.

Possibility thinkers have the potential to not only impact their own life, as Muhammad Yunus demonstrates, but radically change millions of lives. His unwavering belief in others' potential, despite difficult circumstances, proves an important principal for possibility living. Your possibilities are not determined by where you come from; your possibilities are realized by knowing where were *going*. Mr. Yunus provided the resources and road map that led to possibility opportunities; the people added what multiplies possibilities... resiliency. Your investment in possibilities now can also put you on the road to unlimited opportunities in the future.

The highest use of capital is not to make more money, but to make money to do more for the betterment of life.

— HENRY FORD

STANDING TALLER

Sometimes we inspire and motivate others by sharing what we have experienced. Other times, we share what we haven't experienced. Andre Agassi, a child tennis prodigy, left school in the eighth grade to go on the pro tour. He later completed his education through correspondence courses. When Andre decided to give back to his hometown of West Las Vegas, Nevada, a school seemed the logical thing to him.

A labor of love, the Andre Agassi College Preparatory Academy opened in 2001 for 3rd to 5th grades, which are considered the most pivotal period for the future academic success of a child. Students pay no tuition and are selected by lottery. Many are what are considered "at risk" kids. Each year, another grade is added, advancing the initial students, until the school has a full twelve-year program. Agassi guarantees each graduate a college education.

By its sixth school year, the $4.4 million charter school offered kindergarten through 10th grade, with an enrollment of 530 in classes no larger than twenty-five students. "You wouldn't believe how much has changed there," Agassi says. "There's so much pride. They're getting rid of the graffiti. The respect for the community has grown so much. We've driven in the point that the way to reach a child is through education. But these kids aren't going there simply to stay in school. They're going there because a lot of people are expecting a lot out of them."

Agassi himself pays all the fund-raising expenses of the Andre Agassi Charitable Foundation so that donations – reportedly more than $14 million since 1995 – go entirely to the school. But his support is not strictly monetary. He also drops by the school twenty-five to thirty times a year, often unannounced. However, he is not into self-publicity. If Agassi had his choice, he'd take his name off the building. "But he realizes the importance of it for funding the school in perpetuity," says Roy Parker, principal for the elementary and middle schools. "If he had his druthers, it would just be a charter school. This is a selfless undertaking for him…it is his devotion."

"It's about getting fifty kids off to college each year," says Board of Trustees member Bill Hornbuckle, "and keeping it going. It's a massive project, a massive responsibility. It's a great burden. You can't walk away from it. It's far more intricate and emotional. It is forever."

Parents, teachers, and students all sign a "commitment to excellence" contract. Elementary school parents must promise to read daily to their children. All parents must commit to volunteering twelve hours every year at the school. And each child must memorize and recite the school's code of conduct, which is posted inside the front door:

- The essence of good discipline is respect,

- Respect for authority and respect for others,

- Respect for self and respect for rules.

It is an attitude which begins at home, is reinforced at school and then applied throughout life.

"People are going to know who you *are* here," Principal Parker says. No anonymous dropouts here. These kids are going to *be* somebody.

And Andre Agassi explains what this mentoring has meant to him: "Every year, you see these children...all of a sudden, they're ninth graders. You think, 'You were third graders. Look at you. You're standing taller than I am, speaking better than I speak, having more of a plan for your life than I have for mine.' The kids are the best part of this."

When I read the Academy code of conduct, it revealed an important principal of multiplying possibilities. Respecting ourselves increases our expectations for our future. Self-respect is seeing your value and worth. When you don't respect yourself, you live life as a victim of circumstances rather than a creator of opportunities. Embrace this attitude and you, like those in Andre's school, can overcome circumstances that lead to a victorious life!

WHAT A SINGING PIG TAUGHT ME

Anyone who has achieved multiplied possibilities has had colossal flops! Has anyone ever told you that when you make a mistake, put it behind you? Here's what I've learned: put mistakes in front of you and learn everything you can from the experience!

You may have heard of Pat Williams from his days as General Manager of the NBA Philadelphia 76ers and the Orlando Magic. He gained the reputation as a creative genius in promoting his basketball teams, changing the way others think about possibilities. But not every idea paid off the way he hoped it would.

One memorable event was called the Blind Date Night. Male participants were given odd numbered seats while females were given even numbered seats next to the men, creating a blind date for the couples sitting next to each other. The men thought this was great. Fifty-six of them turned out, but only four women showed up. Not a success.

Pat also tried a promotion where fans were challenged to grapple with Victor the Wrestling Bear between the games of a rare doubleheader. Participants' enthusiasm quickly waned when it was discovered that the bear was both toothless and declawed. Not a success.

Then Pat invited Chick the Singing Pig to perform at a game. The swine waddled out to center court, managed an off-key oink, and relieved himself on the floor. The fans would not let this one pass without making their disapproval known. The following day the newspaper read, "Knicks Whip 76ers – Pig Booed." Definitely not a success.

But Pat Williams is a true possibility thinker. Even after such missteps, he persevered and became one of the most respected innovators in professional sports.

Consider this thought: I want you to fail your way to achievement. Now, that may sound contrary to popular motivational advice, but I believe that failure – big, embarrassing fall-on-your-face blunders and bloopers – is invaluable for your future. The experience of failing, failing again, and finally succeeding is the foundation for maximum achievement. If you ask objective self-observers, you will find they have *failed* their way to success. I remember our tennis coach advising, "Fail and fail fast." In other words, identify what does not work, grow from it, and move forward.

John Maxwell honored me by featuring me his book *Failing Forward*. What a great word picture that title is. Every time you fail, you move closer to your objective. Every defeat is providing you valuable information about your action and attitude. With that data, you can reevaluate, reenergize, and recommit to your possibilities.

If you want to experience a power surge of motivation, here is a thought: Remove the word "failure" from your vocabulary. Replace it with "setback," "learning experience," or "trial run." Watch how your energy expands and your enthusiasm explodes when you use these phrases. You erase anxiety and replace it with the anticipation of future possibilities.

INSPIRING CONFIDENCE: TWO HANDS WORKING

What if you had a workforce where over sixty percent of your employees had disabilities and many had never held jobs before? Could you compete with other businesses? If you said, "No way," *think again*. Just ask Michael Ziegler and a group of parents who once had a powerful vision.

Pride Industries is an organization built on identifying possibilities. It began in 1966 when a group of parents gathered in the basement of St. Luke's Church in Auburn, California, to brainstorm what they could do to create better lives and opportunities for their physically or mentally-challenged children. If anyone had predicted their efforts would result in an organization that is now the world's largest employer of people with disabilities, many would have said, "That's impossible."

Today, Pride Industries is a $100 million business spread across eleven states that employs more than 4,300 people, 2,700 of whom have some type of "handicap." Pride is led by a remarkable leader, Michael Ziegler, who became CEO in 1983 when the organization had 65 employees and $250,000 in annual sales. Mike is the most passionate individual I have ever met. He has an entrepreneurial vision and, most important, he wants to create new possibilities for people with disabilities. He is a "hug-a-minute" kind of guy with an unforgettable and all-encompassing embrace. When I spoke for his organization,

I said, "You've heard of a bear hug. Well, Mike gives you a grizzly bear hug, but one with a positive attitude."

Pride Industries is now a thriving, self-sufficient company. It has a clear mission statement: Provide jobs for people with disabilities. Mike says he is so proud that everyone gets a paycheck and that many employees have gone from receiving taxpayers' assistance to being taxpayers.

One of the most memorable experiences of my life was when Mike took me on a tour of his company. Most people would have regarded many of the individuals I saw as unemployable. Yet, there they were, contributing to the success of this company. When they saw Mike, they got in line for a hug and a word of encouragement. What struck me was that Mike knew their names and something about each of them.

There are four core lines of business at Pride Industries: facility support services, government services, mail and fulfillment services, and manufacturing and logistics services. It has contracts with companies like Intel, Microsoft, and General Motors. It is an organization built on finding possibilities in others, no matter what their circumstances. Michael Ziegler refuses to let this be a token button-sorting kind of job. He wants all the employees to *earn* their paychecks, increasing their self-respect in the process. The supervisors skillfully identify what abilities each employee has and uses them effectively.

One thing I saw inspires me to this day. There were two men with cerebral palsy. Each had the use of only one arm. They had put their wheel chairs side by side and, with one using his left hand and the other using his right hand, the two were assembling gift boxes of Jelly Belly candy!

Mike told me that many people might look at the circumstances of some of his employees and ask, "How could *they* be gifted?" "We ask a *different* question," he said. *"How* are they gifted? When we find the answer and place them in an appropriate job, their lives and possibilities expand enormously."

Michael Ziegler offers us an important principle for multiplying possibilities and effective living. We change our possibilities when we change the questions we ask. And when we ask the *right* questions, we can create possibilities for others.

Disability is a matter of perception. If you can do just one thing well, you're needed by someone.

— MARTINA NAVRATILOVA
FORMER WORLD NO. 1
FEMALE TENNIS PLAYER

HAVE YOU KISSED YOUR ASHTRAY TODAY?

How do you get people to stop drinking, smoking, eating junk food, and engaging in other self-destructive behaviors? Well, obviously not by telling them how bad it is and how weak they are because they can't kick these habits. And not by scaring and threatening them.

Throughout history, such authoritarian approaches have rarely worked, although this hasn't stopped the powers that be from trying. Public health service advertising continues to warn us about heart attacks, strokes, and diabetes; pregnant women are cautioned that drinking may cause Fetal Alcohol Syndrome; and cigarette packs display skulls and crossbones on their labels. But few people are sufficiently influenced by these admonishments to actually curtail their addictions.

However, someone with a different approach to inspiring positive change is Dr. Dean Ornish, Clinical Professor of Medicine at the University of California, San Francisco. Dr. Ornish is widely known for his research on controlling coronary artery disease and campaigning for healthful lifestyle changes that include a low-fat vegetarian diet, no smoking, and regular exercise. To inspire people to make positive changes in their lives, especially when thorny health issues are involved, Dr. Ornish believes that short-term gains are much more motivating to people than the fear of dying.

He has suggested possibilities to millions of people he will never even meet by finding an effective way to inspire them to make positive changes in their lives. "As health professionals," he says, "we often talk about risk factors or offer prevention tips, but most patients think those are really boring. And telling patients 'If you don't change your diet or quit smoking you are going to have a heart attack' is not that motivating in the long run. It's too distressing to think about – so they don't. When someone has had a heart attack, they will do anything you tell them for about a month or two. Then the denial comes back and they return to their old patterns because thinking long-term about health crises is just too scary."

Dr. Ornish thinks that appealing to vanity and pointing out immediate possibilites may work much better. For example, instead of "Smoking causes heart disease, emphysema, and lung cancer" a more effective advertising slogan has turned out to be, "Do your kisses taste like licking an ashtray?" Think that ad increases the possibility of more kissing if you quit smoking? You bet!

"That places the consequences of behaviors in the here and now – in present tense," he says. "And people are always making changes and choices when they see immediate benefits. That's the point. Every day, people are out there making monumentally difficult changes in lifestyle – when they have a child, for example, or when they change jobs – but they do it because it is worth it. My observation has been that for many people, a big change to quit smoking is worth making, not only because it can help them live longer, but also because it can help them live better."

Through his extensive writings, Dr. Ornish's common sense advocacy for better health practices has created possibilities and made a difference in the lives of countless people. Inspiring them to make positive changes in their lives has made him a mentor to millions. The message is clear: the promise of possibilities is far more motivating than potential problems. *Think again* and multiply your possibilities by dwelling on the benefits instead of the barriers.

Faith and prayer are the vitamins of the soul; man cannot live in health without them.

— MAHALIA JACKSON
GOSPEL SINGER

INSPIRING EMPLOYEES

Have you ever wanted to help someone in distress and had your support refused? Did that experience sour your magnanimous spirit? Or did it inspire you to seek new possibilities for generosity?

In the best-selling book *Halftime,* author Bob Buford encourages readers to move beyond success and strive for significance. He says true success is moving beyond your own self-interest and creating possibilities for others. Since I am at the "halftime" of my life, this philosophy has a profound impact on how I think about achievement. As I looked at the people I admire who epitomize providing possibilities for others, the first person who came to mind was Dave Lucchetti.

After floods devastated northern California in 1986, thousands of homeowners wanted to return to their damaged homes but lacked the money to make the necessary repairs. Jim Miller, a salesman for Pabco Gypsum, approached Pabco's parent company, Pacific Coast Building Products, about the possibility of donating wallboard. Because giving back to the community is a tradition at Pacific Coast, President and CEO Dave Lucchetti responded enthusiastically.

Only, it wasn't that easy. All the charitable organizations they initially contacted turned them down, saying they had no methods to qualify recipients for the wallboard and distribute the donation. At this point, most companies would have just dropped the offer, but the staff at Pacific Coast persisted. They finally found a church and then a fraternal organization that agreed to screen applicants and handle the distribution. Within a few days, five truckloads were delivered to the victims in two communities and, soon after, two other disaster areas received more donated wallboard from Pacific Coast.

"For years, I've watched Pacific Coast employees go above and beyond, with selfless sharing at the top of the list," says Lucchetti. Possibility thinking is a mandate throughout the company, and employees have suggested and participated in dozens of projects. Over the years, Pacific Coast employees have taken part in efforts including an annual Paint the Town Project (which provides painting and roofing to low-income homeowners), a holiday season Adopt-a-Family program, Habitat for Humanity, and Susan G. Komen walk to cure cancer. Employees have also lent their support to art programs, fund-raising events, food banks, recycling projects, and environmental concerns. And again, after more California flooding in 1995, Pacific Coast distributed donations of building materials, this time through the Red Cross.

Of course, any company that has survived for more than fifty years has had to do a lot of possibility thinking. Few companies face more challenges than those in the building industry. Both demand and supply alternately skyrocket and flatline in unpredictable cycles depending on the economy, demographic shifts, and random political, meteorological, and social variables. The nimble footwork needed to stay afloat could be compared to that of an old-time lumberjack dancing atop a rolling log on a rushing river.

Pacific Coast started modestly. In 1953, Fred Anderson and his wife, Pat, sold their car and put everything they owned into starting a small, family-owned lumberyard in Sacramento, California. In 1971, Dave Lucchetti started as a "yard man," cutting and loading lumber for customers. Just eight years later he became company president.

What started as a small lumberyard in 1953 has diversified and expanded to offer a wide range of products and services for builders and the construction industry? By being open to possibilities, Fred Anderson and Dave Lucchetti have built a business that now operates in ten states, employs more than 3,400 people, and does $900-million in annual business, frequently expanding into new products and services.

A lot of possibilities had to be considered along the way, and the company's expansion has had as many "downs" as "ups." For example, one of their divisions was acquired when a customer couldn't pay its bill and offered to turn over its contracting business in exchange for what it owed. That was a unique opportunity. Was it the right step toward what Pacific Coast wanted to become? Or could it prove disastrous?

Pacific Coast decided to go for it. Unfortunately, their bank foresaw doom and pulled their line of credit, demanding payment in full – $750,000! "On top of that," recalls Dave, "our large volume of business strained our cash flow nearly to the breaking point. Bankruptcy was a distinct possibility."

To get enough cash to pay bills on time, Dave, Fred Anderson, and others made daily rounds to pick up customers' checks and rush them to the bank, hoping the deposits would keep their own checks from bouncing. "I spent an awful lot of time doing this," Dave says. "Once I walked into the bank with several hundred thousand dollars in checks, just before closing. The poor teller didn't know what to do with them, but we had to get them in that day." The crisis dragged on for months, but eventually their hard work and vision paid off.

"We have taken advantage of opportunities as they presented themselves," Dave told me. "We looked for business that fit with what we were doing. After all these years of expansion, all of our businesses continue to be related."

That last point is important. Pacific Coast Building Products has survived and thrived both by being open to possibilities and by pursuing *only* those that would contribute to their vision of interrelated products and services. The company is now a network of semi-independent enterprises, serving their customers, employees, and communities.

I have been fortunate to call Dave Lucchetti a friend for over 20 years. The generosity of his time and talent has been an inspiration to me. Dave's example of attaining both success and significance has taught me the true meaning of achievement. When you are tempted by all the wonderful possibilities around you, remember to choose the ones that contribute to *your* vision of your goals. Be sure to *think again* about what you should pursue that will bring fulfillment, meaning, and purpose in your life. And a life well lived is not attained by only creating possibilities for ourselves; it is in helping others realize their possibilities too!

I feel the capacity to care is the thing which gives life its deepest significance.

— PABLO CASALS
SPANISH MUSICIAN

STRENGTH IN NUMBERS

You know the cliché, "Don't put all your eggs in one basket." I believe you *should*. Like hunting for Easter eggs, find your personal gifts – what you're really good at and love doing – and then focus all your energy on refining the "eggs" in your basket. You'll achieve a lot more and be a lot happier.

No one is brilliant at everything. Have you ever heard someone say, "Oh, I could never do that because..."? Sometimes it's just because the person lacks one of the several skills needed to achieve the desired result. To increase your possibilities, have you ever thought about *subcontracting* to obtain the skills that you just don't have?

Suppose you're right in the middle of a household project, and you're in need of just the right tool. You dig through your toolbox. There are a couple of tools that resemble what you need, but none is quite right. You have needle nose pliers, but you need a vise grip. If you're like me, you run over to a neighbor who seems to have every tool known to man. Now you're able to finish the job.

Life is like that. You begin an ambitious project, make the necessary plans, and gather what you think you need. However, part way through the project, you realize a vital tool or talent is missing. After struggling with the wrong tool, have you ever noticed how useful "the right tool" becomes?

This is the great benefit of having possibility partners with a variety of tools, many of which you do not possess. Your repertoire and available options expand enormously until you've got more specialty tools than the *Yankee Workshop* and just as much expertise to get the job done. You're no longer faced with trying to use a hammer as a screwdriver.

Take a few moments to think about what "tools" you have and what you might need to achieve your possibilities. Develop possibility partners who will share their tools with you, just as you share yours with them.

In the old days, people looked for business partners (and life partners) who could supply the talents they lacked. One person would be a great people person, greeting customers and motivating staff, while the other was skilled at handling finances and business matters. Or one would be a great designer and the other a dynamite marketer. One might be excellent at seeing the big picture, but poor at details, while the other was just the opposite. Each person complemented the other to create a whole greater than the sum of the parts.

Most large projects use *subcontracting*. Businesses and even countries devote their energies to doing what they do best and then fill in the blanks with outside services. You can do the same!

Suppose your goal is to photograph iron bridges in Europe, but you're weak at plotting itineraries, reading timetables, and booking reservations. Then subcontract the travel arrangements portion of your project. You'd go to an experienced travel agent or get a traveling companion to handle this for you, so you could concentrate on what you want to do and what you do well. What if you need the bridge photos for a book you've written, but you don't know one end of a camera from the other. Subcontract that part of your project to a skilled photographer. Making travel arrangements is a piece of cake for you, but languages are difficult. You could hire a translator or team up with a buddy who has that skill.

Consider some talent and weakness combinations that might be parlayed into possibilities:

- You're a terrific "people person" but absolutely no good at the day-to-day details of organizing and running a project.

- You're gifted at managing *things*, but your ability to motivate and inspire other *people* is low. You always seem to put your foot in your mouth and alienate others.

- You're very creative, but your time management and budgeting skills are weak.

- You're not the least bit artistic, couldn't tell a Monet from a motet, but doing budgets and taxes is easy for you.

- You're super at puzzles, but...

- Sports – or writing – or speaking – come easily to you, but...

You get the idea. We each have *some* things that we excel at. Identify yours and use them to multiply your possibilities to achieve what you want. As we learned in *Amplify Your*

Possibilities, we all have definite weaknesses too. Identify yours and then learn to *leverage* them – which doesn't mean "overcoming" them; acknowledge your weaknesses and use them as a tool. Turn limitations into strengths by fitting them into your big plan.

If you're not sure how to do this, imagine you are an employer eager to match your employees' skills and experiences to the jobs you want done. What unique niche might someone with your particular profile fill? For example, here's a common characteristic that many people would see as failure. Suppose you have enormous energy for starting new projects, but then your interest drops off and you never finish. How could this "weakness" be turned into strength?

There was a formidable Englishwoman named Rachel Kay-Shuttleworth (1896–1967), who specialized in conceiving and organizing social service and public betterment projects, sort of a British equivalent of Eleanor Roosevelt. Once a project was under way, Rachel would find the right people to take it over, organize and inspire them, and then leave them with a clear road map of where to go. Once this was done, she'd move on to a new project.

Rachel made invaluable contributions to infant and maternal health among the poor, juvenile justice and prison reform, the Girl Guides (British Girl Scouts), education, community services, civic betterment, housing, and social services for World War II evacuees. Her passion for needle arts and crafts resulted in many training programs, and she personally amassed the largest private collection of historic needlework, textiles, and quilts in the world, now housed in a teaching museum in Lancashire, England.

Rachel was so beloved by those whose lives she had touched that, when developers threatened to do open strip-mining near her home and she told them she'd get every Girl Guide in northern England to stand in front of their bulldozers, the developers knew that she could. They retreated, choosing instead to change the course of a nearby river! Thus, throughout her life, this dynamic woman made a virtue of the seeming vice of starting projects that she didn't finish herself.

Unlike Rachel, there are people who can't conceive or create a project but who can become super team builders and follow through long-term once they are motivated and given clear instructions. This might be you or someone you are seeking to motivate and inspire. Again, get around the perceived vice and turn it into a virtue.

You don't have to be talented at everything to achieve great results. Consider multiplying your own abilities by finding others who can do what you don't do well. Whether you pay an expert or team up with others to supplement your deficits, you can often achieve your goals by *subcontracting*. Remember, Michelangelo didn't *build* the Sistine Chapel ceiling. He just painted it!

I dunno, she's got gaps, I got gaps,
and together we fill gaps.

— ROCKY'S RESPONSE WHEN ASKED WHY HE
LIKED ADRIAN (FROM 1976 FILM *ROCKY*)

5
QUANTIFY
YOUR PROGRESS

How will you know when you're there?

THE POWER OF
(IM)POSSIBILITY THINKING

I love to tell a story about the three questions a Canadian border guard asked me when I was returning to the U.S. from a business trip:

- Where are you coming from?

- How long have you been there?

- Where are you going?

These questions triggered my thinking about human potential and inspired me to write *How High Can You Bounce?* One group resistant to this book title was an association of skydivers. It seems they avoid anything with the word bounce in it. More recently, the border questions have changed:

- What is the nature of your trip?

- Do you have anything to declare?

- If so, what is the approximate value?

As you've read this book, you've actually been considering these three questions. You started by defining the nature of your trip your dreams and your ideal life. Then you thought about any negativity or pessimism that might be blocking your way. Next, you considered your resources, talents, passions, and uniqueness. Then you reflected on the concept of multiplying the resources you need to pursue your possibilities through possibility partners, mentoring, and subcontracting. Now, in Part 5, you'll consider ways to evaluate, extend, and achieve your possibilities.

"Value" has two distinct meanings. Both are essential for pursuing possibilities. We live, with varying degrees of success and comfort, by our *values* – our beliefs and ethics. And we place a *value* on each of the many conflicting fragments of day-to-day living. But some people, as Oscar Wilde commented, can know the price of everything and the value of nothing.

With all the pressures we face every day, it's easy to be distracted from our beliefs and overlook some of our real riches. We are constantly torn between options, confronting choices, and making quick decisions that can have profound effects on our lives. By declaring our values and the value of our choices, we make our lives infinitely richer and more profound. We can focus on attaining and sustaining our essential core, the gift we give ourselves and the world.

It's fairly easy to be grateful for the good things, but even burdens and frustrations can offer positive value if you know how to look for it. What is the value to you of navigating a difficult situation? When you've come through an awkward or painful time, do you feel grumpy and put-upon, asking "Why me?" Or for having made it, do you feel stronger, wiser, and better able to appreciate and enjoy the good things?

New wisdom is one of the greatest perks of those less-than-perfect times. How often have you said, "If only I knew then what I know now." Wouldn't it be great to replay your life with the wisdom you now possess? Well, we can't go backwards and do it all over again. But we have an even greater gift. We can move forward with our new wisdom. We can respond with improved judgment, greater knowledge, and more patience and understanding the next time things don't go just the way we'd hoped. With our broader perspective, we can define negative events as glitches instead of catastrophes.

When you come up with your own answer to "What is the value of working through this difficult situation?," you become open to using both the positive and negative experiences of your day with a life-affirming attitude of gratitude. With a grateful mind-set, you constantly re-energize your heart and soul.

A friend of mine likes to say, "We have a choice when we wake up in the morning. We can groan and pull the covers over our head, moaning, 'Oh, God, it's morning!' Or we can rise, greet our loved ones, and gaze out the window at the rain or shine of the glorious planet we live on, and gratefully say, 'Oh, God, it's morning!'"

You increase your personal happiness and achievement when you value whatever makes your life enjoyable and challenging, even the smallest things. Your "attitude of gratitude" makes you even more open to noticing and taking advantage of the wealth of possibilities awaiting you.

As you start your day, take a few seconds to focus on what you truly value. As you quantify your progress and celebrate your success, watch how your gratitude grows.

Empower yourself by celebrating and acknowledging all the good in your life. This is how the seemingly impossible becomes possible.

For a long time it had seemed to me that life was about to begin – real life. But there was always some obstacle in the way, something to be gotten through first, some unfinished business, time still to be served, a debt to be paid. Then life would begin. At last it dawned on me that these obstacles were my life.

— ALFRED D. SOUZA

"IF I EVER DECIDE TO WORRY"

As I registered at the reception desk, a young man in military uniform greeted me with a smart salute and handshake. The bustling activity and energy all around us was unforgettable. I wish you could have been there with me.

We were standing at the entrance to Walter Reed Army Medical Center in Washington, D.C. I had been invited to give my presentation called "Challenges are Inevitable – Defeat is Optional" to a group of injured military personnel returning from Iraq and Afghanistan. To be invited to speak to these soldiers was a tremendous privilege, especially for a civilian. I felt both honored and humble, uncertain whether what I had to say would be relevant to these people who had faced so many challenges already.

My escort informed me that he would be my guide for the day. I was to stick with him and not go anywhere unescorted during my visit. As we walked through the rotunda, I thought about all the sick and injured that had been treated here, everyone from buck privates to presidents. The walls were covered with large paintings of famous military leaders, their expressions conveying strength and patriotism.

We went first to meet the Chief of Staff, who also greeted me with a firm handshake. He presented me with a cherished memento, a military medallion that signifies courage. During our conversation, he informed me that several soldiers would be unable to attend my presentation due to their injuries, but they had asked that I visit them in their rooms afterward. Before my arrival, I had sent along autographed copies of my book *How High Can You Bounce?* and many had already read it.

Then I was led into the main auditorium for my formal presentation. When those large doors swung open, I will never forget what I saw. Although I pride myself on showing up early to prepare, there were already two-hundred young men and woman waiting for me. My initial surprise was that the audience wasn't all male. My second surprise was seeing how young they all were. I think of myself as a young man, yet many of them could have been my sons or daughters.

My escort introduced me to the group, and I began my speech. As I looked at the faces of these heroes, a young man to my right caught my attention. He had a great big magnetic smile, a grin so engaging that I didn't realize immediately that both his arms had been amputated at the elbow and that his right leg was missing. Next to him was a woman who, I assumed, was on staff at Walter Reed.

At the completion of my talk, this woman began to clap loudly—so loudly that I was somewhat embarrassed. I felt *I* was the one who should have been applauding everyone in this group. I walked over to her and said how much I appreciated her positive response.

"Roger," she said, "my son asked me to applaud extra loudly for him. He won't be clapping anytime soon." And she nodded toward the young man in the wheelchair. Fighting back tears, I realized this soldier was her child.

I went over to talk to him, kneeling down so I would be eye-level with him. He eagerly shared his plans for his life with me. "Tell me," I finally asked, "where does your courage come from?"

Gesturing with the stumps of his arms, he said, "Roger, I can't wait to see what I can do with this." Adding with a mischievous grin, "At first, I was really down and discouraged, but then I realized there was a bright side. If I ever decide to worry about the future, I won't be able to bite my nails!"

The word courage comes from the Latin word cor, which means heart. Do people with incredible courage just have a heart that does not feel fear? I don't think so! Courage is not discovered; courage is a decision.

You have been my friend. That in itself is a tremendous thing. I wove my webs for you because I liked you. After all, what's a life, anyway? We're born, we live a little while, and we die. A spider's life can't help being something of a mess, with all this trapping and eating flies. By helping you, perhaps I was trying to lift up my life a trifle. Heaven knows anyone's life can stand a little of that.

> — CHARLOTTE
> FROM *CHARLOTTE'S WEB*

Courage is not the absence of fear,
but rather the judgment that something
else is more important than fear.

— AMBROSE REDMOON

Courage is resistance to fear, mastery
of fear—not absence of fear.

— MARK TWAIN

Courage is being scared to death,
but saddling up anyway.

— JOHN WAYNE

HOPING OR HAPPENING?

Once you are well on your way to accomplishing your goals, follow-through is critical to achieving your possibilities. Quantifying and evaluating your progress is the difference between hoping possibilities will work out someday and making possibilities happen. The process helps you identify where you are and serves as a guide to where you want to be. Here is the thinking process.

THE THREE R'S OF QUANTIFYING

Rate where you are. This is reality-based thinking. What are the facts? Have I made the planned-for progress? Am I meeting my benchmarks? Am I taking a global view of my circumstances and a *macro*-look at my possibilities?

Review strategy. Take a *micro*-view of possibilities. What am I excelling at? What still needs work? Do strategic goals need to be redefined? Bring possibility partners into the process. Implement tactics.

Revise. Make any mid-course adjustments needed to advance toward your possibilities. Look for ways to improve and increase efficiency.

"The road to success" is a popular expression, but this image is somewhat misleading. I prefer to think of the way to success as a *path*. When I visualize a *road*, it is relatively smooth and well marked, with identifiable stopping points and speed limits. It is usually well traveled. However, a *path* is typically more difficult to follow. It may be uneven, rocky, meandering, and often desolate. It's easy to stumble and even get lost, and you can go a long way alone without running into another traveler.

Ordinary possibilities may lie at the end of a straight, heavily-trafficked road, but extraordinary possibilities are usually reached by a path. If your journey is challenging, circuitous, and uncertain – often an uphill climb – then extraordinary possibilities may await you.

Security is mostly a superstition. It does not exist in nature, nor do the children of men as a whole experience it. Avoiding danger is no safer in the long run than outright exposure. Life is either a daring adventure or nothing.

— HELEN KELLER

DON'T JUST DO SOMETHING –
SIT THERE!

We have a five-pound Pomeranian named Mac-A-Roon who lets *us* live with *him*. His attitude is much more Great Dane than Pom. He is always showing us his doggie tricks, undoubtedly eager to amuse "his people." One of his favorites is to spin in a circle a few times. His reward is a dog biscuit or, as we call it, a cookie.

Soon after we were married, I heard my wife say, "Sweetie, spin if you want a cookie." I mistakenly thought she was talking to me and spun so rapidly that I became lightheaded and collided with the kitchen table. Mac-A-Roon gave me a look that communicated, "You people are so hard to train."

Whenever I watch Mac-A-Roon spin in a circle, I am reminded how often I feel that way – that I am spinning into things and hard to train. Despite my best intentions, I frequently feel overscheduled and stressed – as if I am running on a treadmill and making very little progress.

Do you remember as a child being so swept up in thought that time stood still? I still recall how wonderful that kind of daydreaming felt. It was a peaceful and harmonious state. Or do you remember how it felt to be so focused on a balloon or a bug that everything else around you was totally blurred? I have watched my own daughter drift off into such a trance-like state, and I have caught myself saying something like, "Earth to Alexa..." or "Anybody home?" One reason we continually have to remind our children to stop doing what they're doing and do something else is that they have a tremendous capacity for this kind of focused concentration.

Why does daydreaming often stop as we get older? Why do we lose the ability to be totally captivated by the moment? Why do we stop cultivating our imaginations? I believe it's because we feel guilty. We've been taught that if we take time to dream, engage in imaginary ventures, or just be still, we are somehow neglecting our responsibilities. Over time, our minds become so cluttered with practical things that there is little room left for anything else. We become, as I said previously, "terminally adult."

One of the valuable lessons I have learned from those who achieve great possibilities is that they are all great dreamers. Too often we buy into the myth that possibilities require constant activity with no time for rejuvenation. Our busy-ness erodes our wonder about what's possible. High achievers do not let everyday concerns get in the way of thinking about their possibilities. They intentionally take time to have child-like dreams about *what if?* Have you noticed that children rarely believe something is impossible? Ask them, "What do you want to be when you grow up?" and their answers are often ambitious and exciting. Give yourself time to evaluate your progress. Think again and imagine possibilities.

So long as we believe in our heart of hearts that our capacity is limited and we grow anxious and unhappy, we are lacking in faith. One who truly trusts in God has no right to be anxious about anything.

— PARAMAHANSA YOGANANDA, INDIAN YOGI

ACT WITH IMPACT

Activity is very different from accomplishment. Some people confuse busyness with importance and bustle with impact. People who achieve great possibilities concentrate on doing the most important thing every day, rather than frittering away their time on a hundred other daily demands. They focus on what will yield the greatest benefit.

Here's an acronym that many people respond enthusiastically at my presentations:

I   Inspiration occurs when your dreams are so compelling that they wrap around your heart. This is the root of passion.

M   Motivation happens when you wrap your mind around your possibilities and decide to take the action necessary to make them a reality. This is where purpose comes into focus.

P   Precision. Possibilities require specific planning and preparation. It is in this process that dreams become possibilities.

A   Acquisition. Possibilities require that we continue to gain new knowledge and expertise. It is in this process of getting better that our possibilities get better.

C   Connection. Possibilities are multiplied when we enlist the energy and encouragement of others. No one does it alone.

T   Transformation. Realizing we can do more and become more transforms discouragement into hope. Hope as it strengthens gives us greater courage, which leads to greater possibilities.

Understanding the meaning of impact is obviously not enough to achieve great possibilities. You must also *act* with impact. Here are four things to accomplish that:

FOUR KEYS TO ACTING WITH IMPACT

> *Get started.* Have you ever watched a horse race, and the track announcer cries, "They're off!" Visualize the beginning of your day the same way. Start your activities with a sprint instead of a trot. Commit to possibility-producing activities and concentrate on them single-mindedly, without diversion and distraction. Realize that every minute of every hour is filled with possibility. Develop a sense of urgency toward important activities, and apply the discipline necessary to complete them. Once you've developed the habit of beginning your day in this way, you're off in pursuit of amazing possibilities.

> *Be a simpleton.* Remember the old putdown, "simpleton"? Well, sometimes being "simple" about things is a strength instead of a weakness. Being able to simplify one's life and work is an invaluable skill for a possibility producer. I loved the commercial that transformed Fabio from young to old with the tag line, "Life comes at you fast." Isn't that true?

> The velocity of change seems to be increasing rapidly. The more change, the more possibilities, but it is a double-edged sword. The solution is to discontinue tasks that move you away from possibilities. When

you reduce low-value activities, you produce peak performance. Earlier, you read about the power of subcontracting some tasks as a way to leverage your strengths. It is also helpful to *eliminate* some of the tasks that you are not particularly skilled in.

Affect your effectiveness. An employee asks his boss, "When will my raise be effective?" His boss responds, "When *you* are!" To act with impact requires maximum effectiveness. Focus on those things you can control. Try to improve every day. Decide to be a perpetual student, always eager for new knowledge and experiences. Dorothy Fuldheim was a newscaster in Cleveland, Ohio for decades. In her nineties, she signed a five-year contract and was asked afterwards when she planned to retire. "When I'm old," she replied.

Focus on solutions. I was watching a morning TV show featuring an expert instructing viewers on winter driving. "When you encounter slippery conditions," the expert said, "steer away from the problem and toward the solution." Life is the same. As you navigate treacherous circumstances, resist concentrating on the problems. Focus on the possibilities – on where you want to end up. The more you dwell on possibilities, the more creative you become at solutions. If you are tempted to focus on difficulties – on where you don't want to go – then the fruit of your mindset will be disappointment and pessimism.

If you steer toward solutions, then inspiration and creativity will be the products of your focus.

Every day there are hundreds of demands, large and small, on our limited time, energy, and resources. If we try to do everything, our most important core goals may get lost in the shuffle.

Identify your high-value activities—those that will have the most impact on achieving your possibilities and goals—and focus on them. Learn to act with impact.

Difficult times have helped me to understand better than before, how infinitely rich and beautiful life is in every way, and that so many things that one goes worrying about are of no importance whatsoever...

— ISAK DINESEN
DANISH AUTHOR

PERFECT TIMING?

"If your ship does not come in," my dear friend Cavett Robert used to say, "start swimming." What a great metaphor for taking action now, no matter what the circumstances. People who, as we say in tennis, "rip it," don't paralyze themselves with endless and repetitive analyzing, organizing, or contemplating. Of course they have a plan, but once they have established their target and route, they move into action mode. They run into the inevitable obstacles, even failures, but they keep going.

So often, we buy into the myth of "perfect timing." Yes, timing is absolutely essential for comedy, cooking, and conversation. Split-seconds count in things like nuclear fission, space launches, and air traffic control. Even Shakespeare wrote about the importance of timing as "a tide in the affairs of men," which had to be gauged carefully before success could be possible. Missing high tide to get out of the harbor meant "all the voyage of their life is bound in shallows and in miseries."

Two actions that will help you progress in expanding your possibilities are:

> *Choose your pain.* No one wants to hurt, but pain is an inevitable part of our lives. Sometimes our only choice is how and when we want to hurt. This

became clear to me when my valued friend, Nido Qubein, said, "We choose between the pain of taking action and the pain of regret." Whenever I'm debating a course of action, I remember his words. Invariably, my decision is to "rip it"!

Concentrate on what you procrastinate. All of us delay *something!* Procrastinate the unimportant activities that produce little or no results. Take action on the possibility producing activities that move you closer to your ultimate objective!

Hindsight reveals that there is rarely an ideal time to start your life's mission. Waiting, postponing, and procrastinating are the saboteurs of possibilities. The most important thing is to *just get going.* How many times have you said, "Someday..."?

Well, today is the day to "rip it." Do not delay. Don't wait for that illusive right moment. Start now. Learn from mistakes. Ask for feedback. Make necessary changes. Keep moving towards your goals. As the Nike Company slogan says, "Just do it!"

While one person hesitates because he feels inferior, another is busy making mistakes and becoming superior.

— HENRY C. LINK
AMERICAN PSYCHOLOGIST

PATIENT? OR PASSIVE?

Sometimes all we want are answers, commitments, and achievements, and we want them now! "It shouldn't take this long," we insist. "Be patient," we are told. "These things take time." Other times, we're all too willing to wait and see what happens... which can be zero. "I held out in this dead-end job until something better came along, but nothing did."

What's the difference between being wisely patient and foolishly passive? How can you tell the difference between expectant waiting and a resigned attitude that tells people, "Nothing good ever happens to me"?

Patience is an active stance, not a passive one. This may seem confusing because most people equate patience with inaction. *Think again!* Being patient means that you have done all you can to prepare, and now things are out of your hands. It's time to sit back and trust that the work you've done will bring the results you want. But if you haven't set things in motion and are still waiting for an outcome, you're just being passive.

> A *passive attitude* means that you continue to wait for what you want, taking no action toward your goal, yet maintaining an attitude that what you want should come your way just because you are waiting.

> *A patient attitude* comes after noticing and selecting a
> possibility, assessing the goal, planning, marshalling
> resources and supports, putting the plan in action,
> and then waiting for results.

What if you want to help your daughter get into the higher
reading group at school? You can complain loudly to anyone
who will listen that you think she belongs there (passive). Or
you can sit down with her and help her improve her reading and vocabulary skills, and then wait for the next regular
reading test to be administered (patient).

Have you ever noticed how different children react to
being told they need to wait? Two kids want new bikes for
summer vacation. They both cut out pictures from magazines and spend hours at the bike shop admiring the bikes.
Their parents say, "You have to be *patient*. It takes *time* to
earn enough money for a bike, and we really can't afford it
yet." Notice that the parents have given the children an important clue. "You must be patient and wait" is only half of
the message. The second half reveals what is needed: money.
One child hears the whole message and takes action, doing odd jobs to earn money toward the purchase, waiting
patiently until sufficient funds are accrued. The other child
does nothing and waits passively.

Patience following preparation is a virtue. Dag Ham-
marsjöld, former Secretary General of the United Nations,
said it well when he described how his mountaineering skills
had prepared him for one of the highest international positions in politics: "Mountaineering calls...for endurance...
perseverance and patience, a firm grip on realities, careful
but imaginative planning, a clear awareness of the dangers,

but also of the fact that fate is what we make it and that the safest climber is he who never questions his ability to overcome difficulties."

Nothing in this world can take the place of persistence. Talent will not; nothing is more common than unsuccessful people with talent. Genius will not; un-rewarded genius is almost a proverb. Education will not; the world is full of educated derelicts. Persistence and determination alone are omnipotent. The slogan 'press on' has solved and always will solve the problems of the human race.

— CALVIN COOLIDGE

WHERE'S YOUR AIR?

Have you ever seen an uninflated volleyball or basketball, one with no air in it? What a sorry sight! When I was a kid, I used to marvel that it was the same air *outside* the ball as *inside* it, but what a difference *location* can make. Moving the air from outside to inside the ball gave it its shape, elasticity, and power.

Remember the old Bill Cosby routine: "Why is there air? To fill up basketballs." I agreed. The concept of breathing and needing air to live, to sustain life, didn't make much sense to me; but the concept of needing air to make a ball be a ball, to make it bounce, made perfect sense. Poke a hole in a basketball, and watch the ball – and the game – disappear. Smash a ping pong ball too hard, and the game is over.

Of course, filling a ball with air isn't a permanent proposition. As it sits in the garage, it will gradually deflate. Even after just a few weeks, it loses much of its bounce. People are the same. Just as we continuously feed our bodies with oxygen, we need to restock our "bounce factor" to nourish our spirits. When our bounce factor is in good shape, we are better able to spot and seize new opportunities, as well as quantify our progress. Get ready to bounce before you need to.

Staying pumped up is a continual process. Start by trying to notice good things every day, no matter how much stress and negativity you run into. It's not always easy, but it's well worth the effort. Each bright, positive moment you notice may offer a possibility. Mentally stockpiling these moments is like creating a reserve of pure oxygen, ready to keep you going toward your goals when your stamina gets low.

Next, to increase your elasticity, work on your attitude toward clearly stressful situations. For example, if someone – a boss, relative, or friend – finds fault with something you've done, listen to the criticism as if it were a gift. Maybe the complaints are valid and useful, maybe not. Try taking the attitude that an appreciative, open mind makes it possible for others to teach you what they know and inform you of their perceptions. Recognize that, if you have an open attitude, your critics may actually become your possibility partners.

Accepting criticism grudgingly is no easier than accepting it gracefully and gratefully. In fact, it's a lot harder. No one enjoys being attacked. Rejecting criticism can make you feel better in the short run because it protects you from admitting you might have something to learn. But *think again*. Does acting defensive really soften the blow? Or would it be better to leverage the energy of the attack, using it to "bounce" you to the next level?

I recommend using the momentum to propel you toward the basket. The person who found fault with you will appreciate your wisdom in acknowledging the complaints, rather than arguing. Except for a few malevolent individuals you'll encounter from time to time, most people would rather praise than condemn. They want things to go smoothly as much as you do.

Delivering criticism requires energy. You can deflect that energy by either lashing back or by bouncing forward. Those seven-foot basketball players can use their jumping ability to push the ball out of bounds, back in the face of the shooter, or toward the basket. Become a winning possibility player by choosing to move toward the goal.

Finally, in the most difficult situations, ask yourself what you have to gain from the experience. Hang on to that nugget of learning. It is pure gold and can open up future possibilities.

Don't pray when it rains if you don't
pray when the sun shines.

— LEROY (SATCHEL) PAIGE
CONSIDERED ONE OF BASEBALL'S
GREATEST PITCHERS

PLAYING TO WIN

During a highly competitive tennis match, as you hover between victory and defeat, the dreaded cement elbow can set in. This happens when you focus on "playing not to lose" instead of "playing to win."

For those of you who don't play tennis, let me describe the condition. It begins when you start responding conservatively, not taking risks. As you do, the net slowly grows taller and your legs begin to turn to rubber. Your mouth feels as if you swallowed a cashmere sweater, and your arm locks up like it's cast in cement.

How do you crack the cement elbow? Like the Nike slogan of "Just do it!" tennis has a saying that conveys the same philosophy: "Grip it, rip it, and forget it." It works like this:

Grip it: Take control of what you can influence. Take the initiative. You cannot control the wind, the sun, or your opponent, so concentrate on what is controllable. Choices can only be made in the present. Don't worry about the last point or the next point. Focus on the present.

Rip it: Take action. Give it maximum effort. Hold nothing back. Lay it on the line. Do not focus on the net (obstacle). Focus on your opponent's open court (possibility). Anticipate success and take your best shot. A victory is made up of hundreds of such shots.

Forget it: Whatever the outcome of the last shot, keep going. Don't spend a second reacting to that miss. Get ready to grip it and rip it again.

This kind of thinking lets you break through anxieties and keep going. Ironically, when you focus on playing rather than winning or losing, you're far more likely to win.

In sports they say there are two types of players: those who play to win and those who play not to lose. Here are the characteristics of the two.

PLAYING NOT TO LOSE

- Cautious

- "Ready…aim…aim…aim"

- Needs reassurance

- Avoids pain at all costs

- Quick to blame

- Risk averse

- Sees obstacles before opportunity

- Looks at failure as final.

PLAYING TO WIN

- Adventurous

- "Ready...aim...fire...fire...fire"

- Believes she or he has what it takes

- Understands that temporary pain can equal permanent growth

- 100 percent responsible for attitudes and achievement

- Ready for risk if there is worthwhile reward

- Sees possibilities before problems

- Willing, even eager, to fail, knowing this brings success closer.

My close friend and fellow speaker Tony Alessandra grew up in Manhattan's "Hell's Kitchen." One of his favorite expressions is so typically New York: "Fahgetaboutit." This attitude is essential when you are playing to win. A tennis match is comprised of points that are won or lost by the shots you attempt. Some shots are clear winners. Others hit the net. Some shots are picture-perfect, while others are hit so awkwardly that the ball disappears over the fence and is gone for good. Life is a lot like that: a series of events – some memorable, others miserable, some annoying, and some astounding.

In tennis there is a tendency to be so caught up in plans for the next point or in bemoaning a missed shot that you don't pay attention to the present. Tennis coaches have a valuable admonition: "Play in the present." The wisdom is that you let go of the past; and the future is not here yet. All you have to focus on is the current shot. In other words, do not make this shot a rehearsal for an imaginary future performance.

When the "game" is over, then there's time to stop and evaluate how you played and what you could do differently next time. Without analyses of your progress, you may make the same mistakes over and over, never learning from them. In the midst of the process, forget the gain or loss that just happened. Concentrate instead on *making the next shot your best shot*, each and every time. Don't paralyze yourself by thinking how the last shot went or worrying about the difficulty of shots to come. Opportunities to win the game open up for positive possibility thinkers.

There is one quality that one must possess to win, and that is definiteness of purpose, the knowledge of what one wants, and a burning desire to possess it.

— NAPOLEON HILL
AUTHOR OF *THINK AND GROW RICH*

BE LIKE MIKE

You likely remember the commercial that showed Michael Jordan flying through the air completing one of his awe-aspiring dunks and the slogan was "Be Like Mike!" He is arguably the greatest basketball player and most popular athlete in history!

What you may not know is that Michael Jordan ranks number one in only one NBA career statistic! There's a popular notion that successful people do everything well and never experience failure. Michael Jordan is someone who disproves this myth. Not that he wasn't amazingly good. Even non-sports-fans know his name. In fact, Michael Jordan became so recognizable that when one ad showed him in silhouette with no identifying caption, just an outline of his famous bald head, people instantly knew it was "MJ."

To ardent basketball fans like me, he will always be "His Airness." The man seemed to walk on air as he completed jaw-dropping jump shots. Millions of youngsters dreamed of being an NBA superstar, and they all wanted to "be like Mike." Fellow player Magic Johnson said, "There's Michael Jordan and then there's the rest of us."

So, what records does Michael Jordan actually hold in career statistics? A lot of people think he must be the most prolific scorer in NBA history, number one in percentage of field goals, or has scored the most points in a single game. *Think again!* Michael Jordan isn't the greatest scorer. He doesn't have the highest field goal percentage, and he's not even the greatest rebounder. In fact, he holds only one top NBA statistic. Michael Jordan has missed more shots than anyone else.

What, then, constitutes his greatness? Could it be in part the fact that he has risked failure more often than anyone else? What if he'd passed on the winning shot in 1998 against the Utah Jazz to win the NBA title? Or hadn't attempted that last-second shot to beat Phoenix in 1993? If he hadn't risked failure by taking those shots, his legendary status would be somewhat diminished.

Here's what we can learn from Michael Jordan. If you seek big possibilities, you have to risk big failures. Some pursue their possibilities only up to the point where they begin to encounter discouragement. Then they choose retreat.

If you can honestly say, "I've never been discouraged," then I suspect you have sidestepped possibilities. If you believe that your path to possibilities means avoiding mistakes and missteps, you're depriving yourself of life's true richness. Have you ever heard of someone sleeping on the floor because they are don't want to risk falling out of bed? It seems they settle for the discomfort of the floor because they are "certain" they will not fall! Possibility producers take the top bunk!

There is a popular saying tennis coaches use to inspire players to take risk. "You miss 100 percent of the shots you do not take!" Don't be afraid to risk some failures on the way to achieving extraordinary possibilities.

BE AN AMATEUR

Suppose you were about to have surgery and the nurse said, "Don't worry–your doctor is an amateur." Or your plane was in a fierce storm and the flight attendant tried to comfort you with, "Relax–the pilot is a real amateur." How would you feel?

You might be tempted to leap out of the hospital bed or even parachute out of the plane. To many, the word "amateur" means someone inexperienced, unprofessional, or unskilled–even someone who is definitely going to make a botch of what they do. But *think again!*

"Amateur" comes from the Latin word for love and is defined as "one who loves or has a taste for anything." When you decide to convert "impossible" to "possible," you start by falling passionately in love with what you want to achieve, and you become a true "amateur."

Lackadaisical or halfhearted just isn't going to hack it. If you reluctantly feel you really *ought* to be doing something, or you believe something *might* be fun or useful if you tried it, what kind of fierce ingenuity and fiery energy are you likely to come up with? If your goal and passion aren't in total alignment, you're just going to spin your wheels and overlook your many possibilities.

What keeps you up at night? This statement is frequently used to identify problems, individually and organizationally. A typical response is, "I'll tell you what keeps me up–*stress!*"

What about taking the thoughts of all the things that generate stress and replacing them with thoughts of success instead? How about using this mindset to quantify your possibilities or ambitions?

Certainly life's challenges can cause restless nights, but have you ever been kept awake by a potential possibility you are pursuing? That indicates you are tapping into your passions. If you are so full of anticipation for the next day or next opportunity that it keeps you awake at night, then you are becoming a true "amateur." You're shifting your focus from the uneasiness of worry to the exhilaration of possibilities.

> *Schedule a "heart scan."* Follow your heart and intuition. Life is short. Don't waste it in pursuit of someone else's dreams. Don't let others' limited perspectives prevent you from achieving abundant possibilities. Avoid people who resist the notion of amateur and want you to do the "right" or the practical thing. This does not require a professional opinion. As an "amateur," you are your own best "heart specialist."

> *Show me the money.* A clear indication that you are becoming an "amateur" is answering "yes" to questions like, "Would I do this for free?" or "Would I even pay for the pleasure of doing it?" When you plug into your passions, money becomes secondary to meaning. Purpose is preeminent over power.

You may have heard the phrase, "Do what you love and the money will follow." A true "amateur" says, "If I do what I

love, joy and contentment will follow." Money has importance, but it never replaces the value of things that energize
our hearts and souls.

DARE TO GIVE UP

There's a popular theory that if you do ten things well and one thing badly, you must concentrate all your time and energy on improving that single deficiency. *Think again!*

Of *course* we might benefit by single-mindedly pursuing perfection in an area we feel inadequate. But time and energy are not infinite. If you make a good faith effort and fail miserably at a single aspect of your project, quantify your progress by asking yourself these questions:

- Can I overcome this deficiency if I try hard enough?

- Must this shortcoming keep me from achieving my goal?

- Could others be harmed if I don't have this particular skill?

If you can honestly answer "no" to these questions, move on to new possibilities. You have my permission to stop beating yourself up over what you do badly and concentrate on what you do *well*. Build on your strengths! Either devise a strategy that eliminates the need for this talent from your project, or subcontract this aspect out to someone else. You can consciously decide that your precious resources would be better devoted to what you are *good* at–to what you're *passionate* about–and move on toward your goal.

One necessary element of realizing great possibilities is to get great at knowing what you're truly *bad* at. We can each do almost anything in life. But we can't do *everything* in life. I learned this life lesson recently at a speaking engagement in Bermuda. An activity was planned in which the attendees would hop onto motor scooters and tour the island. An exhilarating excursion, to be sure, but I got caught up in the excitement and neglected to evaluate my strengths and weaknesses for this activity.

I was so engrossed in anticipation that I overlooked the fact that, with my hands shaped as they are and having limited dexterity, applying the hand brakes on a motor scooter would be challenging–okay, *impossible*. I hopped onto my scooter like everyone else and hit the gas. *Then* I realized that I wouldn't be able to stop! I had to circle the parking lot for several minutes until a speedy hotel employee caught up to me and brought me to a halt. An ignominious but safe conclusion to an endeavor I should not have started. But by daring to give up, I had saved myself a great deal of grief and the tour organizers the cost of a new scooter.

When you quantify your progress and revaluate your potential remember, never let what you cannot do get in the way of what you can do!

Everybody has talent; it's just a matter of moving around until you've discovered what it is.

— GEORGE LUCAS
AWARD-WINNING PRODUCER,
DIRECTOR, SCREENWRITER

DREAM THE IMPOSSIBLE DREAM

Who can think of the words, "To dream the impossible dream..." without hearing the incomparable Robert Goulet belting out the theme from Man of La Mancha? I think we take to heart the commitment of Don Quixote, and we want to follow our own quest, "No matter how hopeless, no matter how far."

The problem is, most of us think our own struggles with everyday life are in the same category as trying to bring peace to the Middle East. We place too much importance on most decisions, agonizing over them endlessly, and not enough on the few genuine, life-changing choices we can make.

If we really distill our life choices, there are only three important questions that define our lives:

- Where do I make my home?

- With whom do I share my life?

- What is possible for me?

Can you think of any other questions that have a greater impact on your life?

Here's an exciting thought, one that fuels my passion about possibilities: *possibilities have never been so abundant.*

We are living in perhaps the greatest era of opportunity the world has ever known. There has never before been a time and a place in which individuals hold so many possibilities in their hands. Think of the myriad of options, knowledge, decisions, and alternatives available to *you*.

The explosion of technology has opened doors to possibilities that just a short time ago would have been impossible. Years ago, the ability to explore possibilities was nearly always limited. You could spend your entire life in the place where you were born. Your profession was determined by what your family had done before you, and your elders preselected your life partner. Your contact with others could have been limited to your tribe or village.

All these limitations are still true for many people throughout the world, but if you are reading this book, it is probably not true for *you!* I hope you now have a new appreciation of how much is available to you, once you begin to notice, evaluate, choose, and pursue *your world of possibilities.*

Each of us has a purpose in life, a passion we were created to pursue. I hope this book has inspired you, through its true stories and bits of wisdom, to look for opportunities of impossible possibilities. I end with lyrics that capture the essence of possibility thinking. May you follow the exciting path available to you as you *think again* and enjoy the quest for an abundant life.

THE IMPOSSIBLE DREAM

Lyrics by Joe Darien

To dream... the impossible dream...
To fight... the unbeatable foe...
To bear... with unbearable sorrow...
To run... where the brave dare not go...
To right... the unrightable wrong...
To love... pure and chaste from afar...
To try... when your arms are too weary...
To reach... the unreachable star...

This is my quest, to follow that star...
No matter how hopeless, no matter how far...
To fight for the right, without question or pause...
To be willing to march into Hell,
for a Heavenly cause...

And I know if I'll only be true, to this glorious quest,
That my heart will lie will lie peaceful and calm,
when I'm laid to my rest...
And the world will be better for this:
That one man, scorned and covered with scars,
Still strove, with his last ounce of courage,
To reach... the unreachable star...

INDEX